Children of Abraham

Children of Abraham

R. H. Martin

www.RHMartin.net

To order additional copies of this book, contact:
Xlibris Corporation
1-888-795-4274
www.Xlibris.com
Orders@Xlibris.com
47913

DEDICATION

This book is dedicated to the leaders of the world's faiths and those that have suffered from religious conflict. It is dedicated to those that hold and control the vast wealth of this planet and to Charlene Dumas, a young Haitian mother who eats cookies made of dirt, vegetable oil, and salt to ease hunger pangs. It is dedicated to what we can do together. It is dedicated to the evolution of the humane being.

ACKNOWLEDGMENTS

Taking on a project concerning religion, in today's world, is an ambitious task. It would have been an impossible task without the help of friends, family, professionals in the field, clerics, people of faith, and doubters.

First and foremost, I thank my wife, Connie, and my children, Kate and Mike, who all provided hours upon hours of listening and invaluable insight in the formative stages. Particular recognition and thanks are due to my wife's sister, Ida Edwards Clayton, who pushed me to work with her for twelve-hour days during the final editing. We both are of strong character; and the arguments over split infinitives, misplaced modifiers, and pronouns without antecedents would fill a book. We came out of it knowing each other better, having developed a profound mutual respect.

Judges Steven Balog and J. Kent Washburn helped me coalesce my thinking concerning the legal implications of the shift from God as a matter of belief to a matter of fact. Ann Washburn added a healthy dose of skepticism to the book's premise and told me, in no uncertain terms, what proof she would need to convince her that the storyline of this book was believable. Her input is certainly represented. Dot Hutelmeyer worked with me to understand the character Claire Medina. Actually, Dot breathed life into Claire in a way I never could.

Thank you to Father Bob of the Blessed Sacrament Catholic Church, the Reverend Sandra Lee Swift of the Center for Spiritual Living, the Reverend Larry E. Covington of the Ebenezer United Church of Christ, the Reverend M. Keith McDaniel of the Elon First Baptist Church, the Reverend Evaristo Lacerdo, Pastor Darrell Cox of the Trinity Worship Center, members of IIASA (a nonprofit educational institution affiliated with Al-Imam Muhammad Ibn Saud Islamic University of Saudi Arabia), members of the Islamic Center of Charlotte, Rabbi George Garten, and Kisor and Chandana Chakrabarti for their help in finding the common theme among belief systems as well as the unique voice of each of them.

I want to express my appreciation to Congressman Howard Coble and his staff, especially Janine Osborne for allowing me to spend time in the Rayburn House Office Building and the Capitol during my research in Washington DC.

I give thanks also to Elon University creative writing majors Ted Dodson and Carolyn Clark, along with religion and history major Patrick Moore. They served as focus group, editors, and critics. The shape of the novel is due in no small part to their efforts. Thank you also to Dr. John Malcolm for consulting with me regarding the medical aspects of characters' wounds, to Mary Kilchenstein of ActiveVoice Editing for pushing me as a novelist, and the Hon. Vic Euliss for his input into the mind of an honest and forthright human being.

I want to thank Bill Livesay, Chuck Basa, Valerie Fearrington, Elizabeth Reed, Albert Kauslick, Gregory Saldanha, Gavin Saldanha, Jack Rutherford, Anna Gerow, Gary Cole, Jim Stiles, Craig Thompson, and Luke Allen for their input into the social, political, and philosophical aspects of the novel.

The final draft was copyedited by Chile Gadingan. She did a thorough and professional job of putting on the finishing polish. She and the entire staff at Xlibris publishing were highly responsive and encouraging throughout the publishing process. Thanks and kudos to them.

Finally, I thank the Divine Creative Intelligence, however It may be named.

If you knew that you would die today and saw the face of God and Love—would you change?
If you knew that you would be alone, knowing right but being wrong—would you change?
—From the song *Change* by Tracy Chapman

CHAPTER 1

My children, please give me your attention.

—God

The view from thirty-five thousand feet was stunning. A few minutes before dawn, Capt. Moshe Nadav gazed through the cockpit of his American-made Israeli F-16 Falcon, mesmerized as always by the perfectly balanced layers of red, orange, yellow, and blue piled upon the horizon. The indigo sky surrounding his plane was empty, and the dark heavens filled him with such a sense of awe and profound peace that, for a few moments, he felt as though he could reach out and touch the face of God. The tranquility offered by his surroundings soon died, unable to exist alongside the brutal knowledge of his mission or the grip of his own inner struggle—his own jihad.

Captain Nadav hated these reprisal bombings. Palestinians had fired missiles from the West Bank and Gaza colonies into Israeli cities. His orders were to destroy a military target in Gaza. He knew his missiles would cause "collateral damage," the deaths of innocent civilians caught in the cross fire. When Israel had occupied Gaza, several hundred thousand Palestinians had lived there. Now several million lived on the same land, crowded together so tightly that it was impossible to take out hostiles without killing two or three times as many innocents.

He was a soldier, an aviator, a pilot in the Israeli Defense Forces. It was his job to carry out orders, even if those orders meant delivering death from the safe haven of his jet's Plexiglas cockpit. He questioned the wisdom of his superiors even as he hoped his orders would somehow help resolve the conflict. The pain of lost life and limb would stir the need for vengeance; vengeance would lead to rockets being fired and Israeli deaths; the Israeli deaths would continue the cycle and send him out on another mission.

Why didn't the Palestinians and other Arabs acknowledge that Jews were only acting in self-defense? *Why* didn't they see that his people were merely asking for what God, Himself, had promised them in the Arc of the Covenant: their just and rightful home in the Promised Land. Could they not understand that Jews and Muslims were both Children of Abraham? Both shared the same history; both shared the same ancestry, and all were Semites. Their God was the same God, and God's words and promises should be respected by all His children.

Nadav reached the proper coordinates and took a hard ninety-degree bank off the now-twinkling blue waters into a head-on course toward the coast. He was mere seconds away from his target. His personal reservations had no place here. Death was represented by the red nipple on top of his flight stick. A jolt of adrenaline shot through him when he placed his thumb on the button. He felt the power of that high, the power of life and death. He heard the high-pitched *beep beep beep* that indicated he'd reached the coordinates and his radar had locked on target. Without another thought, he pushed the button.

Instantly, from beneath the wings, two AGM-65 Maverick missiles streaked outward, in front of him. He watched them accelerate, then arc smoothly downward, leaving a trail of vapor in their wake. He continued watching the signal received from the missiles' nose-cone cameras as they shot toward the marketplace below—a marketplace already teaming with early-morning merchants and shoppers. When the missiles struck their target, Nadav let out the breath that had been imprisoned in his lungs. Once he confirmed the hit, he turned back, heading for Israel's Ramat David Airbase and a hero's welcome.

He did not stay to watch the cloud of smoke and the hellfire that carried the screams of God knows how many dead and injured. Of course, no one on the ground saw the tears inside his goggles or heard the shudder of his sigh.

*   *   *

As the missiles approached, Al-Khalil stood quietly at his mother's side; his right arm stretched upward, his hand reassuringly gripped by his mother. With his left hand, he held on to the wrist of his younger sister, Teeja. His mother was haggling for the purchase of some couscous, dates, and apricots at the sidewalk market outside a large armored and barricaded building. The vendor's display table sat on a four-foot wall of sandbags in front of the armory. Al-Khalil could not see the vendor, but from his mother's excited speech, he knew she was trying to buy the most she could with the few shekels she got from Hamas as a widow's benefit.

She was holding his baby sister, Aleena, in her right arm. Aleena had been born seven months after his father was martyred in an Israeli attack. Al-Khalil held on to his mother's hand tightly. He knew that she was not only his whole world but also his connection to his history, his past, and his traditions.

In the next moment, he saw the grains, fruits, and shards of glass blow over the wall and past him in a pink cloud. His mother's hand was ripped from his as she disappeared in a fog of masonry dust.

*   *   *

"It was more than a dozen years ago, and I remember every detail as if it had all happened in slow motion. The strangest part is—it didn't seem violent at the time," Al-Khalil explained in a voice that was strangely monotone. "It didn't sound loud either. In fact, I hardly heard any sound at all. I guess the wall protected me. I just stood there. I felt like I was watching someone else's life. I did not know what to do—I was just a child. When the smoke began to clear, I started hearing things again; there was yelling all around me. People were running toward me. No, not toward me, they were running toward the people that were blown away from the building. My mother and my sister and . . . I . . . I . . . cannot even explain what they looked like; I thought somebody poured red paint on them. I did not feel anything; I just kept touching my mother's shoe with my foot and saying 'Mommy, Mommy, Mommy!' Teeja just sat on her ankles and cried. I think she was more upset at the explosion—I don't think she really understood what happened because she was looking for our mother the next morning."

Al-Khalil's breathing became harder. The edges of his nostrils flared; his eyes remained dry and steady. He went on, "I never really felt any great pain, but when I see the blue and white of the Israeli flag or one of their Sons-of-Satan soldiers, I feel something then!"

Al-Khalil could see that his American social worker, Angie Gibran, was reacting to the emotion that was flooding into him, even as his mouth was forming the word *Israeli*. She clutched her chest as his face transformed, and his cheeks burned red with hatred. She reached out from under her traditional Muslim abaya and touched the back of Al-Khalil's hand.

"It does not matter if someone is Palestinian or Israeli; it does not matter if one is Muslim or Jewish or Christian or Catholic—the pain of suffering, the pain of loss is universal. I understand what you are going through. I truly understand. I have a connection to your story not nearly so dramatic, but to me just as painful. My mother was a Palestinian. She was also taken from me to be with Allah."

A happy voice came from the direction of the house behind them. It was Teeja, Al-Khalil's now-teenaged sister. She came running from behind one of the columns on the marble patio overlooking the Mediterranean.

"Al-Khalil, Angie, look what Ben and Sarah gave me!" Teeja shouted, holding a pendant that dangled from a neck rope of braided hemp.

At sixteen, Teeja was well developed, even voluptuous. Her face spoke of legendary Bedouin beauty with large almond-shaped brown eyes and full but perfectly proportioned features that framed the soft bow of her lush lips. When looking at her, it was hard to remember that her maturity and her emotions were still very much a teenager's. Al-Khalil had done his best over the last twelve years to be a father, mother, protector, cheerleader, and disciplinarian. He had done a good job.

"I told you I didn't want you to accept gifts from them, and you should call them by their proper American last names—Mr. and Mrs. Gordon," instructed Al-Khalil in Arabic.

"Oh, don't be so stiff," Teeja answered in English. "They told me it comes from the great pyramid in Egypt. Look, it has the mark of the Prophet on it."

Al-Khalil looked at the pendant. It was modest and, he felt, would do no harm. "Okay," he laughed, tickling her, "but wear it under your abaya."

Teeja pulled at the top of the neckline of her clothing and let the necklace slip underneath and out of sight; then she laughed, pushed against Al-Khalil, and ran back inside. Al-Khalil watched her and felt his most common emotion—ambivalence. He loved to see her happy, but he resented the Jews she and he worked for. He knew she didn't remember their parents' deaths—her world and his were miles apart.

He turned and asked Angie rhetorically, "What am I going to do with her? Sometimes she acts as is if there is no difference between us and the Jews."

"There is no difference—except for how you think of each other," Angie offered.

"Yes, that and the power they wield, and the suffering they cause!"

"There is great suffering; that's for sure. Perhaps that is a good reason to allow for whatever small happiness she can find."

Al-Khalil was about to continue when Mrs. Gordon and her cousin, the American congressman Max Silverman, came out onto the well-manicured lawn. Sarah and Ben Gordon had made the aliyah, the return of a Jew to the Holy Land, in the mid-1980s. They were now Israeli citizens and owner-operators of two thriving Starbucks coffee shops in Tel Aviv. Al-Khalil immediately stood up—bowed his head ever so slightly and began to move toward the pump house.

"Al-Khalil, you don't have to go. I didn't mean to interrupt your talk," Mrs. Gordon said.

"There is still much to do," Al-Khalil replied in a tone that cut off debate.

Al-Khalil turned on the water and began to spray the emerald green grass. As he watched the sod suck up the clear water, he thought of the foul, brackish water that most Palestinians drank in the refugee camps and their segregated ghettos. He would do anything not to work for a Jew and have to pretend to be grateful, but there were no other jobs, and he had a mission. If it were not for Teeja, he long ago would have martyred himself by exploding a crowded bus or a busy marketplace. Then he would have peace and justice for his mother and father.

After his mother's death, Al-Khalil and Teeja lived in a refugee camp in Gaza with their uncle. Six people lived in one room. There was no breeze; it was hot, smelly, and the floor was hard. After two years, a group of Hamas freedom fighters came to the camp asking questions of the children. After Al-Khalil told them that both his mother and father had been killed by the Israelis, they selected him and Teeja to attend one of their boarding schools.

At the school, they had beds and ate well. The walls of the school were covered with banners, slogans, and posters cursing the occupation by the Israelis and extolling the virtues of the Palestinian people generally and Hamas specifically. In class, they were fed propaganda and were taught a violent form of Islam by radical mullahs.

Hamas's propaganda was not necessary to fuel the fire of Al-Khalil's hatred. He had his own personal reasons for hating the Israelis. No philosophy, no religion, no rhetoric could trump his desire for revenge. So when he was asked to become a *sleeper,* a future suicide bomber planted in an Israeli city, he agreed. It was by knowing his life would end in short order that he rediscovered how to appreciate each day; to revel in the flowering of his younger sister; to feel, touch, and taste the experiences with which Allah blessed him. In choosing death, he gained life.

Although hatred propelled him forward, some part of his humanity, his compassion, his soul, survived. Even as hatred seethed within him, he was moved, sometimes to tears, by Teeja's eternal optimism and resiliency. She was the one light of his life. Even more important than his desire for revenge was his vow to buffer her from the ugliness around her, and the hatred within him.

Working for the Gordons was both a curse and a blessing. They were genuinely good people. They treated Teeja and him no differently, he imagined, than any parents would treat their children. He was especially, albeit begrudgingly, appreciative of the nurturing way they had with Teeja. He loved Teeja. So much, in fact, that it was hard to maintain hatred toward anyone showing her kindness. Still, they were Jews . . .

Mrs. Gordon approached them from the patio with her guest. "Angie, I would like you to meet my cousin, Max Silverman. He is a member of Congress from Manhattan. Isn't that where you come from?" she asked.

"Well, actually, I grew up in Brooklyn, but my father works in Manhattan."

"What does he do?" Max Silverman joined in.

"NYPD," Angie left it at that.

"New York's Finest," Max added.

"My cousin is a very smart man," Sarah said as she held Max's arm. "He just came from a congressional fact-finding trip about all the killing in Africa; he heads up a commission on genocide. In September he's going to give a major speech at a human rights conference in upstate New York."

Max was in his midsixties. He was a bit short at five foot seven inches but athletically proportioned. He was bald from his forehead to the crown, which was covered with a yarmulke. The white hair that went around the sides and neck also constituted a short well-trimmed beard and mustache. He was handsome in an easy way; his most striking features were his clear hazel-green eyes and a quiet but infectious laugh.

He was also a sex addict.

He eyed Angie during the introduction. Max eyed every female he met, and he did have preferences. After a moment of ogling, Max seemed startled out of his fantasies as he noticed Angie was talking to him.

"So I joined Amnesty International, and they sent me here because I speak Arabic."

"Uh, uh . . . Amnesty International, yes, they're a good organization. They, uh, give us a hard time; I mean the government. They give the government a hard time every once in a while, but they're a good group," Max stammered as he tried to make sense in response to what he did not hear.

Sarah Gordon said, "Angie, I want to thank you for the good work that you're doing with Al-Khalil. He doesn't talk to us much about his growing up, but I can just tell that he had a hard time. You're doing such a good job with him—you're being a very good friend to him."

"Thank you, Mrs. Gordon," said Angie, acknowledging Al-Khalil with a nod, "I think Al-Khalil has done good work in letting go of some of the anger and hatred he holds inside; and working with him has taught me a great deal about the Palestinian experience. I know it is not very professional of me, but sometimes it seems that he and Teeja are more like family than clients. I don't think

I've ever met someone with more joie de vivre than Teeja." Angie and Al-Khalil smiled warmly at each other.

Ben Gordon came out from the house beckoning to them. Whatever he wanted, it seemed urgent. "Come, come inside. You must look at what's on the TV!"

Everyone moved inside, crowding around the television. The set was tuned to CNN International. The report had already begun.

> CNN has learned that it is not the only network where the messages have appeared. Reports are coming in from the BBC, MSNBC, and other news agencies all the way from Russia to China to Chile. All networks are reporting that the same two messages have appeared on their news tickers:
> *My children, please give me your attention.—God* and
> *Your actions have consequences—in this existence and the next.—God.*

> The first message appeared on the seventh minute of the seventh hour past noon on the seventh day of July, the seventh month of the year, in each time zone. The second message appeared at 7:07 PM and seven seconds the next day. The messages came across the news tickers on the bottom of the screen in the language and alphabet used by each broadcast station. All stations are denying any involvement in producing the messages. We cannot show you video of the messages as they do not appear on any videotape, although they reportedly were seen live by innumerable viewers. Again, two messages, allegedly authored by God, have made mysterious appearances . . . .

The announcer continued speaking, but the enormity of the news caused the listeners to glaze over. The people standing there did not have much in common, but at that moment, they shared a common expression—one that said, "What? What does that mean? What am I supposed to do with it?"

After a few more moments of headshaking and tch-tching, they began to catch each other's eyes with questioning looks. Angie and Mrs. Gordon were not really thinking; they were too busy trying to figure out how they felt. Ben Gordon figured it was some kind of trick and was already trying to solve the question of how it was done. Max Silverman was working out his response, should he be publicly asked for a reaction. Teeja was anxious. Al-Khalil believed the report had to be an Israeli hoax. As a Muslim, he knew God only communicates with humankind indirectly, through signs and messengers like Moses, Jesus, and Muhammad. He wondered what nefarious scheme his enemies were creating. Teeja grabbed his hand, and he patted it reassuringly.

"What do you make of that?" Sarah Gordon quizzed.

"It's gotta be some hacker pulling off the joke of the year," replied her husband.

"Of the century," added Angie.

"What do you think, Max?" asked Ben Gordon.

"I'm not sure. The world is certainly in enough of a mess for God to issue a midcourse correction, but it could certainly be some kind of hoax. Whatever it is, it will sure make people think. It'll be interesting to get back to Washington and see what the hotheads are going to say on the floors of Congress—whatever it is, I hope some good comes of it, even if only for a little while."

Those sage words received nods and grunts of approval. Al-Khalil kept silent and listened. Teeja trembled ever so slightly. Ben broke the reverence.

"Well, Max, we've got to get you to the airport, and, Angie, we've got to get you home. Al-Khalil, would you give them a ride in the Citroën?"

Al-Khalil nodded his assent and went to get the keys to the French-made car. Good-byes and hugs were traded all around. As Al-Khalil returned, he saw Max patting Teeja's cheek.

"I'll miss you most of all, pretty one," said Max in a pseudo-fatherly way.

There was something about what he said that gave Al-Khalil a tug in his stomach and a short burst of cold sweat. Something in the tone of Max's voice, or it might have been that he was standing just a tad too close to Teeja, or maybe it was a look in his eye; whatever it was, Al-Khalil didn't like it—not one bit.

"Ahem," Al-Khalil cleared his throat. "Mr. Silverman, Angie, shall I bring the car around?"

"That'll be fine, Al. Max's bags are in his room," interjected Ben Gordon.

As he left to follow Mr. Gordon's instructions, Al-Khalil bristled at the shortening of his name. After loading Max's bags, he brought the car around to the front door. He got out and opened the passenger doors. Teeja was waiting to get in.

"You stay here with the Gordons," Al-Khalil said.

"But, brother, I love to go to the airport and see the planes. I think that maybe someday I will travel to another place, maybe even America."

"No, you must stay," Al-Khalil said in Arabic for emphasis.

He didn't want Teeja in the same car as Max Silverman, much less next to him in the backseat. Angie and Max got in the back. Al-Khalil placed Max's hand luggage in the front passenger seat, and then ran around to the driver's side, slid behind the wheel, and pulled off.

"So what do you do for Amnesty International?" asked Max, petting Angie's knee.

Angie gave Max a look that only lasted a mini-second but clearly said, "Back off." She adjusted her tunic and, by doing so, managed to move a few inches farther away from Max.

"I'm a social worker. I came here because my family is, was, uh, well, my father is Lebanese and my mother was Palestinian; she passed away. I speak English and Arabic, and I learned Islam from my mother, so I asked to be sent here by Amnesty International because there's so much pain and need here."

Max looked at her kindly. Even though her voice had been strong and free of shudders, the thickening of the moisture in her eyes exposed the pain she held inside. Angie sighed and went on, "Maybe that message, the one we saw inside, really was God, and maybe he's going to do something. I hope so . . . I've seen so much . . ."

"From your lips, to God's ears," Max said softly and fell into a reflective silence looking out the window.

As they traveled south toward the airport, they were treated to beautiful views of the Mediterranean and a tapestry of humanity. Arab and Jewish citizens of Israel walked together in business suits, thobes, t-shirts, tunics, and Jakarta shirts.

Al-Khalil brought the car to a stop. Gush Shalom and Peace Now, two of the older and larger liberal Jewish antiwar groups were holding a demonstration and parade. Their car crept behind people holding signs calling for a stop to Israel's attacks on the Palestinian people and an end to the occupation of Gaza and the West Bank territories.

"I wish that people back home could see what we're seeing. Many of my constituents think that Israelis think with one mind.

Many of us understand what it feels like to be persecuted. Both my parents were killed in Nazi death camps. We hate to be thought of as persecutors, but then we have to protect the land, don't we?" said Max. Then, changing his tone to his lecture voice, he continued, "This is clear proof that Israel is a democracy—with right wing and left wing groups, liberals and conservatives, hawks and doves. How many Americans know that many Israelis oppose war?"

Al-Khalil was surprised to hear Max's confession of internal turmoil. His reality was that Jews were unrelenting, ambitious, and heartless. He began to feel the stirrings of empathy for this fellow orphan. Then he brushed off Max's comments as so much babble. After all, how could a nonbeliever say anything significant?

They arrived at Ben-Gurion Airport. Since May of 1972 when there were two terrorist attacks at the airport killing twenty-six and injuring eighty, Ben-Gurion Airport had become the most secure airport in the world. Al-Khalil drove past layers of fencing where armed soldiers stood guard. There were dozens of surveillance cameras. They stopped at three different security booths on the airport road. Each of them had to produce identification as they went under intense scrutiny and questioning.

Finally, they pulled up to Terminal 3. Al-Khalil put the bags on a baggage cart and pushed it inside. The first thing he noticed was groups of people crowded around televisions tuned to news stations. Max offered his hand, but Al-Khalil bowed his head and returned to the car. Angie moved to the front passenger seat.

"It's hard for you to be around them, isn't it?" said Angie as Al-Khalil moved into the flow of traffic.

"Yes, yes it is, and I hate that. I get mad at everything they say. Later, when I think about it, I won't know what it was that I got so mad about."

"Sometimes we are already angry and are just looking for something to glue our anger onto," offered Angie, wearing her social worker hat.

Al-Khalil indicated his agreement, even though he did not really understand her. He was thinking about other things. They rode in silence a short while, and then he began thinking aloud.

"My father taught me that Allah is kind and merciful, and that we must be kind and merciful too. How can we do that in a world that is not kind and is not merciful? My mother was the most kind. She always said nice things, and she always smiled—you could see it in her eyes above her veil. I want to be like her—but they murdered them; so does that make her right or wrong? That man sounded sad because his parents were killed. Well, my parents were killed, too—and they were killed by his kind. So why should I feel sad for him? It's twice as bad because he knows what it feels like and does it anyway."

Al-Khalil pulled up to the entrance of the apartments where Angie lived. She was relieved because she did not have an answer to Al-Khalil's questions. She grabbed his hand and, with gentle eyes, let him know that she understood.

She got out of the car and walked toward her building. As she walked, she started thinking about her mother again. Her mother had taught her that Islam was a peaceful religion, a religion that honored human rights and dignity. It had clarity; it laid out duties to family, each other, and Allah. It taught that Allah was infinite, wise, and compassionate. It instructed Muslims to treat People of the Book, the Children of Abraham—Muslims, Christians, and Jews—with special courtesy and respect.

In spite of her faith, Angie's mother had been a fragile woman, no match for the driving negativity of Angie's father. His envy of others, criticism, and psychological pounding had driven her mother to tranquilizers, painkillers, and sleeping medications. The drugs plunged her into a deep depression. She ended her life with a handful of pills.

Angie both hated and loved her father. She despised him and, above all else, wanted him to love her and be proud of her. His self-absorption had left Angie with so profound a sense of unimportance that she was driven to join Amnesty International—driven to find purpose in her life. She had also joined to get away from her father, Louis Gibran, "Louie the Cop." If she'd stayed, she feared she would have followed her mother's path of escape through drugs.

She could hear his woeful promises:

> *"I know you hate to take the train into Manhattan, sweet-cakes. I'll get you a car just as soon as I get that promotion!"*

> *"I know your mom's disappointed, but I'll make it up to her. Joey said he'd let me sell Cadillacs at his dealership, on weekends, to make more money."*

> *"I know your mom needs a program and treatment. I should've got that captain's slot instead of that punk Phil, and then I'd have the money for it. You know, I was ranked ahead of him at the academy."*

It wasn't as if he was like that only with her; he was like that with everyone. He was just like that.

CHAPTER 2

Your actions have consequences—
in this existence and the next.

—God

"Can you believe this crap?"

Louis Gibran, Louie the Cop, was talking to the entire room and holding up the morning's front page of the *Daily News*. The banner headline read MESSAGES FROM GOD? The question mark took up the bottom third of the page.

"I wouldn't call it crap if I were you," said one officer.

"Yeah, St. Peter probably has a whole chapter on you in the *go to hell* part of his book," said another.

The whole patrol squad laughed. Louie the Cop dismissed them all with a wave of his middle finger. He was a sad man, wholly unworthy of sympathy or compassion. Whether Louie the Cop was a jerk because of some deep psychic pain caused by an unfortunate past, or if he was a jerk because he was just plain mean didn't much matter to the other officers in the room. He was still a jerk.

He was a tall man, standing six foot three inches, and weighed 230 pounds; but he was not an impressive man. Slumped shoulders, a potbelly, and pockmarked face accentuated an aquiline nose and small, dark, ratty eyes. The same challenges most people meet, greet, and dispose of gave him a shuffle in his walk and a muffle in his talk. His hat was always cocked back, exposing strands of sweat-dampened black hair; however, he did have a set of beautiful white teeth that would glisten and shine, if only he would ever smile.

Louie the Cop, at least that's what everyone from the soda jerk at the Eastside Diner on 112th Street to the assistant chief in charge of Manhattan's Fifth Patrol District, called him. It was a fitting title and not a complimentary one. Most officers take umbrage at being called cops, but after twenty-nine years of less than stellar performance, Louie the Cop's self-esteem took such a beating that even he came to think of himself with that moniker. Every promotion that came his way passed him by. At fifty-four, Louie the Cop was twenty years past burned out. He was eligible to retire, but he had nothing else to do but grumble and covet what everyone else seemed to get.

The occasion of the gathering was the daily roll call and briefing of the afternoon shift. The briefing room was in the basement of a fortress-like building that housed the 23rd Precinct of NYPD's Manhattan North District. The basement of the precinct house shared its space with the briefing room, C-Com—the Communications and 911 Center, locker rooms, and the offices of the sergeants on duty.

The 23rd Precinct was responsible for the area of East Harlem north of Ninety-sixth Street and from the East River to Broadway. The area was commercial, residential, and industrial. It was home to eleven subsidized housing projects and several luxury high-rise condominiums on the East River that had glorious views.

Officer Craig Thompson came over and sat next to Louie the Cop. He was Louie the Cop's rookie partner. Thompson had grown up on a dairy farm outside of Hershey, Pennsylvania, and he looked it. He was a tad over six feet with a swimmer's body, blond hair, brown eyes, and an "aw, gosh" way of speaking. Eighty percent of the milk produced by his family's farm went into Hershey's chocolate.

"Good morning, Louie. What do you think of that?" Thompson asked, pointing to the headline.

"Not much—it's probably some environmental group wanting us to think green," said Louie the Cop, rolling his eyes and making the "quotes" sign with his fingers.

"Uh-huh, well, maybe there is something to it. Did you see the last one? It said, '*Love one another. Work together. Your nature is to be interdependent.—God.*'"

"Well, tell you the truth, I don't give a rat's ass where or who they come from, but I do know this: nothing and nobody has given me a break in this life, so I don't expect to be a poster boy for eternal bliss in the next one . . . . Did you pick up today's login codes?"

"Uh, no."

"Well, why don't you go do that—you're the rookie," instructed Louie the Cop as he turned his attention back to the paper to check how the Yankees were doing.

Thompson got up, walked over to the communication center's Plexiglas window, and leaned down to talk into the semicircular pass-through at counter height. The area had been kept secure ever since onboard, wireless network-access computers were installed in patrol cars. The computer communications were developed to foil criminals who monitored police activity through radio scanners. The computer access codes were changed every day to maintain the security of the network.

"How you doin', Sergeant Sam? Car 5151," Thompson said, flashing his ID.

Sergeant Sam Shómogee responded with the okay sign and then pulled a clipboard off the wall behind him, lifted the blank cover page, and checked the name against the car number. He pulled the tag containing the day's randomly generated username and password off the weekly printout and handed it to Thompson, who returned to his seat next to Louie the Cop.

"Okay, settle down, people," said Shirley Kaminski, the sergeant on duty, as she assumed the podium. Glancing around to assure she had everyone's attention, she continued, "All right, listen up. We got some announcements and some intel. First item—Barney McNulty's wife had a baby boy, eight pounds, eleven ounces—ouch! The jar is set up in the back. Be generous. Second item—Captain Capriati announced his retirement."

There were moans all around.

"Yeah, I know he was a good friend to patrol. Dinner's going to be at VFW Post 165 on Flatbush Avenue at 8:00 PM next Saturday, August 28.

"Third item—we have some stats since the God messages began that show behaviors are changing out there. Church, synagogue, and mosque attendance is up; but car break-ins and grab and runs are up too, usually during and after the services. Domestic violence and rape up—property crimes down. And here's a big one, no murders—not one, zilch, nada. In the same period last year we had five.

"Next item—this is from legal, and I quote—'Be aware of, and sensitive to, freedom of speech and freedom of religion issues.' I asked what that meant. Best I can figure is, someone talking on a soapbox, that's free speech; someone spray-painting REPENT on the wall is not. Carrying signs is okay—blocking sidewalks is not. Remember your actions have consequences, and don't forget that you may be the consequence of somebody else's action. Okay, that's it. Be careful—things can get scary fast out there."

"Hey, Sarge, is some people carrying signs and walking in a row a parade?" asked an officer as the squad began standing up and shuffling out.

Sergeant Kaminski turned around and shrugged her shoulders. "If it walks like a duck, quacks like a duck, and looks like a duck . . ."

"It's a duck," finished the young officer with a smile and a nod of his head.

Louie the Cop and Thompson walked out to the precinct parking lot and got into their squad car. Thompson entered the day's login codes into the computer, started the automated sign-on process, put the car in gear, and eased out of the precinct parking lot, turning uptown toward 112th Street.

"You know, if I hadn't picked up a rookie partner like you, I'd be drivin' a full-sized squad car instead of this tin can, not-made-in-America piece of shit," said Louie the Cop.

Thompson suggested, "At least we're saving gas and not contributing to global warming. You know, I saw this movie about the polar ice caps . . ."

"I don't wanna hear about that liberal crap, you tree-hugging Chicken Little," Louie the Cop interrupted as Thompson turned onto 112th Street and headed east in silence.

On the East Side, 112th Street was one of those peculiar neighborhoods where subsidized housing projects were nestled in the armpit of high-rise condominiums with killer views and even deadlier price tags. The elite, living six hundred feet in the air, had their groceries delivered by food emporiums with names like Gristede's, Nature's Menu, and Holistic Health. The poorer folks shopped at corner convenience stores, where they paid just as much—the economics of poverty. During the day, kids attended after-school programs at the First Baptist Church of Harlem, the Islamic Unity Mosque, Upward Bound, the B'nai Brith Synagogue, and St. Mary of the Immaculate Conception. The gangs ruled the night.

Thompson slowed down and pulled over next to the playground at the First Baptist Church of Harlem. The eight-story building was a landmark because of the fifty-foot-high cross of white brick set into the grey masonry of the west wall. Underneath the cross was one of the few uptown playgrounds that actually had a grass playing field.

"It really bothers me when I see them hanging around the playground wearing colors," said Thompson, motioning toward the three boy-men leaning around a light pole wearing fire engine red and silver, the colors of the 112th Street Gang.

"So whaddya gunna do? You can't touch them for fear of *harassing* them, you can't search them 'cause they *got rights*, and you can't order them to move 'cause *it's a free country*," Louie the Cop said as he turned the page of the *Daily News*. "You know, back when I started out you could . . ."

Thompson didn't hear the rest of Louie the Cop's historical analysis. He was out of the car and moving toward the gang members. "Hey, guys," he called. His gun was in its holster. His nightstick was in the sheath of his utility belt. Both of his hands were visible to send the message that he was approaching in peace.

"Look, I know this is your turf, and that you guys rule . . . and I know you're not selling any dope to these young children so . . . ," Officer Thompson started.

"Yo, man, you're that new cop, ain't you? What's your name?" The tall one peered closely at Craig's nametag. "Yeah, Officer Thompson, I heard you was a'right—a little too white maybe, but a'right."

"I just don't know how you can partner up with Louie the Pig over there," the small one said.

"It's Louie the Cop," Thompson politely corrected him. "So like I was saying, in a few hours all these children will be finished and . . ."

The group started stiffening. They did not like being told what they could and couldn't do and where they could and couldn't hang out.

"Okay, okay, just hold on a second. You know that you guys with your cool jackets are kind of, you know, a distraction, and . . . it takes them off their game," Thompson said.

"Yeah, well, their game ain't our game."

"We're just fine where we are, man."

"I like the view from right here," said the third one, ogling one of the girls on the playground as she shot a basket.

"And you know we all gotta remember that our actions have consequences," Officer Thompson finished, quoting the alleged message from God.

With his last three words, the energy in the air shifted.

"Yeah, man, okay, that's cool. We got some shit to take care of on 114th anyway," said the tall one.

"Long as you ain't telling us what to do," said the short one.

"That's cool—later, man," the third one added.

As they walked away, they all stood a little bit taller, as if to show they were moving by their own choice.

As Officer Thompson got back in the car, Louie the Cop's face was still buried in the newspaper. "What was that—some of that

'Relating to Gang Members' psychobabble bullshit they're teaching you guys at the academy these days?" Louie the Cop queried out of the side of his mouth.

"Why, you thick-skinned old geezer, you were watching me after all," Thompson exclaimed.

At least Louie the Cop knew something about watching your partner's back. He wasn't a total loss. In spite of the outwardly calm exchange, both officers knew that any contact with gangs had the potential of devolving into violent, even deadly encounters.

*   *   *

A short walk from the First Baptist Church of Harlem was one of the few remaining clusters of privately owned brownstones in the area. The homes had passed down for at least three, if not six or seven, generations. Although modest, land values had risen so much over the years, many of the owners would no longer have been able to buy their homes.

Tillie Clidson had inherited her house from her mom. Her dad had died in the Korean War, and her brothers had been killed two years apart in Vietnam. From the time she was twenty until she was thirty, Tillie had taken care of her mom, who had never been the same after her sons died. Tillie had borne three children before a stroke had paralyzed her husband's left side. He had died soon after, having lost his will to live.

With all the loss and heartache, Tillie was still warm, inviting, and gracious. She loved her children Brenda, Joe, and Billy. They gave her meaning, purpose, and happiness. Ever since Joe had started bringing over his playground playmates, she had been the quintessential Kool-Aid mom.

Like most brownstones, the bedrooms were upstairs in the narrow building. The stoop, or front steps, went straight into the living room where Tillie's old console television was always on. She bought it new before there were remote controls. The last time it was repaired, she was told she probably would not find any more replacement vacuum tubes. She liked not having a remote. It was one of her little ploys to get attention.

"Joseph," she would call, "come put on Oprah for me," or "William, find me something to watch without so much fighting." She never asked Brenda. When Brenda wasn't working, she was home tending to Tillie. Sometimes when she was talking to her children, Tillie's eyes would well up, blood would rush to her head, and her breath would shorten and take on shudders. A psychologist might say it was repressed grief and anguish from her lifelong history of loss. Tillie would say it was gratitude that the Lord had blessed her with three such beautiful children.

The curtains were closed, even in the daytime, but the bright light of a clear, late summer afternoon came snaking through the cracks. The room had a soft golden glow from the low wattage light bulbs and a not-yet-quite-musty smell from the upholstered furniture, which could qualify as antique. The family was devout Baptist. One wall boasted a beautiful print of Black Jesus; on the credenza was a porcelain crèche, which was left up all year 'round. Tillie had placed the Ethiopian wise man and his camel in front of the other two.

She often watched the television preachers. She liked that young boy from Houston best. Since God had made Himself known (there was no thought of hoax in Tillie's mind), everyone had been talking a lot about the messages. She did not understand why anyone was making such a fuss—after all, she had always known God existed. Hadn't he always given her strength?

The United States representative from her district, Congressman Max Silverman, was on the television from his conference in the Adirondacks. The cameras were around him, and they were asking him what he thought of the messages.

"Well, I don't think we should jump to any conclusions until we know more," suggested the politician. "Congress will be starting hearings Monday, and I understand the National Security Council is already trying to determine if there is any threat to national security."

"How could a message from God impact national security?" quizzed a reporter.

"If they *are* messages from God . . . if not, we've got someone hacking into the worldwide communications network—and that could be worrisome."

Another reporter asked, "SETI, the Search for Extraterrestrial Intelligence, is reporting that its radio telescopes and those of other agencies are receiving the same messages all over the world at the same moment in Morse code and in the language of each country. Do you have a response?"

"I haven't seen the report, so I don't want to speculate, but look . . . we can all choose how we want to understand these messages. For me, I've always been a spiritual man, and so until we know the facts, I'm going to hope that this is some form of helpful divine intervention. Lord knows, and I say that literally, we've got some problems down here. If we started realizing that our actions, individually and as a nation, do have eternal consequences, we would be better off. Thank you."

"Amen," Tillie shouted.

CHAPTER 3

You have everything you need to make
your world a paradise
or to destroy it.

—God

Billy was bouncing his basketball on his bedroom floor when he heard his mother, Tillie, call his brother's name.

"Joseph, you take your brother out to the basketball court so he can let loose some of that energy!" she yelled up the stairs; and then as she returned to her easy chair, she followed her admonition with, "Lord, Billy, you're going to drive me crazy with that thumping, thump, thump, thump. One of these days you're goin' to knock the plaster down around my head and then what are you goin' to say—oh, Mama, I'm so, so sorry—well, you better not do that!" She gave out something between a sigh and a groan as she fell backward into her cushions.

Smiling, Billy caught the ball, which he'd known was hitting the floor over his mother's head. At fifteen, he was the youngest, tallest, and smartest kid in the junior class at his high school. He loved to talk about calculus, Einstein, and black holes—mostly because of the ooohs and ahhhs he got from adults when he did—but he loved to play basketball even more. At 147 pounds, six feet and a half inch tall, he'd have been called a geek if he weren't so deadly with his three-point shots. Taking his ball with him, he headed for his brother's room. His mom wouldn't let him go to the courts without Joe this late in the afternoon—they weren't safe after sunset—but he didn't mind. Joe, who was known on the streets as Joe-24, wasn't as much fun has he used to be before he broke his leg in college, but they were still close. Besides, Billy didn't mind Joe-24's celebrity rubbing off on him.

Joe was asleep. He slept a lot lately. Billy sat on the bed next to Joe and bounced the ball off his brother's shoulder blades a couple of times. At first, Joe didn't move; then his right arm swung around in a blur, and his hand met the ball. The ball stopped dead in the air as if it were glued to Joe's huge mitt of a hand. Billy got a small flutter in his stomach, wondering what Joe was going to do next.

Joe slowly lowered the ball to the floor, then rolled onto his back. "I guess it's time to get up, huh?" he said, rubbing his eyes and yawning. The first few minutes of the day were the best, the few moments before he remembered that he couldn't play football anymore. Joe's question was rhetorical, but Billy answered it anyway.

"Yeah, it's time to get up you big lazy has-been."

Joe came up fast but then laughed and just rolled his brother off the bed onto the floor. No one but Billy talked to him like that and got away with it. In spite of everything—his career-ending injury, dropping out of college, not getting a job—Joe knew his brother idolized him. He also knew Billy was the only person with whom he could be himself. Around his little brother, he didn't have to pretend not to be sad, didn't have to pretend to be anything other than the injured athlete that he was.

Joe launched himself at his brother, pulling him back onto the bed, and attacked with the ages-old brotherly tradition of the underarm tickle. As Billy squirmed and screamed and laughed, Joe wondered if the kid had any idea how much Joe idolized *him*—idolized him for his intelligence, loved him for his sweetness, and respected him for his dreams of the stars.

A shrill Mama-yell cut short the reverie, "You boys stop that! I told you—no fighting! I'm trying to watch *Dr. Phil* down here."

The boys stopped going at each other and said in turn, "Yes, ma'am," and secretly chuckled and winked at each other. It only took a few minutes for Joe to get dressed; then they headed down the stairs with Billy dribbling off every other step.

"Joseph, now you watch out for your little brother."

"Yes, Mom."

"And don't walk around with your chest open like that, or you'll catch your death."

"Yes, Mom," Joe said in a sigh.

"Joseph Roosevelt Clidson, you're not listening to a word I say. You know, just 'cause God is around doesn't mean you don't have to be careful. I've known lots of righteous men who aren't always doing the right thing."

Joe stopped at the door, turned, and went back to his mother. He cradled her face in both of his large hands and looked her straight in the eye.

"Don't worry, Mom. Nobody's going to mess with skinny Billy while Joe-24's around," he said, then pushed up his sleeve to show off his thigh-sized biceps.

Tillie seemed satisfied. She reached up and caressed Joe's cheek with her palm. No other words had to be said.

Joe and Billy walked down the stoop and turned west toward the Fiorello LaGuardia Community Center. Joe's appearance was so different from Billy's that it was hard to imagine them as brothers.

Joe was compact, where Billy was stretched. Where Billy's face was long, Joe's was round. Where Billy's face was mature, Joe's was boyish.

From across the street someone yelled, "Yo, Billy, for three."

Billy push-passed the ball to the young man; it flew across the street in a line drive. The boy caught it, dribbled twice while doing a 360-degree turn, and lofted the ball up in a perfect arc into Billy's hands.

The boy shouted, "Three!"

Billy shouted back, "Three!"

They waved at each other, smiled, and went on their way. Everybody knew Billy. He had won the New York City Science Fair by building a model of a futuristic colony on the planet Mars. He built a replica of a canyon on Mars and then put a roof on it, installed a miniature ventilation system, created a city inside it, and then showed how algae could breathe oxygen into the thin Martian atmosphere. When one of the judges, a NASA scientist, revealed that NASA itself was using the same concept in its strategic planning, Billy won first place and a headline on the front page of the *Daily News*.

As they rounded the last corner, they ran into Joe's ex-girlfriend, Lori Blount. Lori was a few inches shorter than Joe. She was slim but not delicate. Her cheeks were perpetually rosy, even without blush. She had teardrop shaped eyes, long eyelashes, smooth skin curving gently over high cheekbones, and exceedingly kissable lips.

Whenever Joe saw Lori, it filled him with so many emotions, but awkward was the only thing that came out. Seeing Lori always brought Joe down. It made him think of what was—and what could have been.

"Uh, eh . . . hi, Lori."

"Hi, Joe. I was just going over to see your mom."

"Uh-huh, yeah well, she's home," Joe said, trying to be helpful.

They both shuffled a bit. Too many seconds went by in silence.

"I . . . I was just takin' Billy to uh, to play some ball," Joe explained.

"Yeah, I guess . . . well, you best go on. It's getting kind of late, see ya," Lori responded.

"Yeah, I guess I will. Well, see ya," Joe said.

"Mhmm," Lori said with a slight smile as she turned and walked on.

Joe-24 watched her walk away feeling foolish, helpless, proud, and mad all at the same time. He still loved her, but he wasn't about to admit it to himself. His intoxication with pride pushed her away as surely as any other addiction. Now that he was a wounded warrior, his pride wouldn't allow him to reach out to her.

"You know she really loved you. When you were away, she always came over and talked to Mom about you, even after y'all broke up," said Billy. Then he added in a whisper, "she still does."

Joe-24 heard the whisper. He looked at Billy with questions written all over his face—questions to be left among the unasked.

"I don't want to talk about it" was all Joe-24 said.

Billy and Joe-24 walked onto the basketball courts, and Joe went over to his spot in the corner of the fencing where a little patch of weeds had struggled up through a crack in the blacktop. He picked up a few blades of what seemed like grass, started breaking off quarter inch pieces, and mindlessly throwing them toward his feet. His brother was already in a pickup game of three-on-three.

Joe first started playing pickup football on this very same court. *Man, did I go home with all kinds of cuts, scratches, and road rash*, he thought. His mother would scold him from the time he got home until she cleaned the wounds with hydrogen peroxide and put on the last Band-Aid.

He looked up, watched the basketball sail on a crosscourt pass, and remembered how many times a football had sailed like that into his arms for a touchdown. Joe had been an extraordinary football player. At a muscular 210 pounds and five foot eleven inches tall, he was the ideal size for an NFL running back. He was like a bowling ball. Once he got the football and tucked it into his gut, opposing players bounced off him like so many bowling pins. His childish round face and broad grin endeared him to everyone he met.

Joe had broken every football record at East Harlem High. He became a neighborhood icon even before he graduated. He had a fairytale romance with Lori, the captain of the cheerleading team. They started dating in their sophomore year, and everyone said they were soul mates. Joe was recruited by Syracuse University in upstate New York. He became a starter in his freshman year, wearing number 24. By the end of his first season, he was already a Big Man on Campus. Being a star brought parties, adoration, and, of course, women. Everyone said that Joe had pro potential.

When he came home during the summer between his freshman and sophomore years, he still had stars in his eyes. Lori became just a girl from back home. Joe had moved on, at least in his perception of himself, to bigger and better things. Lori was heartbroken but always told him that he would come to his senses. How could he not? Their relationship had been so special.

In the sixth game of his third collegiate season, in a short yardage situation, things changed for Joe. It was third down with two yards to go. Joe lined up behind the quarterback.

"Two . . . 12 . . . 8 . . . Hut . . . Hut!"

The center hiked the ball to the quarterback, who stepped back, turned, and placed the ball in the center of Joe's body between his folded arms. Joe cradled the ball, put his head down, and exploded into the hole created by his offensive blockers between the center and guard. The linebackers were on a blitz, so once he cleared the defensive line, he was into the secondary and three steps away from an open-field sprint to the end zone. That's when he went down. The sickening crack was heard all the way up to Row LL in the stands.

The referees' yellow flags flew out all over the field, but it wasn't much consolation to Joe-24. He had been the victim of an illegal move, in technical terms, a facemask infraction. An opposing team member grabbed his facemask and spun him sideways. That didn't cause the injury, but it did cause his right foot, which was planted solidly with cleats into the turf, to turn at an odd angle—just enough of an angle to make the bones of his shin and ankle vulnerable to be crushed by the weight of a pursuing linebacker coming from the other side.

The stadium fell into a hushed silence. Trainers came running out onto the field, took one look at Joe's leg, and called for the motorized cart. It drove onto the field and drove Joe off the field after the last play of his career.

They gave Joe a shot of morphine, and he fell into a drugged sleep. When he woke up in a hospital, his leg was in a cast and in traction. His team members came by to visit with sad beagle eyes. They felt bad for their fallen friend, but Joe could see that they mostly felt relieved it had not happened to them. Each one of them thought, *There, but for the grace of God, go I.* Career-ending injuries are life changing—and not for the better.

Once Joe got out of the hospital and was walking around, he got plenty of pats on the back and well wishes, but they didn't last long. After a while, his team members would cross the street to avoid him. He knew it wasn't because they had anything against him, but because he was a constant reminder of how fragile their own futures were. In time, they stopped calling. Joe lost the advantages of being on the team. He no longer ate at the training table; he no longer had the tutors and mentors that helped him handle a sophisticated, academic college load. By the end of his sophomore year, he was on academic probation and decided not to return for his junior year.

When he came home, he was still a hero in the neighborhood— that never changed; but getting a job was a different thing. He had been concentrating on the art and science of football for almost a decade. He was lost without it—lost and depressed. He had such pride, and now it was all gone. He saw Lori from time to time, but the hurt prevented them from getting back together. He spent his days mostly in bed and running errands for his mom. He was on a downward spiral.

A cold shudder ran through Joe due both to his thoughts and the temperature drop from the setting sun. As the light failed, the game broke up. Billy came over, slapped Joe-24 on the knee, bringing Joe out of his reflections.

"You wanna drop by Sandy's and get something to drink?" Billy asked.

It was a rhetorical question since they always stopped by Sandy's for something to drink. Joe answered anyway, "Yeah, sure."

Joe stood up and limped. He always limped for the first few steps after his ankle had been motionless for a few minutes and stiffened up.

Habib's delicatessen and convenience store on the corner was called Sandy's by the locals. The awning over the door said so, and neither of the last two owners had changed it. Habib had four employees on the books and a few under the table. Once a week, when Billy came in with Joe, Habib gave Billy the list of employees and hours worked. Billy kept the hourly rates in his head and knew the percentages for federal and state payroll deductions. Inside of five minutes, Billy would write down the gross pay, the deductions, and the net pay for each worker. He did it all without a calculator. In return for Billy's "bookkeeping" services, his family got sodas and sandwiches whenever they wanted, as long as they didn't abuse it. They never did.

While Billy was taking care of Habib's business, Eyeball and 4x4, two members of the 112th Street Gang, wearing their colors, came in. They were in good humor and passed palm slaps all around. Eyeball got his name from having incredibly acute vision. Local lore said that once he had spotted a penny while walking by a pile of dead brown autumn leaves; Eyeball swore it was from across Amsterdam Avenue. The origin of 4X4's name was more obvious; he stood five foot nine inches tall and packed 305 pounds.

They'd been trying to recruit Joe-24 since he came back from Syracuse. His size and toughness would be a real asset to the organization, not to mention the increase in status the gang would achieve by assimilating someone that already had the respect of so many locals. Although Joe-24 grew up with most of the 112th Streeters, even liked some of them, the gang life just wasn't his thing. Joe didn't drink, much less do dope, steal, rob, or rape.

Football had always been his drug of choice; any violent urges that arose in Joe-24 played out on the gridiron.

After the usual shoulder shots and barbs, Eyeball grabbed a beer, reached around Billy to hand Habib the cash, and headed out the door.

"You can't walk on the street with an open bottle," Habib warned.

"Yeah, I sure don't want to go to prison," Eyeball responded with his signature roll of the eyes.

Billy finished up with the math, folded the payroll sheet in half, and gave it to Habib at the front counter. He grabbed a Dr. Pepper, and Joe selected a Gatorade. They turned to leave. Billy fell into formation behind 4x4 as Joe stopped to grab a piece of baklava from the counter.

*   *   *

A black General Motors SUV with tinted windows slowly turned at the far corner and slid along the parked cars. The darkened back window slid down smoothly, and a dark hand gripping a black Beretta peeked out. The streetlights glinted off the gold-nugget ring on the trigger finger.

*   *   *

As 4x4 filled the doorframe, Eyeball saw the action in the SUV and let out a high-pitched whistle. He motioned to 4x4 with his hand spread out, palm down, and hit the sidewalk. 4x4 didn't have to think; he flew forward, rolled, and buttressed up against the car parked at the curb—leaving Billy exposed behind him.

Joe saw some motion at the door from inside the store. He looked over and saw Billy's soda bottle explode. At first, he thought it was the carbonation. Billy turned to look at Joe with pure curiosity for a second that seemed to take minutes to pass. His eyes rolled back, his head followed, and then his whole body just seemed to sink into his feet as he fell backward into the store. That's when Joe saw the widening red stain on the front of Billy's shirt. The scream that erupted from Joe's throat and his movements were automatic. It seemed that someone else was yelling using his vocal cords. Joe cradled Billy's head; he could feel Billy's breath. He pulled back and looked at Billy's face; his brother was still conscious but bewildered.

"You're going to be okay! You're going to be okay!" Joe pleaded, spitting tears. Then he shouted at Habib, "Call 911!"

Habib seemed stunned. When he heard Joe-24 yell, he was startled out of his shock. He fumbled with the phone and dialed in the report. Eyeball ran after the SUV to try to get a description, and 4x4 was on his cell phone to the 112th Street Gang to tell them about the drive-by.

*   *   *

The call came over the radio in under a minute.

"Shots fired. Man down. Sandy's delicatessen on 113th Street in between Second and Third avenues . . . still acquiring information from reporter."

The district supervisor picked up the broadcast and radioed out, "Car 5151 or any other cars in the vicinity report Code 3. EMS and fire rescue stage on Second Avenue in between 112th and 113th Street."

An EMS van and a fire rescue truck headed toward Third Avenue to wait until the officers responding cleared the scene of any danger, so they would be safe to attend the wounded.

"This is car 5151. We are in route. ETA under a minute."

Officer Thompson switched on the blue lights and siren, did a screeching U-turn on 112th, and was the first responder to the scene. He brought the squad car to a halt at a forty-five degree angle to the front of Sandy's delicatessen so that the car could be used as a shield should any shooters still be in the area.

Eyeball came running over, shouting about the black car. From behind the passenger's door, Louie the Cop yelled for him to put his hands in the air and to stop in his tracks. Eyeball did as he was told, then spoke more coherently. "It was a drive-by, man. They were in a black SUV. They went that way," Eyeball shouted, pointing west.

Thompson and Louie the Cop came up from their protected positions and surveyed the outside. Louie the Cop covered his partner as he entered the store, did a quick scan, and then asked Habib if he was okay.

"I'm okay, I'm okay. They're gone, they gone away," Habib said breathlessly.

"We're clear in here," Thompson shouted out to his partner then clicked the shoulder speakerphone to call in EMS, "EMS come in. The scene is secure. We have one man down, gunshot wound to the chest."

Joe-24 was rocking back and forth, holding his brother and stroking his hair. The back of his left hand was already wet with tears that thinned the blood as he shifted between holding his brother and clearing his eyes. He was talking gently to Billy, but between the grip grief had on his throat and the short breaths he could manage between sobs, his words turned into nothing more than an undulating moan.

Louie the Cop was outside debriefing 4x4 and Eyeball. Once he had a rough idea of what happened, he called in a Be on the Look Out for the black late-model GM SUV within a five-mile radius. The orange and white NYC EMS ambulance pulled up, followed shortly by backup patrol and unmarked cars. EMS officers went straight to Billy and gently pried Joe-24 away.

"Please, sir, you have to stop moving him. Let us get in there. We are here now. You've done a good job. You have to let us do ours now!" said the EMS officer gently but firmly.

Joe-24 allowed himself to be pulled away and half blindly stood up. A flash of rage tore through him. His fist barreled down on a rack of fried pork rinds, slicing through the top three shelves and throwing bags and chips all over the floor. In the next moment, a blanket of defeat enveloped him. Louie the Cop heard the crash and asked a couple of bystanders to help Joe-24 outside.

By now, a crowd was starting to form. The news sprinted down the sidewalks, across streets, and around the corner. A light-skinned twenties-something man with dreadlocks—pushed into his green, yellow, and red knit cap—walked up to the ladies sitting on the sidewalk in front of Tillie's house.

"Ms. Clidson, they say something happened over by Sandy's. It was something 'bout one of your boys."

It took all of a second for what the man said to sink in. Tillie exhaled with a shudder, "Oh, oh, oh, what is it? What happened?"

"I don't know ma'am, just that something happened with one of your boys. I got Sammy comin' over with his car."

Tillie grabbed at her sweater and clutched her purse. She began folding her chair, as if on auto-drive. Her friends waved her back.

"Don't worry about your chair, we'll take it up."

"It's okay; everything is going to be okay."

"Nothing's goin' to happen to those good boys of yours."

The reassurances came fast but were halfhearted. In this neighborhood, getting uninvited news was always unwanted. As a local expression puts it, "Bad news travels fast, and good news don't travel at all."

A faded green and primer red 1986 Buick drove up. The young man driving the car, Sammy, opened the driver-side rear door, and the neighborhood women ushered Tillie over to the car with encouraging comments. Brenda came down the stoop still buttoning her coat and jumped in the passenger seat.

"Mama, oh, Mama," she said while reaching back to grab her mother's hand.

Tillie patted Brenda's hand in an act of false bravado. They spent the rest of the short ride in silence. Silence, that is, until they turned the corner and saw the red and blue flashing lights. A uniformed officer was stretching yellow police tape around the door of Sandy's.

"Oh, Brenda," Tillie said as Sammy eased to a stop next to the ambulance.

Tillie got out of the car and came head-to-head with the gurney Billy was on. Billy was conscious but very tired. He recognized Tillie.

"I'm sorry, Mama, I'm sorry," Billy whispered through half-closed eyes.

"You don't need to be sorry. You just need to live!" Tillie prayed, holding his hand while moving with the gurney.

The legs of the gurney hit the back of the ambulance and folded up with a metallic clank. The EMS officers jumped in and told Tillie they were taking her son to the trauma center at Columbia Medical Center. They closed the back doors, cutting Tillie off from her son. The siren started up, and the ambulance sped away, leaving nothing behind except the smell of diesel and burnt tire tread.

Tillie just stood there in the middle of the street, not sure of what had just happened. Brenda put her arm around Tillie's shoulders and led her to the curb. Tillie saw Joe on the sidewalk against the wall of Habib's store. His cheeks were shiny with smeared tears and blood. *Dear Lord, why couldn't he keep my Billy safe*, she thought as a jolt of despair flashed through her. She looked for the ambulance, and then back at Joe. Even through her fear of the horrific, her dread of what might have happened to one son, her Mother's pain for the torment she knew her other son was going through pulled her toward Joe.

She walked toward him—arms outstretched. She lost sight of him in a blur of tears. She rubbed her eyes. When she lowered her hands, all she could see were the flashing red lights. There wasn't enough air. The concrete felt like it was still wet. Her head started to spin. She fainted—she fainted right there on the sidewalk, just barely ten feet from where her son was shot.

When Tillie came to, the first thing she noticed was the familiarity of her own living room, its warmth, and the sound of her own television. She was having a hard time remembering when she lay down on her couch. Then the cold, hard images of the flashing lights, the gurney, and the crowd of people fired in her consciousness; and she sat bolt upright.

"Billy, my William, where is my boy?"

Her plea woke the room up. There were more than a dozen people in the room, all quiet, all somber. Brenda, Joe, Lori, the sidewalk ladies, and some of Billy's friends were there. Their expressions scared her. Brenda came over, knelt, and took Tillie's hand.

"Mama, you fainted, and the doctor gave you something to help you sleep."

"Where's my boy?" she asked again but more quietly. She feared she already knew. She looked deeply into Brenda's face but got no answer. Moving her gaze from face-to-face, her fear was confirmed. She let out a sorrowful wail, and then turned her face into the couch and cried. The combination of grief and medication shortly eased her back into a merciful sleep.

CHAPTER 4

Love one another. Work together.
Your nature is to be interdependent.

—God

Habib Rashid had pushed back the scissor gates protecting his store at 5:30 AM every day for the past seven years. There was always a delegation of the city's homeless asleep on the sidewalk along Lexington Avenue and down 112th Street. Sometimes he felt sorry for them, especially when it was raining or cold. He knew that the Quran required him to give alms to the poor. He justified ignoring them by telling himself that they probably weren't Muslim or, for that matter, not even Children of Abraham.

The years since 9/11 had been difficult, especially for an American citizen of Persian descent. True, his Middle Eastern appearance evoked hard looks and uneasiness, but the aspersions cast upon Islam and his devout beliefs were more difficult to deal with. It seemed for him and other Muslims that freedom of religion had was a right owned by others. He hated being pressured by public opinion to choose between being a Muslim and being American. For many Americans the expression "For God and Country" is clear. For Habib it was an oxymoron like a "patient New Yorker" or a "fun tax audit."

With the images of Billy's shooting swirling through his mind, he did not sleep well. He had become nauseous cleaning up the blood, and he grieved the boy he considered a friend. Violence seemed to assault his senses daily. The number of killings due to religious warfare in the Middle East and between People-of-the-Book—Jews, Christians, and Muslims—worldwide was never ending and growing in viciousness. He was grateful that his religious leader, the imam of his mosque, was moderate and interpreted the growing violence as signs of Allah's displeasure. He felt that the recently reported messages from God bordered on being a sacrilege; nevertheless, he did take note of the mysterious nature of their appearance.

Perhaps it was these thoughts that brought him to the decision that would forever change his life and the lives of countless others. On this day, he decided to feed the few souls outside his store.

He unlocked the side door, turned on the lights, and turned up the heat. The small convenience store was modest at best. It still had a tattered awning with the name of a previous owner and what Habib called plate-wood-windows—glass where they hadn't been broken, planks where they had been. There wasn't much room inside. The aisles were so small that two people had to turn sideways to pass. Even though clean, the lack of light and age made the store look dusty and dingy. Habib filled the basket of the BUNN coffeemaker with grounds and hit the start button. The refrigerated display case still had a dozen or so wrapped subs from the day before and half a tray of rich, honey-soaked baklava pastry.

Upstairs, a studio apartment, of sorts, was built into an old storage space. Omby, Habib's night clerk lived there. It was part of his so-called compensation package. It also provided a little extra security during the night hours. Before the coffee was finished, its aroma drifted upstairs and prematurely coaxed Omby from a solid sleep. Six minutes later, Omby was coming down from his upstairs bedroom.

"Mornin', boss," Omby said with a yawn. "What's all the commotion?"

"Come, come," Habib motioned him over. "Here, fix up six coffees to go—regular."

"Ah . . . Boss, we ain't even open yet. There's no customers— what time is it anyway? It's not even light out! I need to go back to sleep," Omby declared as he looked around at the still-darkened store and scratched his butt.

"*Tut, tut, tut, tut, tut,*" Habib machine-gunned. "Come fix coffees, fix, fix, fix."

Habib was concentrating on cutting the baklava into squares. He was licking the honey off his fingers as he had done at his uncle's store in Tehran, when his Mother wasn't looking. He was smiling the same way too. Omby dutifully finished his assigned task.

"'What next, boss?"

"Take that table outside the front door."

"What table?"

"That one, the one where the dolls are."

"Boss, those aren't dolls. They're action figures," said Omby with a lighthearted jab.

Habib noticed Omby's tone. "Action figures, dolls—dolls, action figures," Habib sparred back with an over-exaggerated roll of his eyes. "Get the table ready—put outside."

Omby did as he was told. Habib put the subs in a box with the tray of baklava on top and carried them out to the table with its red Formica top floating like a magic carpet above the concrete sidewalk.

"Bring the coffees," shouted Habib over his shoulder.

Omby, by habit, lined the coffee cups up, still looking for the prospective customers. All he could see was some bums sleeping in the crook of the sidewalk and the building. He was drop jawed when he saw his boss walk over to the closest one and begin shaking her awake.

"Food, food, coffee, hot coffee," said Habib, pointing at the table. The homeless woman just looked at Habib blankly. She pulled back at first, not comprehending what was happening. "Food, food, coffee, hot coffee," repeated Habib more urgently.

The woman shifted and pushed herself up. Habib watched as she tentatively walked over to the table and carefully reached out to cradle the warm cup, half-scared that Omby would swat her hand. Omby was still shaking his head in disbelief. Once the woman saw that she was safe, she began grabbing at the baklava. Omby finally came out of his trance and took the woman's arm gently, giving her a sub as he did it.

Habib went to each person in turn, shaking them and pointing them to the table where they could enjoy coffee and food. By now, it was getting close to six o'clock in the morning, and there were others walking along the street and down the sidewalk. They stopped and watched what was happening. Those that were poor and hungry came across, looking for warmth and food also. It didn't take long for a crowd to gather. Habib started to feel the warmth inside during acts of kindness. He rested for a moment, putting his hands on his hips, and looked over at Omby and gave a smiling wink.

"Yeah, boss, at first I thought you were plumb crazy, but this feels good. It's kinda cool," replied Omby to Habib's unspoken affirmation.

Both of them were now going in and out of the store, making more coffee, pulling out rolls and cold cuts, making up sandwiches, and bringing them outside. The crowd continued to gather and grow. Two teenage girls came across the street and watched. They whispered to each other a few times. Finally, the blonde pushed the brunette closer.

"Stop," she said to her friend. The brunette turned around and found herself within a few feet of Habib. "Can we help?" the shy girl asked.

"Of course, of course," Habib responded. Then he turned to Omby and said, "We need more sandwiches. Get more food from the storage closet and show them how to make sandwiches."

Omby went back inside and walked through the store to get to the storage room. He walked into the dry storage area and pulled open the door to the small walk-in refrigerator. He did not see many cold cuts, but he retrieved what there was and brought them to a prep table. He pulled several loaves of bread off the shelves and some jars of mayonnaise. He showed the girls how to make various sandwiches.

When Omby went back outside, the line stretched down to 112th Street and around the corner. Across the street, a crowd of spectators had begun to form. At least half of them were talking, text messaging, or taking pictures with their cell phones. He shook his head.

"Holy Moses, boss. Are you sure we know what we're doing?"

"Allah is generous; we must be generous. The Quran instructs us to give alms to the poor."

"Yeah, but it doesn't tell you that you have to do it all by yourself!"

"Hush, hush. Go. Get more sandwiches; make coffee."

Omby had three pots of coffee brewing at the same time and still couldn't keep up. After a few trips, one of the girls came over and tugged at his elbow.

"Mister, we need more stuff for the sandwiches."

Omby wasn't quite sure what to do. He went back to check the walk-in just to see if there was anything else he could use as a sandwich filler. He opened the door and stood there as if a blast of cold air from inside had frozen him solid. The two girls saw him standing there motionless with his hand still on the outside knob of the door. They walked gingerly to where Omby was and carefully looked around him. That's when they, too, were struck dumb.

All manner of meats and cheeses stocked the shelves of the walk-in. There were racks of perfectly seasoned roast beefs, tubes of baloney, salami, and liverwurst. Wheels of cheese were stacked six feet high. Fully cooked turkeys—waiting to be carved—and trays of chicken salad, tuna salad, egg salad, potato salad, and macaroni salad lay waiting. There were honey cakes, chunks of pineapple, baskets of mixed fruits, fruit juices, and gallons of milk. There were no pork products. There was barely room to step inside the walk-in. When they looked back at the aisles in the store, they saw cases of fresh breads, bagels, and rolls.

Omby started walking toward the front door slowly and cautiously. As the enormity of the situation began to sink in, he developed an I-know-something-you-don't-know smile. He went outside and walked over to stand aside and slightly behind Habib.

"Uh, boss, you gotta come inside and take a look at something."

"Not now, I'm busy."

"No, boss, I'm serious—you need to come inside, right now!"

Habib looked at Omby and saw the Cheshire cat smile on Omby's face. Curiosity got the better part of him, and with a shrug, he followed Omby inside. They walked over to the walk-in refrigerator, and when Habib saw the treasure within, he let loose with a shriek of wonder and began laughing until tears came out of his eyes. Omby was not quite sure what Habib's reaction meant; perhaps he had lost his mind.

"A miracle—Allah has sent us a miracle. Allah has sent us a miracle—a miracle, a miracle!," Habib chanted as his hand went from shelf to shelf, breaking off and tasting little pieces of beef, turkey, and chicken.

All four began jumping up and down and hugging each other. Habib called his wife and told her to get their children and bring them to the store so that they could participate in the wonder. Both Habib and Omby fell to their knees and prayed.

They got up and, with a sense of urgency, started to set the foods out and prepare more sandwiches. By the time they got outside, the line was even longer, and the crowds across the street were even larger.

Habib danced around his serving table, giving testimony to the miracle that had occurred inside. The crowd laughed and cheered, and more volunteers came across the street. Soon, an entire production line had been set up in his store, and they were feeding the poor.

By 10:00 AM, word was spreading all through Upper Manhattan and had reached the ears of the media. A skycam truck from *NY 1*, New York City's twenty-four hour news station, pulled up. A camera crew and reporter, Alice Hoffman, got out and scanned the scene. She stood on the corner with a camera in front of her so that the serving table and the line of homeless were in the background. She began to report.

"An apparent miracle occurred today in a small convenience store in the upper East Side. Habib Rashid, the owner, decided to feed the homeless and found his own stockrooms filled with a bounty of meats, cheeses, salads, breads, and fruits. As you can see, the line of the homeless stretches down the block and around the corner. Not only is food appearing but volunteers are also showing up to help."

As she reported the story, she slowly walked, with the camera behind her, over to where Habib was serving food. The cameraman filmed the action a few seconds before Alice Hoffman got Habib's attention to ask him questions.

"Mr. Rashid, tell us what happened here."

"It is a miracle! It is a miracle! Allah has graced us. Go back; see what is inside. There is food everywhere. The refrigerator is full. The shelves are full. It is a miracle. We are grateful that Allah has chosen us to be the messenger of his miracle."

"When did you discover the food?"

"Earlier this morning. We were just about to run out. We were down to the last loaf of bread, the last package of meat, and then we looked again. There was food everywhere. Now, people eat."

"How long will you keep serving the people here?"

"How long will I keep serving? As long as Allah wills it—as long as Allah continues to fill my store with food, I will serve his blessings."

When she was done, the news crew jumped in to volunteer as well.

Within hours of the broadcast, Muslims all over New York City began giving to the poor. They dropped quarters and dollars into the pencil cans of the disabled, shared their lunches with the hungry, and found clothes for the tattered. Those of other faiths saw the happiness and glee on the faces of the generous ones and soon joined in.

Perhaps the giving would last for a day; perhaps more, but at least one thing was certain: human beings had demonstrated what they were capable of and the collective consciousness had shifted. The shift may have been a small one, but it was a permanent one.

*   *   *

About the same time Omby discovered the treasure in the walk-in refrigerator, Congressman Max Silverman was waking up in his hotel room on the banks of Lake George in the chilly Adirondack Mountains of northern New York State.

The windowsill at the new Lake's End Hotel and Convention Center had a thin layer of morning frost on it. The gas fire logs of the twelfth-floor penthouse suite kept the room toasty in the morning, toasty enough for Max Silverman to think of sex, again.

He rolled over and spooned with Alice, or was it Debbie or Sue? All he could remember from last night was how boring the keynote speaker at the Human Rights conference was and how soft the skin of the woman in front of him, the woman in his bed, was. She welcomed his excitement, and they became the most important persons to each other, at least for the next eight minutes.

Max looked at his watch. "Ah, crap! I've got a breakfast meeting with my aides."

"I want to go with you. I'm starving. You know, we missed dinner last night," said Alice-or-Debbie-or-Sue.

"I hear you, sweets, but my aides are going to be there, and one of them is my wife's sister."

His wife was an only child, but Silverman knew this one always worked. While they hurriedly dressed, Alice-or-Debbie-or-Sue turned on the TV, and the news anchor was talking about the strange messages.

> This message, like the messages previously seen on the ticker at the bottom of several news channels, has mysterious overtones. The source of these messages, allegedly signed by God, still has not been determined. A spokesman for the NSC, the National Security Council, in the White House has indicated that the messages are beginning to take on a high priority as it relates to homeland security. The most recent message states: *I do not impose my will upon you. By what logic do you impose your will on others?—God*

> Within hours abortion rights groups claimed the message was an endorsement by God of a woman's right to choose. Right-to-life groups countered that the message regarding consequences of actions endorsed their position, also citing the commandment prohibiting murder. Groups advocating different political, environmental, and social positions are beginning to wade into an increasingly heated debate over the meaning of the messages. There seems to be a shift in the commentaries from whether the messages are indeed from God to what the significance of each message is, assuming they are, in fact, authored by God.

> It is important to note that, as of yet, there has been no technological proof or remaining physical evidence pertaining to the source of these messages. Academic scholars, religious leaders, and politicians are beginning

to weigh in as well. Our London correspondent, Stephen Morrow is standing by. Stephen, I understand that you are at a conference being attended by the Dalai Lama.

Exactly, Jim, we are here outside the Royal National Theater in the center of London where the Dalai Lama has been attending the annual Science and Mind Conference. He stopped for a moment to share this response with us . . .

> This whole thing is very, very interesting. It is good reason to be happy today. We will want to see what scientists and other investigators have to say. If true, we will have much to discuss, maybe even change some old ideas. For now, the important thing is that all advice given is good advice, true advice. It is not important if you are Buddhist, Christian, Jewish, Muslim, Hindu. However, love is essential to all religions; we could speak of the universal religion of love. Just be kind. This is what is important, be kind—and be happy.

As you might know, Jim, this Dalai Lama, the Fourteenth Dalai Lama, has long been interested in the connection between spirituality and science. His Holiness has often said that as science advances and we learn more about the universe, religious thinking must harmonize with discovered truths. At least he's consistent. Back to you, Jim . . .

Max tried to turn a deaf ear to the news, but the words still wedged their way into some portion of his consciousness.

"Now listen, if you come down to the city and have any trouble, any trouble at all, you call my office and we'll take care of it," Max lied as he pressed a twenty-dollar bill into his night partner's palm. "This is for breakfast," he finished with a smile.

They walked into the elevator. He pressed lobby; she pressed three. When Max arrived at the lobby, Antonio Bortzi was waiting for him.

"Good morning, Congressman. I was about to come get you. We gotta go over today's agenda, and more important, breakfast is almost over."

"You're a good kid; you understand the priorities," Max joked, then his smile became somber. "But don't you ever, ever come get me in the morning. Call if you have to, but don't come to my suite!"

"C'mon, Congressman, I've been with you for a dozen years. Don't ya think I know what's going on?"

"I'm not thinking about me Tony, I'm thinking about you. Didn't you ever hear of deniability? You're a good kid, but you haven't learned how to testify yet," Max said with a nod and a wink.

Antonio Bortzi was a good kid. His grandparents entered America through Ellis Island when Mussolini came to power in Italy. His family pillars were loyalty and appreciation for America, obedience to God, and love for the Pope. Max knew that sometimes Tony struggled with Max's promiscuity, but Max also knew that all the bills he had championed for education, the poor, the elderly, the sick, and the middle class had impressed his aide.

They entered the hotel's plush dining room. Three large plate glass windows lined with light purple chintz and gauze overlooked a thirty-two-mile-long lake of certified drinking water. It was overcast, and the lake was mirror smooth. The lake islands, which offer campgrounds in the summer, were draped with a clinging fog. The surrounding Adirondacks were mere silhouettes against the slowly moving striated blanket of clouds. From time to time, the sun made itself known as a circular patch of a lighter shade of gray.

The canvas covers were stowed for the winter, leaving the boathouse roofs skeletons of green piping. A single evergreen stood among fallen leaves and naked birch trees. The breakfast room was, by now, empty, and the only sound was the Brandenburg concertos playing ever so softly from speakers squirreled away in the corners. The only movement was a slight drizzle of rain rippling soft puddles on the concrete walk outside. It was a moment of awesome calm and intense serenity. One might say a moment divine. Max noticed it when he walked in, but the feeling was too scary. The one person Max didn't like being with was Max Silverman.

"That's pretty." And with that, Max dismissed the scene from his mind.

As they sat down, Tony pulled out some papers and started to talk, Max drifted off.

"Congressman Silverman . . . Congressman . . ." Tony had to say it three times before getting Max's attention.

Max was thinking about screwing their waitress from behind while she was draped over the back of that couch in his suite and wondering if it would be a good fit for his short body.

"Congressman Silverman . . . Congressman . . . ," Tony continued to repeat as Max came out of his stupor.

"Huh, ahh, what did you say?"

"I was going over the speech you have to give next week at the Columbia University students' chapter to the National Organization for Women," Tony said with more than just a little irony in his voice.

"Never mind that, tell me about the agenda."

"Well, actually it's pretty light since we are up here at the convention. Of course, first thing on the agenda today is a speech that you have to give on the main floor. It's your standard Genocide/Not on My Watch speech. Another thing—remember that young boy Billy Clidson—the boy you gave the trophy to for winning the whole city science fair for the colony on Mars exhibit?"

"Yes."

"Well, he was shot a few blocks away from his home yesterday; he was DOA at the hospital. The funeral is tomorrow."

When Max heard of Billy's death, he remembered meeting the boy and was saddened. He also remembered thinking about what effect low gravity or no gravity would have on sex. Max pushed that thought out of his mind. After all, he did retain some vestige of dignity.

"He was a good kid; I want to go to the funeral. Find out who's making the arrangements. Ask whether I can say a word or two. We'll check out tonight and drive back to the city, so I can wake up in my own bed and be fresh. What's next?"

"We should have a staff meeting sometime today to talk about further responses to the God messages, and you have a meeting with Clay McRae in Washington set for the end of the week. Everything else is SOP." It didn't matter; Max wasn't listening anyway. As Tony continued to talk, Max's gaze drifted out over the lake. He was amazed at the natural beauty and the curves of the mountains. He focused on two. He was amused at how much they reminded him of a pair of luscious tits.

CHAPTER 5

I have given you free will.

Use it to make choices for the good of all.

—God

Billy's viewing started at 9:00 AM in the chapel of First Baptist. Tillie's family had lived in the neighborhood for generations, and decades of neighbors came to pay their respects. Billy's world included schoolmates, teachers, friends, and even a congressman. Joe-24's schoolmates, friends, and admirers also came. The line of mourners snaked around the sanctuary, and others milled around outside. The 112th Street Gang posted an honor guard outside the front steps. The viewing lasted throughout the day with the services slated to begin around 4:00 PM.

Billy was laid out in a beautiful casket; it was one that the Clidson family could never have afforded. The 112th Street Gang knew Billy took a bullet meant for one of them, so they chipped in and helped to pay for the funeral. Sitting on a podium above the casket was Billy's science fair trophy and pictures of him from all the newspapers.

Joe-24 wasn't very good at grief. Except for the last couple of years, everything had always gone so positively in his life. A tragedy like this was something he didn't have much experience with. He

stood strong and greeted people as they came in. Underneath his
hulking frame, all he wanted to do was crawl into a small dark corner
in a back room and be by himself. He looked over and saw his mother
rocking back and forth in a small arc; her eyes were fixed on an
imaginary point somewhere in front of her. He went over to console
her. She allowed him to move her hand, but her face didn't change.
She was beyond grief. She stayed that way until Brenda came over.

As Brenda approached Tillie, she lifted her eyes up hesitatingly.
She took her hand out of Joe's and, with both hands, reached
toward Brenda, pulling her to sit. Holding Brenda's right hand in
her left palm, Tillie began stroking her daughter's hand and just
repeating over and over, "Oh, Brenda. Oh, Brenda. Oh, Brenda."

Joe had never felt so alone. His brother was dead, and his mother
seemed to have no need for him. He didn't know why. Perhaps it
was anger over his inability to stop the fatal bullet; perhaps she
just needed a female's touch, or perhaps it was a mother's need
to be with a daughter during traumatic times. The reason didn't
matter. Joe just felt an aching loneliness—a loneliness that was
born of more than loss, born from a sense of impotency, of not
being able to do anything, accomplish anything, be anything. For
Joe, not having a sense of pride was a living death.

*   *   *

Louie the Cop and Officer Craig Thompson sat across the
street from the funeral. Louie, the veteran partner, thought that
it wouldn't be a bad idea to keep an eye out for any disturbance
since the killing was gang related.

"Well, this is how it is—you get something going, and they shoot
you down like a dog," Louie the Cop said, obviously referring to

events that went beyond the funeral, perhaps to the events of his own life.

"Yeah," Thompson breathed.

They both drifted off silently into their individual worlds. The onboard computer beeped twice and began to read out a report called in by a neighbor on the fifty-second floor of luxury apartments down 112th Street on the East River.

East River Towers were three narrow fifty-six floor high risers that have a Frank Lloyd Wright look. Each floor houses only four apartments. The monthly maintenance fee for these residences would pay for a penthouse most anywhere off the island of Manhattan. A single space in the parking garage went for over two grand a month.

Thompson suggested to his partner that they pick up the call since they were right down the street. Louie the Cop just shrugged. Thompson typed a response into the computer, shifted into gear, and rolled down 112th Street.

When they walked down the hall of the fifty-second floor, there was no noise coming from apartment 52C. Louie the Cop knocked on the door, waited a few seconds, and knocked again. He kept his eyes on the peephole watching for it to go dark. When it did, his hand went back to rest on the butt of his pistol. The door opened and stopped at the length of a shiny brass chain.

Louie recognized the face at the door. It was Tomás Medina, a high-powered lawyer that mostly represented clients charged with drug offenses. Louie had seen him around the Manhattan County Courthouse, most often yelling at the clerks, his clients, or opposing lawyers. Louie had never had a case with Tomás and did not want to. The lawyer's anger was intimidating.

Tomás was wearing black silk elastic-top house pants and a ribbed sleeveless undershirt. He boasted the soft glow of a

Mediterranean tan. Even so, his shoulder-length black hair, black eyebrows, and black eyes caused his skin to seem fair by contrast.

Louie the Cop said, "NYPD," as if the uniforms didn't speak for themselves. "Uh, Mr. Medina, we've received a complaint regarding a possible fight or property destruction at this apartment. May we come in?"

Tomás's eyes flitted back and forth. He hesitated, evidently considering his options, and then nodded his head in reluctant agreement. He pushed the door forward momentarily, released the chain, and opened the door. By now Tomás had changed his posture to be more gracious, even if he didn't completely remove the sarcasm in his voice.

"Yes, officers, please come in, come in," he said, half bowing at the waist and swinging his hand as if he were a cabaret announcer directing the audience's attention to the next act.

It would be impossible to talk about Tomás Medina without sounding out a series of clichés. He was tall, dark, and handsome without question. He didn't work out, but his muscle definition and the shadow of six-pack abs said he did. He had just enough of a Spanish accent to be exotic but not so much as to hide his wit and brilliance. His eyes could be soft or fierce; his passions were both strong and gentle. He was a lady's man, but he was also a man's man.

The two officers entered the apartment together. The first thing that Thompson did was move toward the wife, making sure she did not need medical attention. Louie the Cop took a few purposeful steps, but then went into the same trance a child goes into upon entering a toy store. His attention was drawn to the visual candy in the apartment and the magnificent view over the East River.

Tomás Medina shared this luxury high-rise condominium with his wife, Claire. The apartment was decked out, as if it were an estate tagged with a name like Carnegie, Rockefeller, or Kennedy. The foyer had a dark hardwood floor. In the middle was a round antique table on top of a Persian rug so thick it would eat your toes. Above the table was a rich chandelier of lead crystal that sparkled rainbows around curved walls that funneled into a living room. The living room had dual fireplaces on the right and left and plate glass windows in front with a broad-enough angle of view that you could see the Cloisters on the north end of Manhattan where the East River and the Hudson joined.

Louie the Cop walked by the stereo system, custom set into the wall, with brand names he didn't recognize. He heard soft music that was coming out of nowhere and everywhere at the same time. He saw photographs detailing the history of Tomás and Claire Medina covering the wall, together with awards, certificates, and newspaper clippings attesting to their achievements. Arts, crafts, and baubles collected in travels around the world decorated shelves and tables.

Louie the Cop saw Claire Medina sitting on the couch in the living room with her head bowed and rubbing her forehead with her right hand. She was a tall woman with soft flowing, dirty blonde hair and striking blue eyes. Her face was long rather than round, and her nose was just crooked enough to give an imperfection to her face that created a sense of approachable beauty—and vulnerability. Her eyes revealed a baseline fearfulness, or perhaps it was sadness.

Louie looked at the pictures on the wall and saw her standing in front of her office door at Halliron Corporation, one of the largest energy, transport, and civil engineering companies in the world. The plaque on the door said Vice President, Finance. In another picture, she was in a glamorous gown at a formal affair in Lincoln Center, and in another, dirt from a garden covered her as she reached into a pile of ripe compost.

"Mrs. Medina, my name is Officer Craig Thompson. We received a report of 'loud voices and things thrown' from a neighbor, I wonder if we could step into another room for a moment?"

"Eh, well, Officer, everything is just fine. I'm just fine," Claire offered. Claire glanced in Tomás's direction, but he was busy showing Louie the Cop how the stereo system worked.

"I'm sure you are," said Thompson. "Even so, I would appreciate it if we could step into another room just so that I can speak to you privately. Standard procedure, you understand."

"Oh, of course," Claire glanced at Tomás again. This time he was looking at her but did not react, one way or the other. Claire continued, "That would be fine. We can step into the den."

They walked into the adjoining room while Tomás continued to give Louie the Cop a tour of the residence. Louie always thought of rich people being stuffy and stodgy. He never imagined wealth used for such fun things. Louie could see himself sitting in the easy chair in front of the huge high-definition plasma television mounted on the wall with his array of remote controls—in charge of his life and captain of the universe.

"You know, Mr. Medina, this apartment, besides being luxurious, is just plain cool," Louie said.

As they moved from one center of attraction to another in the apartment, they came across a row of framed pictures sitting in a curio behind glass doors. In one of the pictures, Tomás was standing in front of his top-of-the-line, forty-eight-valve, twelve-cylinder 760Li BMW, leaning back, his legs crossed casually, one hand on the hood.

"Wow, that sure is a beauty," Louie said, referring to the car.

"Yes, it is," Tomás boasted. "It practically reads your mind and drives itself. How'd you like to go for a ride in it?"

"Jeez, really? Yeah, of course I would," Louie said without thinking.

A fleeting, surprised look passed across Tomás's face. It engendered an equally fleeting pang of guilt in Louie the Cop. Louie wondered if he had revealed too much.

"Sure, I'll take you for a ride," said Tomás, recovering. "When would be good for you?"

Before Louie the Cop could respond to him, Thompson and Claire came out from the other room. Thompson motioned for Louie the Cop to come over and speak with him in a far corner of the living room.

"Look, Louie. The wife says he didn't hit her, but I think she's holding something back. I can't see any sign of physical violence, but she seems awful, fearful, and teary-eyed. I think she's really scared."

"Does she want to file a complaint?"

"No."

"Well, she says that she didn't get hit; you don't see any sign that she did; and she doesn't want to file a complaint. Seems like a no-brainer; there's nothing we can do."

"Yeah, Louie, I know. I still think there's something going on here, something that we haven't been told."

"Well, whether you think something's going on or not, it don't matter. Without any physical evidence, without a statement by her, and with no desire to prosecute, we got no case—nothing we can do. Just write it up and go."

Louie the Cop noticed a curious look on Thompson's face and felt a little tug from his conscience at the same time. Not wanting to appear to take the husband's side over the wife's, Louie the Cop walked over to check in with Claire even if it was for nothing more than to soothe his partner.

"Ma'am, are you sure that everything is okay here?"

"Yes, Officer—we just got in a little bit of an argument," Claire explained. She shifted her weight and tugged at her sweater. Her caution suddenly changed to impatience as her voice became more grounded and gained a tad of indignation. "My husband has a quick temper, but he's never hit me; I assure you I'm just fine," she finished.

"Okay, I guess we're all done here. C'mon, Thompson, let's get going."

Louie the Cop looked at Claire and then at Tomás. Tomás winked, and Louie acknowledged the wink with a nod. Something in his gut didn't feel quite right about that, but he was already so drunk with the taste of luxury that he didn't want to think about anything that might stand between him and having even a sliver of the life Tomás enjoyed.

Claire closed door behind the two officers and turned around to look at Tomás. He had a stern expression, but she was relieved to see that the intense anger had subsided. She walked quickly toward the kitchen. Tomás moved to one end of the sofa and patted the center cushion, beckoning to her.

"Querida, come. Sit down. Let's talk this thing through."

"Okay, just let me put the milk away."

There was no milk to put away, but Claire needed a few moments to compose herself. She poured a quick shot of Chivas Regal and let it slid down her throat. Claire understood numbers; she liked it when debits and credits balanced. She liked to live in a simple world with simple answers and tasks that had clear beginnings and endings. She liked the feeling of completing a job and getting a task off her desk.

She hated these "talks" with Tomás; they were really lectures. She always felt like such a little girl, but at least it was better than suffering his anger. She felt she was smart, but Tomás was an intellect. He never saw things simply; he had the talent to immediately perceive situations in a rich tapestry of multifaceted colors, emotions, perceptions, and motives. He loved to weave an argument while all she ever wanted to do was cut to the chase.

She didn't understand why he had gotten so angry. All she tried to do was talk to him about the pressure she was feeling at work, about the rising discomfort of having to fudge on certain accounting reports. She just wanted him to hear her, to listen to her. It seemed that he had less and less time for her. Maybe she shouldn't have told him that. She just wished he loved her enough to put his client files down and pay her some attention.

"Querida, are you ready?"

"Uh . . . yes . . . I'll be right there."

She opened and closed the door of the refrigerator to sound like she was putting the milk away. Claire shook her head and then pulled her hair back and rubbed under her eyes just to make sure there were no residual smears from earlier tears.

She sat just off the other side of the middle cushion and turned toward him with her best listening face on. She hoped she would be able to keep focused on what he was saying, just in case he checked her listening by asking her to repeat something he had just said. Her eyes were slightly pink and watery, hiding their natural blue beauty. She felt fragile, even submissive. She began to feel the fear return as she noticed emotion flow back into Tomás.

"I just do not understand why you allow yourself to be taken advantage of by a bullying crook like your boss. You're an intelligent, responsible, strong woman. I've told you a thousand times to just say no to his illegal and unethical business practices. I just wish you loved me—or, I guess, trusted me—enough to take my advice and stop being a pushover and giving in to what is clearly an abusive situation."

Tomás stopped short. Claire could see the wheels turning in his head. He recomposed himself with a relaxing sigh and dropped his shoulders. "Look, Querida, perhaps I jumped without hearing you completely. Please finish telling me what you wanted to say."

Claire was surprised but just for a moment. She quickly remembered that Tomás was often kinder after his temper flared up and would let her talk without interruption.

"Are you sure? I don't want to make you mad again," Claire ventured.

"I'm sure. I'll just take off my Latino passion and put on my Anglo ice pack."

Claire giggled. The little laugh relaxed her and helped her open up. "Honey, I know you have a lot of work, and I understand that your work is important and complicated. Mine is too, and sometimes I feel that you don't understand the pressure I'm under or just don't have enough time for me."

"I . . ." Tomás started but then put his hand over his mouth and signaled her to go on.

"I feel caught between a rock and a hard place. I feel so dirty and so guilty all the time. They're asking me to do things at work that just don't feel right, but I'm scared to say no because I don't want to get fired. I mean, I know that you make a lot of money, but without my salary to go along with it, we could never afford this apartment and living in Manhattan. And besides, I'm worried that not going along with them will cause the whole company to cave in. If that happens, there are a lot of people in the lower floors that will lose their jobs, they might even lose their pensions. I worry about them, and I worry about us."

Claire reached up and took a clip out of her hair, hoping that would release some of the tension that was gripping her chest. She shook her head with a sigh and clutched her sweater tight around her waist before continuing.

"I didn't feel so bad until those crazy messages from God, or whoever, started coming on the TV. Now, I'm walking around feeling like there's somebody watching over my shoulder all the time. Watching everything I do, making a record of it. I ought to have a conscience and do what's right on my own, but I feel like I'm cornered, and I don't know which way to turn. I hate to say it, but I don't feel like I get much support from you. I know that you've got your own pressures and your time is valuable, but I remember when we were in law school . . ."

Claire got up and started pacing quietly. She walked over to the picture wall. She looked at their graduation pictures, at the picture of Tomás jokingly flexing his muscles on South Beach, the view from the room at the Pink Sand Hotel in Bermuda during their honeymoon, and the one of Claire at her first accounting job buried under a mountain of papers during tax-time.

"You were studying so hard. We were living in married-student housing. We got by on just one salary; we had that old clunker of a car. It seemed that we were a lot happier then. I remember touching and kissing a lot. I remember lying in a hammock and gently swinging in a warm breeze and feeling the sweat run down where our bodies touched. We don't seem to have time for those things anymore. Don't get me wrong. I'm not saying that I think that the love is gone; I just think that our priorities have gotten real screwed up. I don't know; you seem to be distracted an awful lot. Maybe you don't find me attractive anymore?"

"That's not so."

"I don't know. I just wish I could put my finger on what's wrong. I'm overwhelmed by problems that once were easy to solve. I used to bounce out of bed in the morning, and now I have to drag myself to work. Do you think that maybe I could be depressed?"

"First of all, Querida, I want you to know that I find you attractive, as attractive as the very first day I laid eyes on you. You are a beautiful woman inside and out, and I suppose that is what frustrates me so much. It seems that you're stuck in your situation. You have come to me many, many times and asked my advice about dealing with your work situation. I tell you what I think is the right thing for you to do, but you don't seem to take it to heart—and I don't understand that. But I'm sure of one thing, and that is—drinking can't be any help."

When Tomás mentioned drinking, a cold chill ran through Claire's body. She didn't mind discussing anything except alcohol. Her father was an alcoholic and had uncontrollable anger. She hated her father's drinking, but lately she had become more and more isolated and was drinking more and more.

Tomás had come close to mentioning it on several occasions, and she was getting more and more afraid he would confront her directly. She started looking for a way out of the conversation, but she just sat passively and tried to maintain a poker face so that Tomás wouldn't be aware of the dagger that struck so close to her heart.

What Claire didn't know was that Tomás was struggling with his own demons. Tomás represented some of the biggest crime bosses in New York, and lately they had been pressuring him to go over the line. They wanted him to become involved with bribing police officers to get inside intelligence concerning routes and patrols in the lower Harlem area. Now that he met Louie the Cop, he felt he had identified someone he might be able to turn. That prospect scared him profoundly because it brought him one step closer to the point of no return—the point of crossing over from being a mob lawyer to being a mobster.

Tomás had worked all his life to have the wealth and power to determine the course of his own life, and now he felt he was in the pocket of the bosses. When Claire complained to him about her feeling of being trapped at work, a small part of his anger dealt with her, but most of it was self-anger that he threw out on her.

Tomás had waited for a reaction from Claire, but when there was none, he continued, "You say that you feel stuck between a rock and a hard place, and perhaps you are, but you are the only person who can get yourself out of it. I wish I could help you. I wish I could go to your Clay McRae and take him down a peg, but that's not something I can really do. If I did, it would only piss him off. Eventually it would come back to bite you. Is there nobody you can go to?"

"Not in the company—the only people I could go to would be the regulators, but if I did that . . . ."

"I understand. I understand. Well, I really don't know what to say anymore. If you had dealt with this back when it wasn't such a big deal—it's always better to deal with an oak when it's an acorn—it wouldn't have developed into the problem it is now. Well, I don't want to be an 'I told you so.' I can see that all these things have had an effect on you. You asked me if I think you're depressed; well, you just may be—I don't know—I'm not a psychiatrist. Maybe you are depressed, and maybe you're drinking to self-medicate. I think it would be good idea if you see a therapist. Would you be willing to do that?"

"I . . . I suppose so," Claire said, but her tone said—*you win*.

"Bueno," Tomás said with a tone of finality, "I know some really good counselors from court; I'll set you up with an appointment."

Claire patted her knees twice in agreement, and with an "Okay then," she got up. Walking toward the bedroom, she said over her shoulder, "Well, I think I'm going to visit with my sister for a bit. Are you okay for dinner? We still have some *carnes parilladas* and *humitas* in the 'fridge."

"Yeah, I'm fine."

He was intellectually proud of himself. He allowed Claire to make her statement first, without revealing his hand, thereby gaining a tactical advantage. He was able to turn the discussion from not paying Claire enough attention to focusing on her problems. Many professionals leave their jobs at the office. Lawyers rarely do. Even so, he told himself, it probably would be a good thing for her to see a therapist anyway; she actually did seem somewhat distracted lately. Still, there was something unsettling about the conversation. It seemed like a hollow victory. There was something gnawing at his insides, something that just wouldn't let go.

CHAPTER 6

You have a conscience for a reason.

Pay attention to it.

—God

At a couple of minutes past 7:00 PM, Tomás picked up the remote control and pushed a button to turn the television on. It was already tuned to CNN. The reporter was in midstride with his story . . . .

It is now 7:04 PM. Just as Americans and viewers all over the world sit in anticipation to see what will happen in the next three minutes, so do we here at CNN. As we know, all of the mysterious messages have appeared on the ticker of our screen at seven minutes and seven seconds past 7:00 PM. In a few minutes, we are going to turn our attention to the monitors in our studio, as I am sure you are turning your attention to the ticker on the bottom of your screen.

As none of the messages have shown up on our internal videotaping devices, we have decided today to film CNN's actual TV screens to see whether or not the message can be captured on an external videotape. If you look behind me, you can see several cameramen preparing for this evening's message by setting a high-resolution camera in front of our broadcast monitors. As you know, CNN and other news stations are reporting that millions of people have seen the messages. It continues to be reported that people see these messages in their native languages; the messages appear in French on French-language stations and in Spanish on Spanish-language stations. There have been rare reports of people who speak different languages reading the messages in their own tongue while watching the same station at the same time. They always appear at the same time in each time zone. To date, there have been seven distinct messages broadcast. They are the following:

My children, please give me your attention.—God

Your actions have consequences—in this existence and the next.—God

Love one another. Work together. Your nature is to be interdependent.—God

I have given you free will. Use it to make choices for the good of all.—God

Be kind. You will be happier.—God

I do not impose my will on you. By what logic do you impose your will on others?—God

You have everything you need to make your world a paradise or to destroy it.—God

It is now 7:06 PM and fifty seconds. Please stand by, 7:07 PM and three seconds, four seconds . . .

Exactly at seven seconds past 7:07 PM, these words scrawled across the bottom of the screen:

"You have a conscience for a reason. Pay attention to it.—God"

Tomás didn't listen to any of the commentary after the message scrolled off the screen. He didn't have to. This message felt like it was there specifically for him. He didn't need any of the talking heads on television to tell him the significance of the message. Tomás had been brought up Catholic, at least to the extent that he was brought up in any religion at all. He hadn't attended church for many years, but he did understand conscience, and he did understand guilt.

*   *   *

In 1970, Tomás was nine years old, and his only concern was getting out of school to play fútbol—soccer, as it is called in North America. He lived in an upscale neighborhood of Santiago, Chile. Life was good until the Marxist, Salvador Allende, came to power. Things got worse when Gen. Augusto Pinochet swept into power in a CIA-backed coup. After his mother died, he and his father fled to America and were naturalized—thanks to their political refugee status. Tomás hated the chaos and vowed to amass power and wealth enough to protect himself from political or social winds.

Two months into his first year of law school, Tomás was at the University of Miami library doing research when an assistant approached his table to tell him the library was closing.

"I need half an hour," Tomás muttered.

"Sorry, you gotta go," said the work-study student.

"I said, I need half an hour," Tomás replied, stabbing his pen into his notes.

A silent, tense moment passed.

"Joey," said a female voice from somewhere behind Tomás, "you have to close up and stack books, don't you? Why don't you do that and let Tomás close out his notes and then we'll all leave together?"

Joey hesitated. He took another look at Tomás's face and said, "Alright," nodding his head and walking off.

Tomás turned around, "How'd you know my name?"

"I've known your name ever since you gave Professor Peters a piece of your mind two years ago," she answered.

Claire Howard was studying for her CPA exam. She had taken an undergraduate accounting course with Tomás and was always impressed with his strength of purpose, convictions, and not least of all, his good looks.

They dated for the next year and married the week after she got her CPA. Then they moved into married-student housing at the law school. She happily supported him through law school, and he gratefully appreciated her faith in him. The income of a new CPA wasn't much to live on in Miami in the eighties, but it was enough.

After he graduated, Tomás interned in the Dade County State Attorney's office. Janet Reno was his boss. By the time he graduated law school, he already had three felony trials under his belt and was hired directly into a felony court trial division, bypassing the two to three years of traffic and misdemeanor court most prosecutors go through. His performance was stellar. Within two years, Tomás transferred into the Major Narcotics Division and a year later was division chief. Tomás built up a fearsome reputation among those in drug trafficking circles as a hardball prosecutor. Two years later, he left to find his fortune in private practice.

In Miami, during the nineties, criminal defense work was drug work. Rather than being suspicious of a recent state attorney, those that were savvy knew that aggressive prosecutors made aggressive defense attorneys. Tomás's practice took off.

A rookie defense attorney representing drug-involved clients started out representing users. As clients expressed satisfaction, street-level dealers started showing up for legal services. Then distributors, then wholesalers, then traffickers, then importers came through the door. At the highest level were the bosses who were never charged—and claimed not to know anything. They connected the dots of a vast network of manufacturers, transporters, suppliers, dealers, and muscle. They knew people— people who could refer clients in need of a defense attorney.

The day that Tomás met Giovanni Pericolo marked a change in the way Tomás did business. That day, Tomás had an appointment with one Robert Matisse, a Haitian. Robert Matisse came into his office with another man, a European, who wore Armani slacks and an Izod polo shirt. The two men sat down. The European spoke first—and exclusively.

"My name's Johnny. We've heard good things about you," Giovanni Pericolo said in a gruff voice with a heavy Brooklyn or New Jersey accent.

"Thank you. What can I do for you?" Tomás asked.

"I wanted to introduce my friend, Robert Matisse, to you. He's a good man. He has a packing and delivery company over on NW 79th Street and Second Avenue in Little Haiti. Unfortunately, sometimes his employees get arrested, and he may be referring them to you."

Tomás's attention perked up. He was about to get a windfall of a client. Tomás knew how the bosses worked. They never had employees; they simply introduced you to someone who would be the referral source in the future. But the message was clear. When Robert Matisse referred clients in the future, they were really coming from Pericolo, and Pericolo would not want them to turn state's evidence. Pericolo then continued his interview of Tomás Medina.

"How do you feel about working with clients who want to turn state's evidence—you know, testify for the prosecution?"

"Well, Mr. uh, Mr . . . . ," Tomás began.

"Pericolo, but please, call me Johnny; that's what Giovanni means, John—or Johnny."

"Thank you, Johnny," Tomás continued. "As you know, the drug-trafficking laws call for extremely severe mandatory sentences. Just for possession of a few ounces of cocaine, you would be looking at fifteen years with no parole—that means day for day. The only way to get relief from such harsh sentencing is for a defendant to give information. The prosecution is only concerned with the dealer's wholesaler. That's how they go up the ladder."

Tomás studied the faces of the two men. The Haitian was looking around the office. As he had not yet said a word, Tomás did not know what language he spoke or if he was following the conversation at all. Johnny, on the other hand, was earnest and intense.

"Look, I run an ethical practice," Tomás stressed, "and I emphasize honesty with me and with the courts. This is not because I feel holier-than-thou, but because strategically it gets the best results for my clients. If the client comes to me and wants to work with the government, that's the client's decision, not mine. It's my job to listen to my client's desires and try to make them happen. But I suspect I'm telling you something that you already know."

Johnny's smile had a wink built into it.

"I'm glad to hear you say that you are ethical and honest. A lawyer that's not honest with the court won't be honest with his clients. This can sometimes be a scary and dirty business. There are a few things I think a good lawyer does that keeps him effective—and safe. He should never promise anything he can't deliver; he should never guarantee anything that's not 100 percent predictable. He should never sugarcoat results, and he should always keep his clients informed—and informed accurately.

"I understand, and I agree wholeheartedly," Tomás replied.

Johnny continued, "Some lawyers refuse to work with clients that want to rat. They have a reputation for it. They advise their clients of it at the very beginning . . . so as not to run into any conflicts of interest. When a client goes belly-up and informs against his friends, it can cause all kinds of problems."

Johnny peered at Tomás to see his reaction. Tomás had his hands pressed together lightly, touching his index fingers to his lips as he thought deeply about Johnny's comments and their implications. Tomás decided that he could work with this man as long as it was clear that Tomás intended to stay on this side of the law. By following Johnny's guidelines, he would be able to honor his oath as a lawyer and build his practice. He nodded in agreement and then responded.

"I understand what you're saying, and I agree that such practices are ethical. I want us to be clear about what I am and am not willing to do. It can raise a problem if someone, other than my client, were paying the fee. For example, should Mr. Matisse," Tomás said, acknowledging the silent man in the room, "pay the fee of my client. Such situations are uncomfortable. You understand that it is my obligation to represent my client, regardless of who pays. My obligation to represent my client's interest is not for sale. I personally prefer that my clients pay their own way. That way there's no question about my loyalty."

"And I am sure that they will. Robert's employees are well-paid, and should they ever act indiscreetly and bring trouble upon themselves, they should have the funds to pay their own way," Johnny said with an almost imperceptible wink. "I think you can expect that they will bring their fees in on their own—in cash."

"You do understand, of course, that I should never be paid more than nine thousand five hundred dollars in cash. Federal tax law requires that I report any payment of over ten thousand dollars in cash directly to the IRS, including its source. Now, with those understandings in place, if a client tells me that he doesn't want to work with the government—in spite of the fact that he may have an excellent chance to reduce his sentence—perhaps because he is fearful of his own safety or the safety of his family, then it is of course my duty to get him the best results possible without turning belly-up."

"I understand," Johnny agreed.

Johnny stood up and offered his hand to signal an end to the conversation. Everything about Johnny showed that he was gracious, polite, and had a good sense of propriety. Everything about Johnny also showed he was a man to be respected—and feared.

Many things were left in the unsaid, and the things that were said communicated much more than the words uttered. That conversation began a long, enduring relationship that brought Tomás from a single office three blocks from the courthouse to a suite of offices on Brickle Avenue.

Tomás and Claire visited with Johnny on social occasions. Tomás never did any legal work for him, except for an occasional civil matter like a will or property closing. They met his wife and children; they visited with Johnny, his family and friends on Johnny's yacht, at his Miami Beach condominium, and at his vacation home in Antigua. They never talked business—they just built their relationship.

After another three years or so, Johnny again visited Tomás at his office.

"Tomás, you've now been practicing for many years, and things have gone well. I have come to trust you and, more importantly, respect you. Anyway, I have some friends in New York City that have asked me to move up there to, umm . . . consult with them. I am certain that they would wind up being referral sources for you that would make Robert Matisse look like he was in kindergarten. I would like to see our relationship continue to grow. Would you consider moving to New York?"

"Well, of course, I'll consider it. I'll have to talk to Claire, but her family comes from the North, so I'll bet it won't be a hard sell."

Tomás ran the idea by Claire who was immediately for it. She had always enjoyed the white Christmases of her growing-up years in Connecticut. She missed the change of seasons. Christmas never felt like Christmas when it was eighty degrees in the shade. They moved to New York, and although the cost of living tripled, Tomás's fees increased fivefold.

Not only was Tomás's income stratospheric, but after moving to New York, Claire got a job as the assistant chief financial officer of Halliron, a company with its worldwide offices in the Wall Street district of Manhattan. Adding the two incomes together, Tomás and Claire could no longer be considered middle class.

*   *   *

Claire came out of the bedroom with a light jacket on. She could see that Tomás was disturbed. She didn't know if it was residual anger from their quarrel or if something new was on his mind.

"Darling, are you all right?" Claire's question brought him back to the present.

"Uh, yes, er, no . . . I'm not sure."

Claire looked concerned. It wasn't like Tomás to be ambivalent about anything. He could be angry and he could be loving, but he was never uncertain. This was a new face for Tomás.

"What is it, honey? What's going on?"

After a long pause, Tomás answered her, "It's this God thing on television. I'm not sure what to think about it. How does it affect you?'

"Oh, I don't know. I'm sure it will all make sense eventually . . . I think . . . hope . . . it will," Claire said.

She blew Tomás a kiss and was out the door. All of a sudden Tomás felt lonely—a different kind of lonely—a lonely that had the flavor of being disconnected and vulnerable. It was the kind of lonely one felt on a crowded train with no one to talk to.

Claire punched the elevator button to G, street level. She folded her arms tight. It was beginning again, that feeling of panic that started in her stomach and threatened to travel to her throat. She pulled her arms tighter into her waist, trying to push the panic away. The elevator seemed to sway, and she toppled into a corner. She pressed against the wall with her eyes closed, willing it to stop. When the elevator doors finally opened, she flew across the plush lobby, shoved through the circular doors to the street, and gulped the night air.

Edward stood under the domed red awning that led to the curb. Edward Patrowski had been the doorman at the towers for over thirty-five years. He lived and worked by the motto: "Never a minute late and a spit shine all the time." Short and muscular, he looked a bit like a penguin under his knee-length topcoat. Everyone in the neighborhood knew it would be an act of foolishness to make fun of this once contender for the light heavyweight title. He was an enthusiastic, infectiously happy, and deeply religious man who loved his job. He was one of the perks for the residents, and for him the residents were like family.

Edward saw Claire Medina coming through the door. *Now there is a fine woman*, he thought. She was one of his favorites, always smiling and never too much in a hurry to stop and talk. She remembered the names of all his family and kept up with how the grandbabies were doing.

"Edward, I need a cab," said Claire, trying to hide the tremble in her voice.

"Yes, ma'am," said Edward, hearing it anyway.

Edward was equipped by the building's management with a Secret-Service-quality two-way radio, complete with a spiral wire earpiece and wrist microphone. The transponder had three buttons; one for police, one for fire-rescue, and one for taxis. He whispered into his cuff and then touched his ear.

"We'll have one for you in under a minute, ma'am."

"Thank you, Edward," Claire said, touching Edward's arm and clutching her coat against the evening breeze.

"Mrs. Medina, I'm gonna need to bring you in some good Polish pierogies, put a little meat on you before one of these days a gust of wind blows you away."

Claire laughed and took Edward's arm. He always seemed to know the perfect thing to say to brighten her mood.

"Now, Edward, you know there is not a gust of wind in New York City that would dare do any such thing while you're around."

"You got that right, ma'am. Where will you be going tonight?"

"To my sister's."

A Yellow Cab drove up. Edward opened the door to the backseat. Claire just stood there, lost in thought for a moment. Edward, always the gentleman, held his posture with chivalrous patience. Then with a slight shake of the head, Claire took a deep breath and climbed in.

"Sixty-Fifth and Second," Edward said to the cabbie and, then with a softer face, turned to Claire. "Now you have a good evening, Mrs. Medina."

"Thank you, Edward."

They both knew their final exchange communicated more than the words. Claire knew Edward had picked up on her upset and was letting her know that he cared and wished everything would turn out all right, whatever everything was. Edward knew Claire was thanking him for his concern and respect. They had obeyed the rules set out for residents and staff but, nonetheless, shared an intimacy.

As Edward closed the door, the cabbie switched on the meter, glanced into the rear mirror, shifted into gear, and with a grunt from the front seat, they were off amid the lights of New York City—lights so bright that the Big Apple has been tagged as the City That Never Sleeps. Vendors hawk, groups file in and out of restaurants, couples walk arm in arm into clubs, and bicycles vie with busses for the right-of-way—24-7.

Claire saw none of it; she could have been on the moon. She stretched her stiff neck by pulling her head forward and then rested her head against the back of the seat. *What is happening to me?* she asked herself over and over. The fight with Tomás kept playing in her head, mixing with long-ago memories of her father screaming and cursing at her mother. There were police at her house then too.

The taxi stopped suddenly for a panhandler trying to earn a tip by washing the taxi's window with a dirty rag. The cabbie leaned on the horn, jolting Claire back to reality. The cabbie shouted at the beggar, who started pounding on the hood of the taxi. Claire put both hands over her ears and realized her face was wet; she was crying.

CHAPTER 7

To find comfort, you must confront discomfort.

—God

Steve Blaylock was a cautious and determined man. He stood tall but slight of build and balding with hair that used to be red surrounding his ears and lapping his neck. He had an artificial right leg from the knee down, a reminder of shrapnel that he picked up in the Mekong Delta during the Vietnam War. He wore his wire-rimmed glasses halfway down his nose, which always made his staff feel like he was peering into their souls. He was a heck of a reporter and an even better executive publisher. His domain, his world, his universe was the *Burlington Daily Register*, and he was master of it.

Burlington, North Carolina, is a small to midsize sleepy Southern town with three exits off I-85. Back in the day, it was famous as a textile town and home to Burlington Mills. More recently, with the outsourcing of textile jobs, Burlington had come to be known as a bedroom community situated between Research Triangle Park to the east and the furniture factory centers to the west. It is also home to the corporate headquarters of LabCorp. Except for those two claims to fame, Burlington is no more or less uncommon than hundreds of towns of similar size across America.

On the morning after the first message appeared, Blaylock had spent most of his time reviewing the Associated Press and United Press International reports and calling around within his network to find out what others knew about the strange messages. Most of his colleagues in the papers had been pretty much in the dark, just like he was. There was no consensus as to whether the messages were authentic or some kind of scam. Most people in the newspaper business had been leaning toward a scam—cynics that they were. There certainly had been an animated discussion in the news-budget meeting that morning.

Blaylock had assigned one of his reporters to investigate the story. As he expected, since this was a story of media reporting on media, a highly competitive industry, there was not a great deal of cooperation. The situation was even colder than Blaylock had expected, as this was a story where print media was reporting on electronic media. There is no love lost between those two news sources. Calls to broadcast networks resulted in responses like:

"This story is our story, and we're keeping it in-house."

"We really don't have any information that we can share with you."

"You'll just have to keep watching our network to find out the results of our investigation."

As is normally the case, Blaylock's editorial staff had focused on public response, which was certainly varied and massive. The reporters documented responses from pastors of the area churches, captains of business, the chamber of commerce, district attorneys, police chiefs, and school superintendents—all of whom gave responses to the paper.

Inside news-budget meetings, there was great discussion about how important the story actually was. The general feeling was that the story eventually would be determined to be some sort of prank or scam. Perhaps it was a marketing scheme by the networks to boost their ratings, or a joke by some teenage hacker who was slicing into the electronic stream of worldwide news reporting to earn his fifteen minutes of fame.

Nevertheless, it was a news story of some importance even if it was only judged by the skyrocketing ratings received by the networks. More and more people worldwide were watching news reports on television now than at any time before in history. All of the news agencies were at a loss to explain the messages. They regularly stated that they had not been involved in placing the messages into their ticker tapes.

All of this resulted in a certain sense of levity and a chuckling that went on behind closed doors in the *Burlington Daily Register* offices. A certain glee arose when staff began to imagine what must be going on inside the newsrooms of the networks. It's always nuts when you're both the story and the reporter. How the staff and techs must be running around the production rooms was the common laugh. There were all kinds of speculations from the malevolent to the benign.

Day by day, the number of television stations where the messages appeared spread until they covered the entire world with one exception. Arabic television stations and stations that broadcast to primarily Muslim audiences had no such messages. Even the exception was notable, considering the difference in culture between the Judeo-Christian and the Islamic traditions.

In the Islamic tradition, it would not be credible for Allah to speak to Muslims through television tickers. If Allah wanted to communicate to a Muslim, it would come in other ways, ways that were culturally appropriate and spiritually correct, through signs or messages—never directly. In Islamic tradition, nearly everything from a tsunami to a stubbed toe can be a sign from Allah, and religious leaders often interpret the events.

It was clear, however, that Muslim communities were not being ignored by the force that authored the messages. First, there was the miracle of unending food at a delicatessen owned by a Muslim in New York. At the last count, the miracle subsequently occurred at over 270 places around the world. From fresh water springs and soup kitchens to one-on-one acts of charity, wherever Muslims followed the Quran and gave alms to the poor, their supplies were replenished.

Every imam and ayatollah had decreed it was Allah's will that the hungry be fed. Sunnis and Shiites stood shoulder to shoulder to do Allah's will. Unfortunately, they also still stood face-to-face across battle lines, killing each other over what each faction believed was the will of Allah.

Steve Blaylock woke up on the autumn equinox as he did every other day. He dressed and had a cup of coffee. He never read the newspaper in the morning since he put it together the day before. When he got to the *Daily Register*, he was handed a fistful of messages at the front desk and was told that his answering machine was full. He thought sarcastically, *This looks like it's going to be a great day!*

When he got into his office and started looking at the messages, all of them were expressing various forms of celebration or outrage at the placing of a letter to the editor, allegedly from God, in his newspaper. He opened a copy of the newspaper and found that what the readers had noted was true. There, on the op-ed page, the letters-to-the-editor page, of the Burlington newspaper was a letter to the editor from God. It appeared in a font he had never seen before. It was calligraphy, a handwriting font—a beautiful font. Actually, it looked like handwriting, but of course, that would be impossible in a printed document.

His first thought was that someone at the copydesk had come up with an idea for a joke, but whoever that person was had made a serious error in judgment. He started going through the staff in his mind, wondering who was skilled enough to pull off something like this. His face was flushed, and his anger barely controllable as he walked out of his office and down the short hallway to the cubicles that made up the city room and the copydesk.

Although small, the *Daily Register* was a modern-technology newspaper. There were four computers with large screens to typeset and organize the paper using software. As is the case in many modern newspapers, the *Daily Register* has a Kodak direct-to-plate offset machine that takes the copy from the city desk in digital form and burns it directly onto offset printing plates. Once the city desk approves the final copy and gives the "print" command, the machine processes the tin printing plates and spits them out with no more effort than if they were paper copies. No human being intervenes between computer screen and printing plate.

The print master would then pick up the plates and clamp them on to the huge rollers of a web printing press. After inking, they would be ready to roll. The web press draws paper from tree-size tubes. Within the press, the papers are printed and folded. Assembled newspapers come out at the end of the process. The papers are then stacked, bundled, put in their appropriate delivery cars, and sent out for delivery.

Steve Blaylock marched out to interrogate the day shift at the copydesk. "Who put the paper to bed last night?" Blaylock got the names and told his secretary to call them.

He asked to see the computer file of the paper that was sent to the platemaker. He looked at the op-ed page and compared the paper he had in his hand to the paper that appeared on the monitor. Everything on the screen was on the paper, but not everything on the paper was on the screen. There was the not-so-small matter of the letter allegedly signed by God. In order to get the letter to fit on the page, slight adjustments were made to the surrounding columns that resized them just slightly smaller to create room for the letter. Otherwise, the pages were identical. What he was looking at was impossible.

"Is this the final version? Is this the copy that was sent to the plates?" Blaylock asked.

Everyone shrugged. One of the copywriters raised his hand sheepishly. Blaylock motioned for him to talk.

"Mr. Blaylock, as far as we know, it is. There doesn't seem to be anything that's in the computer after this one. This is the last file we can pull up in the computer's chronology. There's nothing after this."

"Mr. Blaylock? Mike, the typesetter from last night, is on the phone," interrupted a secretary, holding the phone up.

Blaylock picked up an extension phone and mashed down the button for line 1.

"Have you seen the paper today?"

"No, sir, I was just sleeping."

"Well, go outside and get your paper and take a look at it—I'll wait."

Blaylock waited on the phone for the typesetter to get back. He looked across the copy room. The staff was shuffling around. He could see fear in their expressions. He knew he was tough, but he didn't think he was that fearsome. Then he realized they were afraid of something much bigger then he was, something they didn't understand, and he realized that he also felt the fear. The typesetter returned to the phone.

"Okay, boss, I've got the paper here. What is it you want me to look at?"

"Look at the op-ed page. Look at the editorial page. Do you see that letter from God at the bottom of the page?"

"Yeah, I see it, boss. I see it, but I don't know where it came from. I didn't do that. At least it wasn't like that when I left the paper last night."

"What do you mean you didn't do that? You're the one who put the paper to bed last night, and we don't understand what's going on here. We looked at the last file in the computer, the one that was supposedly sent for printing—it didn't have this letter in it, and yet this letter is in it. There's got to be an explanation," blustered Blaylock, talking over himself.

"I . . . I . . . don't really know what to tell you, boss. It's like, well, I just don't know what to say. I can't explain it."

Blaylock slammed the phone down. He was furious now. He stormed into the print room and looked at the rollers of the huge web printing press. The plates were not on the rollers. He called the print master over.

"Where are the plates from this morning's run?"

"Mr. Blaylock, it's almost 10:00 AM. We've already cleaned up from the run. We're about to go home."

The print master made his comments respectfully but with a slight undertone of, *Uh, open your eyes and look around.* Blaylock noticed the sarcasm.

"Well, that ain't happening. You, everyone, can plan on some overtime today. Where are the plates from today's run? I want to see page four of the A section."

The print master noticed Blaylock's seriousness. He whistled for his two assistants. "They're over here in the garbage, Mr. Blaylock. Pete, Bobby, help me dump this out."

The three of them tipped over the fifty-gallon drum, and dozens of thin tinlike shingles slid out onto the floor. It was a mess. The ink was still wet and left black streaks wherever it touched. The three printers waded into the pile. Feeling Blaylock's urgency, they didn't even stop to put on gloves so their hands started turning black as car tires. Finally, Bobby held one of the plates up triumphantly.

"Bring it over to me. Let me see it," Blaylock commanded.

Blaylock opened the newspaper he was carrying to page 4. He compared the print on the paper version to the offset on the plate. The plate was an exact duplicate of what he had seen on the computer screen at the city desk. The paper he was holding in his hand had everything that was on the plate plus the letter with God in the signature line. He held the newspaper up a few inches from the face of the print master.

"How do you account for this? How do you account for the fact that this letter signed by God appears here in the bottom of the paper, and it does not appear on the plate? Look at it. How do you account for it? How do you account for it?"

The print master scratched his head and looked dumbfounded. He took the paper out of Blaylock's hand and walked over to a worktable. He put the paper down and then put the plate next to it. His eyes went back and forth from the paper to the plate, and then from the plate to the paper. After a few rounds of going back and forth, the turning of his head transformed into a—*No, this can't be.* He scratched his head and shrugged. His two assistants were standing by, not knowing what to do or think.

"I don't know what to say, Mr. Blaylock. I can't account for it."

"Well, I'm going to tell you what we're gunna do. We're gunna run it again, and we'll go watch it come off the press. That's what we're gunna do."

"But, Mr. Blaylock, do you know what you're talking about? The presses have already cooled down; we're going to have to warm them up again before we can even put the plates back on. We'll have to clean off all these plates, reattach them, ink them up, and put on another roll of paper. Are you sure you want to go through all that?"

The print master didn't need any answer. He just took one look at Blaylock's face and said, "Yes, sir. We'll get right on it."

Two hours later the city editor, the copydesk chief, the print master, the publisher of the paper, and Steve Blaylock waited for the presses to roll off the first copy of the second running of the day's paper. As soon as it came off the press, Blaylock snatched it up and turned to the op-ed page. The letter from God was there. Everyone looked at the letter and then slowly walked back along the press until they got to the plate in question. They looked at the plate, and the letter was not there. They looked at the paper, and the letter was there.

Each one of them felt a shiver. Someone from the outside might think that this was a joke, some kind of technological heebie-jeebies that an electronic wizard had schemed up, but the people in that room, at that time, understood the process. They understood that there was no method of tampering that would yield these results. A printing plate prints what is burned onto it. The printing process is a touch-to-touch, contact process. If something is on the plate, it gets printed. If something's not on the plate, it doesn't get printed. There is no way to physically make happen what they had just witnessed.

Then they just looked at each other in baffled silence.

"Let's everybody take a half hour break. We'll meet in the budget room at, say 1:30," said Blaylock.

Blaylock walked slowly and quietly back to his office. The air seemed thick, and he felt as though he was walking with a sack of bricks on his shoulders. He had just seen something that perhaps no other human being had ever seen. The "God thing" had been funny when the networks were dealing with it, but now it was in his lap—squarely, front and center, smack dab in his lap. But more importantly, what he had just seen convinced him that this was no scam. This was not a marketing scheme, a joke, or a hoax; this was the real thing. He was scared, and he was wrapped in wonder.

He got back to his desk and sat in his executive chair. He leaned back and looked out the window pensively. This sky was "Carolina Blue." Steve Blaylock was a University of North Carolina Tar Heels fan. The Tar Heels' colors were sky blue and white. Among Carolina fans, it is said that God painted the sky Carolina Blue rather than the other way around. Blaylock wondered if jokes like that would still be told. Then he thought of more disturbing things.

He thought of all the Vietnamese he had killed in the war; he thought of the time he didn't spend with his wife and son. He thought of candy he stole when he was a child, and he wondered if he was a good person. He squeezed out the remaining tears in his eyes with the palms of his hands. Regardless of whatever personal history he had to account for, he had been thrust into the history of humankind. He was a reporter, and he had the story

of the year, maybe of the century, maybe of all time. He picked up
the phone to call his good friend Abraham Holt, the United States
congressman from North Carolina.

"Is the congressman available? This is Steve Blaylock with the
Daily Register in Burlington."

"Oh, Mr. Blaylock, let me see if I can interrupt him," said the
aide, putting the phone on hold.

"Steve, hello. Hope the news is good news," greeted Congressman
Abe Holt.

Abe Holt was one of the most senior members of Congress,
and his offices were welcoming and well lived in. He was a
comfortable-looking man of medium height and medium weight.
His youthful blue eyes offset his wispy gray hair. He had an
impeccable reputation for being not only honest but also a straight
shooter. He was considered a mentor to many other congressional
representatives, including New York's Max Silverman, whose office
was next door to his on the third floor of the Rayburn House Office
Building.

"Well, Abe, I am not sure exactly how to classify this news . . ."

"Hmm, okay, What's going on?"

"A letter materialized on our editorial page today . . ."

"Materialized . . . ?"

                    *   *   *

Earlier that morning, Clay McRae had walked down the hall of
the third floor of the Rayburn Building. As he looked into the open
doors of the congressional offices, he could see the rotunda of the
US Capitol framed like a postcard in the draped rear windows.
Each office had a brass plaque outside the door with the name of

the congressional representative and the state represented. After passing the office of Abraham Holt, congressman from North Carolina, he arrived at the office of the congressman from New York, Max Silverman. The office was sleek and clean, albeit a bit austere. There was an L-shaped counter facing the open doors with pictures of the congressman with each of the last three presidents prominently displayed. Clay McRae walked in.

"May I help you?" queried the young man behind the counter.

Max was smart enough not to hire females for his staff. He had gained a reputation for being a lecher around Congress, and the last thing he needed was for scandal to come out of his own office. One way to deal with temptation was to avoid it.

"Yes, I have a 10:30 appointment with the congressman," said Clay McRae.

"You must be Mr. McRae."

"Yes."

Clay McRae was a snake in a suit. You wouldn't know it to look at him. He was in his mid-fifties, five foot ten inches tall and had rich black hair swept back with little marks of gray on the sides. He had the chiseled features and aquiline nose of someone with good Anglo-Saxon breeding. He wore three-piece suits and, somewhat anachronistically, shirts that took cufflinks, and he wore collar pins underneath his ties. He dressed as if he didn't really understand good taste but was able to imitate it well, very well, by looking at pictures in magazines like *GQ*. Eighty percent of sociopaths end up in jail; the other twenty percent end up in corporate boardrooms.

"Congressman Silverman told me to expect you. The congressman has been called to the floor of the House of Representatives for an important vote. He told me to tell you it had something to do with the SEC, the Securities and Exchange Commission. He said you would understand."

"Uh, yes . . . I do."

McRae was irritated easily with people who were not available for him when he expected them to be. The explanation, in this case however, proved to be effective. Getting a certain ruling from the SEC was the sine qua non of his trip to Washington. He was glad to see that the cost of the several dozen five-hundred-dollar-per-hour professional ladies he had used to buy Max's friendship would not go unrewarded.

Clay McRae had started walking down a path. In time, the path had become a tight rope and, even more recently, started to look like a plank. He had been juggling the books at Halliron. With each passing quarter, he had to manipulate the figures to make the current quarter seem profitable as well as make up the slack left from the manipulations of the prior quarter. Quarter added to quarter until his house of cards was close to collapse. His accountants suggested that he employ an aggressive and creative form of bookkeeping called mark-to-market accounting. Mark-to-market accounting would allow him to place a value on a contract recently made with an outside corporation, and then project that amount into his profit-and-loss statement as if it were a current gain. Used judiciously, this kind of accounting would give stock analysts and investors a reasonably sure window into what Halliron expected its path of growth to look like.

Of course, the word *judicious* was not even in Clay McRae's vocabulary. It was his intent to use the accounting system to prop up his fraudulent persona as a Wall Street wonder boy. With mark-to-market accounting, Clay McRae would be poised to go on a binge of creating dummy corporations and dreaming up breakthroughs in new technologies that would be the basis of magnificent contracts. Once Halliron signed such a contract with the puppet company, McRae would issue a press release, setting an arbitrary value on the contract and then adding that value to the corporation's bottom line in its next quarterly report. The stock analysts would still recommend a buy, and the company would look healthy in spite of a growing aneurysm in the belly of its economic structure.

"Mr. McRae, Congressman Silverman signed a gallery pass for you and said that if you care to go over, he would look for you from the floor. If not, he'll come back here when he's done."

"Excuse me?"

"The congressman suggested that you meet him in the Capitol. He signed a pass that will allow you to sit in the gallery above the floor of the house and watch the members working. Congressman Silverman would be able to see you from the floor and meet with you after the vote . . . or you could wait here."

"Hmm, I guess I'll go over. How do I get there?"

"I'll be happy to walk you over. The congressmen emphasized that he did not want you waiting in any lines."

"Thank you."

The young man got up, slipped on his suit jacket, and asked another staffer to mind the reception area while he walked Mr. McRae across the street. As they walked out, they passed small groups of business-attired people huddled together intently thumb typing into their phones.

"The age of the Blackberry is upon us," said the young aide.

"So I see," mirrored McRae.

McRae's eyes were open wide, and he was busy scanning and mentally recording the sights and sounds of government—not because he had any sense of civics or national pride, but because he knew the information might prove valuable in the future to add color and credibility to a pitch he might try on an as-yet-unidentified mark.

They walked along the paths through the Capitol lawn to the side of the iconic building. After passing security, the aide guided McRae through the awe-inspiring rotunda and down Statuary Hall. They made a right turn to stand before a set of elevators. The doors to one opened, and McRae started to move toward it. The aide quickly reached out and gently touched McRae's arm.

"Ah, Mr. McRae, that elevator is for members only."

"Members?"

"Members of Congress," replied the aide.

"Exclusive club, huh?"

"Yes, sir, very exclusive."

They waited for another elevator to arrive and went up three floors. After walking McRae through more security and handing the gallery pass to a USCP, United States Capitol Police officer, the aide escorted his guest onto the gallery and found him a seat. He looked down at the floor of the house. Less than half the legislators were in attendance. Within seconds, he spotted Max and pointed toward him.

"There is Congressman Silverman now. It doesn't look like it'll be long. As soon as he's done, he'll look up here for you. When he catches your eye, go to meet him in the gift shop. Do remember where that is? We passed it on the way in."

"Yes, I remember."

"Great, is there anything else I can do for you at this moment?"

"No, I don't think so. Thank you."

"Okay then, just make yourself comfortable in these small seats. I swear, you've got to believe people were smaller when they built this place. Anyway, enjoy watching your government at work. Here's my card so you can call me, once you get your cell phone back from security, should you two miss each other."

McRae settled into the narrow stadium-style seat. He never had much of an interest in government except in terms of what it could do for him. But at least from this vantage point he had the ability to see most of everything that went on, just in case he ever had to prove to someone that he had been in Washington for one reason or another. The gallery, etched out of a dark hardwood, followed the curve of the half-moon shape of the House of Representatives. The speaker's podium, which he had seen while watching the President's State of the Union address, was directly in front of him. Democrats were to his left, Republicans on his right.

A congresswoman was addressing the House from a lectern on the left. There was grumbling coming from the right, along with a few blurts of the word *outrageous*. McRae smiled slightly; from above, the objections sounded like the croaking of pond toads. The speaker was beginning to raise her voice.

"For too long have we Democrats sat idly by while Republicans, with their borrow-and-spend policies filled the pockets of liars, murderers, and thieves at the expense of our seniors and children. God, our Holy Creator, has commanded us to be kind to one another. What is kind about giving tax breaks to cigarette manufacturers, allowing pharmaceutical companies to gouge the sick, and for weapons manufacturers to charge thousands of dollars for a toilet seat when homeless people outside this very building do not even have a pot to . . . urinate in? If we are going to be a people, a country, a nation under God, we must maintain a social safety net that is whole, that has integrity—not one that is made of tricks, traps, and black holes. Remember, our Lord Jesus Christ, declared that what we neglect to do unto the least of us we neglect to do unto the Lord Jesus. I yield the floor."

"For what reason does the member from New York rise?" said the Speaker of the House.

"To respond to the member from New Hampshire."

"Does the member from Arkansas yield?" asked the Speaker.

"We yield one minute to the member from New York."

Max Silverman rose and spoke with an earnest tone, "I thank my colleague from across the aisle for her passionate pleas on behalf of her Lord. I stand as a reminder that at my synagogue the jury came in with a different verdict. I remind her that her Lord is not my Lord nor is her Lord the Lord of millions of Americans. We still don't know the origin of the messages. Even assuming that they are divine, I have looked at them very carefully; and it seems to me that there is a clear absence, almost a meticulous avoidance, of endorsing any particular belief system. Perhaps we here in Congress would be wise to follow suit. Let's have cooler heads prevail until we know all the facts. It is no surprise that God exists, nor would that have surprised our founding fathers. In spite of their knowledge that God existed, they still wrote the separation of church and state into our Constitution. I yield my remaining thirty seconds to the member from South Carolina."

The elderly statesman from South Carolina needed some assistance to rise from his seat. Even before he opened his mouth, he raised his fist. "My respected Democratic colleague speaks as if God is a Democrat, and that Democrats have a monopoly on kindness. I remind her that Jesus came to make us all fishermen not to enable us to be sheep in a welfare state. True, we must be kind, but is it kind to make capable and competent people into dependent wards of the state through unbridled entitlement programs? What *is* kind is to maintain a system where everyone has the freedom to compete in a fair market where the rules are stable—a place where we all strengthen our souls and our bodies by free competition and thereby strengthen and lift ourselves and our nation up to the glory of God."

Clay watched as Max Silverman dropped his head into his hands and nodded sadly. It was clear that Max's call to rationality in the face of wild speculation had influenced the discussion in the House of Representatives as much as a gnat might influence a stampeding rhinoceros. He was clearly frustrated and had had enough for the day. Even so, the diatribes continued.

In a few minutes, Max leaned over and spoke to his Chief of Staff, who then began gathering papers up off the broad desk. Max turned and scanned the gallery until he caught McRae's eye. Max pointed toward the door, patted his aide on the shoulder, and walked off the floor. Clay McRae left the gallery, picked up his cell phone from security, and headed downstairs.

They met and greeted in the gift shop. Max pointed down a long narrow flight of marble steps that lead out to the expansive Capitol veranda. The view from the veranda was one of the best in Washington. It looked down on the Capitol Reflecting Pool, out across the Mall, and toward the Washington and Lincoln monuments in the distance. From both sides of the veranda, majestic stone steps curved down to ground level.

It was noon, and the baritone chimes of the National Cathedral filled the air with a reverence. USCP officers armed with modified M-16s, equipped with night-vision scopes or top-of-the-line Birelli semiautomatic twelve-gauge shotguns, took up stations at strategic points on the veranda and surrounding grounds. Max ignored the incongruity and paid attention to the view.

"It still gives me chills," Max said, breathing deeply.

McRae didn't understand chills, but he took a deep breath as well. As he exhaled, he internally mimicked Max saying *It still gives me chills* to himself. It had seemed an emotionally appropriate comment, so he added it to his repertoire.

"It's nice to walk around sometimes, you know, to clear your head. Join me?"

Max motioned toward the large lawn area known as the Mall that stretches from the Capitol Building past the Washington Monument, all the way to the Lincoln Memorial. He started down the path that goes past the Capitol Reflecting Pool and a statue of Gen. Ulysses S. Grant. Clay fell into step.

Each time Clay began to talk, Max interrupted him with trite comments on the history of the construction of Washington DC. Clay wondered what was going on, at least until they arrived at the Museum of the American Indian. At the entrance to the museum is a twenty-five-foot tall, multilevel waterfall that produces roaring sound. They walked up onto the stone steps and stood near the thundering water. No parabolic listening device would be able to decipher their words through the sound of the falling water. The two men stood close so that they could hear each other.

"So what news do you have for me?" Clay asked.

"Nothing good—but it's not hopeless . . . yet," said Max sadly. "The problem isn't so much getting the ruling you want from the SEC. Although that's not going to be easy in the current environment, the problem is more from some investigations that are beginning to surface in one of the congressional watchdog committees."

"Is this a new investigation?" asked McRae with growing concern.

"Have you heard of Renewable Energy Corporation or RenEn Corp?"

"Yes, I have. We hold some very promising contracts with them. They've come up with a new technology that will help fossil fuels burn cleaner, bringing carbon emissions down to almost zero."

Max was asking about one of Clay's puppet corporations, one of his little frauds to artificially inflate the stock value of Halliron. Yes, there was a RenEn; and yes, it did have a contract with Halliron, but it did not have any valid patents on any new technology. And in time, its relationship with Halliron would prove worthless. Of course Max did not know this, and Clay was not about to tell him.

Max went on, "Well, from what I understand, the committee is concerned about the fact that several board members of RenEn have had run-ins with the IRS and the SEC before. Because RenEn is a major business partner with Halliron, I believe that subpoenas are going to issue. You will have to come testify as to what the relationship is between the two corporations. I hope that's not going to cause too many problems for you."

"No, I don't think so," Clay lied, "but thanks for the heads-up anyway."

"There are some new regulations that we're working on in regards to the importation of Middle Eastern oil that probably will have an impact on your financial forecast. I'll be able to get you more details on that before they're released to the public. In terms of the SEC, I hope I can pull a rabbit out of the hat for you."

"Thanks, Max. As always, you know I appreciate anything you can do for me. Will you be back in New York soon? I've got some 'friends' that are excited about meeting you."

"I'll be in and out of the city over the next couple months. The next time I'm coming in, I'll give you a call. We can go out for the night. In the meantime, let's take a little walk around the Capitol building."

Eventually the two men worked their way back to the Rayburn Building. When they got to the front door, Clay told Max that he had a plane to catch, but before he left, he had one other request.

"Max, there's just one other thing," said McRae.

"Yes, Clay, and what is that?"

"Max," Clay began hesitatingly, "I'm not very good at testifying, and to tell you the truth, Halliron is not doing as well as the quarterly report might indicate. I think I might be retiring soon, and I might want to take up residence overseas—somewhere the American dollar goes a long way. I've got quite a lot of stock options and cash. I was wondering if you had any idea how I might be able to move it without leaving a path that, you know, pesky reporters or other investigators might be able to follow."

Max looked around quickly to see if anyone was close enough to overhear. You can't be careful enough in Washington.

"Clay, I can't imagine that you're asking me to help you launder money. You know I can't be involved in anything like that. Giving you some information ahead of time, before it goes public, is one thing. Breaking a dozen federal laws is another."

Max paused for a moment, trying to think if there was anything he could do to help his friend out. At last he put his hand on Clay's shoulder and said quietly, "You know, Santa Claus doesn't always wear red. Sometimes Santa Claus is a big, fat man in a white suit." Max didn't have Clay's cunning or alacrity; it was the best he could do on short notice.

They shook hands and said their good-byes. Clay had no idea what Max meant by his reference to Santa Claus, but was sure he would find out eventually. He made a note to keep the reference in the front of his mind when Max came to New York.

Max turned, walked into the building, and took the elevator up to his floor. When Max came around the corner to his hallway, he saw that there was a crowd of people outside of Abe Holt's office. He walked past his own office and started elbowing his way through the crowd to get inside. People were crowded around something in small groups. As Max got closer, he saw that everyone's attention was directed at copies of newspapers.

CHAPTER 8

As is each of you, so are your families,
communities, and nations.

—*God*

Max saw Kris Tucker, Abe Holt's Chief of Staff, and got his attention by tugging at his sleeve. "Kris, what's going on with all the commotion?"

"It's the messages, Congressman Silverman. Now they've come out in a newspaper, in our newspaper, the *Burlington Daily Register*. There's a letter to the editor signed by God, and, well . . . you've got to see this because I guarantee you've never seen anything like this."

Kris grabbed two copies of the newspaper and led Max into a quiet room. Once in the room, Kris opened the two papers to the op-ed page and put them side by side.

"Look, Congressman, the letters seem to be handwritten. If you hold them up to the light and put one over the other, you can see that there are slight discrepancies. The letters are not in exactly the same place; there is a slightly different slant to the words, and the spaces between the lines are a bit different. It looks like they were individually handwritten, but there are literally thousands of these letters that all came off the press of the Burlington paper at the same time. What's really weird is that nothing appears on the printing plate."

Max looked at the papers. He held them up to the light with one page over the other and saw that Kris Tucker was correct. He put the pages back on the table and then noticed the date of the newspaper.

"These papers are from today! How did they get here?"

"When Congressman Holt got the phone call from the editor of the *Burlington Daily Register*, he called over to the White House. The President took the call directly. They decided to scramble two F-16s to the Burlington Executive Airport where they were met by sheriff's deputies with a hundred copies. The jets landed at Andrews, and the papers were helicoptered to the White House lawn. As a courtesy to the congressman, staffers in the West Wing sent ten copies over here by courier."

Max was feeling disoriented. Things were going too fast. There was too much information to take in, and the information was too important. He might go on telling himself that these God messages were not authentic, but with this evidence, he was convinced they were. The one thought that came into his mind, front and center, was—this changes everything!

"Where's Congressman Holt?" Max asked.

"Umm, he was in his office a little while ago, and then I saw him in the reception area. Give me just a second, and I'll find him for you. Wait, there he is," said Kris, pointing and then beckoning, "Congressman, Congressman."

"Oh, Max," said Congressman Holt as he walked through the parting sea of people to where Max Silverman was standing, "I'm glad you're here. I'd love to get your read on this. Come, step into my office where we can talk like gentlemen."

The two men made their way into Abe Holt's personal office and closed the door. Once they escaped the crowd, both men took deep breaths. Congressman Holt walked over to his worktable where several copies of the newspaper were laid out. He motioned for Max to take a seat at the table as well. Max sat down, and both men looked at the newspapers again, just to make sure that what they had seen before was actually what they had seen before.

"Well, Max, what do you think of all of this?"

Max looked down at his hands. He rubbed the knuckle of his left thumb and slowly shook his head. He gently shrugged and said, "I'm not sure—anymore. What I've been saying when they ask me is that I'm a man that believes in God . . ."

"We both do," Congressman Holt interjected.

"So my position's been that I don't know who the author is, but we can sure use some help, but now, now, I don't know how there can be any doubt—any doubt that it's . . . it's . . ." Max's voice trailed off.

The two men looked at each other. It takes a lot to render a politician speechless. This was a lot. In their silence they heard the muffled hubbub outside the door. Abe Holt got up, walked over to the window, clasped his hands behind him, and began rocking from the heels to the balls of his feet as he gazed at the Capitol dome. Max joined him, hands in pockets and flat-footed.

"We have to be careful about how we play this," Max said softly.

"We have to be very careful—but let me take the position of well, you know, the devil's advocate," said Abe and both men laughed. "I've got to question it so that I can complete the scenarios, all the different scenarios in my mind—to put me at ease and to put me in a place where I can feel I'm making the right decisions."

"What are the scenarios?" Max asked.

"Well, the scenarios are one, it's all a hoax, and it's not God at all; two, it is God, and He remains neutral to all faiths and all countries; three, it is God and He anoints one religion as the true religion or endorses one country as His favorite country. Things will be very different in the world depending on which one of those scenarios plays out."

"And what issues will each of those scenarios raise?" Max asked, pushing Abe a little harder.

"I suppose that each one of those would have different implications for national security, environmental issues, legal issues, issues regarding the separation of church and state. Cripes! I can even see it affecting questions ranging from abortion and public education to mother's milk and the fluoridation of water. Max, I think the only way that we will ever make any sense of this entire thing is if we hang tight to what this country was founded on—freedom of religion and secular government. Remember, give unto Caesar what is due Caesar and unto the Lord what is due the Lord."

"And of those three scenarios, which do you think is the best and the worst."

"The best case is that it is God and He remains neutral. I think the worst-case scenario would be that God would point to one religion or nation as His favorite."

"Do you really think so? You don't think people would move to all get under the same umbrella?" Max looked over at Abe. Abe raised one eyebrow and looked back at Max. "No, I guess not," said Max, answering his own question. "I can't imagine that Christians would ever agree that the Islamic concept of Jesus was correct—even if God said so! I also can't imagine the reverse.

I guess you are right. The best scenario would be for the proof to make it evident that it is God, and that He is neutral. That way, we might find common ground between the different belief systems. As Shakespeare said, 'Ah, 'tis a consummation devoutly to be wished.'"

Abe reflected, "World history teaches us that most nations, especially in time of war, claim to own God. Is the fact that God has made his presence known going to inflame the whole thing, or is it going to make people feel more trusting? Wars create history, and history is always written by the man who wins the war. Of course, God was always on the winning side."

"The only thing that really sticks in my craw is that I just don't know about the rest of the people in this world. We have such a division of haves and have-nots. I'm worried that the haves still won't be willing to share. Remember, the *protestant ethic*, the concept that if God favored you he demonstrated it by making you wealthy. We have churches around that are preaching prosperity as a right. I'm worried that expectations will be raised and not met. That can lead to disillusionment and unrest. Although, on the other hand, if there was ever a time that the world was moved to be generous and kind, this is that time." Max paused for a moment to picture what a wonderful thing it would be to feed the hungry and to see the end of genocide. He continued, "A couple of days ago, I was driving down Broadway, and you can certainly see that the messages have had an impact on people there. Street vendors were selling rosaries, and people were grouped together having prayer meetings. In Central Park and other areas around town, places have been set aside for Muslims to answer their call to prayer. It is having an effect on the street, and I think that this letter to the editor from God is going to take everything to an entirely new level."

"I wonder if this is going to change anything at all, in the long run. You know, our constituent groups are all claiming God is on their side—and you heard that mess in the House this morning," noted Abe.

"Yeah, but I think that's all going to change with this newspaper thing," Max suggested. "You know even without God endorsing any one position, we will still be left with all of the questions about what's right and what's wrong."

"That's true. I wonder if this is going to make any difference at all. After the shock wears off, it may all wind up to be just the same old, same old."

"I think you just hit the crux of it," Max said with a shake of his index finger.

Abe continued, "Weeks, months, or years from now when we get over the shock, is it really going to make any difference in the way we represent this country or the way the nations of the world are going to act? Are we going to slip back into the same old foolishness and foibles that we're used to? How many times has an alcoholic tried to stop drinking? How many times have I told myself that I need to push away from the table? You know we sure hate suffering, but we sure love the causes of it."

"What do you mean?"

"Well, I mean that I hate to be fat, but I sure do love food. The alcoholic hates to be a drunk, but he sure likes his booze. The smoker hates cancer, but he sure likes his smokes. You follow my drift? If these messages are in fact from God, and He has the power to put a handwritten letter into thousands of copies of newspapers in the blink of an eye, we had better think about what He has to say—real careful like. If we don't take heed with the way we're headed right now, with suicide bombers around every corner, terrorists looking to take us down, and us walking around like lords of the universe . . . well, it just doesn't look like we're doing so well on our own."

Kris Tucker knocked on the door but came in breathlessly, without waiting. The two men were startled.

"Sorry to barge in—you've gotta see this," Kris said as he quickly moved to the television and turned it on.

It was a news broadcast, already in progress.

> We continue to receive news reports from all through the
> Middle East. We just received film from Tel Aviv showing a
> failed attempt by a suicide bomber. Take a look at this.

The screen changed to a grainy color film. It showed a busy street in Tel Aviv. A man wearing a light-colored suit paced back and forth for a moment in front of a busy café. He then raised his hands and said, "All glory to Allah. Let the words of Allah be heard, and let me be his messenger."

The man raised his hands above his head. In his right hand was some sort of device with a wire running into the vest of his suit. He pressed his finger onto the detonator. Everyone on the street as well as Max, Abe, and Kris braced for the explosion, but nothing happened. The man was surprised. The patrons of the café jumped up and wrestled him to the ground. Within seconds, police were there, turning him over and handcuffing them. Then the camera shook and fell to the ground. The TV screen returned to the announcer.

> This failed suicide bombing was typical of the events that
> occurred earlier today and yesterday. When the bomber's
> explosive packs were examined, they had turned to salt.

Let's go to our Tel Aviv correspondent, Brian Schott. Brian, what can you tell us about the reaction in Tel Aviv?

George, there is no one word that can describe it. Stunned, amazed, afraid, hopeful, perplexed, fearful; all of those words would describe the reaction of people here. This morning the entire military machine of Israel came to a halt, just as it did throughout the Shiite and Sunni worlds. The sight of tanks, Humvees, and military trucks frozen in the streets is eerie. Even the security gates at entry points and military bases will not operate. I got nonofficial reports that bullets being used for training on the firing range did not discharge. It all seems like a replay of the 1950s science fiction movie *The Day the Earth Stood Still.* The Knesset has been called into emergency session, and the government is being very tightlipped about all it. This is Brian Schott for CNN, reporting from Tel Aviv.

The screen returned to the main broadcasting stage.

Thank you, Brian, for an excellent report. This is a breaking news story of titanic consequence. To recap what we know so far . . .

At 7:00 AM plus seven minutes and seven seconds, Greenwich Mean Time, and continuing for seven hours, seven minutes, and seven seconds—all military armaments and equipment in the Middle East ceased to function with certain notable exceptions: planes in flight, ships at sea, military hospitals, and ambulances. All equipment has returned to its normal operating condition at this time. Bullets, rocket-powered grenades, missiles, bombs, improvised explosive devices—all armaments that were fired and failed to discharge during the seven hours plus of peace—have been examined. The propellants and explosive materials had all turned to salt. The armaments not used during that period seem to be fully functioning and deadly. Both Shiite and Sunni clerics are proclaiming that the events are signs from Allah.

Is the timing of the event, seven hours, seven minutes and seven seconds a signature from the same source that transmits messages and identifies itself as God? Why did these events only occur in the Jewish, Arab, and Persian conflicts? What does this mean for peace in the Middle East? We will be joined by our panel of experts and get their analysis, right after this commercial break . . . ."

Abe picked up the remote and pushed the mute button. He looked at Max with a totally blank expression as he deliberately moved to his desk chair. Max felt a tightness and put his left hand to his chest. With his right hand he steadied himself across the backs of the high-back chairs in front of Abe's desk until he was just two steps from the couch. He let go of his chest to grab the end of the couch and sat down.

Once Max got his air, his thoughts began to condense. He turned toward Abe, and . . . whatever comment he was going to make was cut short when Abe's receptionist came through the open door.

"Congressmen Holt, Jim Stiles is on the phone for you. Line 3.

Abe and Max exchanged looks. It wasn't often that members of Congress got calls from the White House. Abe immediately answered the call from the President's Chief of Staff.

"Abe Holt here . . . Yes . . . Yes, we were just watching it . . . Yes . . . Yes. I know Steve Blaylock. No, he would not dream up something like that! Yes, I can. Congressman Silverman is here in the office with me. He has valuable insights, and it might be a good idea to get the perspective of different faiths. Would one-half hour do? . . . Very good, thank you."

Abe gently and deliberately returned the headset to its cradle. The two aides and Max were staring at him. He turned to Max.

"The President wants to see us."

*   *   *

Down the street at 1600 Pennsylvania Avenue, President Edwards waited in the Oval Office with the same newspapers. He was tall, a large man, with a big chiseled face and a shock of wavy salt-and-pepper hair. His brown eyes were penetrating, and he oozed presence, confidence, and power. He had a low-pitched, booming voice. No matter how jovial he tried to be, he still sounded like a charismatic, evangelical preacher. He grew up in Moultrie, Georgia, as a Southern Baptist and was a devout believer. He was also a Jeffersonian—he believed in a wall separating church and state. Underneath his folksy refrains was a sharp mind, and he was blessed with the ability to see directly into the heart of a problem. He trusted his intuition.

The only other person in the Oval Office with him was his Chief of Staff, Jim Stiles, who was also the President's oldest and closest friend. Jim was a deep thinker and had gone through several evolutions of thought and philosophy. He talked slowly and deliberately. He had wispy gray hair and the spotty redness that comes with an extremely light complexion. He wore glasses that teetered on the edge of his nose, and he always seemed uncomfortable in a coat and tie. He was a man that placed more importance on his thoughts than his appearance.

"What am I to do with this, Jim?" asked the President as he rubbed his chin and furrowed his brow.

"Excuse me, Mr. President," said Jim Stiles, shaken from his own concentration.

"I mean, what am I going to do with this? The content of the messages seems to be consistent with what I would expect God to say to us. Now the newspaper letters make it almost inconceivable that the messages could come from anyone but God. I have to tell you, Jim, I am of the belief—let me restate that—I am of the growing knowledge that these messages do indeed come from God."

"Yes, Mr. President, there certainly does seem to be a growing body of evidence to support your position," said Jim in a neutral tone of voice as if not yet quite ready to take a position himself.

"Jim, two messages keep running through my mind. One talks about our actions having consequences in this life and the next. The other one tells us that the actions of nations are judged the same as the actions of individuals. If that's true, what does it mean for our country? And if so, where does that leave me? You reap what you sow—I certainly don't want to be responsible for sowing any seeds that will lead this country to hell. Lord knows, and I suppose He does, we have enough to pay for already."

"Yes, Mr. President. I understand the issue, and I understand your dilemma."

There was a knock on the door, which Jim answered. He told the President that the group was assembled. The President went to stand in front of his desk, leaning back slightly on its edge. He was a man who liked to think on his feet. Jim beckoned everyone to come in.

The National Security Advisor, the Attorney General, the Director of Homeland Security, and several Senators and Representatives, including Congressmen Holt and Silverman filed in. As each one entered the room, they approached the President, shook his hand, respectfully addressed him, and found a seat. The President began his initial remarks.

"Ladies, gentlemen, I need to make a decision concerning my response to the events and messages. If we are in a new world, I need to figure out how we are going to chart the course of this nation. I called you here today to advise me in these matters. I know you all have much to attend to as today's events have called forth immense public response, so I intend to keep this meeting short by focusing on these questions: Is the force behind the messages and events God? If so, how does that affect the separation of church and state? Will the actions of this country result in eternal consequences? Gareth, I understand there is some information concerning the origin of the messages."

Gareth Rutherford, the National Security Advisor, began, "Mr. President, I have a report here of the most recent assessment regarding the extraterrestrial origin of the messages. SETI first brought the report concerning radio transmissions to our attention. Our worldwide system of parabolic surveillance devices has confirmed SETI's initial reports. The radio transmissions arrive on the same day and are the same message as that which appears on the ticker tape along the bottom of television screens during news broadcasts. Our listening devices in New Guinea, Alaska, Antarctica, and Greenland receive the messages at the same moment in time. The transmissions come in standard Morse code and in the native language of the person receiving the message. The origins of the messages seem to be black holes in space. That, in and of itself, is inconsistent with our understanding of physics. Black holes are areas where gravity is so intense that even light cannot escape. If light cannot escape, then the radio transmissions also could not escape—yet they do.

"What is even more perplexing is that the black holes that are the origin of these messages are located at significantly different distances from Earth. Some are 150 light-years away, some are two million light-years away, and some are fifteen million light-years away. According to our understanding of physics, in order for these messages to reach the Earth at exactly the same moment, the messages would have to have been sent 150 million years ago, two million years ago, and fifteen million years ago—precisely. The power transmitting them was, evidently, familiar with Morse code and was also able to predict the native language of the person receiving the code—all at a time before language was developed on this planet."

"Well, that's enough science to convince me. Still, can we ever be completely sure?" asked the President.

Max raised his hand tentatively; he had only been to the Oval Office three times in all his tenure, and those times were only for ceremonial events.

"Mr. President, when I can't be certain of something, I'll ask myself if it's possible for the opposite to be true," said Max, even as he scolded himself for acting and sounding like a schoolboy.

"What do you mean?" asked the President curtly.

Max stammered, "Well, uh . . . I . . . I might ask if it was possible that it wasn't God?"

The President faced Max with a quizzical look, and then broke into a laugh and said, "I wouldn't want to ask *that* to some of the cabinet. The Secretaries of Commerce and the Treasury already told me it was a grand illusion put on by a conspiracy of multinational corporations and the military-industrial-complex. Interior said it could be aliens, you know, the extraterrestrial kind. Education suggested it could be the anti-Christ." Then more seriously, "It's a good suggestion, Congressman. Okay, I'll ask the question. Can any of you tell me that it's not God?"

The room was silent, except for a sigh of relief coming from Max.

"All right, then let's consider that answered. Let's go on to the implications—separation of church and state?"

"Excuse me, Mr. President, may I weigh in here?" asked the Attorney General. When she received a nod of acknowledgement from the President, she continued, "Mr. President, I'm beginning to understand the point you're getting at. When we speak about the separation between church and state, we are not saying that there is no God. Our currency says *In God We Trust*. The founding fathers all believed in God. If God were to become known to us as a factual power, a power such as electricity or magnetism, and there was an undeniable acceptance of God, then the legal argument for the separation of God and state would be as meaningless as an argument for the separation of gravity and state."

"Is it your legal opinion that there is no barrier between God and state?" the President asked.

"The First Amendment states 'Congress shall make no law respecting an establishment of religion, or prohibiting the free exercise thereof . . .' It really goes to different organized schools of faith. As long as you are meticulously careful not to favor one religion over another, or hinder any religion, I think you will be on safe, legal ground."

The President asked the others in the room if they could propose any constitutional counterargument to the Attorney General. Again, the room was silent. The President continued.

"So then, as I perceive it, the consensus is that if God is a scientific fact, if God is no longer a question of faith, if God belongs to no particular religion, and if He has made his presence known in a way that is undeniable, then it is appropriate to respond to His messages. The power that has been demonstrated is a power that far exceeds our own; it's a power that can conceivably reduce us to ashes with a shrug—I suppose we better pay attention. Okay, let's move on to our actions and their consequences."

Rutherford spoke next, "Mr. President, your job is to protect America. If you make decisions based on messages from God, you will be making the same decision people throughout history have made to their detriment. These kinds of decisions, decisions based on divinities, have caused the fall of the Roman Empire, the Crusades, and the misleading of the German peoples in the last century. Anything that is charismatic and leads people to forget reason and forget defense is dangerous and cannot be abided."

"I hear what you're saying," the President said. "Let me hear from Homeland."

The Director of Homeland Security responded, "If you do, in fact, go public and say that these are truly messages from God, somebody is going to come back and say—*Which God?* What are you going to answer to that?"

President Edwards stood, stretched his legs, and arched his back. He walked up to the world map and began to trace country borders in the Middle Eastern section. The department heads murmured and discussed matters among themselves. Once they got into it, it became clear that the issues raised from all political, philosophical, and spiritual points of view were exceedingly complex.

Rutherford could stay silent no longer. "It is a terrible and dangerous mistake to just drop into faith when you have a phenomenon that you cannot explain. That's why I urge caution as to what you say to the world."

"What says the Secretary of State?"

"Mr. President, from the reports we've just received, we understand that as a result of the seven hours of peace in the Middle East, Shiite and Sunni clerics are coming together and planning a peace summit. Word has leaked that they are interpreting the freezing of the military machines as a sign from Allah, a sign that He intends for there to be peace in the Middle East. There may be an opportunity here of historic proportions."

The room was getting stuffy. All of the participants were beginning to get tired and frustrated at not being able to create any clarity in the matter. Abe Holt, in particular, seemed as though he had had enough. He had a dry sense of humor, so he threw out a total non sequitur.

"Why don't we just surrender? If it is God, we'll be home free. If it's not God, there is probably very little that we can do against such a power anyway, so the game is over. That's my vote, total and complete surrender."

Everyone leaned back in their chairs and laughed. It was good to have the comic break as things were beginning to get a little bit too hot. Every person in that room had excelled in his own profession. Each one of them had risen to be powerful and even more important to have access to power. None of them were sure of their advice, and that was not a comfortable place for any of them to be.

After the laughter died down, Max innocently added, "Mr. President, is it possible that we are making too much of this? Perhaps, all that is necessary to say is that the government is aware of the events, that we're investigating, and ask each person to look into his heart for the answer. Perhaps, all they need from you is a little encouragement and a sense that everything is okay."

"Well, that's all fine and good, but what I want to know is what do I do tomorrow about covert operations? What do I do about executive orders to assassinate? What will I do when I'm faced with the Jack-Bauer moment? I have had to do things in the national interest that have bothered my conscience. Our country has been involved in situations that resulted in the death of thousands to no discernible positive end. We have engaged in covert operations to overthrow governments and sovereign states like Chile or Cuba. We engaged in warfare in Vietnam resulting in the death of over fifty thousand of our servicemen and women, all for something called the domino theory—which proved to be incorrect. We went into Iraq on another theory called weapons of mass destruction, which didn't pan out either. When are we going to learn from our mistakes? Many times our fighting men and women came back, and we didn't have the compassion to adequately take carc of their wounds whether physical or psychological.

"Is this the country we want to live in? If we call ourselves people of faith, *why* do we not act like people of faith? If we say that we believe in a God, *why* do we go sneaking around telling half lies and exaggerations to the public, not to mention our wives and friends? We do it as if we were doing something in private, when there really is no such thing as private, as it pertains to God. How covert is a covert operation—really? Why do we go around acting like we've got to get ours before the other guy gets it? Instead of thinking God's on our side, shouldn't we be asking if we're on God's side? I don't even want to think of what consequences we might be in for if we're not on God's side."

Max shifted uneasily in his chair. The President's words had ripped into his conscience. He thought of all the rooms he had snuck in and out of with so many women. He was a man of faith, yet he did somehow believe he was able to hide his actions. All of a sudden he wondered if his unquenchable need for sex was really a need to connect. But connect to what? Was it the Divine? Another person? Something from his past? Yes, that was it—something about the orphanage—something terrible. The intense discomfort of his thoughts brought him back. He then realized that to go down this path, he would have to consider facing his discomfort and curbing his promiscuity. That was something his addiction would not allow. He shook off his reflection and returned his attention to the Oval Office. Rutherford was speaking.

"It is not necessary for us to violate the Geneva Convention or any other treaty or law in order for us to maintain our defenses in a ready, capable, and able fashion. As you mentioned yourself, Mr. President, if you allow for the possibility of the existence of God, you must allow for the possibility of the existence of evil. You took an oath—I was sitting two rows behind you when you did—to protect and defend this country. You must follow your oath. Let your oath be your conscience."

"And that is going to be the last word. Ladies, gentlemen, you have come here and you have given me what I asked of you. You have given me your heartfelt responses, and I will consider them."

Jim Stiles got up and opened the door for the group as they left. Jim stayed and sat on one of the couches. President Edwards sat opposite him.

"Well, Jim, what do you think?"

"I'm not sure what I think, Mr. President. But I do think I know what you think. I think that you believe the messages originate from God, and, more importantly, that your duty to God and that your duty to this country have become aligned. Am I correct?"

"Bull's-eye!"

"Mr. President, you are going to catch hell in the polls."

"I'd rather catch hell in the polls than in eternity. I hope the same is true of where I lead this country. Why don't you put some notes together? I will too, and we'll see if we can work up a speech that makes sense."

CHAPTER 9

The answer is simple; I am that I am.

—God

Waiting by the oversized gilded elevator at 495 Park Avenue, Claire took stock of the lobby. Everything spoke money. Pots of fresh flowers topped gleaming mahogany tables, screening intimate groupings of overstuffed settees and wingbacks. Even the people quietly chatting were polished.

The elevator arrived with a subdued ding. Claire, eyes lowered, joined the half dozen people already in the elevator and pressed the button for the thirty-third floor. The elevator was paneled with insets of rich Moroccan tapestry. Claire wanted to hide in the pattern of the fabric and wished the elevator would never stop. *I, Claire Medina, am at a therapist's office! What am I doing here?* she kept asking herself. Too quickly the elevator arrived at her floor, and Claire grudgingly got out.

She pulled her appointment card out of her shoulder bag even though she had everything on the card memorized—Dr. Mark Jacobs, Suite 33C, Family Therapy. *Get off the elevator and turn left* were the directions from the throaty female receptionist when Claire called earlier in the week for an appointment. Claire glanced around. She was alone. The deep carpet muffled her steps as she started down the hallway.

She arrived at Suite 33C and entered the unlocked door. There was a small waiting room and a desk for a receptionist, but no one was there. She had a seat. As soon as she sat down, she began to talk herself out of staying. She began to stand just as a casually dressed man came out of the inner office.

"You must be Mrs. Medina."

"Yes."

"I'm Mark Jacobs," the man said, motioning her toward his office. "Please come in and make yourself comfortable. Here, have a seat."

"I have to tell you I'm a little bit uncomfortable being here."

"I understand. Some people feel a bit uncomfortable the first time they come in. Have you ever seen a therapist before?"

"No, I haven't. My mother once went to therapy but . . ." she stopped.

"Well, I'm going to give you a chance to catch your breath. Let me tell you a little about therapy. First, anything said here, stays here. I'm only interested in providing you with helpful feedback. I want to hear you and understand you. That way we can work together to develop new ways to think that may work better for you. How does that sound?"

"That sounds fine."

Claire looked around the office. It was tasteful and sedate. The drapes over the window were semitransparent to let in just enough light to be comfortable. There was a desk in the corner, but the room was primarily furnished by a small three-cushion couch and two upholstered armchairs, which were facing each other. Mark and Claire naturally gravitated to the two armchairs.

"As you may have noticed, I'm a man," Mark said with lightness in his voice.

"Mmmm?"

"Well, sometimes women are looking for, or think they would feel more comfortable with, a female therapist. I'm wondering how you feel about that?"

"I guess I'm comfortable with it. My husband's a man, and maybe, who knows, you might help me understand how he thinks," said Claire, trying to be pleasing.

"I practice a form of therapy called solution-focused therapy. I don't do the Freudian thing, where you lie on the couch and say whatever comes to mind, and I sit behind you with a notebook and nod my head wisely."

Claire giggled and started to feel more at ease.

Mark went on, "The way I conduct therapy is very interactive. You tell me what's on your mind, and I ask you questions about it. If I sense that something needs to be looked at more deeply, I'll ask you about it. I try to quickly help you discover what's interfering with your happiness."

"And my husband's happiness," Claire interrupted.

"Let's make sure we focus on your happiness. Your husband's happiness will be a natural byproduct of your happiness. You've heard the expression, 'When Momma ain't happy, ain't nobody happy?'"

"Yes, I have," said Claire with a smile—she was beginning to like her therapist.

"Once we've identified the problem, it's just a matter of looking at workable solutions and options to find healthy ways of dealing with it. How does that sound?"

"That sounds wonderful. I guess what was the most uncomfortable about coming here was that I thought you would be analyzing me—looking into my brain, dissecting me, and figuring out what makes me tick."

"That's what most people think. I feel that most of us are much more alike than we are different, and more complex than we realize. I know you think that the problems and issues you're dealing with are unique, and I don't know whether this will make you feel better or disappointed, but most of the issues we deal with are common. That means you're not alone, but you are among a special class of people. You had the insight to recognize that something was making you uncomfortable, and you have the courage to seek out help for that. That puts you in the minority, and I applaud you for it."

"Thank you. I am feeling more comfortable.

"Great. So tell me, what's on your mind? Why are you here today, and how can I help you?"

"I am mostly coming for myself, but I'm also coming because of some concerns of my husband."

"Some concerns for your husband or from your husband?"

"From my husband. Recently we had a couple of fights and I . . ."

"When you say fights, are you talking about something physical?"

"No, just yelling, I . . . well—I'm not sure what to say!"

"Please don't worry about whether you say something exactly right. Take all the time that you need. You can always say what's on your mind and then go back and clarify it. I promise that if I don't understand something I'll ask you about it. As I said, the most important thing to me is that I hear you and understand you."

"Well, you know these messages that have been happening lately . . . ."

"Messages?"

"You know, these God messages that have been going around. They really have me spooked. I feel like I'm walking around with someone looking over my shoulder making judgments on everything that I do or think."

"You're not alone; a lot of folks share those very feelings."

"Well, I guess I've been thinking about them a lot and thinking about my life and the decisions I've been making. My husband is, uh, seeing me as . . . I guess it's always been difficult for me to . . . to stand up to people. With my husband, with my job—my thoughts are all over the place. I'm trying to, um, I'm trying to put them into some sense, but they're all over the place. I get the feeling that my husband doesn't think I'm strong enough. That's something that we often fight about, and I don't know where I get this . . . this . . . weakness. At least that's what my husband calls it. It just feels like nausea to me. I've been dealing with it all my life. I'm always worried about the way people see me. I always worry about others and don't really stand up for myself. I think it affects my marriage, my work, and my everyday life. At work I'm being pressured into doing something that I don't want to do. I really wish that I was able to sit and speak to my husband more and get more support from him, but he often seems distant lately. I know that this probably isn't making any sense to you; I just don't know how to start explaining my entire life to you."

"I know it's a lot—let me see if I can help us sort through it. You said that you're here for some concerns that your husband had. The decision to come and make an appointment to see me today, was that your decision or his decision?"

"Well, he made the suggestion, but I didn't think that it would hurt to come and talk to somebody."

"So then, the decision to come is yours?"

"Yes, well, I'm not being forced into it. So yes, I guess the decision is mine. I want to make my husband happy. I mean—

maybe I think it's an opportunity to figure some things out for myself. So here I am."

"Okay—that's good. Do you have children?"

"No. We really want to, but when we moved up to New York we got so wrapped up in our careers we just put it off," Claire whispered as her eyes teared up slightly.

"I can see that's something you really want in your life. I would imagine you want to be in the best relationship possible with your husband before you add children to the mix."

"Yes, I do."

You mentioned before that you think your husband sees you as not very strong. How do you see yourself?"

"Well, it's difficult because I have opposite—or whatever you would call them—feelings. I've been very successful in my life, but somehow I don't feel very successful. I feel that I'm smart and that I'm a good person, but there are also times when I feel like I'm a fake. There are times when I'm presented with something, and I know I can handle it; but rather than deal with it, I just want to go run away or have a drink. Maybe I'm like my father."

"So things were a little hard growing up? Tell me a little more about that."

"I never really talk about it. I had to go through quite a lot as a child. My father was an alcoholic. He fought in Vietnam. When he came back from the war he was changed; it was like I lost my father. I was twelve at the time. He intimidated me until he died . . . in a way, he still does. I was never able to go to him for anything. After he came back, my mother became distant. We became a very superficial family. I never got much support from either of my parents. I guess, my role in the family was just to be quiet, not really make many waves . . . do well and be invisible for the most part. You know, my mother always covered up for his drinking. She always told me to hush and not say anything. I was frustrated that she never stood up to him and tried to make a better life for us. I had to really be strong through all that, but I did grow up eventually and become successful. So in that way, I see myself as a strong person, but at the same time I see myself as a very weak person. I guess I've got to figure out who I am."

"So tell me a little bit about your husband. By the way, what's his name?"

"Tomás."

"What kind of person is Tomás? How do you feel toward him?"

"I very much love my husband. He is a very strong man. He's a lawyer, a very successful lawyer, and, uh, he's a very passionate person, an emotional person. He's also a very angry person. He's very judgmental, and lately he makes me feel worthless."

"That must be difficult for a person as accomplished as you are. Has it always been like that?"

"No, we met quite a while ago. We built our life together. When we started we didn't have anything, but we . . . we always had each other. We were very close and had a good friendship along with our marriage. There were times that were difficult, and we certainly had our challenges, but we faced them together. Lately it seems we are on our own, that each of us is dealing with our own stuff by ourselves. I just don't know if I can do it on my own. I know that I certainly don't want to do it without Tomás."

"So what is it that's creating conflict for you?"

"I guess it's that Tomás just seems frustrated with me lately . . . that and a little insecurity. We're not communicating a lot, and as I said earlier, he seems very distant. I don't know if it's something going on with all the craziness lately. I don't know—I'm not sure."

"Does he work long hours?"

"Yes, he works a lot, lately more than ever. We're not giving enough time to each other, and our marriage is suffering for it."

"You mentioned that he was angry?"

"Yes, he is angry. He has a temper. When he gets angry, he can be very intimidating—very intimidating, very intimidating . . . ," Claire said as her voice trailed off, and then added, "Can I stand up for a minute?"

Mark nodded, and Claire stood up and stretched. She wandered over to the bookcase and read the titles of some of the tomes: *Family Systems Theory, Dialectic Behavior Therapy, Setting Boundaries with Borderlines, Treating Codependency as Addiction,* and *Getting the Love You Want* by Dr. Harveil Hendrix—there were three copies of that one. She returned to her chair and let her posture say she was open for the next question.

"You mentioned that you have some pressures at work. What's going on with that?"

"Well, if you'll excuse my language I have an asshole for a boss. Ever since I've worked there . . ."

"Where is there?"

"Halliron. I've tried to make them happy. There's always pressure and lately, even more. They want me to go along with some practices that I think are fraudulent. I feel very uncomfortable about it. I know it's not the right thing to do, but I don't want to lose my job, and I don't want to cause anything bad to happen to the company. It's just that I would almost sign the papers so I don't have to deal with, you know, him being angry at me. I don't know what to do right now. I seem stuck. I know what the right thing to do it is, but I just can't seem to bring myself to stand up to him."

"Claire, are you talking about several people or just one? You used 'they' and 'him' in the same sentence to describe the source of your discomfort."

Claire felt heat rising in her. He was picking her words apart, and she didn't like it. She didn't want to start feeling that she had to walk on eggshells. She took a deep breath and tried to look at her thinking, giving Mark the benefit of the doubt. She realized he was right—the cause of her upset, the sickening feeling in her gut was just one man.

"Just one—Clay McRae," she said with clarity and a sense of strength and focus that was new to her.

"Claire, hold on just a second and let me see if I've got a handle on what you've said so far. I don't mean to put any words in your mouth, but I'm putting together the things that you said with the emotions you express, and I'm beginning to get a picture of what's disturbing to you. What I'm hearing you say is that you remember a time when you had a better relationship with your father. Then he went off to Vietnam, and when he came back, he was a changed man. He was angry and he drank. You feel that you lost your father, that he abandoned you, and that your mother betrayed you because she enabled his drinking. She tried to placate the situation, making everything seem superficial. I would imagine that you must have wanted your father to love you enough to put down the bottle and stop being angry. I also would imagine that from your twelve-year-old perspective, somehow you felt it was your fault that your father was the way he was—perhaps, because you weren't a good enough daughter to bring him around."

Claire teared up. Mark allowed Claire the privilege of taking care of herself. She reached for a box of tissues that was nearby, pulled one out, wiped her eyes, and blew her nose. Mark didn't make any fuss of it, and Claire appreciated his acceptance of her emotion.

"I'm also hearing you say that you are married to a man you love, and with whom you had a good relationship, but more recently has become a workaholic—not an alcoholic but a workaholic—and is an angry man. I would imagine that you must want Tomás to love you enough to put away his work for long enough to pay attention to you and to understand you enough to be more patient. Perhaps through the same eyes as that wounded twelve-year-old, you feel that, in some way, it's your fault. Somehow, you're not being a good enough wife to bring him around."

Claire was shocked and dumbfounded. He was speaking the words that ran through her mind, tracing an endless Möbius strip in her consciousness. How could he know her most intimate thoughts?

"You're also telling me that at your workplace you have a boss that mistreats you and is doing things that put you in an uncomfortable legal or ethical situation. You're surprised at yourself, nevertheless, for wanting to please him. I imagine you feel that you want him to appreciate you enough to treat you the way you feel you should be treated. Can you see where this is going?"

Claire was stunned. For the first time in her life she realized that she was caught up in a repetitive pattern that's main purpose and goal was to please other people, at her own expense.

"I think we've done enough work for one day. I'm guessing you've got a lot of new thinking to assimilate, and if you don't think about your thinking, you can't change it." Mark retrieved a book from his shelves. "Here's some homework," he said, handing her Dr. Hendrix's book.

"You're right—it's a lot to think about. What's next?"

"When you're ready—and you'll know when that is—we'll set up another appointment. There are still some threads we need to pull together."

"I'll do that. You know, I liked this—I'll be back," she said in the best Arnold Schwarzenegger voice she could muster.

They laughed and shook hands. Shortly she walked through the circular door of the building out onto Park Avenue. She hailed a cab to take her back to Halliron. She felt something inside— something good.

*   *   *

Manhattan County Courthouse is located in Lower Manhattan, just a stone's throw from Chinatown, Little Italy, the Bowery, Chelsea, the Financial District, and Wall Street. It is a busy, thriving, crowded part of the city with uniformed police officers directing traffic at almost every intersection. Throngs of people, poised like Olympic sprinters at each corner, wait for the red electronic palms-up sign to change to a green walk sign and then dash across the intersection, competing with cars turning onto the street.

Things are not much different inside the courthouse itself. A uniformed police officer stands in a circular booth underneath a sign that says INFORMATION directing people to the various offices and courts as they enter. The huge lobby is a meeting place for clients, lawyers, secretaries, reporters, and translators. The floors and walls are made of marble and granite reflecting all the sounds, raising the decibel level, and making the place seem even busier than it is. Pushing open the eleven-foot walnut doors of Division A, Traffic Court, Louie the Cop and Officer Craig Thompson entered the flow of foot traffic toward the lobby.

"Geez, what an incredible waste of time! I can't believe these people actually go to court over a lousy fender bender. Do they think I don't have anything better to do with my time? Of course, if I give them a ticket they're complaining that I should have better things to do," Louie the Cop said with a scowl.

"For Chrissakes, Louie, give these folks a break. It might be just a fender bender to you, but the damage could be a few hundred dollars. That could be a couple weeks' work to them," Thompson replied.

"Yeah, well, If I spent my time being sorry for all these 'citizens,' I wouldn't have time to do my job," Louie said with just a tad of sarcasm.

Thompson gave Louie the Cop a glance and a shrug as a response. They rounded a corner into the big lobby, and as they were crossing through it, Louie heard some commotion on the other side of the lobby.

It was Tomás Medina. Cheeks red, hair pulled back in a tight ponytail, wearing a silk suit and wool overcoat, he was towering over and blasting a rookie assistant district attorney. Though Louie didn't hear the words through the din of the lobby, he could hear the anger and a now-more-pronounced Spanish accent. It started to look like Tomás was actually going to haul off and slug the young prosecutor.

"Hey, just give me a minute here," Louie the Cop said to Thompson as he rushed toward Tomás, hoping to diffuse the situation.

"What are you . . . ," Thompson began, but Louie was already out of earshot.

"Hello, Mr. Medina. Fancy meeting you here, but, eh, well, I mean . . . I guess this is where you work, I suppose," Louie let out with a little laugh to cover his awkwardness.

Tomás turned his attention toward Louie, releasing the intimidated ADA from his gaze. Even though Louie was older than the lawyer, he knew that Tomás had acquired much more and achieved much more than Louie had ever hoped to. Besides, Tomás Medina had so many of the things that Louie the Cop hungered for that Louie wanted to make a good impression; he wanted to look good. As usual, the more Louie tried to look good, the less good he looked.

"Oh, Officer Gibran," said Tomás, sounding formal for the benefit of the ADA. Tomás's radar had picked up on Louie's envy and neediness at the apartment. It was serendipitous that Louie should show up at this moment. Tomás was due to have lunch with the bosses, or as he thought of the group, The Cartel. Seeing Louie now would give him more to report to his clients. He was sure that Louie would get hooked on the bait Tomás had to offer.

"Look, we can work this out later, okay? I'm sorry if I got a little hot-headed," Tomás said to the prosecutor.

"That's okay, Mr. Medina. Just let me know what your client wants to do about the plea offer," responded the ADA, taking the opportunity to escape.

"Officer, I was hoping I'd run into you soon. I was really serious about going for that ride. Are you up for it?" Tomás asked, cooling off.

"Up for it? Hell, yeah, I'm up for it. I kind of thought you were kidding, but my mind's been thinking about it ever since you mentioned it—and you can call me Louie."

"Well, then let's do it, Louie! I've got a break in my court schedule tomorrow. Whaddya say we leave in the morning and take a ride out to the beach?"

"That sounds great," Louie said, almost licking his lips.

"Okay then, why don't you come by my place in the morning? I gotta run now, gotta lunch date, but I'll see you tomorrow morning bright and early," Tomás said, shaking Louie's hand and then waving to him as he walked toward the front door. Louie the Cop walked back to where Thompson was waiting.

Tomás walked out into the bright midday sun. Skies in New York are in some ways like New Yorkers; they are either overcast or crystal clear and not a lot in between. Today the sky was deep blue, without a hint of a cloud. It matched Tomás's mood—clear, bright, and certain—at least for the moment. Tomás headed toward and across Canal Street and then weaved his way east through the vendors of knockoff designer pocketbooks and fake Rolex watches. He reached Mulberry Street and turned uptown.

When he got to the corner of Mulberry and Hester, Tomás stopped for a moment, as he always did. Like so many, Tomás had a dark fascination for pop-culture icons that arose from the legends of the mob—the Mafia and the Cosa Nostra. The spot he was standing on was the exact spot where Crazy Joe Gallo was gunned to his death on April 7, 1972, while eating a plate of shrimp and calamari Fra Diavolo in front of one of Little Italy's clam bars.

From the appliance store across the narrow street, he saw the screens of multiple televisions showing clips of overflowing church parking lots and Muslims meeting for prayer in mosques and open parks. He crossed the street to hear the voice-over.

After yesterday's surprise appearance of a letter allegedly signed by God in the *Burlington Daily Register*, a daily newspaper in North Carolina, the paper published this banner headline today: WE'RE BAFFLED!

Strangely enough, another letter appeared on the op-ed page, in today's *Daily Register*. This is that letter:

Dear Editor,

Of course you are baffled. I understand. The answer to your question is simple: I am that I am. There is no reason to be afraid. My messages do not signal any impending doom. Any healing or harm is entirely in your hands. Over the next few weeks, I will be sending a few suggestions on how to get back in touch with those things that are important to your happiness—and survival.

—God.

In other news, we have a report from St. Patrick's on Fifth Avenue . . .

The newsroom video broke to throngs of people waiting in line to attend the confessionals in the huge cathedral. Many people made the crucifix when walking by. Environmental and animal-rights groups had information tables set up, and a group of thirty-or-so people wearing peace sign t-shirts was holding a vigil for the world's ongoing armed conflicts. The reporter lifted her microphone.

Although starting as a trickle, church, temple, and mosque attendance has more than tripled over the last few weeks in response to the mysterious messages. Of course, not everyone is accepting the messages in a positive way. Alcoholism and anxiety-related crimes, such as domestic violence are also climbing, mental health admissions have nearly doubled, and if you want to see a therapist, you now have to book an appointment two to three months out. Just up the street in Central Park, areas have been cordoned off so Muslims can express their faith during the call to prayer without blocking pedestrian traffic or having to worry about joggers colliding with them. In economic news . . .

The voice trickled off as Tomás continued toward Mott Street where he turned uptown. The reports of physical evidence of God's messages perked his interest as an attorney. For Tomás, however, the jury was still out. The evidence was still mere hearsay. He wanted to see more before declaring a fact of what he already, privately, knew to be true. He was shaken, however, by the idea that God, Himself, had just eliminated any possibility that He would reach down and miraculously cure unsolvable problems.

He arrived at Angelo's Italian Restaurant and Clam Bar. He had been going there often enough and for long enough that he knew the entire staff on a first-name basis, and they knew him as Mr. Medina, a big tipper. He had met the guys whose pictures were on the walls. They were all great actors who had played terrific roles as mobsters. Today Tomás was having lunch with the real thing—the lords of Manhattan's drug empire.

At a certain level, the various organizations—the Italians, the Colombians, the Haitians, the Afghans, and the homegrown gangs— all talk to each other. They have different cultures but one common goal: to move cocaine and narcotics into and around Manhattan as hassle free and profitably as possible. The Colombians hooked up with the Italians to bring their poison into New York through Haiti. The Italians had been using Haiti as a staging area to bring narcotics into New York Harbor due to its French connection with Marseille. Marseille was where Thai opium was refined into heroin. Once the smack left Haiti, the mob influence on the docks of New York assured its safe passage into the city. Once in the country, homegrown gangs formed an efficient, territorial, and deadly distribution system. The Afghans were the new kids on the block, thanks to the explosive growth of poppy fields while under Taliban rule. Not having an efficient distribution system, Afghan warlords collaborated with Turks, who had developed their smuggling routes and contacts distributing Hashish.

Tomás was lucky, or unlucky, enough to represent all of them. As he walked into the warmth of the restaurant, Tomás caught the eye of Sam, who was dressed in the career-waiter's uniform of black shoes, black pants, white shirt, black tie, and white apron. Tomás held up his hand and spread his fingers indicating five, pointed at his chest, and held up the thumb of his left hand for a total of six. Sam gave an almost imperceptible nod and swung his hand to the corner table, nestled into two walls and not exposed to the plate glass window fronting Mott Street. It was the only vacant table left during the busy lunchtime hour. It was vacant precisely to fill needs such as this.

The table could seat nine but had six seats with their backs to the wall. Sam wisely removed the three seats with exposed backs as Tomás took the inside most seat so he could keep an eye out for his clients. Sam brought him a Corona without being asked.

Tomás pushed the lime into the bottle and swallowed deep, following the liquid down his chest as it cooled the constant heat in his soul. Tomás looked around and had a rare moment of contentment. It was nice to be known, really known. Not a word had been said, and here he was sitting on *his* throne with *his* drink about to hold court with *his* clients. If only the rest of the world understood what little he asked for, he wouldn't need to get so mad all the time.

Gee-spot with the 112th Street Gang and Mustafa, the Turk representing the Afghans, came in together. By the time they were seated, his premier client Johnny Pericolo walked in, along with Jacquie, the Haitian, and the Colombian, Enrique. After the usual settling in, hellos, and menu scanning, the group got down to the serious business of relationship building by feigning personal interest in each other.

"You takin' good care of that pretty little wife of yours?" Johnny asked Tomás in a fatherlike tone, and then wagging his finger at him, he added, "The last time I saw her she looked sad, a little down. You know, we're all busy here, but a man's got to take time out for the family."

"We're doing fine, doing okay," defended Tomás.

"Yeah, well, she was looking a little bit nonplussed," countered Johnny.

"Nonplussed, nonplussed—what kinda word is that? Seems like some cheap dance pussy—nonplussed," queried Gee-spot.

"Ahlo, my young friend, is not a good thing to do, call a man's woman that kind of name," advised Enrique in a thick Spanish accent.

"Yo, Man—I wasn't callin' Tommy's squeeze a pussy, I was jus' sayin' the word, the word—nonplussed, sounds like a pussy. Man, be cool."

"Still, you should be more respectful of the women. They are fragile creatures," counseled Enrique.

"Oui, but very often a woman's *no* is much stronger than a man's *yes*," Jacquie said in a French-Caribbean patois straight out of his native Haiti.

"Especially when you're married to them," said Johnny, obviously speaking from experience and closing down that conversation. Changing the subject, he looked straight at Tomás and asked, "So how's the practice?"

"I can't complain. Life is good thanks to you and your referrals," Tomás answered diplomatically then added, "but before we get down to business, let's order."

"So what's good?" asked Mustafa in a flat tone.

"Well, this is Angelo's famous clam bar," responded Tomás.

"Yeah, famous fo' what?" asked Gee-spot.

"Well, it started out as a Little Italy clam bar. They served fried shrimp, calamari, and scungili with mild, medium, or hot marinara sauce. Then they grew into this big restaurant, but the original stuff is still the best," explained Tomás.

"Now what is different in mild, medium, and hot?" asked the Colombian.

Johnny took up the challenge. "Well, mild gives you a warm glow, medium makes you sweat, and hot burns going in and coming out."

The explanation seemed satisfactory, and they all fell into their individual worlds while considering their choices. Sam came over. With his assistance, each member of the group was able to define his particulars. Sam disappeared, and they were in private mode again.

Johnny leaned in, just enough to signal confidentiality, looked at the saltshaker in his hand, and then looked up as if he was looking over bifocals.

"Tommy, things are good. Business is improving, and I think I'm speaking for everyone here,"—he looked up, everyone nodded— "that as things improve for us, they will improve for you too."

Johnny's face asked the question: do you understand? Tomás answered with a nod. He didn't like being called Tommy, but he would take it from his best client.

Johnny went on, "We have new friends and better relations with old friends . . ." Again Johnny scanned the group and got confirmation in every eye contact. "In many ways closer ties, a stronger chain is good, but in some ways it is also dangerous. You know, we're businessmen; we believe in globalization too," Johnny laughed, and the table laughed with him. "When you do business with so many diverse interests, trust is important; you get to know each other. We get to know each other's work, family, friends . . . and if one of us should get arrested . . . you know with the pressure these feds can put on us, with the new laws and this terrorism stuff . . ."

"Yo Man and dos messages . . . ," Gee-spot chimed in.

Tomás saw Johnny's face change in a New York second. From calm and pleasantly businesslike, Johnny became tough, mean, and flushed. Gee-spot said nothing that in and of itself was anger provoking, but Tomás surmised that what Gee-spot said must have hit a nerve somewhere in Johnny's soul, a nerve that was covered up by a mountain of denial. Johnny pointed a trembling finger at Gee-spot.

"Don't you ever say I don't respect God. I go to church every Sunday with my family you little bla . . ."

"Hey, Johnny, calm down, don't draw attention. We're having a nice lunch here," Tomás interceded. Color started coming back to Johnny's face.

"Whew," Gee-spot whistled, "yo, bro, chill, man, I wasn't talkin' 'bout you, man—was talkin' about those messages—just sayin' it's some weird shit ya' know—like it gives me the heebies. I'm hearin' all kinds of shit from my old lady and my Ho', and I'm tellin' ya the pigs on the street are really getting religion—that's what I'm talkin' 'bout. Know what I mean, yeah, they really gettin' religion."

Johnny visibly relaxed, shook his right hand, and said, "Give unto the Lord what's His and give unto Caesar what's Caesar's . . . anyway—Gee-spot makes a good point. The cops are getting religion, they're getting harder to bribe, and that makes getting inside intelligence more important than ever."

"Johnny, Enrique, Jacquie, Gee-spot, Mustafa," Tomás started, acknowledging everyone at the table, "you've been asking me for some time now to arrange for more protection using inside intelligence from the police department and even to find officers that might, shall we say 'alter' their normal patrol routes to stay away from certain areas at certain times. I've had a good relationship with some of you for as long as fifteen years. The reason our relationship has been so good is that I have never promised something that I could not deliver, and I have never lied to you."

"That's true. You listened, you learned, and you've been rewarded. You've always been good for your word, and we've appreciated it," acknowledged Johnny.

Tomás went on, "I have hesitated and held you off for the last few weeks because I have not been sure that I could do the work that you asked and at the same time guarantee your safety. After all what you ask is highly risky, and I was not comfortable with any of the personnel I interviewed. However, this has recently changed. I have come to know a policeman that I believe has the appropriate prerequisites for the job. He's been a patrolman for twenty-nine years and has never advanced. He is greedy and envious and wants to have riches. I offered to take him for a ride in my BMW tomorrow, and he's accepted. I'll talk to him then. How much am I authorized to offer?"

At that point, Sam came up with the lunch platters. The group fell back into their personal patter until everyone was served, and Sam disappeared again. The members of the Cartel exchanged glances and a few words. Johnny spoke for everyone when he said, "I think twenty-five thou' a month ought to do it."

Tomás was surprised. "I think ten to fifteen thousand would be enough."

Mustafa made one of his infrequent comments, "We do not mind spending the money if this policeman understands the discretion necessary for the job. If he would do it for less, I would be concerned that he truly does not understand the ramifications of his assignment."

Tomás understood, and he said, "I'll make sure he fully understands what he's getting into, and I'll be happy to spend your money. At the same time, I don't want to make his head spin with newfound riches so that he gets careless."

Johnny reached out, patted Tomás on the head with his big padded hand, and told him, "You're a good lawyer, and you understand people."

Tomás smiled, but his smile covered a new nervousness in his guts. This meant that he was really stepping out into unchartered territory. After this, for better or for worse, he would be, in every sense of the word, a criminal lawyer, not a criminal defense attorney—ever again.

With business out of the way, everyone got down to having a good lunch and joking around a bit. Tomás looked out at the rest of the restaurant and noticed the television at the opposite corner. He couldn't hear what was being said, but he could see scenes engendered by the God messages. This stuff was always on and always in his face. He didn't understand why the other guys at the table weren't a little bit worried about all this, a little bit uncomfortable; he certainly was. But not so uncomfortable that he was willing to give up everything he had worked for over the last fifteen years.

Tomás walked out of Angelo's Clam Bar full of mixed feelings and anger. Tomás was smart but not insightful. He was master of his intellect but at the beck and call of his emotions. He was high on the professionalism and mastery he displayed at his lunch meeting, and he was leveled by the feeling of having no control at all. He did well, but he didn't do good. He knew if his father was looking down, there would be pride about how he handled himself, but not what he handled. He was master and slave at the same moment.

Of course, to Tomás, none of this rose to the level of thought. It was all a combination of undifferentiated, sequential body sensations left in the undefined. Any other person might have felt conflicted, but Tomás was an angry man; and when he felt conflicted, it came up as anger. Any other man might have felt anxious, but when Tomás felt anxiety, it came up as anger. Any other man might have felt guilty, but guilt only made Tomás madder.

New Yorkers have a certain radar and etiquette as they walk along crowded sidewalks. They may be looking forward or down (never up, that's for tourists), reading the paper or adjusting their watches, paying attention or lost in thought, but they make the appropriate bobs and weaves that keeps contact with oncoming pedestrian traffic down to arm brushes. When a mistake is made resulting in a jarring shoulder contact, a sharp look from the offended and a short "sorry" from the offender is usually all that's called for.

Tomás was in no mood to follow the custom. His short walk back down Canal Street to his car parked on Broadway was as-an-arrow-flies straight. His jaw was set, brow furrowed, and eyes fixed on a spot that looked through the crowd in front of him. Those that noticed him stepped aside. Those that didn't bounced off him.

Tomás gave his claim ticket to the parking attendant who trotted off to the corner of the ground level lot. Tomás's BMW was buried behind four cars, which had to be moved to get his out. All Tomás wanted to do was get into his shower's steam bath and sweat out his pissedoffedness, but he had to wait for his car and he just got hotter. His car pulled up; the young boy got out and held the door open. Tomás came around the door and noticed the boy's hand out, palm up. Usually Mr. Medina was good for at least a five-spot.

Tomás looked down. His eyes narrowed; his face closed in; he didn't blink. "The next time you bury my car, I will spit in your sweet upturned palm," said Tomás, sliding into the seat. The boy started to close the door, but Tomás yanked it closed first. The boy was literally taken aback. Tomás accelerated across the sidewalk until he was stopped by a car blocking the driveway. Cars that block intersections, entrances, and exits were one of his pet peeves anyway. All he could do was pound the horn.

Once he finally started creeping uptown and crosstown in the encapsulated privacy of his car, his anger subsided to a patter of muttering. He still didn't know why he was angry. A dozen reasons were circling a holding pattern around the center of his mind, but what he felt most of all was the creepy feeling of losing control of his life—becoming what he had always feared becoming—an indentured servant, a slave.

He decided to drive uptown on Broadway for a change. The traffic was miserable, but there was always something going on to notice. After a while he just slipped into numbness. At Columbus Circle he cut crosstown to Third Avenue and then back uptown to 112th Street where he turned right.

As Tomás slowly drove east on 112th street, he passed three young men wearing the red and silver of the 112th Street Gang. They were not a part of Tomás's world, and so he paid them no mind. That's not to say they weren't noticed at all.

From the window of her classroom at the First Baptist Church of Harlem, Lori Blount looked out, her stomach sank, and tears rose in her eyes. One of the gang members, one of the young men wearing red and silver, was Joe-24.

CHAPTER 10

*Do the right thing because it is the right thing to do
and for no other reason.*

—God

Lori was devastated. She slowly walked closer to the window and folded her arms across her chest, more to hold in the pounding of her heart than for comfort. She came to stand at a forty-five-degree angle to the window, next to the wall heaters that touched gently against her hip. The heat radiating out from the wall combined with the heat radiating out of her body caused her to break into a clammy sweat. She could feel the heat and didn't know whether it was anger or fear. She watched, as well as she could through the tears, as Joe walked down 112th Street until he was out of sight. Eventually she shuddered.

Lori gathered up her jacket and pocketbook and was out the door. She walked down the hallway and out the 112th Street exit and turned toward the East River in the direction that she had seen Joe walking. She decided to walk over to the Clidson's brownstone to see if he was there. She wanted to check on Tillie Clidson anyway. She hadn't seen Mrs. Clidson much since Billy's death and worried about her on a regular basis.

The sidewalk ladies were playing cards, as usual, except Tillie Clidson's chair was unoccupied. "Afternoon, ladies. Where's Mama Clidson?" Lori asked.

"She was out here for a little while before, but then she went inside—said she was tired," responded one of the ladies.

"Yeah, she doesn't stay out very long anymore, not since . . . ," said another lady.

"Billy was shot," finished the third lady.

"By the way, have any of you seen Joe Clidson come by in the last few minutes?" Lori asked.

All the ladies nodded or grunted no. Lori thanked the ladies and walked up the stoop to ring the bell. She waited for a moment, and when she got no response, she opened the door and stepped inside. The television was on, and Tillie was asleep in her armchair. Lori walked over to turn the television down, approached Tillie, and touched her gently on the shoulder.

"Oh, Lori—I'm so glad it's you, my sweet, sweet Lori."

"Mama Clidson, have you seen Joe? I'm looking for him."

"Lori, I don't see much of Joe anymore. Doesn't seem like he's ever home much anymore. Comes around here with all kinds of new friends—I'm not sure if I like them. Some of them use language that's not pretty. Oh, Lori, I sure hope that boy isn't doing anything that can get him in trouble. You go find him now and tell him to come home and sit with me. I need somebody to change channels for me—I need my Joe."

Lori walked down 113th Street to the corner. She went to the right and saw four or five young man wearing the red and silver. She turned and walked straight toward Joe-24.

"Joe Clidson, I want to speak to you right now," said Lori.

Joe-24 could see the other gang members were watching him. "You talk to me in that tone of voice, girl, well, you can just keep on walking by," Joe said.

Lori hesitated, her tone changed, "You're right, Joe, I'm sorry. Actually, I need some help; I was hoping that you would help me out with a situation."

The other gang members, true to street ethic, moved off the stoop, away from the wall they were leaning on, and wandered off down the street to give Joe-24 privacy.

"Joe, what do you think you're doing?"

"Why, what's wrong? What are you talking about?"

"What have you turned into? Is this what you've sunken to—being in a gang?" said Lori, hands on hips.

"What do you know? Everything is going just fine for you. You get to go into a nice building, stand up in front of your nice class, teach your nice lessons with your nice degree. I think you forgot what things are like out here on the street. Nobody wants to do nothing for you. Billy got shot and what happened? Did you see any big police investigation? Did you see anybody get arrested? Oh, it's fine sitting up there, being all holier than thou. Just tell me one thing—are you going to take any action about what happened to Billy? At least me and my boys, we are going to get justice for Billy."

"You know, I thought that you—I thought there once was a time that you loved me—but that doesn't matter anymore. What's really scary is that it looks like you don't even love yourself anymore. Here you are, a gang member, and you're throwing your life away. Okay, so you hurt yourself and you can't play football anymore, but it seems like you don't even care. You don't care about me, you don't care about yourself—you don't care about anything."

"What is there for me to care about? Everything in my life that ever meant anything to me has been taken away. The only people that really care about supporting me are my boys. At least they went out and found out who killed Billy. We know who he is, and he needs to go down. Maybe that will get me some relief."

"I just can't believe you. I just can't believe that you would resort to being in a gang and somehow that would solve all your problems—somehow that would bring Billy back. You need to just look within yourself and find yourself and maybe stop being so sorry for yourself. Maybe you need to be thinking about helping somebody else instead of killing someone. I know you, Joe Clidson; you can't fool me. How long since you've seen Pastor Abrahms?"

Lori waited. Joe wanted to say he didn't need the advice of any pastor, but the words wouldn't come out. Pastor Abrahms had been like a father to both Lori and him. He tried to shake Lori's question off, but it stuck to him like a tick, engorging itself on his thoughts. He tried to say something once or twice. Finally he just looked at his shoes and sighed.

"I know that you're a kind and good and smart man," continued Lori. "What you're doing wearing those colors is a disgrace to your brother and a disgrace to your mother and to everyone who's ever cared for you and supported you. You know you didn't get to go to Syracuse just because you are Joe Clidson. You got to go because a lot of people believed in you; they still do, and by wearing those colors you're letting every one of them down."

"Well, yeah, there once was a time I had some strong feelings for you. But ever since I came back, every time I see you, you got your nose fifteen feet in the air, like you're too good for me."

"Me—me being too good for you—you've got to be kidding," said Lori. "What happened when you went to college and you were such a big man on campus with all the booze, all the women up there?

You came back, and I was nothing but a neighborhood girl. You talk about me having my nose in the air; you wouldn't even give me the time of day. What am I supposed to do—come running back like a little puppy dog when you whistle? No, I'm sorry, Mr. Clidson, life don't work like that. When you came back that very first summer—I felt like I didn't even know you. I didn't want to have anything to do with you, ever again."

"Well, if you don't want to have anything to do with me ever again, what are you standing here in front of me now for?"

"I'm standing here because I know that you're better than this. We were both brought up in the same church. We went to the same Sunday school, and Pastor Abrahms baptized both of us. I know that you believe in God, and I know that you have to be affected by the messages that God has been leaving us. Go talk to him, talk to the pastor. I know you know the difference between right and wrong, and I know that you know what you're doing is wrong."

Joe was beginning to feel the power of Lori's words. He knew that she was right but couldn't bring himself to admit it. He couldn't deny it either. He felt control over the situation slipping away from him.

"Somebody's got to take up for Billy. If I don't do it, who will?"

"And if you do it, Joe Clidson, and they come back, and they do it back to you, like you know they will—what's that going to do to Mama Clidson? Billy may be gone, but your mother's still here, and she needs you. If you go off and get yourself killed, they might as well build a coffin for two people because she won't survive it—and I might not either."

"What are you saying? Are you telling me that you really care what happens to me?"

"Joseph Clidson or Joe-24 or whatever it is you call yourself these days, sometimes you are *so* stupid. You don't even have sense enough to know when someone who loves you is standing right in front of you."

Joe-24 hung his head in shame; he had nothing left to say. Lori spun on her heels and marched away, but not before Joe could see the tears . . .

Joe stood there. He was alone on the sidewalk, and he was alone in his soul. He joined the gang to recapture a sense of being connected to something, but he still felt connected to nothing. He envied Lori's relationships at First Baptist. Most of all, he felt disconnected from hope—and God.

He had nowhere to go but felt a magnet pulling him. Frozen in indecision, his feet, nonetheless, began walking toward First Baptist and stopped in front the entrance stoop. He willed his legs to step back—they would not. He told himself to turn and walk away, but his body disobeyed. He knew that if he went in the door, he would feel the deep ache that lay under his anger and give power to it. He was defeated and deflated. The pride he had had in his accomplishments was dead, and pride in himself was still unborn. Finally, the hurt within took over his body—taking him back in time to when he knew how to cry. His legs began to shake, and he sat on the stoop and cried—cried like a baby.

"Are you all right?" came the familiar voice of Pastor Abrahms from behind and above him.

Joe turned around and saw the pastor's face wrinkled in concern. Pastor Abrahms was a giant of a man, a full neck and head above most other men. He was completely bald, and his ears were slightly cauliflowered. He'd been wearing the same wireframe glasses for so long that the ends of the frame had made permanent indentations along the outside of his ears. He had droopy, sleepy eyes that bespoke an extraordinary kindness; and although he was dark complected, the visible interior portions of his lips were bright pink. From his neck, arms, and legs, you could tell that he was once a tall, thin man; but the years and gravity had taken their toll. He now sported a midsize paunch that pushed the front of his brown pants down just a bit. He always seemed to be wearing the same scruffy brown shoes and black suspenders under a white shirt. His trademark, though, was his bowtie.

He could have been a beat generation poet, a tenured, past-his-prime professor at New York University, one of the half-crazy proselytizers that inhabit the New York City subway system, or one of those avid readers that takes up permanent residence at a particular table in the New York Public Library on Fifth Avenue. He was, in fact, a Doctor of Divinity, the senior pastor of the First Baptist Church of Harlem, and the principal of the church elementary school. He had been there for over a quarter of a century.

"Are you all right?" the pastor asked again, although he knew the answer.

Joe stood and faced the pastor. He tried to frame an answer, but none would come. He could not unclench his fists. He could not wipe away his tears. He just stood there, now feeling foolish, along with the cacophony of other feelings playing within him. Finally, all he could do was gently shake his head no.

"No, I don't suppose you are," Pastor Abrahms said. "Come, it's warm in here."

Joe moved toward Pastor Abrahms. The first step of the stoop was the hardest. On the second step, some of the chill went away. On the third, he didn't care what anyone thought about him. On the fourth step, he felt a yearning begin to stir within him, and by the fifth, he was ready. As he stepped through the opened door, the pastor opened his arms and gently folded Joe's powerful frame into his chest. Joe could feel the protection and knew that he was in a safe place. He let his emotions out and cried and sobbed and heaved. Pastor Abrahms patiently held him in his gentle, fatherly embrace until Joe's spasms subsided and the catharsis was nearly complete. When Joe began to regain his composure, he pulled ever so slightly back. Pastor Abrahms opened his arms so that Joe could have the space he needed.

Joe started to wipe away the tears on his face. Pastor Abrahms reached into his pocket, found a clean handkerchief, and offered it to Joe. Joe blew his nose with a honk that surprised both of them.

They walked down the hall to one of the classrooms and stepped inside. Pastor Abrahms pulled the teacher's chair out from behind the teacher's table and invited Joe to sit in it. The pastor half sat on the teacher's table and stroked his chin.

"Joe, I look at you, and I can't believe you've become such a man. Do you know that you were one of the first babies presented in this church when I came here?"

The change of subject was just enough to bring Joe out the blackness. Pastor Abrahms had a way of bringing lightness to even the darkest of times.

"Yes, Pastor, you've only told me a couple of hundred times or so," Joe replied.

"Well, I can certainly understand why you cried then, but please, pray tell, what is it that brings you such sadness today?"

Joe stood up. He took off his red-and-silver jacket and held it out to the pastor. When Abrahms didn't take it, Joe slammed it to the floor, turned, and looked out the window. Pastor Abrahms followed him and stood with him, looking out onto the street, but looking at nothing at all.

"How bad was the initiation?" the pastor asked.

"Not too bad. It was three minutes—three minutes of standing still while four of them pounded and kicked between my belt and neck. It wasn't anything I ain't felt before from a half-decent linebacker. It didn't hurt as much as when Billy . . ."

A moment of respect passed in silence.

"I've seen too many young men fall victim to the street," Pastor Abrahms said. "Your brother's loss was the hardest, the saddest."

The pastor gently took Joe's arm and led him back to the chair.

"Joe, I've known your family for as long as I've been here. As a matter of fact, your mother helped move books into the library when we moved into this building from uptown. How can I help you today, Joe?

"Pastor Abrahms, I just don't know what to do—don't know what to do and don't know what I feel. There's something changin' in me . . . I don't know if it's for the good or for the bad. I . . . I . . ." Joe shook his head. "You know how much football meant to me—I'll never be able to play again. I've lost that—and Billy too. I can't get a job. My mom blames me for Billy's death—maybe she's right, I don't know. And the way I've treated Lori . . . the way I've treated Lori . . . she didn't deserve the way I treated her. She deserved better. She's got good reason to be disappointed in me—everybody does."

Joe's long, cathartic cry had served its purpose. He was talking to the pastor in a problem-solving mode now, no longer through an emotional cloud. His strength was returning to him with each word uttered, with each deed confessed, and with each flaw recognized and confronted. Pastor Abrahms was an excellent counselor. He knew how to listen and when to listen; he also knew when to speak and when to move a troubled soul forward.

"Joe, I could listen to you, commiserate with you—show sympathy, compassion, empathy—but I've got too much respect for your strength, your strength of body, and your strength of character. So I'm going to talk straight with you. Can you handle it?"

Joe was surprised by the pastor's approach. He sat upright, listening harder. "Yeah, I can handle it. Lay it on me."

"Okay, Joe . . . so tell me—who are you?"

"Whaddya mean—who am I?"

"You heard me—who are you?"

When Joe realized that the question was a serious one, the upset flew out of him, leaving nothing in its wake. It was a question Joe had never asked himself. Who was he? Was he Joe? Joe-24? Joseph Roosevelt Clidson? A football player? Billy's brother? Tillie's son?

"I . . . I don't know."

"Joe, it's not such a tough question; you're just looking too deep. Who you are is one of God's children."

Joe took a long, shuddering breath and nodded yes.

"If you are a child of God, what do you believe your purpose on earth is?"

"I thought it was to play football, but it ain't that."

"No, it ain't that. Christ said it was to love your God with all your heart and to love your neighbor as yourself. That's not as easy as it sounds."

"No, it ain't. 'Specially when there's justice to be done."

"Yes, especially then. How do we get from here to there? How do we get from lost pride to rebirth in Christ? I suppose we have to go all the way back to the beginning—back to Genesis."

"Genesis?"

"Yes. Remember that God gave Adam dominion over all the plants and creatures. Well, when God gave us that wondrous gift, I believe He intended for us to be responsible, to be good stewards. We're not doing a very good job. Maybe that's why the messages have come. Anyway, in order to be good and wise rulers of the earth, we first have to be rulers of ourselves—our emotions, thoughts, passions, egos—and pride."

"How do you do that?" Joe asked.

"How did you become such a good athlete?" Pastor Abrahms shot back.

"By being the first one on the field, and the last one off it. By doing laps around the field as if they were touchdown runs. By playing every play as if the game depended on it—as if my life depended on it. By getting hit hard and getting back up and into the game. By letting every loss give me the motivation to win the next game. By telling myself I was unstoppable, and believing it so hard there wasn't a mustard seed of doubt."

Joe looked up. Pastor Abrahms was rubbing his chin, nodding his head, and smiling. Joe got it; he got it as clearly as the nothingness that existed just moments before. Football was an allegory for life. Joe had known the solution all along; he just didn't know that he knew it.

"Joe, whose team are you going to be on—the gang's team or God's team?"

"Is that my purpose then, to be on God's team?"

"No, Joe, but that is the way you will find your purpose. If you want to be on God's team, you have to be in training. You know what that's like. You have to give a hundred and ten percent. Like you said, you have to take the hits and get back up. You have to take the challenges that have been given to you, confront them and overcome them—even transcend them. You have to gain dominion over yourself; God doesn't want uncontrolled people on his team."

"But there are so many challenges, and they hurt so badly," Joe said.

"God doesn't give you anything you can't handle. Whatever doesn't kill you makes you stronger."

"What will I do?"

"The Lord doesn't close one door that He opens another."

"But what about justice for Billy?"

"An eye for an eye makes the whole world blind," Pastor Abrahms replied.

"Damn . . . uh . . . I mean dang, Pastor, you got an answer for everything," Joe said.

"No, I don't—but God does. Look, Joe, this is how it works. First, you go and take care of your original purpose—to gain dominion over yourself. Start living the life that you choose to live. Live the life God intended you to live, instead of the life that has been thrust upon you—thrust upon you by pride, pain, anger, hurt, desire and the wants of others. When you've done that work, when you've learned how to substitute the message of Christ in your heart for the message of the pride that was there, then . . . then God will reveal to you your true purpose—the purpose that will lead you to your highest and greatest good. You will know that it is *your* purpose because it will call you to use your skills, abilities, and talents to the glory of God. That's how it works. You have to do your work first, and then God will do His. It's a partnership; never forget that. Since we're in a classroom, I'll put it to you this way. You have some homework to do."

They walked out of the classroom and down the hall to the door. Pastor Abrahms began to tell Joe about all of the new services the church was offering and about the "Celebration for God" that was being planned. Joe was lost in his own thoughts and plans.

When they reached the foyer, Joe turned sharply to face the pastor, "What about Lori?" Joe asked.

"Joe, I know something about that question. I promise you that it will not be as big a problem as you think. You just do what you need to do. Then let go and let God take care of it. You can trust me on this," Pastor Abrahms said with a knowing wink.

The two men exchanged nods of thanks, shook hands, and Joe turned to step back down the stoop. Joe took with him four new pieces of knowledge. He knew he didn't want to die. He knew he didn't want to kill. He knew he didn't know where he was going. He knew what he had to do to find out.

CHAPTER 11

What you sow, you reap.

This is a law of universal energy response.

—God

Claire woke up at 7:30 AM. She rolled over and realized that she was alone. Hearing some conversation coming from outside the bedroom, she slipped a floor-length silver-gray Bergdorf Goodman robe over her red silk pajamas and walked into the den, tying her waist sash.

The chatter of a morning show was coming from the TV. Tomás was spread out on the couch, asleep from the night before. A glass was on the coffee table. It had a small pool of condensation around it and a clear layer of melted ice above a shot or two of scotch. She reached across the arm of the couch, picked up the glass, and downed it in one fell swoop. Her face grimaced in the pain of the burn and the pain of the guilt. She walked into the kitchen and picked up a bag of Costa Rican Tarrazu coffee beans, Tomás's favorite, and began preparing a continental breakfast. The sound of the coffee grinder stirred Tomás awake.

"Oh, good morning, dear. I must have fallen asleep on the couch."

"So I noticed. I'm making you Tarrazu coffee. Would you like toast? I've got some fresh Jewish rye . . ."

"With seeds?"

"Yes, or would you like an English muffin?"

"What kind?"

"Cinnamon raisin."

"Hmmm, I'll take the rye."

They were both being courteous. It was just too darn early to risk another argument. Tomás and Claire loved each other; they shared a bond, a deep connection that even they did not understand. They both would be surprised to find out that the initial attraction, the fireworks, the love-at-first-sight effect was for them, as it is for most people, a recognition that they each had found the perfect person to cast as their partner in each of their life dramas—whether those dramas were comedies or tragedies. Tomás adjusted himself on the couch and then got up.

I'm going to jump in the shower real quick. I'm taking someone for a ride out to the beach today."

"You don't have court?"

"Not today. That's what I love about being my own boss."

"Who ya going with?"

"A cop named Louie, you know that cop that came up here the other day," Tomás said, disappearing into the bedroom.

Claire stopped buttering the toast in midstroke. She put the knife down. She started to follow him into the bedroom, still holding the toast, then stopped . . . and returned to getting breakfast ready.

Tomás came out a few minutes later in brushed herringbone casual khaki pants and a high-end fleece crewneck t-shirt. He carried his suede Eisenhower jacket over his arm.

"Coffee ready?" he asked, running his fingers through his long, still-damp black hair.

"On the table, dear."

They both sat down and enjoyed the tastes and sites in peaceful silence. From a distance, the East River, Brooklyn, and Queens looked pristine and orderly in the early morning light. Tomás retreated into his inner serenity. But it didn't last long. He was disturbed by the uncomfortable thought of negotiating a bribe with Louie the Cop. On top of that, and perhaps even more painful, was keeping it all secret from Claire. He knew she wouldn't approve, especially after he blasted her for not standing up to her boss and not doing the right thing.

She needed to stop the raping of the company by its chief officers, to stop the hemorrhaging of cash out of company accounts into fake corporations owned by the CEO and his lackeys. He knew she was worried that standing up to them it might cause the collapse of the company. If that happened, all of the employees would lose their pensions, and their 401(k)s would become worthless as Halliron stock bottomed out—not to mention the loss their jobs—and hers. He wanted to be supportive, more helpful, but he always became so critical and so angry.

His introspection was cut short by a knock on the door. It was Louie the Cop. He had on a pair of jeans, a Yankees sweatshirt, and a Mets ball cap.

"Hey, Louie, come on in, come on in. This is a whole lot better than the last time you were here, huh?"

"Oh, yeah," Louie the Cop agreed

Tomás looked at Claire and could see that she was ill at ease. All of a sudden, he also felt a little odd. What was this high-powered lawyer with the cashmere-looking shirt in designer pants doing running around with a New York City beat cop? There were warning bells going off all around the three of them, but it was all pushed into the unsaid—each for his own reasons.

Claire finally said, "Well, if you're going to take the car out, you can give me a ride to work. You know one of us has to try to bring home a paycheck. Give me just a minute, and I'll be ready to go."

More at ease, thanks to Claire's comment, Louie the Cop and Tomás walked over to the plate glass. Tomás pointed out some landmarks: the Tappan Zee Bridge, the Triborough Bridge, and the Arthur Ashe Tennis Center. From their vantage point, they could see planes flying in and out of LaGuardia and Kennedy airports, subway trains crossing the East River on trestle bridges, cars and trucks on the Brooklyn Queens Expressway, and tugboats chugging along the East River. The city was certainly dynamic. Even New Yorkers never tire of marveling at the immense scale of the Big Apple.

Claire came out with a smile, and her ergonomic purse slung over her left shoulder. "Okay, I'm hot to trot and rarin' to go—another day with Clay McRae."

Tomás, Claire, and Louie the Cop all turned to the front door and walked out of the plush apartment. Tomás pushed a button that would notify the parking attendant that they were coming down. Tomás's Beamer was purring expectantly when the elevator doors opened. The concrete and steel of the underground parking level bounced the gurgling of the tailpipes around, amplified the sound, and made the motor sound even more powerful.

Louie the Cop went for the backdoor, but Claire stopped him, "I'm getting out first, so I'll take the back. That way you won't have to change seats."

"Are . . . are you sure?" stammered Louie the Cop.

"Uh-huh," murmured Claire as she made herself comfortable in the back.

Whatever uneasiness Louie the Cop had, it disappeared when the last door closed with the whump of rubber gaskets sealing the cabin. Louie the Cop felt the increase of inside pressure in his ears and suddenly had the sensation of being on holy ground. The smell of leather, the quiet, the barely noticeable hum of the running engine, the orange dashboard lights, and the softness of the seat that enveloped him were intoxicants. Drunk on comfort, any remaining dis-ease was cured.

Tomás eased out of the underground garage, up onto 112th Street, and swung onto East River Drive. Traffic was light, and a few minutes later, he was in the Financial District, easing up to the Halliron building at 12 Finance Drive.

Claire walked around the car to Tomás's open window. "Have a good ride," she said, and then as she lowered her head to give him a peck on the lips, she added, "whatever it is you're up to."

Tomás doubled back to take the Brooklyn Battery Tunnel to get onto the Belt Parkway, which follows New York Harbor around Brooklyn. They drove under the world's largest suspension bridge, which spans the Verrazano-Narrows and past Coney Island where the famous parachute-jump ride was hibernating for the winter. Tomás merged off the Belt onto Flatbush Avenue. They passed by the old, deserted army air corps hangers of Floyd Bennett Field. Just before they got to the toll booths of the Marine Parkway Bridge, Tomás broke the relaxed quiet of the ride.

"See that guardhouse and gate over there?" asked Tomás, pointing to his left about one 150 yards down a side street.

"Uh-huh."

"That's where Sonny got machine-gunned in the *Godfather* movie."

"Really. No kidding. Oh yeah, I can see it. That's really neat. I didn't know they filmed that out here."

Tomás slowed down to pay the toll, and they were onto the bridge, over the outlet of Jamaica Bay and into Rockaway, Queens, New York.

At the southwestern end of Long Island are two boroughs of New York City: Queens and Brooklyn. No one who lives on the island of Long Island north of the two boroughs considers them part of Long Island. No one living in Queens and Brooklyn considers himself a Long Islander—the heck with maps and geography.

Rockaway, a peninsula that sticks out from Queens to run along the coast, is one of the lesser-known treasures of New York City. Only about four blocks wide, it has Jamaica Bay and Brooklyn on one side, the Atlantic Ocean and Europe on the other. Only a forty-five minute drive from Manhattan, it offers one of the richest beaches on the East Coast. In its heyday, Rockaway was home to an amusement park, five-star beachfront hotels, and a honky-tonk boardwalk. The residents were mostly Irish and Italian. There were a hundred taverns with names like Flanigan's, Gallagher's, the Irish Circle, the Blarney Stone, O'Gara's, along with some cross-cultural ventures like Boggiano & McWalters. About all that's left is the one hundred block stretch of boardwalk overlooking white sand beaches—sans honky-tonk.

In the winter, there is a strange feeling in the air. Rockaway was really designed for throngs of beachgoers seeking relief from the city heat. By October, it seems nearly deserted. Except for moms strolling their babies or the occasional jogger, the thirty-foot-wide boardwalk is almost empty—the perfect place for a serious and confidential talk.

The two men walked over and sat down on a bench facing the beach. Tomás leaned back and crossed his feet on the boardwalk railing. They sat in silence for a few moments, paying respect to shades of sky and sea, seduced by the gentle movements and sounds of the surf. Louie the Cop spoke first.

"Mmmm, I love the smell of the salt," he said, breathing deeply.

"Yes, I remember this smell from my childhood in Chile. My father would often take us to the beach in the summer during our Christmas vacation."

"Huh? Well, I guess it's summer all year 'round down there where you come from," said Louie the Cop.

Tomás was accustomed to the seasonal confusion that comes from living in different hemispheres. He responded to Louie the Cop's geographical faux pas in a kind and friendly tone.

"My country goes so far south you can almost throw a stone at Antarctica. Our winters get very cold, and since we are in the southern hemisphere, our winter is the same time as your summer."

"That's weird," said Louie the Cop. "So what was it like growing up down there; did you eat chili?" Louie the Cop chuckled, thinking he had come up with an original joke.

Tomás ignored the attempt at humor. "There was much political mischief and war when I was growing up. When I was nine years old, my father was taken political prisoner by the Pinochet regime, which, you know, was backed by your CIA. We didn't see him for two years, and when he came back, he was a broken man. My mother committed suicide shortly after that, and my father and I fled to the United States as political refugees. When we got here, we were very poor."

"I'm sorry."

"There's nothing to be sorry about, it wasn't your fault . . .
personally."

"Still, it sounds pretty tough. I know what that's like. I lost my
wife to suicide too. So with all that, how did you come to be so,
so . . . ?"

"So rich?"

"Yeah, so rich."

"My father was pretty much of a pushover. He tried to be on the
side of whoever was in power and look at what he got. My mother
prostituted herself to get us by, once he was arrested. When he got
back, she killed herself from the guilt. I promised myself I would
find some way, do something to make sure I had enough power and
money so that those things could never happen to me. I figured
the law was a way to do that. After I graduated from law school,
I worked for the state attorney's office in Miami, that's like your
DA's office, for a while then I went into private practice. I picked
up a good client. That's made all the difference."

"So you were a DA.?"

"Yes, I was a DA."

"How come you switched over to the other side, and . . . Can I
ask you another question?"

"Sure. And I bet I know the question you want to ask me—you
want to ask me how I can represent my clients, especially if I know
that they're guilty, right?"

"Right."

"Well, I get that question a lot, so I've got a good answer for you.
First, I do it because that's my job. I get paid to do it. You wouldn't
think very highly of me if I took my client's money, and I didn't
give them the best representation I could, would you? Secondly,

I do it because that's the nature of the system—adversarial. If I didn't give it my all, do you think that the DA would take it easy on me? But the real reason is because defense attorneys are really prosecutors."

"Prosecutors?" Louie the Cop said, "what are you talking about?"

"Yeah, you guys on the law enforcement side enforce the law. Those of us on the defense side enforce the Constitution. You guys go after people because they violate the law; we go after you guys when you violate the Constitution—search and seizure, forced confessions, stuff like that. If you think about it for just a moment, criminal defense attorneys and tax lawyers are the only people that stand between the power of the government and John Q. Public. As one of those high-profile lawyers said, 'We are the Guardians of Liberty, and the Trustees of Justice.' What's really funny is when you take one of those conservative, law-and-order types, you know—the kind who's always screaming about criminals getting off on technicalities—take one of those guys and watch what happens when their daughter's purse gets searched because a cop like you smelled her smoking pot. Then all of a sudden they're shouting about how their civil rights were violated, ain't that so?"

Louie the Cop could hardly get a yes out through his laughter, "Okay, okay, I see what you're saying. I never thought of it like that, but you're right. Now I see why you're a lawyer. You sure got the gift of gab, and you know, you're really not such a stiff after all. Irregardless, you sure got a nice car."

"Yeah, it is. When things get really crazy, it's nice to get inside and feel like you're in command of your environment. You feel more powerful, more in control, especially when you have a full tank a gas."

"I hear you. Maybe that's what I'm missing."

"A full tank of gas?"

"No, not a full tank of gas . . . I mean, what you said . . . about being in command—that's what I'm missing."

"You know, you don't have to miss anything."

"Uh . . . what are you tryin' to say?"

"Well, Louie, remember when I told you that when I first started out in private practice I got a really good client and it made all the difference. It's been over a decade, and I still have the same client. He's a good client. He's always been straight up with me, and I trust him completely. He's in the, you know . . . 'import-export business.' I had lunch with him the other day, along with some of his partners, and they tell me that certain details of their business are getting more difficult because of all of this God business that's going on. He would like to buy some extra insurance that would help them steer clear of patrols."

"Wait a minute—I don't know if I like where this is going."

Louie the Cop wasn't a pristine, squeaky-clean police officer. He had certainly taken his fair share of free lunches, deep discounts on purchases, and free Yankee tickets to turn and look the other way when private garbage was dumped in city containers or water meters were bypassed. But this, this was an entirely different ball game. This kind of thing could be career ending, this kind of thing could land you twenty years in Attica or worse—Leavenworth.

"What I'm talking about is keeping your partners out of harm's way," replied Tomás, "whether you do this or not, the business of my client will go on. You've been around the beat long enough to know that no amount of enforcement is going to stop the distribution of product, but what you don't want and what nobody wants is for the two sides to clash with each other and, God forbid, someone gets hurt. What we're talking about here doesn't hurt anybody; it doesn't put even one of your brother officers at risk. It's kind of a "don't ask—don't tell" policy for the streets. And what's more important, it gives you the opportunity of getting what you deserve after almost thirty years on the force—a comfortable life."

Tomás hit perfectly on the two issues that would have to be resolved in order to win Louie the Cop over. The first was to satisfy him that no one would get hurt, and the second was to grease the greed button. It worked.

"So what are we talking about?" Louie the Cop queried.

"You mentioned you liked my car; well let's say you get a car just like it for a down payment and, on top of that, fifteen thousand dollars a month."

Tomás knew Johnny and his friends would spring for the car, especially since the monthly would be lower than expected. Tomás could see that Louie was doing everything he could not to show that he was chomping at the bit.

"What do I have to do?"

"You'll get a phone call on your cell phone identifying a place and a range of time, all you have to do is call back with a specific twenty-minute span when that location will be safe. Do you understand what I mean?"

"I understand. You know, what you're asking doesn't seem that hard."

"No, it's not. Good, I'm glad we got that out of the way because to tell you the truth, fresh air always makes me hungry, and they've got some really good seafood restaurants out here. How about lunch?"

*   *   *

Clay McRae held the door open for his wife, Jennifer, as they entered the plush restaurant for lunch. The Restaurant at 14 Wall Street, on the thirty-first floor of the building by the same name, was once J. P. Morgan's residence and has that old-world look that just oozes wealth. Power brokers meet for power lunches while looking down like gods on the entire Financial District.

Clay ordered the chef's special—cooked liver with mashed potatoes and a parboiled string bean cold salad with roasted beets and walnuts. Jennifer McRae ordered brook trout with fennel, lightly smoked and served on a wooden plank. For dessert, they ordered a sample of crème brûlée, three dainty cups of custard flavored with Amaretto, vanilla, and pistachio. The period was put on the meal by cups of Jamaican Blue Mountain coffee.

"Jen, when I was in Washington I spoke with Max Silverman. I was hoping he would be able to get some rulings from some watchdog agencies that would have, umm, helped Halliron keep up the growth we've had over the past few years. Well, it doesn't look good. Max is still working on it. Matter of fact, I'm meeting with him tonight to see if there has been any progress."

"What will it mean if you don't get what you want?"

Jennifer McRae had been a rising star as a junior executive in Manhattan's cutthroat fashion district. She was Euro-Asian, bright, remarkably attractive, and ambitious. She wasn't ambitious for fame, recognition, love, or awards. Her ambition targeted one thing—wealth. For that reason, Clay McRae really rang her bell, and she was upfront about it. Clay's attraction to her was not needing to pretend he had emotion.

"It could mean anything from a drop in the price of our stock to a bad, bad situation."

"That doesn't sound good. Could it affect us?"

"Yeah, actually it would affect me more than us. I'm the one that's really exposed. You know how it is, if anyone—a board member, a stockholder, an employee, anyone—loses money, they'll come looking for someone, and that someone will be me. Ahh, you know, when you're making money for 'em nobody wants to know anything. If they lose anything, they want to know everything. Well . . . I'm not complaining . . . I understand the field I play on. The point is, that I could wind up being sued, even indicted. We need to protect what's ours."

"Okay, I'm with you, keep going."

"You remember that I have been transferring stock options to you, the kids, and your mother. You had better start exercising those options and selling. Don't go too fast. You don't want to bring the market price down or attract attention. Go to our banks and the stockbrokers and open up accounts in your name alone with the kids as beneficiaries. Transfer everything out of our joint accounts into your account. I've made out quitclaim deeds for all our property except our main home in Garden City. Stop by Brian Bissel's office. His paralegal has all the closing documents ready to transfer the Hamptons estate, the yacht, the acreage in France—everything into your name. Just leave the account that issues the drafts to pay our credit cards as a joint account."

"Why that one?"

"The money I have outside all this is not very liquid. I would like to have lunch without getting your permission first, if that's okay, dear?

"Of course, I was just asking. Doesn't this make you a little nervous?"

In fact, it did make Clay McRae a little nervous. He wasn't good at trusting. If there was anyone he came close to trusting, it was

Jennifer and, of course, Max. He knew where Jennifer stood and what was important to her. He knew that he was a means to her end, and with that understanding, they had an understanding.

"Yes, a bit. I trust you, but with this kind of money, it's nice to have a backup. Look, we're talking about ten, maybe twenty million dollars here. Most folks could live a comfortable life on it, but you're not most folks. I will have access to hundreds of millions after this thing blows over. I've never known you to pass on a good investment, and I'm still a good investment."

'Oh, Clay—you do understand me. I can be patient as long as I get to keep my Tiffany's charge card, that is."

"Not a problem."

CHAPTER 12

Your entire world is my Holy Land.

—God

The company limo pulled up to the front of the Halliron building. As the chauffer walked around to open the door, Clay turned to Jennifer and squeezed her hand.

"Max Silverman is in town, and I'm taking him out for dinner. I'll probably stay in the city tonight."

"I know all about the good congressman and his taste in company. You're lucky I'm not a jealous wife," Jennifer said.

The door opened, and Clay got out. He told the driver he wanted the limousine available by 5:00 PM. As Clay walked into the marble lobby, he melded with the opulence around him. Halliron was in some ways his alter ego. On the outside, there was wealth and fame, but there was nothing inside to support it. He made it about halfway through the lobby when he was approached by the pesky stock analyst from the *Wall Street Journal*.

"Mr. McRae, can I have just a minute?"

"Yes, but just a minute."

"Your third-quarter report was due out last week. The rumor on the street is that it won't be nearly as rosy as has been predicted. Do you have any comment on that?"

Clay knew Halliron would probably collapse within six months. He only had to hold the press off for another half a year.

"Oh, that's just the talk of people who live in a world of limitations. The contract we've entered into with RenEn Corporation, and the patents that come with it, could easily increase our net earnings by twenty-five percent or more. Can I tell you something, off the record?"

"Yes, sir—agreed—off the record."

This was Clay McRae at his best. By pretending to bring the reporter into his confidence and give him a scoop-to-be, he could flatter the twerp enough to get him off his back. The lie Clay McRae was about to tell his prey was a whopper. It was a lie of such enormous proportions that only someone with the chutzpah of, well, a sociopath, could actually pull it off.

"Do you know of Albert Einstein and his equation of $E=MC^2$?"

"Yes, sir."

"Do you know what it means?"

"No, not actually."

"You see, E stands for energy, M stands for mass, and C stands for the speed of light, which is 180,000 miles per second squared. So what Einstein said is mass, you know—matter, stuff—can be changed into energy by a factor of 180,000 times 180,000. So a little bit of mass produces a whole lot of energy. That's why a few pounds of plutonium, when converted into energy, can blow away half of New York State. Are you following me so far?"

"Yes," said the reporter, but his head was starting to swim.

"Well," MacRae continued, "after Einstein came up with his equations, other physicists working in the same field came up with something called the unified field theory. What the unified field theory says is that the different forms of energy—heat, light, electricity, gravity, magnetism, and the weak and strong atomic forces are just different forms of a single kind of energy. The theory suggests that it is theoretically possible to convert any one of these forms of energy into another. That means, for example, that gravity can be converted into electricity. Do you understand the significance of that?"

"I think so, but why don't you lay it out for me?"

"If gravity could be converted into electricity, that means we can take every gasoline motor out of every car, truck, and bus and put in an electric motor instead. Where the fuel tank used to be, we would just install the device that converts the gravity around it into electricity. The motor would be fueled by the same energy that holds the whole universe together. What we're talking about here is an unlimited, pollution-free energy source." McRae leaned in closer to provide an additional sense of confidentiality. "We're six months to a year away from a prototype. Nobody believed the theory would be realized this quickly. Keep this under your hat, and you may just have the scoop of the century, maybe even a Pulitzer. Can you keep your mouth shut?"

"Yes, sir, I can."

"Good. I'll keep in touch. In the meantime, why don't you Google some of those terms I gave you so that when the announcement's ready, you'll understand the science behind it."

Clay turned and started walking toward the elevator. There was enough truth in what he told the reporter to keep him glued to his computer for days on end. He didn't take any pride in putting on an act like this one. This patsy was just too easy.

On his way up to the top floor of the Halliron building, Clay began to calculate. Max would be here in a few hours, and he wanted to be prepared. He thought about the last thing Max said to him in Washington, something about Santa Claus not always appearing in red; sometimes he's a big, tall man in a white suit. He still wasn't sure what that meant, but he surmised that he might be meeting such a man tonight.

He got out of the elevator and turned right across the foyer's Italian marble floor. He pressed his thumb into the fingerprint scanner at the front door of the executive offices. The door buzzed and let him in. He walked along the perimeter of the floor, in between the window offices of his top executives on the right, and the cubicles of the support staff on his left. When he reached the back corner, he entered the fifteen-hundred-square-foot suite that was his.

He had a panoramic view through plate glass windows. To his right he could see the Empire State Building and midtown Manhattan. To his left he could see the Statue of Liberty and the Verrazano-Narrows Bridge. Directly in front of him was Ground Zero, where the Twin Towers of the World Trade Center used to stand. He had been at his desk that fateful morning of September 11, 2001. It was one of the few times in his life that he actually felt emotion. He turned his chair away from the window to look at the relatively bare wall behind him. He liked to look at the emptiness of the wall; it helped him focus on his thoughts.

He knew that dealing with the kind of people who could move the kind of money he contemplated would require trusting them. McRae was not very good at trust. He wondered how it would all work. He began to wonder exactly how much money he was dealing with. He spun around to face his desk and reached out to get an open line on his telephone. He made some phone calls to the various brokers that handled his stocks, and then to the underwriters who handled the stock options. He reached into his bottom drawer, pulled out his personal ledger, and made some calculations.

Five . . . hundred . . . million dollars. Once he figured in commissions, fees and "transportation" charges of 10-15 percent, he would be looking at a net result of four hundred and twenty-five to four hundred fifty million dollars. That was a comfortable enough sum. He started to figure what he might be able to produce if that sum was partially invested.

In the middle of his calculations, Claire Medina tapped on his door and walked in. Even though this was their normal way of operating, she still seemed tentative. She was holding two files against her chest, almost in a defensive posture. Even though Claire had been working at Halliron for five years, she still wasn't comfortable around Clay.

He didn't want to talk to her at that moment, but then again he didn't want to raise any suspicions that he was thinking of flying the coop.

"Yes, Claire," he said as he looked up from his paperwork.

"Oh . . . sorry to disturb you, Clay," Claire said. "I . . . um . . . was just looking at the third-quarter figures, and I'm a little concerned. You remember that in both the first-quarter and the second-quarter reports we included figures that we expected to be realized from our contracts with Arctic Oil Corporation and that newly discovered oil field in Datong, China."

As she talked, her voice became more stable. She moved to the chair in front of Clay's desk and sat down. Clay became more upset with the direction he thought she was going. He began to tap his pen. He knew that the tapping signaled to Claire that he was annoyed.

"I . . . I know I brought this up to you before, but neither of those predictions have materialized yet," Claire said. "I do understand that you expect them within the next six months, but by carrying them forward onto the third quarter, we're really beginning to blow up a balloon that might pop. Now on top of all that, you're asking me to include predicted profits from the contract with RenEn Corporation."

"Yes, do you have a problem with that?" Clay asked.

"Well, I'm afraid that if we keep putting prediction on prediction, and then cover those predictions with other predictions, we're going to get to a point where it all collapses—or at the very least, pick up a federal audit and a place on the front page of the *Wall Street Journal*. I know how you feel about this; I just want to tell you that I'm concerned."

Clay threw his pen down and stood up. He walked over to his window and looked uptown. He stood there silently for just long enough to allow Claire's nervousness to rise up again. Then he turned around. "Do you think I care about your concern? I don't need your concern. What I do need is your signature on the bottom line of the third-quarter report; and I need it quickly. The report is overdue."

Claire clutched the two files she was holding tighter. She shifted in her chair and looked like she was about to say something when Clay pressed on.

"You've been with us five years now, haven't you? That's five years getting, what, fifty thousand shares in stock options a year? That gives you a quarter million shares. Do you want all of them to drop in value? If you don't care about your own stock, what about all the stock that's sitting in the 401(k)s of the employees that are outside and downstairs? I want that third-quarter report on my desk in forty-eight hours."

She nodded in agreement. Her eyes welled up; she turned her back to Clay and quickly left his office. Outside his office, she leaned against the wall to catch her breath.

McRae got the best of Claire again, and he knew she hated it. He needed her signature on those reports . . . and he was going to get it. He thought about the contract with Arctic Oil Corporation and the Datong oil fields and knew that Claire would no longer pretend that they were anything more than a fiction. Of course, she was right. He thought about the message that said *I gave you a conscience for a reason, pay attention to it* . . . He knew it somehow applied to this situation, but since he didn't have a conscience, he didn't understand how. Besides, there was too much at stake.

Moments after Claire left Clay's office, she also left his thoughts. He reached over and picked up the phone. He dialed the phone number and waited to hear a familiar voice at the other end of the line.

"Hello, this is Clay McRae."

"Clay, do you think you still have to identify yourself to me? Don't you think I can recognize your voice by now," said the sultry female at the other end.

"I need Andrea, Rose, and Charlie for tonight. My limo will pick them up at 5:30 PM."

"Do you mean Charles or Charlene?"

"Charlene, of course. Have I ever asked for a man before?"

"Let me just take a look at the schedule here . . . I can get you Charlie and Rose, but Andrea is already spoken for. Clay, I keep asking you to give me a little bit more notice than this. I know you want them at their best, and two hours is not a lot of time to get them ready."

"I want Andrea, the blonde; she's his favorite. Would an extra couple of grand per girl be able to make that happen?"

"I think we can arrange that. Are there any special requests?"

"I want them in evening gowns—not too much cleavage showing—he likes the mystery. Bras, no panties. I want Andrea in the back, driver's-side seat, and Rose in the back, passenger's-side seat. Make sure that they leave enough room for my guest to sit between them. Put Charlie in the seat facing them. Charlie needs to wear a gown with a long side slit. Tell her to make sure she flashes my guest while we're riding to the restaurant. Just tell Andrea and Rose that they'll be with my regular guest. They've been with him before; they'll know what to do. The limo with the girls will pick up my guest and then me. I need a teaser, a squeezer, and a pleaser."

"I got it. The girls will be ready at 5:30 PM, correct?

"Correct."

At six o'clock sharp, Clay McRae walked out of the front doors of the Halliron building and stepped to the curb. Two minutes later, the stretch limo pulled up and stopped. The chauffeur got out and walked around to open the door, allowing Clay to get in. Max was busy tickling and getting tickled, so without a word, Clay just took a seat in the front, next to Charlie. Andrea was teasing Max by tickling his earlobe; Rose was squeezing him with her hand embedded solidly in his crotch.

"Stop it. Now, stop it for just a second; I want to say hello to my good friend," said Max, trying to push the girls' hands away but not trying very hard. "Hello, Clay."

"Don't mind me. I'll just chat with Charlie," said Clay.

Max looked at the voluptuous brunette sitting next to Clay. As soon as their eyes met, Charlie slowly pushed her left thigh against the slit of her evening gown, opening her legs just enough for Max to get a peek at the treasure within. Max became even larger and harder in the redhead's grip.

After the limousine passed Grand Central Station on Park Avenue, it turned right along the side of the Millennium Plaza Hotel. The driver then turned right into a narrow entrance behind the hotel that was reserved for celebrities only. He approached the security gate and told the guard that there was a reservation in a private room under the name of Clay McRae. The gate swung open and the long black car proceeded within.

It pulled up to beautifully carved wooden doors. A doorman appeared out of nowhere and pulled the door open so that the party of five could enter. They were met there by the maître d', who escorted them to a private dining room. This part of the Plaza, unknown to most of the population, was specifically set up so that celebrities could enjoy themselves without finding their pictures plastered all over the tabloids next day.

The table in the private dining room was round. Max took a chair facing the doors with his back to the wall. To his left sat Rose. To his right sat Andrea. To her right sat Charlie, and Clay McRae took the seat closest to the door. As soon as the maître d' had them seated, another waiter came in with a bottle of Dom Pérignon champagne and poured the glasses. Clay had already arranged the menu. It was typical of Clay to remember what people liked and did not like—not because he cared about them, but because it was a good tool to accomplish his own ends.

The dinner proceeded without interruption. There was lots of giggling, teasing, squeezing, and pleasing. Clay was bored. Near the end of the main course, a waiter came in with a small folded card. Clay opened it, and the only thing appearing inside were the words Merry Christmas. Clay asked the waiter where he got the card, and the waiter whispered that a man in the sports bar off the main lobby had given it to him. It was what Clay had been waiting for.

"Uh, Max, will you excuse me?

"Of course, of course. You're leaving me in good company."

Clay offered his apologies to the ladies and started out of the room. Before he got to the door, he heard Max call out to him.

"Uh, Clay, aren't you forgetting something?"

Clay turned and smiled. He reached into his front pocket and pulled out two gold keys on a single ring. One was to enable the elevator to go to the exclusive floors that housed the executive suites. The other was the room key. He tossed them to Max. Max removed his hand from Rose's breast just long enough to catch them. Max nodded his thanks. Clay turned to the door and, with a flick of his wrist, signaled to the waiter to lead on.

Clay followed the waiter through a labyrinth of hallways that led upstairs to the main floor. They crossed the lobby and approached the sports bar. The waiter nodded to Clay. Clay pressed a five-spot into his palm and entered the lounge. Even before his eyes had a chance to adjust to the dimmer lighting, he noticed that the only sound coming from inside was the sound of the television. There did not seem to be the hubbub normally present.

When his eyes adjusted, he spotted a tall, large man in a white suit leaning against the bar. The man's attention, like all the other patrons, was glued to the TV. Clay wasn't even curious about what it was that demanded such focus. Instead, he approached the man and touched his shoulder.

"I'm Clay McRae," Clay said to get the man's attention.

The man turned around and put a finger over his lips. He then directed Clay's attention to the television. The camera was zooming in on the President, who was seated at his desk in the Oval Office. The President began to speak.

My fellow Americans, I, and the presidents that have come before me, have often sat at this desk in this office to address you in times of crisis.

Today I do not address you because of a crisis, but rather because of a reason to celebrate. As you know, many messages have been appearing in both electronic and print media carrying the name of God as their author. From the very first time these messages appeared, I ordered a technological, political, and philosophical investigation regarding the authentic origin of these messages. All of our investigative agencies have been working on that charge. The CIA, the FBI, and the National Security Council have used all of their technological expertise and state-of-the-art equipment to analyze the messages, their placement, the means of their appearance, and their content. Those agencies have fully briefed me, and I have had thorough conversations with the heads of other sovereign nations. The agencies have brought me the results of their investigations, and it is at this time that I want to share them with you.

There is a consensus among the Intelligence Community that the origin of these messages is not discoverable. The consistent theme of the messages is responsibility, peace, and love toward one's neighbor. No physical evidence or testimonial evidence has been uncovered that would indicate that these messages are any kind of plot, plan, or fraud. Most importantly, no one involved in the investigation has any proof whatsoever that these messages do not come from God.

Without presuming upon a higher authority, it is nevertheless my responsibility to make a determination of the facts so that this country can proceed forward in setting policy and determining the propriety of its actions. A nation, like the individuals that make it up, has a psyche, a conscience, and a will. Like an individual, a nation is free to exercise its will according to its principles and philosophy. Therefore, as your President and for setting our nation's future course of action—I hereby declare that God does exist and that the actions of this country have consequences.

This country was founded on freedom of religion; and therefore I do not make this declaration in political, moral, ethical, and philosophical terms. I make this statement only as a declaration of fact, as we know it from the evidence. I do not impose, nor will this declaration impose, on any individual a requirement of belief. That is up to each of you to decide. I am well aware that making this declaration will require us to review many of our policies—particularly those policies regarding global warming, involvement in the internal affairs of other governments, engagement in war, covert actions resulting in death, the construction of our social safety net, education policies, and the like.

Changes in these policies may affect each of you. In the short term, we may have to put more of our resources into the development of new technologies. Each of us may be called upon for some measure of sacrifice. I have no doubt that harmonizing our national policies and actions, to run along with the letter and spirit of the messages, will be in the best interest of each and every American, nay, I would say, of each and every human being.

Things have been done in the national interest that were not always morally correct. Our motto claims that we are one nation under God. We have always felt that we were in God's grace, that He blesses us, that He was on our side. From this day forward the principal question for our nation will be—are we on God's side?

At the end of speeches such as these, the President traditionally ends with the statement—God bless you and God bless the United States of America. I no longer feel those words are fitting. Far better, let us ask God to bless all of us and the planet we all share.

Good night, and thanks be to God.

Mustafa turned to Clay. He didn't offer his hand or an introduction. Instead, he nodded his head and tipped his cup of espresso in a perfunctory toast, then chugged the last sip. "This is an amazing world we are living in these days. What do you make of all that?"

Clay didn't make anything of it. He didn't much care. What he did care about was—what this stranger was going to be able to do for him. Clay just shrugged his shoulders. Seeing that Clay, like so many Americans, was tunnel-visioned on his business, Mustafa came directly to the point.

"I understand you have some funds you need to transfer," said Mustafa.

"Yes, that's correct."

"How much are we talking about?"

Clay hesitated. Mustafa waited, sizing up his new client. Mustafa determined Clay needed a small prompt.

"When Santa Claus used to ask you what you wanted for Christmas, did you hesitate?" Mustafa asked.

"Five hundred million," Clay whispered.

"That is a large order to be sure. The beauty of my business is that the route one dollar takes is the same route that many dollars take. We can do what you ask. The shipping charge is 20 percent."

"Let's go with 15 percent," Clay counteroffered. "It seems that would be a fair amount for a quantity discount."

"Fair for whom?" Mustafa asked.

The big man reached into his pocket and pulled out a wad of bills. He peeled two ten-dollar bills off and tossed them on the counter. He turned to leave. Clay gripped his arm.

"Okay, okay. Twenty percent, agreed."

Mustafa turned back to Clay and said, "The next thing we have to consider, Mr. McRae, is the question of trust. We both have confidence in one mutual acquaintance. Is that sufficient for the sums you speak of? I think not."

"What do you propose?"

Mustafa called the bartender over and told him to have the concierge check him out and then to bring over his hotel bill.

"Can I do that?" asked the bartender.

"This is the Millennium Plaza Hotel. Can you say no to a guest?" Mustafa asked. The bartender nodded and was off. In a few minutes, he returned with a three-page invoice. Mustafa looked it over, and then showed the bottom line to Clay. "Why don't you pay this for me?" Mustafa stated, more than asked.

"Four thousand, seven hundred, and seventy-three dollars," exclaimed Clay in surprise. "Why?"

"Make it four thousand, eight hundred, and seventy-three dollars, which would include a one-hundred-dollar tip for this nice bartender. Why, you ask? Let's just say, it's a matter of trust. You have a credit card that will cover it, I trust."

Clay looked at Mustafa. He didn't even know the man's name, and he was asked to lay out almost five thousand dollars. He looked into Mustafa's eyes. There was not even a hint of a joke there.

Clay pulled a credit card out of his wallet and gave it to the attendant.

"And one hundred dollars in cash for the bartender. You know, as a Muslim, we don't believe in taxes."

Clay was becoming irritated, but he reached into his pocket and pulled out a fifty-dollar bill and three twenties. He pushed them into the bartender's hand and told him to keep the change.

"It's good to be generous," Mustafa said.

As they waited for the young man's return with the charge card slip and canceled invoice, Mustafa gave Clay instructions on the next step.

"There is a small electronics store on Eighth Avenue between Forty-second and Forty-third Street. It is the only one on that block. Meet me there tomorrow at 3:10 PM. I will only be there for a few minutes. Bring one hundred thousand dollars in cash. Ninety-eight thousand should be in a box from a clock radio. The box should be wrapped in gift paper suitable for a little boy's birthday. The other two thousand should be in used one-hundred-dollar bills and placed in a regular white envelope."

"Why do you want—"

Mustafa cut him off, "Let's just say, it's a matter of trust."

Clay studied the large man. He wondered why he was being asked to do things in such a convoluted way. Then he asked himself why he would do such a thing, and he understood—he was being tested.

The bartender returned. Mustafa snatched the canceled bill and was gone, leaving Clay behind to sign off on the credit card authorization.

At precisely 3:08 PM next day, Clay McRae walked into the small electronics store on Eighth Avenue. Mustafa was at the counter talking to a sales clerk behind it. Between them was a boxed, new laptop computer and an invoice for one thousand nine hundred and ninety-two dollars.

Mustafa looked up, "Ah, you're here. Perfect timing."

Clay stood next to Mustafa. He wasn't clear on what to do. Mustafa thanked Clay for the birthday gift for his son and took the box from Clay.

"Please, give this good man the other envelope," directed Mustafa.

Clay didn't expect this. It didn't seem that he could put a halt to it either. He pulled the envelope out of his breast pocket and laid it on the laptop box. The sales clerk opened the envelope and counted the twenty one-hundred-dollar bills inside. Mustafa picked up a card off the counter of the electronics store and wrote a number on the back of it. He slid the card over to McRae and told him to refer to himself as Mac when he called. He then returned his attention to the clerk.

"Keep the change, my good man," Mustafa said as he picked up the laptop box by its handle and walked out of the store. At the sidewalk, Mustafa turned toward Forty-second Street. Clay was following behind.

"Excuse me!" Mustafa continued walking smoothly. Clay jogged around to be in front of Mustafa, then turned and faced him. "Excuse me! What is going on?" Clay demanded.

"Oh, yes, how rude of me. I was so excited about how much my older son will enjoy the computer that I couldn't wait to get it home to him. Please forgive me. When you're ready, please come visit me. Give me a call at the number on the card for directions."

Mustafa began walking around Clay. Clay moved in such a way to stand in front of Mustafa again.

"Just a minute. Whatever your name is. Yesterday, I paid your hotel bill of nearly five thousand dollars."

"I think it was four thousand, eight hundred, and seventy-three with the tip."

"All right, four thousand, eight hundred, and seventy-three. Today, I just handed over a hundred thousand to you, and you used two thousand of it on a computer for your son. All I get is a phone number to who knows who?"

The two men stood facing each other. Mustafa offered the gift-wrapped box back to Clay. "I would be perfectly content with having my hotel bill paid and this laptop, if that's what you prefer."

Clay was finally getting the message. Things were going to be done the fat man's way, or not at all. Clay took one step to the left. Seconds later, Mustafa disappeared down the steps to the A Train of the Eighth Avenue subway.

Chapter 13

You have the power to heal each other.

—God

"Claire, how would you finish this sentence—I wish my father would have loved me enough to . . . ?" her therapist, Mark Jacobs, gently asked.

"I wish he wouldn't have been so angry with me all the time. The bottle was more important to him than I was. You know a bottle of whiskey costs about ten dollars. I guess I felt that I was worth less than that to him. He didn't really understand me. I tried to please him so much, but everything I did was the wrong thing to do. So I guess I wish that my father would have loved me enough to understand me and to appreciate me . . . I wish he loved me enough to love me."

"What I really liked about my father was . . ."

"He was passionate. I think he really did love me; I could see that he really loved me when he wasn't drinking."

"I wish my mother would have loved me enough to . . ."

"Stand up to my dad and . . . I mean she was my mom. I wanted her to be my mom, not the person she told all her little secrets to, complained about my dad to. She made me her best friend—I already had best friends—I wanted to be her daughter. By being my best friend, I lost having a mom."

"One thing I loved most about my mother was . . ."

"That she was kind."

"Let me step back for a second and give you some feedback about some of the dynamics that I think might be at work here. I want to throw some ideas out to you and let you try them on. Okay?"

"OK."

"Our brain, our mind, doesn't really have an accurate sense of time. You can test that out for yourself by thinking about something that happened in the past. The moment you remember something, you remember it with all the sights, smells, and feelings associated with it. It's almost as if it just happened. Have you had the experience of remembering something sad in your past and tearing up about it?

"More than once."

"So then you know that once you remember something like that, it's just as if it happened today. What lets us hold on to some of the thrills and joys of childhood also causes us to hold on to some of the wounds of childhood. We want to somehow heal those childhood wounds. We try various ways to do it; some are healthier than others.

One of the most common ways that we try to heal our childhood wounds is to find someone who wounds us in the same way that we were wounded when we were children. Then we try to get that person to change in the same way we wanted our childhood caregiver to change. So it's normal that the child of an alcoholic, who had a roller-coaster relationship with that parent, would marry someone who creates the same wound, although perhaps in a different way. In your situation it might be your husband's work. If you think about it, you might very well say to yourself, I wish that Tomás would just love me enough to give me some attention instead of being buried in his work—instead of bottle—all the time. I wish I could have him more consistently. Are you with me?"

"It's a lot of information; it's hard to take it all in. I . . . I . . . think I'm with you."

'You're absolutely right. This is not easy stuff. You're doing really well. Can you hang in there just a little bit longer?"

"Go ahead . . ."

"We have a tendency to select mates that have similar emotional profiles as our childhood caregivers, both the good and the bad sides. You say your father was a passionate man who loved you. Tomás is a passionate man who loves you. You say your father was an angry man. Tomás is an angry man. So why do we do this? Well, if we can find someone who wounds us in the same way and we can get that person to change and become the person that we wanted our parent to be—then that would accomplish what our childhood desire was, and it would put aside the childhood frustration that we felt. Does any of this map on for you?

"Yes, it does . . . it's just that this way of thinking is so new; it's hard to take it all in at one time. But I feel like I'm following you because there's something about what you say that just seems right, seems like it makes sense."

"Great. Now, if we can accomplish that, if we can get our partner to make that shift, we would finally have closure around the issue, and the wound would go away. The proof of that is this: if Tomás were to change and he loved you enough to understand you, enough not to be angry with you—if he loved you enough to put his work aside and give you the attention you yearn for . . . . would it matter so much to you that your father was unable to do that?"

"No, it wouldn't really matter, I suppose . . . but if all this is true—how come I married him? I don't remember thinking Tomás was going to hurt . . . or as you say, wound me, and I certainly didn't think I had to change him. He didn't show any of these traits then. We both thought we had found the perfect mate.

"You did find the perfect mates. I know this feels confusing. It was exactly those feelings—romantic love, fireworks, and passion that helped you avoid seeing the traits. The problems you perceive are really opportunities for healing, if you can bring yourself to see them that way."

"This is all fine and good, but what do I do about it? It's one thing to know what I need. It's another thing to know how to get it."

"You're right. That is the million-dollar question. Before we look for the solution, let's take a look at the other side of the equation. Let's take a look at it from Tomás's point of view. Tomás may have picked you for the very same reason. He had a father that he didn't respect because his father didn't stand up to things and a mother that didn't maintain her virtue, although the reason for her not maintaining her virtue may have been her great love for Tomás. She was willing to do anything for that young child."

Claire was enraptured by Mark's insight. She was all ears.

"He has married someone who, you say, he also perceives as somebody that doesn't stand up for herself and, by going along with the corrupt practices of your boss, hasn't maintained her virtue, at least in his perception. From your descriptions, it seems he understands you enough to know that you love him so much you would sacrifice almost anything for him. I would imagine that

Tomás feels that if only you loved him enough to change and stand up for yourself, he would have the perfect spouse. So you can see that there's a kind of symmetry in the way this connects."

"Yeah. I never thought about anything like this before. But still, this is all a nice theory. How does knowing this make anything different?"

"One of the wonderful things about this is that healing can come out of it. I know re-wounding each other feels like throwing salt on old wounds. It appears to be a negative. But if you are conscious about the dynamics, if you are aware of them, and if you are both willing to put each other first, you can turn it into a positive. The original attraction that you had for each other, that you are exactly the perfect persons to heal each other, would come forward. These dynamics have to be something that you know of, something that you are aware of, because if you don't know they're operating on you, you have no access to change how they manifest. There's a word we use—*metacognition*."

"Excuse me?"

"It's a fancy word that means thinking about your thinking. There are three types of knowledge. There are things that you know about and you know that you know them. For example, I know there's something called therapy, and I know that I know something about it. Things like that are 'known-knowns.' Then there are things you know about and you know you do not know anything about them. For example, I know there is something called automobile mechanics, and I know that I do not know anything about it. Such things are 'unknown-knowns.' Then there are the things that you do not know, and you don't know that you don't know about them. For example, if you had never heard of DNA, you would never be able to study it or learn about it because you didn't even know that it existed. These are 'unknown-unknowns.'"

"Okay . . . I'm following you."

"Up until now the effects of childhood wounds were unknown-unknowns; you didn't have access to them. If you are not aware of them, you can't work with them. If you are aware of them, you can work with them. Since you have taken the effects of your childhood wounds out of the realm of unknown-unknowns and moved them into the area of unknown-knowns, you can study them and turn them into known-knowns."

I see . . . I think," Claire said as Mark continued.

"Once you become conscious of it, you can become more aware of how it works. If the two of you become aware of how these forces weave you together, you can work with them together to heal each other. What I'm hearing is that the two of you love each other very much; you just need to understand the vital part you each play in each other's healing. Ultimately, this is why you are together—to grow the positive and heal the negative. Does this make any sense to you?"

"Yes, it does. It is very interesting. It gives me hope. I mean, I do understand that it's something that we have to work on. I hope that I can share this with him. I hope he'll work on this with me as well."

"He's an intelligent man. If you want to ask him to come here with you, we can talk about this together. It would be an excellent next step."

"Yes, I would like to do that. I would like him to join me."

"Just make sure you don't run home and dump this on him all at once. Remember, it's taken you a few weeks of assimilating the information. I would suggest you Google 'Imago Therapy' and read more about this kind of thinking. I'm not a certified Imago therapist, so if the two of you want to pursue this learning, I will refer you to one."

"Thank you, Mark. The other thing I wanted to talk to you about is these messages from God. They are disturbing to me. I mean, they make me wonder if I've made the right choices in my life, if I'm good enough—from signing off on the papers at work, to the person that I am and have become. Frankly, they scare me a little. I don't know what to believe at this point. They definitely have me looking at myself a lot more—and my choices. I'm wondering if I'm good enough, if I've accomplished enough, if people like me . . . if God would approve of me."

"Those are very personal matters, things that have much to do with our belief systems. I can't tell you what you should believe because there is no right or wrong when it comes to beliefs. There are only beliefs that work or don't work in your life. I can only tell you what my take on it is, and what I can glean from the messages."

"Yes, what do you think?"

"From my perspective, as a therapist, what I can tell you is that the power that left these messages, the power that calls itself God, is an excellent parent. What God has told us so far is that our actions have consequences. I believe that those consequences are not meant to be punishing, evil, or bad. He has never used the word *good* or *bad*. He only uses the words *comfortable* and *uncomfortable*. What I get from that is that forces were set in motion so that we could grow and mature. That's exactly what a good parent would do; that's exactly the way a good parent would act. There should be rewards and punishments in life, but the rewards and punishment should not come out of anger or because the parent wants to be evil or have control. They should come so that children can learn how to guide themselves. Children do some things that lead to their lifelong happiness. If they move in that direction and something comfortable happens, it reinforces it. If they go in the opposite direction and something uncomfortable happens, that is also a good thing because it helps them to understand where not to go.

"What you've gotten from the messages is the opportunity to reflect on your life and to take a look at what you've done so far. If you deal with that with an attitude of gratitude, if you look for the purpose in the mistakes, you will see the opportunity to make corrections and changes. If you do that, then you will be right smack in the middle of the system. You will be doing everything that is expected of you. We're not expected to be perfect, but we are expected to be responsible for our development. We are expected to learn."

"You're a smart man."

"Thank you, that's why I get the big bucks. As far as the whole God thing goes, what I am amazed at, awed at, is that when I think about the healing of childhood wounds I can see a perfect symmetry in the process. Imagine, each person takes his own wounds and wraps them together in a relationship that creates an opportunity for mutual healing. It just depends upon the choices, love, commitment, and awareness the partners bring to the task. There is a perfect symmetry to it. As a therapist, I look at it and think that there is no human intelligence that could have created that system. It is too perfect."

"Wow, I can see what you mean. So you think God had a hand in all of that?"

"You know, there's a recently coined term, *intelligent design*. Well, this particular design sure seems intelligent to me."

They both sat in silence. Within a few moments, Claire felt an odd sensation begin to flow over her. It was not a familiar sensation, but there was nothing scary about its lack of familiarity. It had both the comfort of walking into your own home and the energy of a new adventure. It was a feeling of humble confidence, a feeling of gentle power. She was ready to surrender the identity the world had imposed upon her in favor of the person she or God or the partnership of the two of them wanted her to be. There was the possibility of having a say in the matter of her life, in becoming fully self-actualized, in becoming the person she, all along, was meant to be. There was both death and rebirth. The slightest tremble ran through her.

"I've got goose bumps," said Claire, rubbing her upper arms.

"Are they bad goose bumps or good goose bumps?" Mark asked.

"Good goose bumps."

"I love it when that happens."

When Claire stepped out onto the sidewalk, the day was crisp and clear. She looked right, then left, up and down the block. Was she imagining it? Were her senses actually more alive? Colors seemed brighter; sounds seemed clearer. The smell of roasting chestnuts and pretzels coming from a street vendor seemed more pungent. She looked at the people passing by and felt a deeper understanding of what each of them was feeling: this one was in a hurry for an appointment, that one was enjoying the weather, this one was chewing on a pleasant memory, that one was anticipating something to come. Everything was the same, and yet, somehow, it was all different. The difference was all in the quality of her experience; it was in a feeling of being connected to the people on the street, in the city, on the planet, and beyond. Her cheeks began to ache slightly from the broadness of her smile. She took both index fingers and pressed both cheeks inward, but the smile kept bouncing back. She started to laugh and to cry. She wanted to hug everyone around her but knew that there had to be some limits to her celebration.

She thought about Clay McRae. All of a sudden, he wasn't such a problem. Why had she *ever* thought that saying *no* was such a big deal? She began to anticipate stepping up to the plate, telling him that she was going to do the right thing, and relishing the expression on his face. For a moment, she stopped and felt guilty. Would it be right to take glee in someone else's misfortune? Maybe not; but then again, maybe this was one indulgence that she would allow herself. There were things she would have to do to prepare herself. She wanted to approach him without his having any power over her. She committed to doing whatever it would take to be successful in standing up to him.

She thought about Tomás. Now she understood exactly what it was that he was urging on her. This is how he wanted her to be. She realized that he didn't want her to be this way for his sake, but for hers. She understood what Mark had been talking about, that although Tomás had hurt her, the result was that through the pain she molted into the butterfly that was just itching to come out.

She could see that, in some perfectly symmetrical way, the very forces that created the suffering in her life were the forces that delivered her highest potential. She felt an incredible wave of love for Tomás come over her. That love gave rise to a sense of empathy for the trials and tribulations that Tomás was going through. She could only imagine the frustration and troubles he must be experiencing without the benefit of her newfound understanding.

She resolved to be the healing force he married her to be. She wondered where he was and when she would see him.

*   *   *

Tomás was indeed feeling the frustration and trouble Claire imagined. The messages and letters from God had been burrowing their way into his consciousness and below. His life, at least since his childhood, had been committed to power and control. He now began to feel that those were false securities. He'd been exposed to God early on, and he remembered feeling awe and wonder, both under the high ceiling of the church and under the night sky. Deep within, he sensed that some part of him, maybe his heart, was connected to something outside him, something greater than he was. He knew that his sense of the glorious and the foul came through that connection. He had divorced himself from those feelings and that thinking for a long time now.

As he thought he walked. After a while he stopped, so he could look around and see where he was. He was standing in front of the steps to St. Mary's. Without thinking, he climbed the steps and walked through the open door. Father Fitzgerald was arranging some things at the altar. Tomás began to walk up the aisle between the rows of pews. He stopped to take a knee and genuflect. When he stood up, Father Fitzgerald had turned around and was walking toward him.

"How can I help you, my son?"

The child deep within Tomás began to cry. For so long, that child was waiting for his father to ask him that question. Tomás, the adult, decided he would not allow such weakness to show. He said to himself, *I am not going to allow myself to look like a child*, even as tears filled his eyes. He told himself, *I can control my emotions*, but when he opened his mouth to speak, the words could not come out.

He became scared; something like a panic began to stir inside. There was nothing about it that felt adult. It was the same feeling he had when his father was taken away. The same feeling he had when his mother died. It was the childhood sensation of being alone . . . and being powerless. He also felt a yearning to be rescued. It had very little to do with what was going on in his life at that moment. It had everything to do with what constituted the foundation of his very identity. He understood none of it.

"You seem confused by the strength of your emotions," the priest said, sitting next to Tomás and stroking him gently on the head.

How could he know just by looking at me? Can he read my mind? Tomás thought. The priest seemed comfortable waiting, so Tomás took time to let the wave of emotions flow over and out of him.

"So what's the matter? Why the tears? This is an exciting time in the world and in the church. What troubles you so?"

"I don't know. I don't even know. I was walking along the street outside, thinking, and I just stopped. I looked up; I saw the church, and I walked in."

"Well, don't discount that. God speaks to us in gentle ways. I don't believe it's a coincidence; it may be a gift from God. If you open up your heart and let God fill it, you will hear what He wants you to hear."

"Well, you know about all these God messages?"

"Yes, the whole world is talking about them. We certainly have seen a change in attendance in the congregation. They're making a lot of people pretty excited these days."

"I turned on the TV the other day. I saw one of the quotes, and I felt like it spoke directly to me. It said something like: I've given you a conscience for a reason, pay attention to it. It hit me like a left hook."

"Um-hmm, is there something that's weighing heavy on you—something that has gone against your conscience? That's normally where our conscience gets bothered, when we know better, but make exceptions."

"That's what I'm so confused about. I'm a lawyer; it's my job to live in that world, where you push as hard as you can up to the line without going over it. I used to be a prosecutor. I could do what I felt was right . . . now I'm a defense attorney. I don't have any problem with that, now mind you."

"Um-hmm."

I don't have a problem with representing guilty people. This is confidential, isn't it?"

"It's privileged conversation, for the most part. Are you a Catholic?"

"Yes, well that is, I was brought up a Catholic. I haven't been to church in many, many years."

"Have you received the sacraments and the first reconciliation?"

"Yes, yes, I have, when I was still young in Chile."

"Well, if you want to enter into a moment of the sacrament and reconciliation, we can do that. The sacramental seal is something that cannot be divulged in any arena. The first step would be that I would welcome you back to the practice of faith. If you want to do that, we can move over to the confessional."

"Well, I haven't been to church in so many years. I would have so much to confess. I, I don't know if I'm comfortable just yet. Can we just talk?"

"Yes, my son, of course."

"I have a client. I don't know how else to say it, but well—he's a mobster. He hired me, and he's given me many clients. My entire practice revolves around him—around him and his associates."

"I see."

"I know what it is they do. I know that he and his people own the docks of New York; and they bring in heroin, cocaine, and other poisons. They give it over to the gangbangers in Harlem for distribution. It's impossible to ignore it. Now the day has come where he's asked me to do something to cross the line. He's asked me to do something I can't rationalize; something I know is immoral, illegal, and something my conscience bothers me about.

"Are you representing these people because you truly believe in the law and that everyone's entitled to a fair trial? Is it for the excitement, or are you doing this because it pays extremely well and fills the coffers?"

Tomás got up and walked over to the stained glass windows at the side of the sanctuary. He clenched his hands behind his back and considered the father's question deeply. He didn't want to face the answer, but he knew the true answer. He turned and faced the priest. He slowly walked back and took a seat. His head was bowed.

"I remember when he first came to talk to me. It was exciting; I was going to be a player. When we first talked, the conversation was full of innuendo and double meaning. I thought I was so smart . . . so cool. I knew my stuff. I knew what not to say and what to say . . . and how to say it. Yeah, I was smart—smart enough to walk myself right under his thumb. It was for the excitement, yeah . . . the excitement."

"You know what else is exciting?" asked the father, and then answered his own question. "To become the person that God created you to be—not becoming the person we think we need to be, or the person that's looking for affirmation from others. The only affirmation we need comes from God. It comes from your knowledge of becoming the person God intended you to be. How exciting the world would be if everybody took that seriously. Can you imagine what kind of world that would be?"

"I can't imagine that."

"The reason that your conscience is bothering you is that at some level you know that what you're doing is wrong. As much as it may be exciting for you to do, as much as it may help you pay your mortgage, there are other ways for you to be validated without having to be involved in a vicious cycle that brings other people down while promoting yourself."

"I close an eye to the fact that I know that people are receiving this poison and are being hurt by it," Tomas paused, thinking of something from long ago. "My father was a puppet to the political winds in Chile when I was growing up, and so was my mother. I swore that I would never let that happen to me. I would never let anybody pull my strings . . . and look at me now."

"Are you a puppet?"

"That's exactly what I am."

"Yes, that is exactly what you are. Somebody else is pulling your strings. All those things that you've accumulated came because you've done what other people have told you to do."

"If I take this extra step—do this thing they want me to do—I don't know . . . I mean, it's my job to walk as close to the line without going over it as I can. That's what a lawyer's job is. But this is going over the line. This is definitely over the line. If I go over this line, there is no coming back. But if I don't, I'll lose my life."

"You don't know that."

"Well, I'll lose my client. I'll lose my business, my income."

"So you say that you'll lose your material possessions—that's not your life. What will you gain?"

There was a long pause

"Freedom?" Tomás asked.

"Self-respect?" Father Fitzgerald asked.

"Self-respect," affirmed Tomás.

"One of the hardest things about making these choices is that doing so leads you into a future that is unknown and unpredictable. Life is not always about walking in our comfort zone; sometimes life is all about walking in the mystery. Sometimes we stay along certain paths because they're fixed, and we know what's going to happen. Other times we reach out and walk on a path we don't know. That is the trust I'm talking about. God is speaking to you through your inner voice and directing you along a path. You have to trust that He would not lead you along the wrong path."

Tomás wasn't quite following the father. His face showed it.

"Here, look at it this way," the father instructed. "Think of the man on the flying trapeze. He's facing backward, holding a swing in his hands. He falls off his perch and falls down and then up. At the very height of the arch, he has to let go of his swing, turn around, and grab a swing from the other side. When he lets go of his swing, he doesn't have knowledge that the other swing is going to be there. Yet he allows himself to be suspended in the air with nothing to support him. Then he turns around, and the other swing is there. He grabs it and gracefully moves to his perch on the other side of the trapeze. You are at that point now, my son. It is scary to let go of the known and trust that God will put in front of you what you need. Is that not what your inner voice is telling you to do?"

Father Fitzgerald held Tomás's hand in his. Tomás felt odd for a moment as he felt the warmness and intimacy of another man's hands. The oddness soon melted into reassurance and comfort.

"You know, being a prosecutor was the most fun I ever had as a lawyer. Maybe I can still stay in the game; I just have to switch sides again. Of course, prosecutors don't get paid very much."

"It's an interesting thing about money. We make more money; we get better jobs; we get bigger houses; we buy more clothes; we take more expensive trips. At some point we start getting older and we get rid of the big house and get rid of the car. We tone down because it's too much for us. You know what? It's not really about the house, the furniture, the clothes, or vacations. It's about us and our friends and joy. You can find joy among the simplest things. As a matter of fact, you most often find joy among the simplest things."

Tomás began to feel more at ease and said, "I have one other confession."

"Just one?" the father laughed, and then said more seriously, "I just want to remind you that we are not in the sacrament. We're having a conversation, but we are not in the sacrament, so I just want to make sure that we're clear on that. I can listen to what you have to say, but if we are not in the sacrament, it is not really an act of contrition."

"Well, Father, I want to enter into the sacrament. What I have to say weighs very heavily on me."

There was nobody else in the church, so there was no need to move to the confessional. For this moment, this time, the entire church became a confessional for Tomás. The father's face became more serious. He leaned in toward Tomás and began to speak in confidential and hushed tones.

"Welcome back after so many years of being away from the practice of the faith. May God be in your heart and on your lips, that you may worldly confess your sins."

Tomás told Father Fitzgerald about Johnny's request and Tomás's conversations with Louie the Cop. The father listened and then spoke with great earnest.

"If you go forward with their plan, my son, you will be violating the laws of both man and God. It is my strongest advice for you to get out of this. You know in your heart that your actions bring great harm, pain, and suffering to those who are the weakest and most vulnerable of us. Remember Jesus said that what you do for the weakest of us, you also do for Him. The other side of the equation is that what you do to the most vulnerable of us you also do to Him. If you take a hand in spreading this poison, it is no different than pressing the plunger of the syringe yourself. Obviously, you've come here for a reason. You are in a place where you must make some decisions for yourself. Do you want to continue in this life being bothered by your conscience, or do you want to move away from that and truly concentrate on using your skills and abilities to build up God's kingdom here on earth? It is never too late to make a new beginning. That's what the sacrament and the reconciliation is all about. It is all about making a new beginning."

"A new beginning . . . ," Tomás repeated

"You don't make a sacrament and then leave, planning to continue the same activities that you've confessed to or planning to participate in the same sin. The sacrament doesn't work like that. Now that you have finished confessing this sin, it is important that you make an act of contrition. If you make an act of contrition, only saying the words without really being contrite, then there's a problem," Father Fitzgerald said.

"Tell me about conscience. Tell me about the voice that I'm feeling inside. Is this really God speaking to me?" Tomás asked.

"I think God speaks to us in many ways. God will get you one way or another. God's messages are always around us. Sometimes the messages have to hit us over the head for us to hear them, which sounds like what's been happening to you. The messages hound us until we come to the point where we ask: What is it that I'm doing with my life? What is the purpose? Am I going to be living as a puppet of these people? Can I truly believe that if I give this up God will truly provide everything that I need, perhaps not everything that I want, but everything that I need?"

"There's something else."

"Okay."

"It's my wife. My wife is the CFO of Halliron Corporation. She has a boss who has been cooking the books. She doesn't want to rock the boat. That's what she tells me. I keep telling her what the right thing to do is. I preach at her and tell her what the right thing to do is. I get mad at her, and well, I have a temper . . . I now realize that my anger with her for not doing the right thing is really anger with myself for not doing the right thing. I love her, and I feel terribly guilty about having treated her like this. I didn't realize that until this very moment."

"Then cherish this moment, my son. It sounds to me as if you already know the truth of the matter because you have come to your own epiphany. You know that what you've been doing with your wife is using her as a sounding board to speak to yourself. You've been yelling at her, but you really have been yelling at yourself."

"How do I set that right?"

"You tell her what you just told me. There is no more loving communication between a husband and wife than an authentic acceptance of responsibility for having made a mistake. This is the most treasured moment of trust that passes between two people. Besides, if you think she doesn't already know this, I believe you are mistaken. Go to her and ask her if you both are living the life you intended to live. Include her in your decisions; listen to her thoughts and feelings. A simple, *I'm sorry*, goes a long way. It's not too late to make a fresh beginning. You both may have to make some hard decisions. No one ever said that being a Christian, being a Catholic, is easy. Make your choices together. I don't believe that this problem will be as large as you think it is. You both want to live lives where you don't have to toss and turn at night."

"It's been a long time since I've felt that kind of comfort."

"I am sure you can easily find something that would make use of your talents in a way that builds people up and enhances the Kingdom of God."

"Is there really such a thing as forgiveness?"

"Oh yes, absolutely. When the priest says those words—I absolve you of your sins in the name of the Father, the Son, and the Holy Ghost—we believe that you are absolved of all your sins. We believe that is what God said to us in the scriptures. 'Who forgives is forgiven; those who hold bound are held bound.' It's right in the scriptures, word for word, and so we believe that the sacrament was given to us by Christ for the forgiveness of sins."

"Please, Father, forgive me."

"For penance then, free yourself from your puppet master, but before you go speak to these people, spend some quiet time and pray to God. Pray to be guided to say the right words and have the right feelings, and then it will be okay. Sometimes it's not what you say, but it's how you say it. So go there in peace. Go in peace with yourself, and go in peace with the people that you're talking to. Be prepared to say the right thing, in the right way, in the right tone of voice. Speak from your heart and not your head. Pray for those people your sins have affected. Pray for those people who have given you directions to harm others so that they may hear the word of God and cease their actions. Take a percentage, that you decide upon, from the earnings that have come from these sources and donate that money to something other than the church, something that benefits others. You determine the amount. It should be an amount that you can afford, as it seems your cash flow is about to change significantly. Where have you found it most comfortable to pray?"

"My mother always prayed to the Blessed Mother, we had a statue at the head of my bed. I suppose I most enjoyed the prayers we said at bedtime."

"Why then, let's try a decade of the rosary today at bedtime and then another decade of the rosary tomorrow. A decade is just the ten Hail Marys. I want you to get back into the practice slowly because if you say the whole rosary, all fifty of the Hail Marys, it might be a bit much to start. Just do one decade at a time for the next five days. Offer up those intentions for people that have been harmed by some of the activities you've mentioned."

"I will do that."

The priest then asked Tomás to repeat after him the Act of Contrition,

> O my God, I am heartily sorry for having offended thee,
> and I detest all my sins because of thy just punishment,
> but most of all because they offend Thee, my God,
> who art all-good and deserving of all my love. I firmly
> resolve, with the help of thy grace, to sin no more and

to avoid the near occasion of sin. In the name of the Father, and of the Son, and of the Holy Spirit, Amen.

Father Fitzgerald then absolved Tomás of his sins.

God, the Father of mercies, through the death and resurrection of His Son has reconciled the world to Himself and sent the Holy Spirit among us for the forgiveness of sins. Through the ministry of the Church, may God give you pardon and peace, and I absolve you from your sins in the name of the Father, and of the Son, and of the Holy Spirit.

"Thanks be to God," said Tomás, remembering the reply from some deep recess of his mind.

"Go in peace and sin no more," said Father Fitzgerald, finalizing the ceremony.

"Thank you, Father. Thank you for your forgiveness, your counsel, and your time."

"You're welcome. You might want to think of stopping by on Sunday; we have quite a crowd these days—you might enjoy it."

"I might at that."

Tomás left the confessional feeling so lighthearted he had to check to see if his feet were really touching the ground. When he walked out of the church, he realized that it actually was a bright, sunny afternoon, just like Father Fitzgerald said. Tomás walked back to his condo, thinking all the while of how and what he was going to say to Claire.

Even though he wanted to share the conversation he had with Father Fitzgerald with his wife, something still tugged at him.

Was it that he wasn't ready to finally let go of his façade? Was it that he was still projecting his anger onto Claire? His thoughts were clear but unsure. After all, she still had her situation with Halliron and Clay McCrae to deal with. He had to keep pushing her to resolve it, didn't he? How could he show weakness? This is where the rubber hit the road. Tomás wasn't quite sure how to make that happen.

CHAPTER 14

You are all my children.

—God

When Claire walked into work the next morning, she passed Clay McRae's office. She just got a sideways glance in, but she noticed a look on McRae's face that startled her. He looked troubled, perhaps even a bit desperate. She had never seen McRae display much emotion at all—certainly nothing that would give a clue there was any disturbance under his mask of confidence.

As she turned the corner, she could see several heads of telemarketers over the partition of her secretary's cubicle. When they noticed her, their conversation stopped, and they started to shuffle out.

"No, no, don't stop. Don't leave—it's only me. I don't think I grew fangs last night," she chided.

They stopped shuffling and waited for her. They seemed a little ill at ease. At the same time, they looked like a collective hot air balloon just waiting to burst forth.

"So guys, what's going on over here," she said while crossing her arms.

They looked at her, then at each other, then at Zeta, Claire's secretary, and then back at her.

"Something's going on with the old man," one said.

"He was here before anyone this morning, and you know, he hardly ever gets here before ten o'clock," another offered.

"There was a big argument going on between him and two of the board members."

"He fired Roberta."

"Yeah, then he went to get his own coffee. He burned his hand and threw the coffee pot against the wall."

"Wait, wait just a second," Claire interrupted, "you say he fired Roberta?"

Roberta had been McRae's secretary for as long as anyone knew him. She was the only person who could or would put up with him. She knew him inside, whatever inside there was, and out. She never judged him. She was a rare find and irreplaceable.

"Yes, ma'am, at least we think so. No one knows what happened. She brought the mail into him and came out crying. She picked up her coat and left. She wouldn't talk to anybody," Zeta said.

"That's odd," Claire whispered.

Claire put her overcoat, scarf, and briefcase down on Zeta's desk. She turned pensive and serious. McRae was certainly capable of all kinds of unexpected behavior, but firing Roberta, even running her off, would not be in his best interest; and Clay McRae never did anything that wasn't in his best interest. Something was wrong—gravely wrong.

Claire stepped gingerly back around the corner toward Clay's office. She looked at his door; it was open just a crack. She moved closer and stopped for a moment to hear if there was someone with him. There was only silence.

Claire knocked on the door softly. It was more of a push than a knock. The door slowly opened. When she could see inside, she saw McRae standing motionless at his panorama window looking out at Battery Park, New York Harbor, and the Statue of Liberty. He was holding his napkin-wrapped left hand in his right.

"Mr. McRae?"

Six seconds passed before he moved—for Claire it seemed longer. It wasn't so much what she felt, as what she didn't feel. On any other day, she would have had that knot in her stomach, the clutching feeling in her chest, the about-to-break-into-a-cold-sweat feeling that borders on nausea. A life of trying to keep the peace, of not knowing where the next blowup was going to come from, made the physical sensations of anxiety seem normal—so normal that the new calm, solid, grounded feeling within was a radical change. Radical because it signaled a sloughing off of the Claire that tried to be responsible for everyone else's happiness, and the birth of a free, self-confident, and self-aware woman. She had gained the ability to become an observer of the situation, only as emotionally involved as she chose to be. She understood what Mark, her therapist, taught her about healthy detachment.

Clay broke from his stance into his normal charm-to-disarm mode. The transformation was so quick and so complete that Claire did a double take. Being a couple of steps removed, she easily saw through McRae's calculated pretense of friendliness. She shook her head ever so slightly as she wondered, with some amazement, how she had not seen before how fake this man was. Now she knew he was a put-on, and he didn't know she knew that. That gave her the advantage. She liked that!

"Claire, good morning. I'm glad you stopped by. Would you like some coffee? Oh, you'll have to get it yourself," Clay said.

"Uh, no. I'm good. What happened to your hand?" she asked, knowing the answer.

"Oh, Roberta had to leave . . ."

"Yeah, I wanted to ask you about that, the guys on the floor told me you fired her. I couldn't believe it."

"No, it was something personal, something in her family. Anyway, I poured some hot coffee on my hand."

Claire chose not to press him. She nodded her head and just kept silent, watching and waiting for his next maneuver. McRae moved to his plush leather executive desk chair. Claire sat on the arm of the easy chair across the desk from him—taking the power position of looking down at McRae.

"As I said, I'm glad you stopped by. We need to get the third-quarter earnings report finished and to the printer. The analysts are beginning to get under my skin, especially that one from the *Wall Street Journal*."

"Umm," said Claire, neither agreeing nor disagreeing.

A couple of seconds of silence passed. Claire was content, even slightly amused, to see what would be said next. McRae became impatient and blinked first.

"I mean, there's no point in delay when you have good news, right, Claire?"

Claire looked directly into McRae's eyes. "I hope so," she said flatly.

Claire could see the chill that ran through McRae. The pretense of friendliness faded from his face. The anger didn't surface, but it started to percolate.

"I hope so?" McRae asked.

"Yes, I hope so," Claire said again flatly.

McRae's eyes narrowed. He looked confused by Claire's response. She had moved up the corporate ladder to become liaison to Halliron's independent accounting/auditors (who weren't so independent, thanks to millions of dollars in accounting fees paid annually) precisely because she was smart enough to go with the flow. She had rarely questioned reports that came to her for review. If she did, an explanation from him or a statement from a board member would satisfy her.

Claire knew the timing of her change of attitude had to be particularly bad for McRae. Halliron's stock had gone up fifty points with news of the deal with RenEn to diversify into renewable energy sources. McRae had boasted to her that with the rebirth of God consciousness, people and, therefore, investors would more readily buy stock in clean energy companies. By forging headlong, supposedly into the green energy market, McRae improved the image of his company and pushed up its stock value upon speculation that its market share would increase.

Claire had fielded some questions from a stock analyst from Baron's who was digging into RenEn's history. The analyst was suggesting that RenEn didn't have the patents described in Halliron's press releases. McRae had cooled the analyst down by taking the analyst into his faux confidence and showing him, off the record, RenEn's patent applications for a revolutionary technology.

McRae picked the amount of $372 million out of the air as a value of the (non)contracts with the ghostly RenEn. McRae had provided documentation of this to Claire, and he fully expected her to include it in the third-quarter statement moving Halliron out of a $122 million red column and into a solid black $250 million gain. McRae didn't know that Claire knew that the patents had been denied.

"I hope so too, Claire," McRae said with determination. "I don't need to remind you that you have a fiduciary duty to his company to file reports in a timely manner. Those reports have an enormous effect on the financial health of this company and its stock price. The jobs and retirement plans of your coworkers depend on optimistic forecasts, not to speak of the value of the thousands of shares you have in stock options. Oh, by the way, your husband practices criminal law, doesn't he? He doesn't do corporate litigation, does he?"

"No, he doesn't."

"That's too bad, just in case you become involved in litigation arising out of this. In that case, I suppose you'll have to hire one of those expensive Park Avenue lawyers."

Claire straightened her back and pretended to show concern. She got up, walked over to McRae's file table, and fingered through the files until she saw RenEn's file. She picked it up.

"Here's RenEn's file. I'll go through it tonight and make the appropriate and proper adjustments to the report. I'll have a rough draft of it for you tomorrow, okay?" Claire soothed.

Clay relaxed. "That'll be fine, I've got to go out now anyway. I've got a financing meeting over at the bank."

Claire was headed toward the door as Clay got halfway up from his chair. She turned. Her voice was deadly serious.

"Mr. McRae, I want to thank you for being concerned about my legal situation, and by way of returning the favor, I want you to know that my husband, the criminal defense attorney, will be happy to represent you when the indictments come down."

With that, she was out the door. McRae didn't see the smile on her face. As she walked back to her office, the smile got bigger and bigger. She closed the door of her office and let out a full laugh. Once she got control of her breath, she curled her right hand into a fist and pounded it into her left hand accompanied by a loud, "Yes!"

McCrae sat down to plan his next move. He didn't sit long. A ruddy, potbellied officer with an unusual gray shirt showed up at the door to McRae's office.

"McRae, Clay McRae?"

"Yes."

"I'm Deputy Sheriff Totter with the Civil Process Bureau. You are married to one Jennifer McRae?"

"Yes."

"I'm sorry, but I have some papers to serve on you. This is a complaint suing you for divorce, and this is a TRO, a Temporary Restraining Order, preventing you from disposing of any marital assets and ordering you to go before Judge Richard Allen in ten days to show cause why the TRO should not be made permanent. Oh, it also says that you are not to go on or about your residence without your wife's permission."

"A restraining order?" McRae asked in shocked surprise.

"Yes, sir."

"For what?"

"It's all in the affidavit. Will you sign for it or should I issue a sheriff's certificate?"

"No, I'll sign."

Totter handed McRae the court papers and the sheriff's return of process. McRae signed it and was reading the affidavit by the time Totter turned to leave. The officer knew better than to say, "Have a nice day."

Jennifer was alleging abuse using veiled threats McRae actually had said, taken out of context, and made to look even worse by the crafty pen of a well-versed lawyer. McRae was mad. He wasn't angry at the false context of the allegations or any hurt caused by being sued for divorce or for being described as an abusive monster. Clay McCrae was furious because she, his ex-wife-to-be, had gotten one over on him. He thought she was under control, but she turned out to be the spider—and he the fly.

The paperwork said that he had to be in court in ten days. He went through a mental checklist of factors. He couldn't depend on Claire's cooperation anymore. The *Wall Street Journal* and Baron's were sniffing around and getting uncomfortably close to piercing Halliron's veil of profitability. Board members were spooked. The news about his divorce would hit the financial papers, and there would be speculation about distractions affecting his ability to lead the company.

Ten days . . . ten days until he had to be in court; well, that wasn't going to happen. With a nod of his head, he made his decision. A calming sense of resolve came over him as he downshifted into survival mode. His first call was to Pierce-Champion and Associates, a midsized investment banker that had bankrolled some of Halliron's earlier schemes. As he had no personal accounts there, they would be outside the tightening circle of scrutiny.

"Hello, this is Bruce Schmidt."

"Bruce, hello, how are you? Clay McRae here."

"Mr. McRae, good to hear from you. We haven't talked since wrapping up that public offering last year. That was a real . . . mutually beneficial deal, huh?"

McRae could feel Schmidt's wink over the phone. He ignored the subtext of the comment and got straight to the point. "Look, Bruce, I have a situation here that needs a certain amount of discretion and confidentiality."

"Mr. McRae, here at Pierce-Champion we purposefully stay smaller to give our clients the personal service and trust they deserve."

McRae knew the comment was bull, but he also knew the banker was beginning to salivate. Higher fees can always be charged when transactions need "special handling."

"Well, I've just been served with divorce papers. I suspect this might have some effect on Halliron's stock price when the papers get hold of it."

"I'm sorry for your bad news, and yes, I agree with you. Anything affecting the CEO of such a large company is bound to have repercussions."

"The complaint has been filed, so it's public record. We don't have to worry about insider trading implications." McRae didn't mention all the other pieces of inside information he had that would combine to bring about the imminent collapse of the energy giant. McRae continued with his instructions. "I'm holding options for over three million shares of Halliron. I want to exercise those options or sell them outright. This morning it opened at 159. I'll take down to 157 for the first million and 150 for the next two. I need to complete the transactions within eight days."

"Eight days? Hmm, that'll put downward pressure on the market price."

"Yes, I know. That's why I'll take less on the second two million," snapped McRae.

"To move that many shares, uh, quickly, I'll have to lay some of that off to other brokerage houses. We'll have to have a surcharge of 3 percent to cover the commissions of the others involved."

"You want 3 percent on top of your 6 percent—9 percent? I won't do that. 7.5 percent is all I'll pay. That's over twenty-five million for a week's work. That ought to be enough."

"That'll be fine. I'll open the account and get the paperwork ready. Can you stop by, say, in an hour, to sign?"

"Not this morning. How about two o'clock this afternoon?"

"That'll be fine. You've given us a big order, and we want to jump on it ASAP."

"Okay, two o'clock."

"Right! Two o'clock."

McRae punched up a new outgoing line and started to dial. He didn't know the number by heart. Reaching into his wallet, he pulled out the card of the electronics store with a number written on the back. He finished dialing.

"Hello."

"Is he there?"

"Who's this?"

"Mac," said McRae, using the agreed-upon name.

"Wait," the response came back.

McRae heard some talking in a language he didn't understand. He assumed it was Turkish.

"Hello."

"It's me."

"Oh, Mac, good to hear you, good to hear you. I'm just going to have coffee; come join me."

"Thanks, but something's come up. It's important I speak with you—this morning. We need to speed things up."

"Umm . . . Okay, okay, sounds important. Meet me at Mustafa's Coffee House on the four hundred block, Bleecker Street"

"In the village?"

"I like Greenwich Village; people don't stare at you there. Give me an hour, I have to get dressed."

Some colleges and universities have a street along their edge with bistros, bars, pubs, bookstores, and boutiques full of the fashions and fads of the current college set. For New York

University, that place is called Greenwich Village, and Bleecker Street is at its heart.

Mustafa's is located in the middle of the block, squeezed between a coin laundry/beer joint called Wash n' Brew and a comic book/celebrity photo/antique postcard collector's shop. The wood of the storefront lost its varnish about the same time Bob Dylan was starting his career as the troubadour of the counterculture hippies. The glass looked like it was frosted over, even in summer.

McRae pushed the door open; the smell of coffee and tobacco slapped him. He peered down the dimly lit row of tables for two. The fat man was sitting at the last table talking with the coffee-bar tender. He was wearing off-white linen pants, a white shirt, and an open matching vest.

McRae nodded from the front door, the Turk finished his comments, and then shifted in his chair to face forward to the table. He waited quietly for McRae to sit down. "Coffee? The beans come straight from Istanbul," Mustafa offered.

"No, no, thank you."

Mustafa waived the waiter away. He leaned forward and hushed his voice. He studied McRae's face. "Talk to me, my friend. Your face seems calm enough, but your eyes tell me there are many thoughts running around inside."

The comments won McRae's instant respect. McRae was good at reading people, but he rarely met someone who could see behind the mask that he was choosing to wear.

"What do I call you?"

"You may call me"—the Turk looked up at the signage on the front of the shop—"Mustafa."

McRae didn't know if the Turk just picked the name out of the air, whether it was real, or if he was the owner of the coffee shop. He didn't care.

"I've just been served with divorce papers and . . ."

"I'm so sorry to hear that. It is sad when the family breaks up. My wife and I are married now forty-two years. Do you love her?"

"Enough to transfer twenty-five million dollars in bearer bonds and negotiable instruments into her name and safety deposit boxes."

"And it was after this that she filed the papers?"

"Yes," said McRae, feeling more embarrassed than victimized.

"I understand your problem. In my country, we would not bother with the divorce. We would just kill her."

McRae toyed with the idea and then dismissed it. Mustafa went on.

"So what is it you ask of me?"

"I am supposed to appear in court in ten days—some hearing on a restraining order. When I show up, it will start a media frenzy, and I will be dogged wherever I go. If I don't show up, the word will still get out, but it probably would take a few days. Either way, I will become a media target and lose the . . . uh . . . convenience of moving around freely."

"Go on," Mustafa said, making the gesture with his hand.

"Have you opened the account?"

"Did you not ask me to?"

"Good. I have two accounts here I can still access. They have about two million in them. I want to wire transfer them now."

"We can do that from the Internet place next door. I will call my son to help us. I am still not comfortable with things that travel through the air. I prefer the comfort of pen and paper."

McRae nodded in agreement. Mustafa signaled the waiter. "Call Achmed. Tell him to meet us here." The waiter moved to the phone. "What else?" asked Mustafa.

"I have over five hundred million in stock options. I'm opening an account right now with Pierce-Champion, and I am instructing them to execute my options and sell them at the best price. I asked them to complete the transaction within eight days. By the time I'm supposed to be in court ten days from now, I want to be in Turkey with my money. Can that happen?"

"I believe we agreed that I would be paid 20 percent of the transfer—that would make my part eighty to one hundred million, depending on the broker's commissions, hmm . . . Yes, I believe I can make that happen. Do you have your passport up to date? Have you applied for a Turkish visa? If you can take care of getting yourself there, I can take care of getting the money there."

"I'll have that cup of coffee now, thank you."

The waiter brought over two fresh cups of Turkish coffee, and the two men waited. When Achmed arrived, all three went next door to the Internet café. Achmed sat down as if he were at home and logged on to the Internet. First, he brought up the homepage of the Guarantee Bank of Turkey. Mustafa gave him the account number and its password. Achmed accessed the account and called up the balance.

He then turned the screen so that McRae could see it. McRae was amazed to see that every penny he had advanced Mustafa—the $100,000.00 in cash, the $4,770.00 hotel bill, and even the $100.00 in cash given as a tip to the bartender—had been deposited, all $104,870.00. McRae appreciated the method Mustafa used to build trust between them.

Achmed then went to the administrative page and brought up the change-password dialogue. He put in the current password and prepared the page for a new password. He turned to the two men.

"The password calls for ten digits. Mr. McRae, you'll put in the first five digits; any combination of digits is okay. You'll do this out of sight of my father. After you put in the first five, you can step away from the computer, and my father will put in the last five. That way you will each be privy to one-half of the password to a numbered account. Neither one of you will be able to access the money through the Internet or at the bank without the other's five digits. This will provide you both with security and a sense of trust and good faith."

Achmed stood up and motioned for McRae to sit down. Mustafa stepped away. McRae put in five digits, got up, and stepped back. Mustafa stepped up to the computer and completed the password by entering the final five digits. On the screen, only simple dots appeared, so neither could see the work of the other. Achmed pushed the enter button and then signed off. After he signed off, he called up the webpage of the bank again and put in the account number. He then invited each of the men to enter their portion of the password. They did, and it worked. Both men nodded to each other and thanked Achmed.

After that, Achmed helped McRae log into his accounts and wire transfer two million to Turkey. McRae was visibly relieved. Even if nothing else went right, he had at least two million stashed away that would give him the beginnings of a new beginning.

*   *   *

As Clay McRae was making his plans to leave the country, Claire was making her plans to leave Halliron. She knew that whatever happened to McRae, her tenure at the company would have to end. Even if she did everything she could to set things right, her actions in going along with McRae's shenanigans required the objectivity of someone else to review the financial matters of the corporation. She only hoped she wouldn't be indicted.

Whatever was to happen, she knew that from this point forward she would be truthful and upright regardless of the short-term consequences. She hoped that if she cooperated with the authorities, things would work out. She also knew the long-term consequences, in this life or the next, would be worth it. One thing was certain; she felt great and wanted to celebrate. She grabbed the phone and punched in Tomás's cell phone number.

"Hello," Tomás answered.

"Buenos tardes, mi amor," Claire said.

"Querida, your voice always takes me away from the mundane ramblings of a poor lawyer," teased Tomás. "How is your day? What's up?"

"Oh, I'm just packing up some boxes."

"Packing up some boxes?"

"Yeah, I'll tell you about it over dinner. Where are you? What's the rest of your day look like?"

"I'm at court. I'll probably be tied up 'til just after five."

"Do you have the car?"

"No, I left it home."

"Good. How does this sound? I'll meet you on Canal and Bowery about six. We'll walk and look in the windows of the jewelry stores. If you see something that absolutely calls out to you, I'll even let you buy it for me. Then we can go have dinner at that little restaurant in Chinatown . . ."

"You mean the narrow one with just one row of tables and hot tea in scratched water glasses?"

"Yeah, that one. Then we'll walk over to Ferrara's and get Italian éclairs and double espressos to keep us up for the long night ahead. We'll take a cab home and make out in the backseat. How's that sound . . . Tomás? . . . Tomás?"

"Querida—you better stop. I'm beginning to sweat, and the judge will think I am nervous about my case."

"Well, you just keep thinking about it. So Canal and Bowery at six?"

"I will be there—with bells on."

Claire put the phone down. She was tingling all over. Maybe it was liberation, maybe anticipation, and just maybe something more primordial. Tomás's tingling was more centrally located.

Tomás was already there when Claire got to the designated corner at five minutes to six. They hugged two degrees longer and three degrees tighter than their norm. Claire turned to face down Canal Street and took Tomás's left arm. Tomás gently disengaged and stepped around Claire from the back and offered her his right arm.

"A lady always walks on the inside, so that she may be protected from what unknown dangers may approach from the street."

"My knight in shining armor," Claire said.

They walked together, looking in the windows of the merchants of New York's oldest diamond district. They tacitly pretended to be a young couple looking for an engagement ring. Halfway down the second block, Tomás stopped and cupped his hand to his ear.

"It's calling out to me. Let's go in here."

Before Claire could say anything, Tomás was ushering her through the door. They stopped along the first glass display case. The owner came over. He was a short older man wearing a yarmulke on his head and a jeweler's loop around his neck. Behind him, a Bunsen burner was spewing blue-yellow flame above scattered gold and silver shards. Tomás motioned to Claire to stay where she was, then he walked up to the front window display with the owner. They spoke and then returned. The owner had a ring in his hand and presented it to Claire for her review.

Claire responded with a sharp intake of breath. She covered her mouth with her hand, and her eyes looked like an eight-year-old's first sighting of Santa's bounty on Christmas morning. The ring was yellow gold. It had swirls of pink and blue opal surrounded by small emeralds and diamonds. In the middle was a multifaceted two-carat Tanzanite heart. The look on Claire's face eliminated any need to ask her if she liked it. Tomás gave the owner his credit card and just smiled at his wife until the owner brought the paperwork back.

They walked out, arm in arm, and crossed the street to Chinatown. Two blocks down Mott Street, they came to the tiny restaurant they used to go to when they first arrived in New York. They entered the long but narrow restaurant and settled into their table surrounded by the fragrances of ginger, garlic, and peanut oil. Tomás went to get them both a glass of tea.

A one-hundred-cup stainless steel West Bend coffee urn filled with hot oolong tea sat on a table with stacked clean but well-scratched glass water tumblers for self-serve. The white Formic-topped tables were attached to the wall on one side and supported by a single aluminum pipe on the other. A tin band, reminiscent of 1950s diners, went around the edges of the tables. In the rear, cooks were shoulder to shoulder at the cook line working their magic with woks.

"So how's your day been?" Claire asked, relaxing.

"It was okay, same old, same old. I got a few good wins in court today. I don't know if I'm just getting to be a better attorney, or the assistant DAs are getting worse; but I tell you, the ADAs in court are not made out of the same stuff they were when I was prosecuting. It's getting to be almost too easy, like shooting fish in a barrel."

"Oh, you're just saying that because it's true," Claire said. She put her glass of tea down and looked directly in Tomás's eyes. "I had an interesting day today."

"I can't wait to hear. You seemed so excited when you talked to me earlier."

"Trust me. I can't wait to tell you about it. Should we order first?"

"Sure."

"What did we use to order here? Was it the orange chicken or did we get General Tao's Duck?" Claire asked.

"I think it was the moo shu pork. I always thought that moo shu was a fun dish—you take all this stuff and put it in a pancake and cram it in your mouth," Tomás said.

"That sounds good. Don't forget how good the chow fun is here," said Claire, licking her lips.

Tomás ordered hot and sour soup for both of them, a platter of moo shu pork, and shrimp chow fun. After the waiter left, they resumed their conversation.

"So tell me what's going on. I am itching to find out."

"Like I said, plenty of things happened today. When I got in, the first thing that happened . . . well, I'm walking in and see that there's a lot of commotion going on over by Roberta's desk. I get over there, and everybody's telling me that Clay is on a rampage and that something's wrong—that he got into an argument with some members of the board of directors, that he got in early, before everybody else, and the strangest thing of all was that he fired Roberta."

"Fired Roberta? She has been with him forever."

"Yeah . . . forever! There is no way that would ever happen. I couldn't understand what was going on, so I walked over to his office. The door was opened just a crack, and he's standing like a statue in front of his window, looking out at the water and the bridge. I waited a couple of seconds. I talked to him, he turned around, and I . . . I've got to tell you, just then the strangest feeling came over me. I . . . I felt this kind of calm inside. I don't know if I've ever shared this with you, Tomás, but I walk around with a lot of anxiety; and I often feel a lot of fear inside of me. Today something just happened. All of a sudden the fear and the anxiety just went away. So Clay turned around and started acting as if nothing was wrong. I saw right through it. I mean, the guy is such a fake; everything he does is put-on. There is not a sincere bone in his body. I just saw through him, and all of a sudden, he wasn't such a big scary thing anymore. He wasn't such a monster. He was just a little man, a little angry man. It was really kind of cool. I felt like I was standing outside of myself just watching everything that was going on. Mark, my therapist, told me about having a sense of detachment, and I discovered what he meant. It's kind of like being an observer of what's going on."

"I remember speaking to you about this."

"Yes, I can't tell you what a good thing it's been for me to get into therapy. Everybody should get into therapy. What I've learned about what it means to be a human being has been terrific; it's been so strengthening. So anyway, Clay turns around and tells me that he wants the third-quarter report."

"I know that you have been struggling with that."

"Certainly not carrying around a burden like that makes you feel a lot lighter, but it didn't seem like I had any struggle at all today. It didn't seem like I had to struggle inside at all. It seemed like it became natural just to listen to what he had to say. And then the son of a bitch tried to threaten me."

"Threaten you?"

"Yeah, he tried. He said something about if I didn't do what he wanted me to do that I'd be involved in litigation and . . ."

"I hope you told him that he better watch it or I would come down there and kick his ass."

"Well, I kind of did. He pointed out that you were a criminal defense attorney, and that you wouldn't be able to defend me in a civil suit."

"He said that?"

"Yeah, he said that. So I let it go for just a minute, and I let him think that he had me. Just as I was about to walk out, I turned and I thanked him for being concerned about my legal liability; then I told him that you would be happy to represent him when the criminal charges came down. The color drained out of his face."

"That's amazing," Tomás said, accidentally spitting out half of a shrimp. "Pardóname! What did you do next?"

"I just walked out and went back to my office. Really, I guess I just took the day off in the office. I made some phone calls; I called my sister. I chatted with some of our telemarketers and took a long lunch. Then I picked up some boxes to start packing my stuff. I don't imagine that under any circumstances I'll be staying there very long."

"What happened to Clay?"

"Well, I don't know. After I talked to him, he made some phone calls and then left the office. He was gone for the rest of the day. I don't know what's going on with him, but whatever's going on, I know I don't care anymore."

They fell silent, basking in the tastes of the foods and the warmth of each other's presence.

"I don't think I could eat another bite," said Claire, leaning back and rubbing her belly through her dark purple silk blouse.

Tomás watched her hands rub the silk material over her skin. The dark color brought out the blond highlights of her hair. He watched the rich material glide over the lace of her brassiere and realized he hadn't felt this turned on in a long time.

"How about a rain check on the pastry and coffee?" Tomás suggested.

"That's fine," agreed Claire with a wink, "but not on the cab ride!"

"Then I suppose it's time to go," said Tomás, pushing back from the table.

They walked outside. The night held the first real chill of autumn. A light drizzle added to the cold. Claire held Tomás even closer. They stepped around some plastic tubs filled with live fish and eels in front of a seafood market. When they got to the curb, Tomás hailed a cab. They got into the backseat of the taxi.

A few minutes later, the cabbie had to turn on the rear window defogger.

CHAPTER 15

When you know what is right in your heart,
you must follow it.

—God

As the taxi pulled up to the entrance of the East River Towers, Tomás took his arm from around Claire and gave the driver a twenty-dollar bill for a twelve-dollar ride. With a smiling nod and a flick of his fingers, Tomás signaled to the driver to keep the change. With a smiling nod, the driver signaled he understood and was grateful.

Tomás got out first and reached back to help Claire. Tomás saw some motion out of the side of his eye and told Claire to stay where she was. Tomás turned to face the motion and saw a man walking toward them. As the man came out of the shadows, Tomás recognized Louie the Cop and exhaled in relief followed immediately by a renewed shot of anxiety. By now, Claire had gotten out of the cab and was standing behind Tomás, looking around his shoulder.

"Tomás, Mrs. Medina," Louie the Cop addressed them.

"Louie, you gave us a scare! What are you doing here? You're not on duty, are you?" asked Tomás, referring to Louie the Cop's civilian clothes.

"No, I'm not . . . uh, Mr. Medina, could I talk to you for a minute?"

Tomás evaluated the situation. He wasn't ready for the conversation that he knew was coming. On the other hand, he thought, *God has a way of throwing things at us when the time for action arrives.* He was surprised at thinking that God was actually a cause of the events in his life. He hadn't thought like that for years—maybe decades.

"Sure, sure. Just let me walk Claire to the door. I'll be right back," Tomás answered. With a gentle pressure, he steered Claire toward the door. She resisted slightly at first, obviously not wanting to go, but then gave in and fell into step.

"What does he want? Why is he here? What's going on between you two? I don't understand. Are you in any trouble? Tomás, I . . ."

"It's okay, it's okay," Tomás said. He stopped with her and looked deeply into her eyes. "At least it's okay, *now*!"

They arrived at the door. Tomás swiped his security card to buzz the door open, and they stepped inside, out of the late evening chill. Once inside, Tomás turned Claire to face him and looked at her lovingly. It was times like this that she wanted to throw words like *liberated* and *equal* into a recycling bin.

"Mi amor," he started, "I am confessing to you that I have hidden things from you, and tonight I will tell you all about that. Right now, I must talk to this man alone. It is important he tell me all that is on his mind. Although I do not deserve it, I must ask you to trust me. Please, go upstairs and make us a nice cup of coffee; we may be up for a while. I will be there shortly."

Claire returned his gaze. His eyes were fierce, but his face and voice were calm. This was his look when he took up a cause that he felt was noble.

"I trust you, mi amor, more than I ever have."

Tomás's eyes glazed ever so slightly and just for a moment. Then he opened and gently directed her through the second door into the lobby. He turned to go back outside to talk to Louie the Cop.

"Louie, come and tell me. What I can do for you?"

"Mr. Medina, uh, Tomás—you know, it's been a little while now since we had that conversation out in Rockaway, and I was wondering what's going on."

"Louie, I'm guessing that there is a little more to it than that. Why don't you tell me what's going on? You look just a bit anxious."

"No, I'm okay; it's just that since we talked about what we talked about, I'm anxious to get started. Tell you the truth, I . . . I just really fell in love with your BMW. Figuring that I was about to have extra income, I stopped by the dealership. Just to look, but the salesman made it sound so easy—and I didn't have to put that much down. Now I have to come up with more money, and I really don't have it, so I really kind of wanted to get going because I used my rent money for the down payment. Yeah, I guess I'm anxious. I've never really done anything like this. I guess that's part of it too."

"I understand what you're saying. There probably would be something wrong with you if you weren't a little nervous over all of this. How much of a payment did you put down?"

"Five thousand dollars."

"Well, I can see how that would get you short with your bills, and I'm sorry that you got involved in this."

"What do you mean you're sorry that I got involved in this?"

"What I mean is—what we talked about is not going to happen."

"Not going to happen?"

"That's correct. It's not going to happen."

Tomás was intentionally keeping his answers short to allow the conversation to drag on. Tomás knew that the information he was giving Louie the Cop would be hard to take.

"I don't understand! I thought this was a done deal; you certainly talked like it was a done deal. What went wrong? Are you working for Internal Affairs? Did you just try to string me along to see if I would take the bait? Why would you do this to me? Now I'm in a terrible position. What went wrong? What's going on? Is it something about me, or is it with your clients? I've got a right to know."

"Louie, this had nothing to do with you. You have done nothing wrong, and I am not working with Internal Affairs. Nothing has changed with my clients. As a matter of fact, I have not yet advised them that this is not going to happen."

"Then what . . . ?"

"Something has changed within me. What has been happening on the television and in newspapers has deeply affected my wife and me. I guess you might say we've gotten the fear of God. Perhaps not the fear of God, perhaps it is more like the love of God. We want to live a life unburdened by our past, and since everything we do today becomes tomorrow's past, I don't want to do anything I will regret. I know this puts you in an uncomfortable position financially, and since it is I who put you in that position, I feel it is my responsibility to make it up to you."

Tomás reached into his jacket pocket and pulled out his checkbook. He opened it up and began writing. Louie watched in disbelief. The opening of the checkbook told Louie that Tomás was not kidding around.

"I don't believe this bullshit! You've got be kidding me! Do you mean to tell me that you actually bought into all that God crap? A smart guy like you? How can you believe that there is a God doing all of this when people are still gettin' robbed, raped, and killed? You got to believe this is some kind of trick. You'll see, pretty soon it's all gonna come out that the government was behind it, or it's some big publicity stunt. Whaddya think, that we've got some kind of guardian angels? Nobody's gonna do anything for you, you gotta get whatever you get on your own!"

"That's certainly one way to look at it. I choose to look at it differently."

"You know you could be wrong."

Tomás could see that he was dealing with a child in a man's body. Tomás felt badly for him and relieved he decided not to go forward with the bribe. It would not take a savant to be able to predict that working with Louie the Cop would surely lead to disaster. Still, he hoped that, perhaps, he would be able to help Louie look at things slightly differently.

"Yes, Louie, I could be wrong. But—and I know that you're angry—but just think about this for a moment. If you are right and I am wrong, what risk am I taking? My decisions will still lead to a happier life, and I'll be more comfortable in this existence even if there is no afterlife. On the other hand, if I am right and you are wrong, what problems would you be inviting into your life? Why take the risk?"

Louie the Cop's lips came together, and he began to utter the *F* sound. Tomás was sure the curse word was coming, but Louie the Cop just reached out and grabbed the check out of Tomás's hand, turned around, and stomped off. Tomás watched until Louie turned the corner and was out of sight. Tomás turned and walked toward the building. Tomás knew that he was walking toward a door that led to an open field of an unknown future—a future he hoped would be full of dreams, hopes, and goodness. A field he would walk on with Claire. A field they would walk on together with God. But for the moment, the walking he needed to do was to walk upstairs and tell Claire all that he had ever hidden from her.

When Tomás entered the apartment, Claire was in the kitchen busily emptying the dishwasher. Claire always puttered around in the kitchen when she was either angry or nervous. He greeted her, but she didn't respond. That was a clear signal that she was angry, not nervous.

"Querida, I have something to tell you." Claire didn't respond. She just kept moving dishes and putting them away. Tomás stood on the other side of the breakfast counter, looked directly at her, and said, "Querida, I have something to confess to you."

Claire stopped her motion in midpath. She froze in her position with a large dinner plate in her right hand. She put the dinner plate away and looked up to him quizzically. Without saying a word, she walked out of the kitchen and into the sitting room. She sat down in the right corner of the couch and waited to hear what Tomás had to say.

"I went by the Catholic Church. You know I haven't gone to church for many years. I took the sacrament, and I made my confession. I asked the priest how I could make things right with you, and he suggested that I might start with a simple, *I'm sorry.*"

Claire nodded that she agreed an apology was in order. Tomás went on and made a full confession. He explained why Louie the Cop was downstairs, what the true situation had been with his clients, what they asked him to do, and how that disturbed his conscience.

That part of his confession was easy. When he finished giving his recitation of the facts, he turned to explain his new understanding of why he had been so angry with his beloved wife. He explained that he was angry with himself, and that he had been projecting that anger onto her. As he spoke, the tears welled up in his eyes, and he began to cry. His vulnerability moved Claire, and she reached her hands out to him. He leaned over, placed his head against her breast, and allowed her to stroke his hair as he continued to tell her how he felt about the way he had treated her. He described it as a knife cutting through his heart.

She pushed him gently back to a sitting position. She dried his tears with her thumbs. She patted him gently on the thigh and looked deeply into his tortured eyes. "Didn't you think I already knew?"

Claire said the words with such love that Tomás began to cry again—this time with thanks, not shame. She got up, selected a CD, and slid it into the player. She stood before Tomás with her hands extended. He took her hands, and she pulled him up as the song began. It was "Hero" by Enrique Iglesias. They held each other and swayed in something that was more than a hug and yet not quite a dance. Claire whispered the refrain in his ear along with the song, "I can be your hero, baby. I can kiss away the pain. I will stand by you forever. You can take my breath away."

They stopped moving and just stood still, holding each other, bathing each other with their tears of love.

Suddenly, Claire pushed back and asked, "Why don't we call Johnny right now?"

"What do you mean we?" Tomás asked, startled at the shift in mood.

"We're in this thing together, sweetheart. You know, I have a relationship with Johnny too, and he kind of likes me," Claire teased.

"I've got a better idea. Why don't we just go off to someplace like, maybe . . . Tahiti?"

"You don't really mean that?"

"No, I don't. But maybe we should hold off for just a little bit—think these things through a little more."

"What is there to think through? You already told Louie it's a no-go. And you have always told me that what Johnny respects more than anything else is to get information, even if it's bad news, as quickly as possible. I know that he's not going to like this, but you haven't done anything to betray him. You're simply telling him that you can't do something that's been asked of you, and he has always instructed you to do just that."

"Yes, I know, but first I told them I would do it, and now I'll be telling him that I won't."

"Tomás, haven't you always told me that integrity is doing what you say you're going to do, or saying that you're not going to do it? I mean, if I'm to lose my job and you're going to lose your client, all we have left is our integrity. Let's hold on to that. Si?"

"Si!"

"Do you think it's too late to call him right now?" Claire asked.

"Not at all. For him, this is just the shank of the evening."

Tomás reached across Claire and picked up the phone. It rang four times, and then a man with a gruff voice picked up.

"Talk to me," the man said.

"Is Johnny there?"

"Who wants to know?"

"Tomás, Tomás Medina."

"Hold on, I'll see," the man said, dropping the phone and allowing it to clatter against the cabinet. Half a minute went by.

"He says hang up. He'll call you back," the man said, then the phone went dead.

Tomás looked at Claire and gave her a shrug. He hung up the phone. In a few minutes, it rang again.

"Hello, Mr. Attorney Extraordinaire," Johnny said, "sorry about all the cloak-and-dagger stuff, but everybody's getting a little bit jumpy these days. What's on your mind?"

"Johnny, something's come up, and Claire and I would like to come down and speak with you."

"Claire wants to come with you? Isn't that a little strange? You haven't been running around on her, have you?

"No, nothing like that, it's just that, well, it's important. We really do need to speak with you. Are you free?"

"Let me see. I know Claire, and it's okay with me, but some of the boys here haven't met her. Let me ask around," Johnny said as he put his hand over the mouthpiece. A few seconds later, he came back on the phone. "It's okay. How long will it take you to get here?"

"We'll leave right away. At this time of night, it shouldn't take me more than half an hour to get downtown."

"See you in half an hour."

Tomás's BMW stopped and waited for the security barrier at the garage exit to go up. Tomás turned right to head toward FDR Drive and downtown. Neither Tomás nor Claire saw Louie the Cop's car pull out from the curb behind them. They didn't notice the lights come on a few car lengths later. They didn't notice the car park up the block when they pulled up to Mustafa's Coffee House.

It was hard to tell whether the business was open or closed. Tomás and Claire got out of their car, walked to the coffee shop, and knocked on the door. The door opened, words were exchanged, and the door closed. Almost a minute went by; the door opened again and they went in.

Once they were inside, Claire looked around and saw Johnny seated at a table in the back. There were people she had met before, and some she had never seen, including a black man decked out in gold. Tomás took her by the elbow, and they walked toward the back. Seated at the table with Johnny was a large man.

"Claire, I'd like you to meet Mustafa. He is the owner of this coffee shop. Mutafa, this is my wife, Claire."

Mustafa stood up and took Claire's hand in his, lowered his lips, and gently touched them to the back of her hand in an exaggerated show of etiquette.

"A gentleman always lowers his lips to the hand; he never raises a hand to his lips," Mustafa said with a smile. "You seem to be the perfect partner for your husband—as beautiful as he is smart."

Claire reacted with a too-cute giggle, then said in a faked Southern accent, "Well, ah do declah, this man certainly does know how to treat a lady!"

"With that complement, I will take my leave and leave the two of you to your conversation with my good friend, Johnny," Mustafa said.

Tomás and Claire sat down. Johnny shuffled his chair a little bit closer to the table and leaned forward. Tomás and Claire followed suit. The rest of those present went back to their conversations, giving the three their privacy.

"Johnny, we've worked together for a long time, and I am very appreciative of all you have done for me, for us. You always told me you want to hear bad news straight and quickly. I don't know that this is really bad news, and quite frankly I was a little scared to even come talk to you, but Claire convinced me that it was the right thing to do."

"I've always considered Claire to be as smart as she is pretty. No doubt, she was right. No matter what the problem, reasonable people should be able to work things out," Johnny agreed. "What's this all about? Give me the bottom line first, and then go back and explain it if you need to."

"Bottom line: what you asked me to do, about getting inside intel from the police department, I'm not going to be able to do that."

Johnny's face turned serious. He looked Tomás in the eye, and then he glanced at Claire. He was more than a little surprised and flustered that Tomás would share such an intimate secret with someone outside the private circle—especially a woman, especially a wife.

Within the Cartel, one of the unwritten laws was that debts and promises are made and paid between the players. Family is kept out of it. That way, families are protected in case something goes wrong between the players. To involve family in retribution is an act of *infamia* and a sin. The exception to that rule is when family is intentionally involved. The look on Johnny's face clearly called Tomás to offer an explanation.

"Claire and I have both been deeply affected by the God messages. In fact, I stepped into a church and gave confession for the first time since I was a child. As a fellow Catholic, I am sure you understand how big a thing that is. Today Claire told me that she refused to go along with some fraudulent practices at the corporation where she works. It probably means that she will lose her job, but she did what she felt was the right thing to do, in spite of the consequences. When she told me about what happened, I decided that for the sake of our marriage, our future, and my future, I had to meet like with like."

Tomás reached across the table and held Claire's hand. He looked in her eyes for reassurance and found it. Tomás continued, "Earlier this evening the cop that I contacted was waiting in front of our condominium building. He wanted me to hurry up the work that we had talked about. I told him that I wasn't going to go through with it. In addition, I feel that, from what I saw of his reactions, it was a fortunate thing. He looks to me like a loose cannon. He almost lost it and said some things that really weren't in his best interest, so I would be concerned if he started working with you anyway. I'm not going to look for someone else because I just don't want to step over that line. I understand that because I confided this in Claire, you won't be comfortable working with me any longer. What we are really concerned about is whether or not we are in any danger."

Johnny leaned back, rubbed his chin, and said, "Danger?"

Tomás just nodded his head in agreement. Johnny looked up. He looked at the clock and around the room, picked up his coffee cup, and rocked it back and forth to ask for a fresh cup.

"Coffee?" Johnny asked. "They have a good espresso here."

Both Claire and Tomás shook their heads no. Johnny talked a little bit about his family and mentioned a couple of old memories from Miami as they waited for his coffee cup to be refilled. After the waiter came and went, Johnny leaned forward again.

"Tomás, you have disappointed me. It is never a good idea to involve family in these things. But you have done it—now it is water under the bridge, but it cannot be forgotten. You are right—after such a . . . a disappointment, I don't see how we could be comfortable as we were before. You did the right thing coming to talk to me." Johnny looked at Claire kindly, and then back at Tomás. "You have a good wife, and you had better treat her well. I have no reason to believe that you would ever betray me. Everything that has gone on is inside of the lawyer-client privilege and as far as this last request goes, well, no harm, no foul. If this man, this police officer has bad judgment, it is perhaps better that we did not start a relationship."

Johnny sat back in his chair. He glanced up and let out a long, slow sigh. "The messages that you speak of have affected me as well, not enough for me to change what I do, but certainly enough for me to respect your decision. I'm a little hurt that you are concerned about being in danger; after all, I am not a monster. You have done nothing to threaten me directly, and I hope, for your sake, that you never do. Save that, go with God, you have my blessing. Maybe it's time you both got a rest, anyway. Claire, you surely must be thinking about starting a family. Isn't it time for a little bambino?" Johnny said, winking at her.

"Johnny, thank you for giving us this peace of mind; I'm sorry that it's time for us to part ways," Claire said.

Tomás smiled and stood up, offering his hand. Johnny stood up, took his hand, and shook it. They walked to the front door. Tomás opened the door, and all three stepped out onto the sidewalk. Johnny put his hands on his hips and took a deep breath.

"It always seems a bit odd to me to take a deep breath of air in New York City, but anything is better than all the smoke in that coffeehouse," Johnny said. Then turning to the couple, he patted them both on the shoulder and said, "You kids go on about your way. Don't bother to stay in touch, but maybe we'll run into each other in this life—or the next."

With that, Johnny was back inside and the door closed. Tomás and Claire looked at each other. Relieved and happy, they walked to their car.

Louie the Cop recognized Giovanni Pericolo, a.k.a. Johnny, a.k.a. Dockside Johnny as a reputed capo and major narcotics trafficker. He knew immediately that this was Tomás's client. He saw the BMW start up and pull off, but he stayed where he was until it was gone; there was no need to follow it. He didn't need Tomás Medina anymore. He just needed to figure out what kind of intel he could get his hands on that would get his foot in that door.

CHAPTER 16

Nothing is done in private.

—God

Clay McRae woke up on his last day in the United States in a hotel room—an extravagant, plush hotel room, to be sure, but a hotel room just the same. It was a cold reminder that he was prevented from going to his home by the TRO. Since he no longer had access to his accounts, the credit cards in his wallet were truly worth their weight in the gold or the platinum with which they were colored.

He had to be at New York's JFK International Airport by 10:00 PM in order to make his midnight Air France flight. Ten hours after that, he would be in Paris, France. After a two-hour layover, he would be on a three-hour flight to Istanbul, Turkey, and his pot of gold.

The week had mixed reviews. On the downside, the congressional subpoenas, which Max had warned him about, were served on him. Once the committee would learn that RenEn was a shell that Halliron had set up to artificially inflate the price of Halliron stock—Pandora's box would seem like it held jewels by comparison. It was obvious they were getting close.

The stock analysts were dogging him too. There was that wretched reporter from the *Wall Street Journal*; he was joined by the financial reporters from the *New York Times*, Baron's, and the trade journals. There were at least eighteen of them due a callback. It all started when the stock value began to slide because of all the options Clay exercised and dumped on the market; he had covered his tracks by selling them through proxies, but it was just a matter of time before he would be discovered and charged with insider trading.

The week hadn't been all bad. He started with almost a half billion dollars in stock and stock options to sell. Things had gone smoothly, especially with the brokers and bankers. Things always go smoothly when someone is getting a percentage of millions in sales. He was left with four hundred and fifty million.

Clay called room service for breakfast of a fruit compote, eggs Benedict, potatoes Florentine, and Cuban coffee. While he waited for his meal to come up, he started going over the day's tasks in his mind. He had been busy, meticulously busy, during the past week. His first stop this day would be at the brokerage houses to wire out the last of the receipts from the sale of the stocks. He had his passport and visa, and he confirmed his reservation at the Swissotel Istanbul Bosporus.

Breakfast arrived. As he ate, he reflected over what he was leaving behind. His wife had betrayed him. He felt sure it wasn't personal, just a business decision on her part—and a bad decision at that. True, she would get twenty-five, maybe thirty million of their money—she would never get a hand on the real wealth waiting for him in Turkey. At least she kept her word and had not closed the account the credit cards drafted. In a couple of days, it wouldn't matter anyway.

He would miss Max. In an odd way, they had formed a bond although it didn't rise to the level of a friendship. Max was the kind of person that never would have liked McRae. It was Max's secret, his insatiable lust, that caused him to connect with someone that knew him as he was—and didn't judge him.

Claire was a disappointment. He had been red-faced angry with her when she let out with that innuendo that he would need a criminal lawyer. He had hired her, nurtured her career, molded her; he expected her to be one of his loyal minions instead of a rebel. Well, she would get what she deserved. She would be a chief financial officer of a major corporation who resigned within weeks of its complete financial collapse. She'd be lucky to get a job as a church bookkeeper.

Admittedly, Clay knew that Claire had very little to do with the acceleration of the implosion. It was coming to a head anyway. Halliron opened at 62 today, down 88 in the last month and the lowest in four years. After some more newsbreaks, it would even fall into single digits.

McRae was worried about Mustafa and the millions of dollars. Those funds weren't just money; they were his life. People are dispensable; wealth is not. Clay never was comfortable putting all his eggs in one basket, and yet that's exactly what he had done. He thought about Mustafa's procedures and transfers from a hundred different angles. He tried to look at what Mustafa had done as if he was running his own scam, and he couldn't figure an angle. He had taken cautious steps. He had a username and password that allowed him to access account information, but he could not move a penny without the ten-digit account access number. Only he, together with Mustafa, each typing in the five digits that each was privy to, could actually touch the money.

He followed up on each transfer. They never went straight into the Turkish account. He transferred them to an account on a list that had been given to him by Mustafa. Those accounts transferred the funds instantaneously to up to twelve banking stations that deleted the transaction files within twenty-four hours after the transfer. Clay never knew the routes, but within ten minutes, whatever he transferred showed up in Turkey. The deposits had remitter memos indicating that the deposits came from Kazakhstan, Afghanistan, South Africa, Yemen, and half a dozen other countries.

Whether McRae liked it or not, he didn't have many options. He wasn't going to leave the money behind, he couldn't carry it on an international flight, and he didn't want the feds to track it to him. Mustafa had been in business a long time. In his kind of work, a person could get dead, quick. Since Mustafa continued to survive, he must be good for his word. As for all the other leeches, hangers-on, fair-weather friends, idiots, and dolts—good-bye and good riddance.

Clay finished breakfast and threw on some casual clothes. Just not having to put on a suit and tie already seemed liberating. As he waited for the elevator, he selected a Godiva chocolate off the snack trays set out for occupants of the executive suite floors and let it slowly dissolve in his mouth. By the time he walked down the steps at the front of the hotel, a doorman was already holding a taxi door open.

"Where to today, sir?" the doorman asked.

"Broadway and Wall Street," McRae answered.

"Broadway and Wall Street," said the doorman to the cabbie.

The cab eased onto Fifty-ninth Street and headed downtown on Seventh Avenue. McRae noticed people grouping around newsstands and magazine stores. Anything even remotely associated with broadcast networks or newspaper publishing was fast becoming a shrine. People praying stood together in group hugs or in circles holding hands. Counterfeit Rolex watches, fake designer pocketbooks, and pirated DVDs were replaced by prayer rugs, rosaries, menorahs, and plastic reproductions of tablets inscribed with the Ten Commandments. Bookstores displayed Bibles, Qurans, Torahs, and the myriad of books interpreting them.

As the cab crawled through the traffic of Times Square, the world's most famous news ticker circling the building on Forty-second Street between Broadway and Seventh Avenue, read out the messages and letters from God. Since the letters had come out in the newspapers—handwritten letters in papers all over the world—the public mood had become more reverent. The President's speech was also a strong motivator toward a consensus—a consensus that God indeed was the author of the letters. For McRae, all of it was nothing more than an interesting phenomenon, something to understand and file away for future use.

McRae got out of the cab at Broadway and Wall Street. He went into the offices of Pierce-Champion and Associates. Within thirty minutes, he finished the last of his business. All the money he owned or had ever owned was now in the hands of his soon-to-be ex-wife or safe in a numbered account in Turkey. He did keep out a few thousand dollars for spending money until he met Mustafa ten days later in Turkey.

Walking out onto Wall Street, Clay had a fleeting sensation of lightness, a sense of being unburdened. That feeling was quickly followed by the thought of being naked without ready access to his millions. That thought also passed quickly. He hailed a cab to take him to Fiftieth Street and Fifth Avenue. From there, he would have his choice of shopping at Saks, Armani, or Bergdorf

Goodman's. He got out of the cab in the middle of Fifth Avenue, as the taxi could not get over to the curb because of the overflow crowd coming out of St. Patrick's Cathedral. Walking along Fifth Avenue, he passed Tiffany's. He thought, *Have at it, a*s he considered his wife's penchant for yellow diamonds.

He pushed through the crowd and walked into Saks. He picked out two suitcases and a carry-on. He tried on and selected a week's wardrobe and toiletries. He then told the last clerk he dealt with to gather his purchases from the various floors, remove the tags, and pack the suitcases. When the bags were ready, they were loaded into a cab that shuttled him back to his hotel.

The bags were put in the security room at Clay's request. Clay sat in the lobby and enjoyed a cold St. Pauli Girl beer. He decided to skip lunch because he was planning a special dinner. Then he went to his room to give Max a call.

"Hello."

"Hello, Max."

"Clay, Shalom."

"Shalom? Are you buying into all this craziness?" McRae asked.

"Well, my friend, I am. You know me, Clay. I try to do the right thing, but for, well, you know—a weakness of the flesh and all."

"How are things?" Clay asked.

"Clay, I can't tell you anything has loosened up. In fact, things are actually getting tighter. I . . ."

"It's okay, Max," Clay butted in. "Don't worry about it anymore; things are going in a different direction."

"Are you sure? I'm still working with a few favors I'm trying to call in."

"Yes, I'm sure. Matter of fact, some opportunities opened up in the Mideast, and I'm flying out to do some fact-finding."

"Good, makes my heart glad. I wish you should find the facts you're looking for. I'm going to see the Saudis on a junket and then vacation with my cousin in Tel Aviv for a week or so. My office will have my itinerary and contact information. Maybe you could meet me. The Saudis treat you like a sultan. Have you ever heard of a sultan's harem?"

"Maybe so, Max, maybe so. I'm going to have a special treat for dinner. Would you like to join me?"

"Where are you going? Let me guess. Del Monaco's? The Palm? The Four Seasons?"

"No, and it even surprises me. What I really feel like eating on my last night in New York is a corned beef and pastrami sandwich from the On-Broadway Delicatessen."

"That's not fair, Clay. Now you're torturing me."

"So come on."

"Can't do it. I've got a fundraiser, but you enjoy."

"Okay, Max."

"Talk to you soon."

"Good-bye . . . Max," McRae said, slowly lowering the phone and letting it drop the last inch into its cradle.

Next, Clay called Mustafa and told him he would drop by around 8:00 PM to say good-bye. It was 4:00 PM. Clay called downstairs and arranged for a 5:30 checkout and a wake-up call for 5:00 PM. Then Clay rolled over and took a nap.

The On-Broadway Delicatessen may very well hold the title of New York's preeminent delicatessen. The sandwiches at On-Broadway are so thick that if you ask for an extra order of bread, they can be split in half and still yield two sandwiches that would be considered gigantic just about anywhere outside New York. The walls of the deli are covered with signed pictures of the guys and dolls of Broadway together with shelves full of jars of pickled tomatoes and cans of sauerkraut.

McRae took a seat by the plate-glass storefront looking out onto Broadway. He ordered a corned beef and pastrami combo, a Dr. Brown's cream soda, and a cube of noodle kugel for dessert. The waiter brought over a pot of kosher half-dill and garlic-dill pickles and an appetizer tray full of coleslaw, beets, and marinated garbanzo beans to nosh on while he waited. A waitress delivered his cream soda. Clay absentmindedly fingered the condensation on the side of the glass as he watched people in various stages of hurry pass by.

As he watched the different sizes and shapes of the people, he realized that he always felt as if he were made from a different cloth, as if he were an alien, and all these people were there solely for his curiosity. His sandwich arrived. He dismissed his reflective thinking to the pile of unneeded and unimportant slots located somewhere in the far reaches of his cerebral cortex.

Forty-two minutes later, McRae put down his fork, leaving two thirds of his noodle kugel on the plate. He sucked bubbles and the last drops of his cream soda through the straw in his fountain glass. He was able to lift a napkin to his lips before allowing a stifled belch to escape and to provide some small relief to his rather full gut. He called the bellman of his hotel, who, being previously tipped, retrieved his bags from security, loaded them into a taxi, and dispatched the taxi to pick Clay up.

Clay paid his bill with a larger-than-normal tip and stood up, taking a quick step back to avoid losing his balance. By the time he stepped out into the brisk night air, his cab was pulling up.

"Mr. McRae?" the cabbie shouted through the passenger window.

"Here!" said McRae, stepping toward the cab and getting in. "Mustafa's Coffee House off Bleecker Street and Fourth, in the village."

"Yes, sir," said the cabbie, flipping down the flag and pulling off. When McRae arrived at Mustafa's, he told the cabbie to wait and keep the meter running. Clay went inside and saw Mustafa seated at a table in the back with some well-dressed men who appeared to be of Mediterranean or Latin descent. There was also a young black man seated at a front table. His hip-hop clothing and the gaudy gold-nugget ring on his right index finger drew Clay's attention as Clay walked past him to the table in the back. Clay nodded to the other men and addressed Mustafa. "May I speak to you for a moment?"

"Of course, of course, my good friend." Then turning to the others at the table, Mustafa said, "Please excuse me for a moment—a private matter."

The others grunted their approval. Mustafa got up with a bit of a struggle and walked toward the front door with McRae.

"Is everything in order? Do you have all the contact information you need?" Mustafa asked with genuine concern.

"Yes, I believe so. All my travel documents are in this pouch, and I have your phone numbers here as well as your family's numbers in Turkey. I also have Achmed's home phone and cell phone numbers. I just got an international cell phone. Here's the number. I am staying at the Swissotel Bosporus."

"An excellent choice," Mustafa agreed.

"I will look forward to your arrival. After we visit the bank, I'll buy you the most lavish night you've ever seen."

"Thank you, but I am a modest man, and after all I should buy you dinner. It's not every day ninety million dollars drops in one's pocket."

"Well, we'll just have to fight over the check, I guess," said McRae, extending his hand.

"That we will. Travel safely," Mustafa replied.

Clay McRae waived good-bye and reentered his waiting cab to head off to the airport.

*   *   *

As McRae's taxi entered the Brooklyn Battery Tunnel, Officer Craig Thompson pulled his patrol car into the Twenty-ninth Precinct parking lot. He parked in car 5151's designated spot and shut down the onboard computer, wiping out the day's username and password.

Louie the Cop was unusually quiet throughout the procedure. "So, Louie, is everything okay?" said Thompson as the two of them went through the end-of-shift mandatory search for any contraband or other items left behind by transported persons.

"Oh, yeah, everything's okay. I'm just a little tired," said Louie the Cop.

"You sure?"

"I'm sure."

"I don't know. You're not acting like you. You're almost being pleasant."

They walked inside, filed their paperwork, and went downstairs. They walked through the shift briefing room and past C-Com, the communications center. Sergeant Sam Shómogee was operating the dispatch console alone because of the shift change.

"Sergeant Sam," shouted Louie the Cop, knocking on the glass.

Sam turned around and gave Louie the Cop a broad smile and a thumbs-up sign. Louie the Cop returned the hand signal.

"You two go back awhile?" Thompson asked.

"All the way back to the academy. Would you believe that bald-headed tub is actually younger than me? We were partners for a while. Then he started putting on weight so they pulled him off patrol, gave him a promotion and a raise, and stuck him in communications. If it was me, they would've suspended me until I took off the poundage."

Louie left out the part about Sergeant Sam studying for and getting masters degrees in communications and computers while they had been on the road. After the small boost in Louie the Cop's mood, he soon fell back into silence. They walked into the locker room.

Craig's locker was on the same row and seven lockers down from Louie's. Both took their service weapons off and locked them in the inside lockboxes. As Louie took off his utility belt, he held it for a minute and looked at the dull, frayed leather. As his eyes darted from pockmark to scratch, to rough edge, to rusted snap, he began to see a reflection of his miserable life—unmaintained, uncared for, and rotting away.

At that moment, an insight came to him. It might have been an epiphany, but Louie the Cop was just not capable of thinking at that level of profundity. He realized that very few of his regrets in life came from making wrong decisions or bad choices. His regrets ran far deeper and were far more disabling. His regrets came from not deciding at all, from refusing to take risks.

He had seen the dumb choices other people made, and for fear of being dumb, he had made few choices at all. He never noticed the wisdoms and creativity around him because he was focused on the mistakes. It was through the mistakes of others that he defined his own self-worth. That's why he was so easily hypnotized when someone like Tomás Medina came along.

He thought, *I'm tired of this shit, and I'm not going to take it anymore. I don't want to be Louie the Cop anymore. I want to be Mr. Louis Gibran. I want to drive a car and dress in a way that gives me respect. I'm going to make somethin' happen. After all, didn't one of those messages tell me that actions have consequences? Well, if I don't do nothing, ain't nothin' going to happen.*

"Hey, can I borrow your polish kit?" Louie the Cop asked Thompson.

"Uh? What?'" Thompson yelped, "Yeah, sure. It's in here somewhere. Oh, here it is. You'll want to take off your pants before you start using it so you don't soil them."

"Thank you, Mother."

"You don't have to be sarcastic. Okay, I'm outa here. Glad to see you're finally going to do something about that ratty belt. See you tomorrow."

Thompson was wrong on both counts.

Louie the Cop pretended to be polishing his belt until the locker room was empty. He stowed his gear, changed into his civvies, went to make two cups of coffee, and walked over to the glass door of C-Com. He knocked with his elbow; Sergeant Sam turned, then buzzed him in.

"Hey, Shamaygay," Louie the Cop said, mispronouncing Shómogee's name.

"Hi, Louie, haven't talked to you in a while. What's up?" said Sergeant Sam, accepting one of the coffees.

"Oh, nothing much—another day older and closer to death. No, I was just leaving and you looked kind of lonely in here, and yeah, we haven't talked for a long time, so I thought I'd stop in for a minute and chat."

"With sixteen squad cars, an old lady worried about her cat stuck in the ceiling, two break-ins, and a bunch of kids raining popcorn from the balcony of the Bijou theater, I don't have all that much time for lonely, but I do appreciate the go-juice," said Sergeant Sam, lifting his coffee cup and winking thanks to Louie the Cop.

"You're more than welcome," said Louie the Cop, returning the gesture. "So how's the desk thing going?"

"It's a living. I've got two kids at City University now. I love them to death, but I'll sure be glad when they graduate and get off my payroll. Maybe then, I can start saving. We've both got what . . . almost thirty years in?"

"Twenty-nine and a half to be exact. Yeah, I hear you. I don't think I could make it on retirement, and I only have to worry about me. I've been thinking of getting into some additional work," said Louie the Cop.

"Like what?"

"I dunno—something. Well, I got to get clear back to Queens. Think I'll move along. You want me to cover for you so you can go get rid of that coffee?"

"Yeah, I could use taking a leak. Can you handle a 9-1-1 call?"

"Yes, Sergeant, we've all had the basics," said Louie the Cop with a pretend salute.

Sergeant Sam pushed himself up out of the chair and headed for the door. As soon as Sergeant Sam left, Louie the Cop was moving toward the clipboard with the printout of the week's usernames and passwords. He removed it from the nail it was hanging on, took off the cover sheet, slapped the printout onto the copier, and punched the button for one copy. The original was back on the clipboard, and Louie the Cop was stuffing the folded copy into his shirt pocket as Sergeant Sam rounded the corner. Louie the Cop buzzed him in and went to leave by the same open door.

"Everything come out okay?" Louie the Cop asked.

"Yeah, just fine. Thanks for the coffee," said Sergeant Sam.

"You betcha."

With that, Louie the Cop was out the door. As the door's hydraulic arm pulled it shut, Louie looked back to wave to Sergeant Sam. He noticed that Sam was looking at something. Louie followed Sam's eyes to the clipboard, which was still swinging on its nail. He looked back at Sam, and their eyes locked. Louie got a sick feeling in his gut, then turned and left. As he went up the stairs, he was already rationalizing: *So what if he looks at it? There's nothing missing. The cover page! Did I put it back on the right way—yeah, I did. I know I did.*

Louie left the precinct house and walked to Lexington to get a train downtown. As he walked, he felt his heart pounding. He didn't know if it was from walking fast because of what he just left, or where he was going.

Louie the Cop came up from the underground and took a cab to Bleecker and Fourth. He walked down the street and turned the handle on the door to Mustafa's Coffee House, but it was locked. The lights were on, and there were people inside, so he knocked on the door. After a minute or so, he saw someone peer out from the store window. After a few more seconds, the door opened slightly. A swarthy man peered out.

"Can I help you?"

"Yes, I'm looking for Giovanni Pericolo."

"I don't know anybody by that name."

"Could you ask for him and tell him that a friend of Tomás Medina is asking?"

The door closed. Louie the Cop stood by, put his hands in his pockets, and took a deep breath. While he was waiting, a squad car slowly cruised by and pulled over in front of a magazine shop about fifty yards down the street. Louie the Cop's palms got clammy as he watched it. The driver got out, leaving his partner in the car, looked over toward Louie, and walked into the shop. Louie wiped his hands on his slacks. There wasn't anything out of the ordinary about seeing a squad car on a street in New York City, but still . . . .

About a minute later, the coffeehouse door opened, and the swarthy man motioned for Louie the Cop to come in. As Louie stepped inside, the door was locked behind him.

In the back corner, he saw a few men at a round table. As his eyes adjusted, the swarthy man motioned for him to come along, and he followed the man into the back corner. When he got closer to the table, he noticed that the man he'd previously recognized as Giovanni Pericolo was seated with a couple of men on either side. The swarthy man returned to his post as lookout.

There was a large man, Mustafa, standing in front of and slightly to the right of the table. As Louie the Cop stood there, Gee-spot moved behind him and to his left. Nobody said anything to him.

"Hello, my name is Louis Gibran. I'm a New York City police officer. I'm off duty, and I am here because we have a mutual friend by the name of Tomás Medina. I wanted to talk to you about that."

Johnny looked up at him, as if he were looking into Louie's mind, and didn't say anything for a long second. Then Johnny spoke quietly and slowly, measuring his words. "Before I talk to you about some man that you've identified as Tomás Medina, and I'm not at all sure who that is, I would like to make sure that our conversation is a private one. Are you wearing a wire or any other surveillance device?

"No, I'm not."

"I'm sure you wouldn't mind if we verified that?"

"No, not at all. Please, please," Louie the Cop said as he raised his hands and submitted to a frisk.

Gee-spot walked up to him and started patting him down. The first thing Louie the Cop noticed was the large gold-nugget ring on his right index finger. Gee-spot patted his sides, reached inside his shirt, pulled out everything in his pockets, and took the gun that was in his ankle holster.

Gee-spot turned to Johnny and said, "He's clean. He had this pistol in an ankle holster." The gang-banger put Louie the Cop's snub-nosed, .38-caliber revolver on the table in front of Johnny.

"As I said, I'm a New York City police officer. We're required to carry an off-duty gun, so that should be no surprise."

"No, it's no surprise, but you can understand it's important that it not be in your possession during our conversation."

"I understand."

"Now, you said that you knew somebody named Tomás Medina and you wanted to speak to me. About what is it that you wish to speak to me?"

"Can we speak in private?" Louie the Cop asked.

"No, these men are my associates. Anything that you say to me you can say in front of them. If you have something to say, go ahead and say it. If not, have a very nice evening."

Louie the Cop looked around and saw that the large man had a bulge under his left armpit, indicating he was carrying a shoulder holster. The black gang-banger behind him was much less subtle.

He had an automatic handgun slipped into his waist. It didn't appear that Johnny was armed, but one can never tell.

"Tomás Medina approached me and told me that he had some clients who were looking to purchase inside intel from the police department, especially information about where our patrol cars would be and at what time, so that movements could be made without detection."

Louie the Cop stopped there and waited for a response. He watched the men pass looks between them, but there were no words forthcoming, so he continued, "When he contacted me, he offered me a price, and I agreed that I would do work for him. Then he . . . he came to me and told me that because of these God messages, he had decided not to go through with it. I'm not sure exactly what went on; but I was ready, willing, and able to fulfill my obligations under our agreement, and I still am. As good faith, I have brought something that ought to stimulate your interest in what I have to offer."

"What is it that you have brought? By the way, you can call me Johnny."

"Patrol cars in New York City now have onboard computers that are tied into a communications network. Once you log into the network, you can get the assignments and the positions of all the patrol cars in New York. I have a list of this week's usernames and passwords. With this information, you ought to be set."

"You have this paperwork with you?" Johnny queried.

"Yes, I do."

Louie the Cop withdrew the folded paper from his shirt pocket and began to unfold it. Before he could finish unfolding the paper and handing it over to Johnny, the swarthy man from the front the door walked up quickly to Johnny's side and began whispering in his ear. The man then backed away from Johnny. Johnny immediately got up and tapped the men on his left and his right and motioned for them to get up. He looked at Louie the Cop.

"This concludes our business. I'm afraid we won't be seeing each other again."

With that, Johnny and the two men stepped into the back room and out the fire exit. Louie the Cop looked toward the front of the store to see what was going on. What he saw was the flash of Gee-spot's gold-nugget ring as it moved toward the gun in his waist.

Louie quickly turned to his right and shoved his hand under Mustafa's coat, grabbing the gun in the shoulder holster. That movement temporarily saved Louie's life. The bullet that came out of Gee-spot's Beretta ricocheted off Louie's fourth rib and continued on to a spot two inches above Mustafa's diaphragm, nicking an artery and causing his lung to immediately collapse. As Mustafa grasped his chest with his right hand, Louie pulled the pistol from under Mustafa's left armpit and turned around pointing the 9 mm toward Gee-spot. Before he could level the pistol, Gee-spot squeezed off another round, exploding into Louie the Cop's voice box. The wound caused Louie's hand to jerk, firing the gun and hitting Gee-spot in the knee.

Gee-spot staggered back and tripped over a fallen chair. The back of his neck came down on the side of the seat of a turned-over chair, breaking his spinal column at the base of the neck, severing his spinal cord and immediately paralyzing him from the neck down.

It took Louie the Cop three-point-four minutes to drown from the blood pouring into his lungs. Mustafa tried to support himself on the table, but as the blood drained from his circulatory system, he gulped for air, and his vision faded.

*   *   *

As Mustafa's limp body fell to the floor, the wheels of Air France flight number 2961, carrying Clay McRae to Turkey, lifted off the tarmac at John F. Kennedy International Airport. As the flight leveled off, McRae relaxed into the quiet boredom of the trans-Atlantic flight.

Chapter 17

If you seek happiness, contribute to others.

—God

Claire opened one eye. The other eye was sunken into the luxurious goose-down pillow of the queen-sized bed she and Tomás shared. Tomás had chosen the queen over a king; he had said that he didn't want too much room between them. She looked over at the digital clock on the black marble-topped night table—10:37 AM. She smiled and stretched languidly like a tiger cub. She rolled over on her back clutching the six-hundred-count cream-colored Egyptian sateen cotton sheet up around her neck. She let out a lazy yawn and stretched her legs again, pulling back on her heels and pointing her toes toward the end of the bed until they trembled. Then she released the tension and let her feet fall into the pillow-top mattress as she felt an invigorating wave of relaxation flow through her.

She thought, *Does it get any better than this?* It was the first day of the third week since she told Clay McRae off and the tenth day of her unemployment. She giggled. It felt so good to be free.

Things were working out just fine. Going to the feds first was one of the best decisions she had ever made. Her value to them in unraveling all the corporate connections and cooked books earned her complete immunity. Even more than that, she was emerging in the public perception as a whistle-blower and a hero. Clay's mysterious departure meant there would be no false explanations and fraudulent counteraccusations for her to deal with. He unknowingly made life very easy for her. The feds even reviewed the sale of her stock and stock options in Halliron. They gave her a preliminary ruling that the sales were not the product of insider trading, and she would be allowed to keep all of the proceeds.

She'd had two hundred fifty thousand shares of Halliron stock under her control from her benefits packages and annual bonuses. When she decided not to sign off on any more doctored accounting documents and just say *no* to Clay McRae, she resolved not to have anything he could use as leverage, nothing he could hold over her head. So she decided to sell her stock.

Since her motive was to divest herself of the stock in order to avoid a conflict of interest, the sale was not the result of insider information. Because of that, the feds approved the sale. The stock was selling then for 156, resulting in a sale of a cool thirty-nine million. Even after taking off for taxes and commissions, it would still be a chunk of change.

She still hadn't told Tomás.

It was such a fun feeling, almost as if they were back in Miami just getting started again. His client roster had shrunk quickly after their meeting with Johnny. He had more time and had been so attentive lately. She thought of what the expression on his face would be when she told him about the money. She giggled again.

"Well, time to motivate," she said to herself, slipping from under the warm covers and into a burgundy and beige robe. She walked into the kitchen sucking up the silence around her.

She sat down with a fresh cup of coffee. Leaning back, she put her feet up on Tomás's chair and looked out through the plate glass. The day was overcast. It looked like it would snow, but that wouldn't come for at least another month. Claire could tell there was a chill in the air. She felt warm and secure. Even better, she didn't have a single thing she had to do.

She heard the front door opening. It could only be Tomás. She stayed where she was, waiting to hear his greeting.

"Querida, I'm home," Tomás called out.

"I'm at the dining table, honey."

Tomás took off his overcoat and suit jacket, hung on the coat tree in the foyer, stopped in the powder room to freshen up, then made his way to the dining room.

"What are you doing home so early? Playing hooky?" Claire chided.

"I am just a little sheep that has lost my way—*baaa, baaa,*" Tomás kidded back, and then replied, "I'm done for the day. I think I've got eight clients left, and nobody is knocking down the door to hire me."

"So does that mean I've got you for the whole afternoon?"

"Yes, it does."

"Fantastico. Let's catch a matinee. We can go stand in line at the extra tickets booth in Times Square and go to whichever show we can," Claire said.

"Si, and aren't you becoming the woman of leisure. Claire, before we think about that, we have to talk about something."

Tomás's tone was serious. Claire put her coffee down and lowered her feet. She turned toward Tomás with her listening ears on.

"Yes, honey—what is it? Is it anything bad?"

"No, but we need to figure out what we're going to do about this place, about where we live. I'm not saying we're poor. We ought to wind up with some change in our pocket after selling this place and getting a home in Queens or out on the Island. I'm going to need to get some kind of a job—we're going to need some income—we can't just live on savings. I talked to the Manhattan DA today . . ."

"*The* DA, not an assistant but *the* DA?" Claire asked. She was trying to keep her voice serious. She was also trying to keep the smile off her face. She figured she would let him stew for just a minute or two more.

"Yes, *the* DA. I approached him about a job, and he told me they were looking for a training officer to take charge of teaching all the new DAs trial techniques and investigation. He said I would also get a crack at some major high-profile cases—you know, the ones I love."

"Tomás, when you're happy—I'm happy. Are you going to take it?"

"It's really tempting. He said he could pay between ninety and a hundred thousand. We couldn't live on that in Manhattan, especially if we want to start a family. I don't know how we would afford it."

"I do," said Claire.

There are two words that can adequately describe the expression on each of their faces at that moment. For Claire, the word would be impish—for Tomás, quizzical.

"Okay, I'll bite. How?" he asked.

"You know those stock options and stock I got from Halliron?"

"Yeah, they're not worth much now."

"Well . . . when I decided I was going to confront McRae, I didn't want to have anything that might have been used against me," Claire spoke excruciatingly slowly; and then after pausing, she continued, "So I sold them."

Tomás was beginning to feel he was the butt of a joke—a wonderful, awesome joke; a joke he still didn't quite understand.

"You sold them before . . . ?"

Claire just nodded her head up and down and grinned.

"Before the collapse—for how much?"

"Oh, it averaged out to about $156 per share."

"And how many shares?"

Claire held up two fingers then five fingers then the zero sign and another zero and another zero and another zero. She was holding the other hand to her mouth, trying to hold the laughter in.

"Twenty-five thousand shares?" ventured Tomás, already excited with that number.

Claire shook her head emphatically no. Then held up her fingers again. This time she emphasized the final zero.

"Two hundred fifty thousand? You . . . you . . . you're kidding!" Tomás almost screamed, as his eyes opened so wide they almost took over his forehead.

Claire shook her head to say, "I'm not kidding." The laughter began to sneak out past her fingers.

"Two hundred fifty thousand! That . . . that," said Tomás, calculating on his fingers, "that's over thirty, maybe thirty-three million."

By now, Claire was in a full belly laugh. The expression on Tomás's face—totally dumbfounded—was priceless. It was worth every minute, every second she had waited to tell him.

"Thirty-nine million," she spat out between the laughter.

"Thirty-nine million!" he repeated.

"Well, you have to take out for taxes and commissions," she said, continuing to sputter.

"Take out for taxes and commissions," he said through his own laughter.

Tomás couldn't take anymore. He fell on the couch. Claire jumped on top of him. They tried to kiss but were laughing so hard they clinked teeth, and that made them laugh even more. The laughs gradually gave way to an occasional guffaw mixed in with groans and moans from the sidesplitting workout they gave their bellies. Finally, they got their breath.

"So now do you think you can afford to take that DA's job?" asked Claire innocently.

"Don't start, I can't take any more laughing. Yeah, I suppose I can. And what about you, Mrs. Get-out-of-bed-at-noon? Are you just going to sit around, eat chocolates, and get fat?"

"Actually it was 10:37 AM, not noon," she said with a cutesy pout.

"Big difference," he said, rolling his eyes.

"I saw a flyer looking for a bookkeeper. It's that church down the block—you know the one; it has the big cross on the side of the building. I think I'd like to do that, do some good. At least for a little while, at least until . . ."

"Until what?"

"Until I am carrying a big black-haired, brown-eyed Latino baby that my husband's going to give me."

"Maybe it will have your gringo yellow hair and blue eyes."

"As long as he . . . or she has your passion!" she said seductively.

"I think I can oblige you."

"When, big talker?"

"How does now sound?"

"I guess we won't be making the matinee, huh?"

*   *   *

Tomás Medina stood at the bottom of the concrete steps leading up to the Gothic columns of the Justice Building. Lower Manhattan still had the fresh feeling of the early morning, and streams of commuters were snaking out of the subway tunnels and buses to stream along sidewalks and across intersections to get to that suite or office or cubicle or desk or broom closet from where they made their contributions to the systems of humanity.

Tomás looked up the mountain of steps with a reverence that bordered on naïveté. He remembered his first day of work at the state attorney's office in Miami so many years ago. The weight of "mob lawyer" was off his shoulders. The heaviness of not being the master of his own destiny had been lifted. He was, you might say, enlightened.

"It feels like déjà vu, all over again," he muttered to himself, quoting Yogi Berra. He took another moment or two taking in the sounds, smells, and feelings of the moment. Then with legs that were suddenly twenty-five years old again, he took the daunting row of steps two at a time.

As Tomás reveled both in past glory and anticipation, halfway across Manhattan, Claire felt trepidation. Her right foot gingerly stepped up onto the first step of the five steps leading to the school entrance of the First Baptist Church of Harlem.

Am I doing the right thing? Am I in the right place? What will they think of me—Ms. Rich Bitch coming to volunteer at a black church? Oh, I don't know if I should. Her thoughts were competing for space in her mind.

Suddenly she found herself at the stoop's landing, and the door opened. Two fourth-grade girls pushed the door open. They were wearing white blouses under their blue pinstripe uniforms.

"Oh, excuse me, ma'am," said one of the girls as she held the door open for Claire. Claire had no choice but to step into a small lobby, perhaps fifteen feet square. The floor was a dark brown industrial Terrazzo, and the walls were painted those beige and green colors found on thousands of school walls. To her left was a gymnasium with basketball goals and two or three groups of students doing some sort of physical education. To her right were what appeared to be administrative offices. There was a small trophy case and a picture of the Reverend Martin Luther King Jr.

Her attention was drawn to the framed photo of Dr. King. This particular picture was taken in Dr. King's office from the side of his desk. It showed him standing behind his desk, chair pushed back, holding and reading some papers in his hand, perhaps his next speech. Behind him in the picture, hanging on the wall to his right, was a portrait of Mahatma Gandhi, Dr. King's hero and role model. Claire moved toward the picture and touched the bottom of the frame. She felt better and less anxious. She knew that whoever hung *this* picture was a person of deep understanding.

"Uh, excuse me, may I help you?" the voice behind her said.

Claire pulled her hand back instinctively. She turned around. In front of her was a middle-aged black woman with an athletic build. She had short hair and dark framed glasses. She was wearing a black-belted dress with white accents. The look on her face was serious but not quite stern.

"Oh, I'm sorry, I, uh, uh, was coming up the steps, and two girls were, uh, coming out. They held the door open, so I, uh, stepped in and . . ." Claire stammered, not knowing if she had needed to ring the bell or otherwise gain permission to enter the building.

"You're just fine, dear. May I help you?"

"Well, yes, I suppose so. I live down the street, and I have some extra time on my hands—my husband and I want to start a family—and well, I know a little bit about bookkeeping, and I don't have to work right now . . ."

The other woman, whose face had been curled into a question mark, suddenly smiled and said, "Sweetheart, do I hear the word *volunteer* in that mess of words coming out of your mouth?"

"Yes, ma'am," said Claire, lowering her eyes for a moment and feeling the slight warmth of a blush come to her cheeks.

"Well, don't be shy now. My name's Rosalyn Bailey. I'm the assistant principal of the elementary school," she said.

Rosalyn stepped forward and put a finger gently under Claire's chin, lifting her face until they made eye contact. "Sometimes I think it's a blessing God made my complexion so dark that other people can't see a blush like that quite so easily."

Claire giggled.

Rosalyn went on, "I don't know who you are, where you come from, or what you've done; but I do know that God put you in His lobby, and you say you want to help us do God's work. That's good enough for me. Pastor Abrahms will sit with you, and you two can figure out where you can help best. Meanwhile, I've got a few minutes; let me give you a tour."

Rosalyn took Claire's hand and started walking with her through the gymnasium. Rosalyn directed Claire's attention to the various points of interest like the restrooms, kitchen, teachers' lounge, and library. She also launched into a brief history of the church and school. Her monologue was often interrupted by the

giving of greetings, admonitions, and words of encouragement to
the students she passed.

Claire was more than impressed; she was wowed by what she
saw. She expected to see her stereotype of an inner-city school—a
place of anger and desperation. Instead, she saw a place of
respect and love. She was chagrined at the realization of her own
prejudice.

As they walked past the classrooms, they stopped at open doors
and looked in. For the most part, they exchanged polite nods with
teachers and moved on. They came to the second-grade classroom
and looked in as usual. Lori Blount was at the blackboard and
looked out to them. They nodded at each other politely, but
somehow their eyes locked for enough of a moment to make it
significant. Claire saw something in Lori's eyes that she had seen
in her mother's eyes. It was a profound sadness that transcends
body language, voice tone, or even a laugh.

A tug on her hand broke Claire away, and she continued
down the hall. After a few more highlights, they came to a door;
the plaque on the side of the door simply read Pastor. Rosalyn
opened the door. There was a short walkway between two desks
leading to another door that was half open. Claire could see the
front half of the side of the desk in the inner office.

"Come on," said Rosalyn, pulling Claire in. Rosalyn nodded
to the secretary on the right and pointed to the left desk, which
was scattered with pictures of young men and women. "This is
my desk, and those are some of my old students. I love to see how
they grow up," she said, and then with a touch of sadness, added,
"most of the time."

Rosalyn stopped at the inner door and gave a slight tap on the
glass with a knuckle. A grunt came from inside. She pushed the

door open. Pastor Abrahms had his back to the door, looking over some paper with columns that Claire immediately recognized as a budget or pro forma.

"Excuse me, Pastor," said Rosalyn, but when the pastor didn't move, she stopped for a moment and coughed, then continued, "this is Claire Medina."

Once Pastor Abrahms realized there was someone else in the room, he swiveled in his cracked old brown leather chair and looked up. "Oh, excuse me," said the pastor, reorienting himself and standing up. He stretched out a hand, "Please forgive me. I was straining to understand this budget. I'm afraid I'm not very good with numbers."

As he reached his full height, Claire looked up at him and accepted his catcher's mitt of a hand. His size was intimidating, but there was such humility and kindness radiating from him that she immediately felt at ease.

"I'm sorry, Rosalyn. Who did you say this is?"

"Claire, Claire Medina. She would like to volunteer."

Pastor Abrahms looked back and forth between the two women and then broke into a big grin. "Well, isn't that wonderful? For a moment, I thought you might be the new inspector from the Board of Education," everyone chuckled, and he continued, "and what kind of volunteer work were you contemplating?"

Claire responded, "Well, I am a CPA, and I was wondering if I can help with any bookkeeping or something."

Pastor Abrahms looked toward heaven and mouthed a silent thank-you. He then motioned to the chair in front of his desk. "Please sit down," he offered.

"Well, I'll leave you two to chat," Rosalyn said.

"Thank you, Rosalyn. Thank you," said the pastor, acknowledging Rosalyn for her contribution. Rosalyn began to close the door and leave but then pushed it open again.

"Oh, Doctor Abrahms, I almost forgot. Rabbi Smulowitz called and said that he would be able to make a commitment on behalf of his synagogue to contribute the soundstage and five hundred folding chairs. And, glory be, we received the permit to close down 112th Street for the day. The mayor included a personal letter saying that he would attend. Mr. Habib Rashid has signed on to provide food out of that miracle at Sandy's Deli. When you first came up with this idea, I thought it was going to be impossible, but it seems you must think in stride with the Almighty because everything is just becoming so easy, and more people are signing up to help than we can even handle. It's going to be one heaven of a party."

"Thank you, Rosalyn. Thank you for all you do. I don't know what I'd do without you," Pastor Abrahms said, knowingly nodding and then toward Claire. "We decided to have a celebration for God, inasmuch as there have been all of these messages, you know. All of the communities are participating; the Jews, the Muslims, the Catholics, the Christians, the Buddhists, Whites, Blacks, Browns, and Yellows. We have a Hindu group that will perform some dances on the stage and even some Hare Krishnas that will lead the street in chanting. We have rap groups, gospel groups, even some country western. Lord have mercy, I never expected it to grow to this size. Rosalyn . . ."

The pastor looked up at the closed door. Evidently, Rosalyn could see that it was time for the pastor and Claire to speak and had gently taken her leave. As the pastor was speaking, Claire had sat down. She looked around the office. The walls were bookshelves full to overflowing, and the little wall space that remained was stark, except for two photographs. One was a picture of a younger version of the pastor with Dr. King. The other was a famous picture from the civil rights movement years. The picture showed police officers using fire hoses and barking German shepherds on Black demonstrators. On the pastor's desk were a mountain of papers and files and a single picture of his family.

Now that they were alone, Dr. Abrahms settled into his chair and rested his head against that dark brown spot that had pillowed his head for years. "So what brings you to our little corner of the universe?" asked Pastor Abrahms.

The large man in front of her seemed to be a vacuum that sucked the words out of Claire. For some reason, she wanted to share it all. She started with her upbringing and her struggles with her father and went on to tell of her romance with Tomás and how they came to live in New York. She revealed her part in the downfall of Halliron and her struggles with finding her inner strength. She talked about her therapy, the lessons she learned there, how she came to believe that God creates a perfect symmetry in life, and that it was her job in partnership with the Divine to find where she could contribute. She talked on and on. It seemed as if Pastor Abrahms didn't have another thing to do; it was as if he had all the time in the world. Finally she was all talked out. Pastor Abrahms changed his position and leaned forward, putting his elbows on the desk.

"Mrs. Medina, or may I call you Claire?"

"Please, Claire would be fine."

"Claire, you come to us at a very special time. We need your talents. Now that God has made his presence known in such an undeniable way, the entire faith community is undergoing a transformation. We don't know exactly where we're going and how we're going to get there, but it's clear that changes are happening. Our attendance is up so many hundreds of percent that we can't even keep track of it anymore. On one hand, we need more funds to attend to the needs of our community, and on the other hand, there are more and more people who are willing to give those funds. We have to find out how to manage this in a responsible way, in a conscientious way, in a way that is in keeping with the messages that God has sent us. That is why it seems to be such a heavenly gift that you come to us."

Claire felt the good goose bumps come back. She rubbed her arms and smiled.

Pastor Abrahms continued, "Your expertise will help us put together the paperwork that we need to take advantage of all the offerings that are out there. We want to provide services to our community and our neighborhood—actually, in this new setting— to the very world itself. You might have come here thinking all we needed was some bookkeeping, but we can put you to much greater use. That is, if you're willing. Hmm, I suppose the deacons will ask me for your references, and if I've checked up on you before we turn our books over to you."

Claire's eyes teared up. She was moved by the opportunity to be of such service. She had spent so much time creating wealth for the greedy that the idea of creating wealth for the needy touched her deeply. She was a little concerned about the time commitment and asked about that. Dr. Abrahms assured her that she could work as much or as little as she wanted. The church and school were sufficiently computerized to allow her to do much of the work at her home should she want to take advantage of that.

"When can I start?" Claire asked.

"Will tomorrow morning be too soon? Don't worry. I'll take care of the deacons. Please think about this over the evening and make sure that this is a commitment you want to make."

"Dr. Abrahms, I don't need the evening to think about it. I have never been more sure of something that I want to do," responded Claire. "May I ask you a question?"

"Of course."

"Looking around this office, I am struck by how little it is personalized. I heard Rosalyn call you doctor, so I'm sure that there is a diploma somewhere. There are probably several licenses and acknowledgments that normally would hang in an office like this, but none are here. There doesn't seem to be anything with your name on it—only these two pictures on the wall, and I was wondering why you chose those two pictures. I was also wondering if you were the one who selected that particular photograph of Dr. King in the lobby."

"Yes, I did select that particular photograph of Dr. King. I worked with Dr. King during the civil rights movement, and that photograph always reminds me of Dr. King's devotion to all forms of righteousness and spirituality. He honored the work of Gandhi, and as we all know, Gandhi was not a Baptist. I try to remind myself to do no less. The reason you don't see all those diplomas and certificates is that *I* am unimportant. I try to think of myself as a vessel for God's will, and I try to keep that vessel empty. Things like letters after my name and licenses keep you somewhat full of yourself. That doesn't leave much room for God to fill me up."

Pastor Abrahms stood up with the stiffness that comes with sitting too long during your second half century of life. He walked over to the wall and stood looking at one of the pictures.

"This picture of me with Dr. King is there to remind me that I am imperfect, that I too suffer the human sin of pride, and therefore, it is important for me not to be too judgmental. The picture on the other wall, the one with a fire hose, I selected to hang because in that picture I am being struck by the water. I keep that picture in front of me because I remember the anger and hatred I felt at that moment and how important it is for me to include that police officer in my prayers. He too was consumed by anger and hatred at that moment. At that moment, more than just a stream of water connected us. We really were not very different at that moment."

What Claire heard was an intense expression of love and compassion. She felt honored to be in the presence of the pastor. She was challenged to help this church make a difference. She asked the pastor where she would be able to work, and he asked the secretary to show her to an office that was on the first floor.

They shook hands gently, and Claire went with the secretary to a small office with a desk, a file cabinet, and a bookshelf. There was a computer terminal and a telephone on the desk and little else. Claire thanked her, and the secretary left. Claire sat down and swiveled in her chair to try her new workspace on and feel it out a bit.

Claire went to the window that looked out on 112th Street and gave herself some time to catch her breath. Everything had happened so fast. What she expected for the day was to find out if there were any volunteer opportunities available, and in less than two hours, she was given the opportunity to make a significant contribution under the direction of a man she could respect. She had come a long way from Halliron.

Claire felt like having a cup of coffee. She stepped across the hall to the kitchen and found a freshly brewed pot. She fixed herself a cup—cream, no sugar—and took a seat at one of the tables. She picked up one of the scattered magazines and started thumbing through it while she cradled the warm coffee in her hand and smelled the sweet aroma of the Java.

A bell rang in the hallway outside, and the sound of students entering the hallways poured into the kitchen. A few moments later, several of the teachers came in to serve themselves from the coffee pot or get their own private snacks from the refrigerator. Lori was the fourth teacher through the door; when she came in, Claire looked up and their eyes met again. The fact that their eyes had locked earlier was not lost on either of them. Lori fixed herself a cup of coffee, came over, and sat down across from Claire.

"I'm Lori Blount. I teach second grade here. We saw each other for a moment when Ms. Rosalyn was with you."

"Yes, I remember. I'm Claire Medina. I just volunteered to help with some of the bookkeeping and grant applications, I'm an accountant. Nice to meet you."

"Nice to meet you. What brings you to our church? Do you live in the neighborhood?"

At this early stage of knowing Lori, Claire was a little embarrassed to admit she lived in the million-dollar condominiums along the East River. Then she decided that she was who she was. She was not going to live her life worrying about looking good in someone else's eyes. It was more important to be who you are, to be authentic. She had finally learned that people who spend a lot of time trying to look good for others don't usually look so good, and those people who are willing to be themselves and not worry about looking good usually look great.

"Yes, I do live in the neighborhood. I live in those condominiums down the street that line the East River."

"Oooh-wee," Lori breathed with an admiring smile.

"Yes, I know. I truly have been blessed, and it's that blessing that gives me the opportunity to volunteer here. I've met Pastor Abrahms, and I am so impressed with him. I have never met a kinder, gentler giant. My husband and I were both facing difficult challenges. We were being eaten up by the situations around us, but thanks to God and His messages and the advice of good people, we made some changes in our lives. I keep hearing that verse from the song "Amazing Grace." You know, the one that says, 'I once was lost, but now am found.'"

With those few words, Claire could see tears welling up in Lori's eyes. Claire reached a hand across the table and touched Lori lightly on her hand.

"I'm sorry. Have I said something upsetting?" Claire asked.

"No, it's nothing you said. It's just that, well, I have a friend, actually he's much more than a friend, and the situation around him is, well, as you put it, just eating him up. I've tried to talk some sense into him, and I think that he knows what the right thing to do is, but I'm still scared—so scared for him."

Claire was surprised that the woman she had just met seemed to trust her. Lori told Claire about Joe, her high school sweetheart, and how he went off to be a college football star. She told Claire how much she still loved him and how things that had gone so badly for him that now he was part of a gang. She expressed how much she was afraid that Joe was going to do something stupid for the gang—maybe do something wrong, very wrong.

Claire gave Lori the gift of listening with both sympathy and empathy. Claire had never been the kind of person people came to for a soft shoulder or to share their troubles. She had always been much more analytical; after all, she was an accountant. Perhaps there were more changes going on inside her than she was aware. Perhaps there was a deeper sense of interconnectedness that settled into her. Could it be a result of working through the pain of challenges? Whatever it was, it gave her an energy that signaled to others that she was a gentle soul. Claire let Lori talk on without interruption. Finally, Lori paused and fell silent.

"Do you feel that you've done everything you can? Is there anything left undone?" Claire asked.

"I don't think that there's anything else I can do," Lori responded.

"My husband, who is Chilean, taught me a saying in Spanish. It goes . . ." Claire paused and her eyes looked up and to the right as she was going over the words in her head, "*Never forget to believe in miracles. For, in truth, God does bless us; it's just that often his vision is better than ours.*"

Lori smiled and said, "That's so nice. It's just what I needed to hear."

The bell ending recess rang in the hallway outside. The two women stood up, stepped to the side of the table, and hugged each other. Claire squeezed her eyes and clenched her teeth, trying to transfer, by sheer force of will, some of her good fortune through the embrace to her new friend.

"Thank you," Lori said.

"No, thank you," Claire said in response.

Claire stepped into her office, and Lori went back to her classroom. Claire sat down at her desk and began to take an inventory of what she had and what she would need to do her job. Her thoughts were relaxed, half on the tasks at hand and half just daydreaming. She looked out the window and watched the traffic on 112th Street.

Patrol car 5151 drove by. Some officer she didn't recognize was at the wheel, and Officer Thompson was beside him. She had no idea that Louie the Cop had been shot and was dead. Her stomach clenched, and she felt a touch of nausea just thinking about the past.

*   *   *

Joe-24 was all cried out. There were no more tears as he stood alone over the storm drain—no more anger, no more pain, just the cold, comfortable sense of numb. Pastor Abrahms was right. Joe-24 had to choose sides—and he knew it was his fate to be on God's team, not the gang's. He was sure about what not to do, but he didn't have a clue of what to do. He was in that state of absolute surrender where he had no choice but to take his hands off the wheel and let God drive for a while. He was in that deep, dark place, just on the other side of not being able to take it anymore, the place from which miracles spring. His fingers eased the pressure on the butt of the pistol, and it slid out of his hands to fall and ring the sewer's grate. Just as he kicked the gun into the underground, patrol car 5151 turned the corner and pulled up to him. An officer he'd never seen before stayed behind the wheel as Officer Thompson got out to investigate.

"What's going on, Joe?" Thompson queried.

"I got rid of a gun."

"A gun?"

"Umm," muttered Joe.

"Talk to me," Thompson said, half demanding and half lending an ear.

"I was going to kill one of the 129ers to get back for them killing my brother." Joe's head was tilted down, just staring at the sewer, his shoulders slumped; he seemed to be half his size. There was no running, no lying, no good, no bad, just what was right and what was so.

At that moment, Thompson saw Joe in a new light. There wasn't a glow around Joe, but it seemed that there was. Maybe it was this God thing, or maybe it was just being with someone in a state of complete surrender, but at that moment Thompson's heart opened up, and he knew he was with a young man who was good and could make a difference.

Thompson reached out and put his hand on Joe's shoulder. "None of that matters now. We're living in a new world."

Joe's eyes were full; the tears were ready to drop. The plea for forgiveness was written all over his face.

"Will you come with me? Can I show you something?" Thompson went on.

Wiping his eyes on his sleeve, Joe allowed himself to be led to the patrol car. He didn't know where he was going. It didn't matter; his hands were off the wheel.

The patrol car rolled up to the playground next to the First Baptist Church of Harlem. There were little kids running around. Someone, about fifteen years old, tall and skinny like Billy, was blowing a whistle.

It took Joe a few seconds to decipher the movements, and then it dawned on him that they were playing ragtag football. No, not actually playing, they were practicing. They kept running the same play. The quarterback handed the ball to the running back, who was able to get through the pass rush but couldn't shake the secondary defenders.

Joe wasn't even aware that he got out of the car, but he became aware that the kids were dead in their tracks, mouths open as this giant of a player strode onto the field. He motioned for the running back to come over. Joe bent down to look in the eight-year-old's face.

"The reason they get you every time is because they can tell where you're going. The next time when they get near, stop . . . just for a heartbeat. They'll think you're going to change direction, and then take off like a tornado the same way you were going. It'll confuse them just long enough for you to get past them. Ya got that?"

"Yes, sir," said the young boy. He didn't know if he was being helped, ordered, or punished as he ran back to the huddle.

"Two . . . five . . . hut . . . hut," the quarterback shouted.

The ball was hiked, then handed off, and the running back headed out on the left slant. The secondary defenders closed in. The boy stutter-stepped as Joe had directed. The defender moved to the boy's right, and then the boy was off down the left sideline and into the end zone. The boy tried to spike the ball, but his small hand couldn't hold on to it, and it flew out behind him. All the players cheered, and Joe laughed.

It was the first time Joe had laughed in a long, long time. The fifteen-year-old with the whistle walked over. He had on a t-shirt that said Coach across the chest.

Aren't you Joe Clidson, number 24 for Syracuse until . . . ?" his voice trailed off.

"Until the injury," Joe finished the question with pride. "Yeah, that's me, coach"

"My name is Jimmy," the boy coach said, reaching out a hand. "Tell you the truth, I don't know much about football, basketball's my game—could sure use your help."

Joe-24 looked at the outstretched hand and stood silently for a moment. Jimmy shifted uneasily. Joe bypassed the hand and bear-hugged him.

"I would love to. I would love to coach with you," Joe-24 whispered.

Looking over Jimmy's shoulder, Joe saw Officers Thompson and O'Hara hanging against the chain-link fence. He winked at them. A tear squeezed out of his left eye, ran down his cheek, and fell into his mouth through his big full-toothed smile. Thompson directed Joe-24's attention to Joe's left by motioning with his outstretched thumb. Joe responded and discovered that Lori and another woman, a white woman, had been watching him all along from the top of the steps leading up to the back door of the church.

Joe-24 ran to the steps and then up them. He cradled Lori's face in his hands. The first thing he noticed about her was how her happy tear followed the exact same path down her right cheek as his had—mirror images of each other.

"I don't deserve you," Joe-24 said.

"That's where you are wrong, Joe. You do," Lori replied.

Claire stood by silently. *Lori was right—they are soul mates,* was all she thought.

CHAPTER 18

You have always searched for a solution.
I have given you one. It is forgiveness.

—*God*

The bus to the Gordon's shorefront home on the Mediterranean coast in Tel Aviv was crowded. Angie Gibran, social worker for Amnesty International, decided to get off a few blocks from her destination and walk the remaining distance barefoot on the beach. When she reached the steps leading up to Ben and Sarah Gordon's comfortable home, she turned and faced the surf to fully experience the warm breeze. She was wearing a neck-to-ankle, long-sleeved, white cotton shift and, of course, a modest headscarf. There were wind surfers catching the breeze and leaping from swells to troughs. It hardly felt like a war zone. For a moment, she forgot that there were still so many scars, both visible and below the surface, that needed healing. The events of the past weeks and months gave new hope for a real, enduring peace in the region. The incidents of violence between Jews and Arabs, as well as between Shiite and Sunnis had slowed to the point of becoming unusual rather than the norm.

If only people could let go of the deep pain of lost loved ones, the cycle of violence might really end. That was her mission, to foster the act of letting go, to open the possibility of forgiveness for her clients—one client at a time. It was Thursday, the day she visited and worked with Al-Khalil.

She turned and followed the stairs that lead up and through the massive stone boulder that formed the foundation of the Gordon's home. No one was on the seaside decking, so she followed the path around to the front door of the house. She rang the electronic chime. In short order, she heard bare feet, in a quick trot, slapping against the marble flooring. She knew it had to be Teeja. The door opened, and sure enough Teeja was there wearing a bright smile. As Angie stepped in, she saw that both Mr. and Mrs. Gordon were at the breakfast table planning for the party set for that evening. Teeja went back to the kitchen to continue preparing a crudités. Mrs. Gordon looked up and spoke to Angie.

"Al-Khalil had to run to the airport to pick up Congressman Silverman. You remember, my cousin from New York. The plane landed over an hour ago, so I expect they'll be back shortly."

Angie was about to respond when her cell phone rang. She excused herself and answered it, "Hello."

"Hello," said the voice at the other end of the line, "I'm looking for Angie Gibran." The voice sounded distant. It was serious and just a bit hesitant. The tone of the voice raised a lump in Angie's throat. She didn't expect to hear good news.

"This is Angie Gibran."

"Good. It's taken us some time to find you. Ms. Gibran, I am Captain Randy Kaplan of the 23rd Precinct in Manhattan. I wish we had been able to locate you sooner, and I wish I could visit you in person, but it is my sad duty to report that your father died in the . . . uh . . . the line of duty nine days ago. In the tradition of the New York City Police Department, he received a funeral with full honors. I am sure you would have wanted to be here, but we had to go through the State Department to locate you, and it just took time."

Angie stood there with the phone cemented to her ear. The Gordons were busy with their plans. Teeja was cutting vegetables in the kitchen. The sun was shining. Outside, the blue Mediterranean extended for as far as she could see, and she had just been told that her father was dead. She was silent. Captain Kaplan was patient. This was not the first time for him; he knew that silence was often the initial reaction. Eventually the words came.

"Thank you, Captain. Is there anything I need to do?"

From her monotone voice, the Gordons could tell Angie had received bad news. They raised their heads and looked at Angie with questions written on their faces. Captain Kaplan mentioned that there were matters that needed to be handled, such as her father's personal effects, pension, and life insurance. None of it was urgent, and he told her that she could take care of those things when she was ready, and that he was available to help her in any way that he could. She thanked him again. They exchanged contact information, and they both hung up. The Gordons waited for her to speak.

"My father is dead. They say he was killed in the line of duty."

Sarah and Ben Gordon moved as one. They rose from the table and embraced her from both sides. Angie felt slightly embarrassed. Her emotions didn't seem to rise to the level that would call for such an outpouring of concern. Teeja came over and tentatively joined in the group hug—acknowledging the sadness yet keeping an emotional distance.

Angie did feel sadness, but it was not from the loss of her father. Rather it was sadness for him. She knew that he never

Children of Abraham

307

experienced self-satisfaction, the sense of being happy in his own skin. Now he was dead. For that, she was sad—sad that he had never experienced the wonder and awe of life.

Behind them, Max Silverman and Al-Khalil were watching through the open door. Al-Khalil watched the outpouring of emotions in silence. Just watching the Jews embrace a Muslim woman stirred primordial emotions. His stomach clenched in disgust, but his heart reached out with compassion.

Al-Khalil's relationship with the Gordons was full of contradiction. They were Jews, more specifically, Israelis—people of the same cloth as those that had killed both his mother and father. Yet over the last years, since they had taken him and Teeja in as house servants, the Gordons had treated Teeja and him with such kindness, gentleness, and affection that it was hard to maintain his hatred for them. Sometimes he even felt a tenderness that he jealously reserved only for Teeja and the memory of his mother.

Teeja was the first to notice that Max and Al-Khalil were in the room.

"Brother," Teeja called out.

The Gordons looked up in response. Ben Gordon stayed next to Angie, holding her arm. Sarah Gordon stepped quickly to Al-Khalil to hug him. Al-Khalil stiffened at her touch but was also warmed by it. Sarah looked over his shoulder and addressed Max.

"Cousin, why don't you put your briefcase down and have a seat in the living room," said Sarah and then redirected her attention to Al-Khalil. Al-Khalil thought it strange that he was the focus of her attention instead of her own flesh and blood.

Sarah placed her hands on Al-Khalil's shoulders and spoke to him quietly, "Angie has received some bad news. Her father, the

New York City policeman, has been killed. They say, in the line of duty."

Al-Khalil moved to face Angie. He wanted to reach out and embrace her, but she was a Muslim woman, and such touching would be improper. He looked down at her with moist eyes and said to her, "I, too, know what it means to be made an orphan."

In spite of their culture, she cupped Al-Khalil's face in her hands and shared his pain, "I know. I know. I understand."

Sarah went into the living room to properly greet her cousin. Al-Khalil brought Max's bags up to his room then joined Teeja chopping vegetables. Ben Gordon stayed with Angie. They sat at the kitchen table.

"How are you—really?" Ben Gordon asked.

"I'm okay."

Ben gave Angie a doubting look.

"No, really, I am . . . I guess. Maybe I'm in denial, or shock, but I don't really feel so bad. I mean, I'm sad but not terribly so. You see, my father and I were not very close. In fact, part of the reason I joined Amnesty International was to be able to travel and distance myself from him."

"Oh, I see. Will you have to go back to New York?"

"Yes, the captain said that there were personal effects, life insurance, and other things that I needed to take care of. I suppose I'll have to make a requisition through Amnesty International for travel expenses. They'll take a couple of weeks, I guess."

"Angie, whether you're just numb, or you truly are okay, you need some level of closure to all of this. I've been to too many funerals not to understand these things. Some of them have been family, and since moving to Israel, I have had many friends pass on—some, like your father, suddenly and violently. I am not about to let paperwork slow you down from paying whatever respects you feel are proper."

Before Angie could object, Ben was on the phone to his travel agent. Within minutes, he had her booked on a nonstop flight to JFK International Airport in New York City leaving at 4:12 PM the next day.

"You have to be at the airport by 1:00 PM to clear security," Ben said.

"Mr. Gordon, you didn't have to do that. I don't know how I can pay you back."

"Yes, I did have to do that. I care for you, Angie. You can pay me back when you get your travel vouchers. Are you going to go home for the rest of the day?"

"Actually, Mr. Gordon, I would rather stay and see Al-Khalil. Then I would like to help you in preparation for your peace party this evening. I think that it's good to celebrate the peace we've all experienced in the past few months and the hope it holds for the future. Besides, I would rather be doing something to keep myself occupied. I think if I go home and am alone, I'll only get depressed."

"Are you sure? You know you don't have to do that."

"Yes, I'm sure."

"Well, then, there are vegetables to be cut, matzoh balls and briskets to be boiled. Spend your time with Al-Khalil, and then we'll put you to work?" Ben suggested that she and Al-Khalil use the outdoor decking since there was bound to be lots of activity inside.

Angie opened the sliding glass door, and both she and Al-Khalil stepped outside. They sat facing each other on the floral-print cushions that graced the wireframe outdoor furniture.

"Someone should be here for you," said Al-Khalil, "rather than you be here for me. How do you feel?"

"I am sad," she replied.

"Are you angry?"

Angie paused for a moment and then replied, "I don't know. Who should I be angry at?"

"The Son of Satan who killed your father, of course."

"I don't know who that is."

"Why does that matter? I don't know who killed my mother or my father, but I still hate them. How can it be that you don't want revenge for your father?"

"It is because I love Allah."

Al-Khalil was perplexed. He asked, "The Prophet, may glory be upon Him, loved Allah; nevertheless, he fought for vengeance."

Angie looked at Al-Khalil with kind eyes and asked him, "Did the Prophet, may grace be upon Him, fight to avenge Himself, or did He fight to avenge Allah, the Most Merciful? Allah not only named Himself Ar-Rahman, the Beneficent, and Ar-Rahim, the Merciful, but He also named Himself Al-Ghafoor—the Forgiving. His mercy overtakes His punishment and anger. He is more merciful to His creations than a mother can be to her infants."

"Then why does He allow His believers to suffer?" asked Al-Khalil.

"Forgiveness is important in Islam. It is often discussed in the Holy Quran. It is easier said than done. It seems very hard to practice forgiveness in daily life. There are wars everywhere. People are fighting and killing each other. Everyone is blaming other parties and neglecting the virtue of forgiveness. Allah wants us to be forgiving because He is the Most Forgiving. If we have not been harmed, how can we learn to forgive?"

"I am scared to forgive. There is great anger within me, but I feel there is something underneath the anger, something that keeps the anger flowing. I don't want to know what that is," Al-Khalil said, looking away.

"I understand, but by holding on to your hatred and planning vengeance, you have sinned against Allah. When we commit a sin, four witnesses are established against us: the place we sinned; the organ we used to sin with, in your case, your mind; the angels who record the deeds; and the physical evidence you will create if you act upon your hatred. With four such strong witnesses, how can you present yourself to Allah? If you repent and forgive, Allah, like a smart lawyer, removes all the witnesses against you. Recording angels erase their records. Organs lose their memories. The earth removes its stains of evidence, so that when that person appears before Allah, there is no one to be a witness against him. In that way, we present ourselves with a clean record. Case dismissed due to lack of evidence."

Al-Khalil sat upright and leaned in. He didn't know these subtleties of the Quran. They gave him hope. Angie smiled warmly at his display of interest.

"What you feel, Al-Khalil, underneath your anger and hatred, is the pain of the loss of your mother and father. You've told me often that when your mother was killed, you felt no pain. That is because you masked it under your anger. What you fear is that if you forgive those who killed your parents, you will begin to feel the pain and grief of your loss. If you are ever to be the person that Allah intended you to be, if ever you are to have happiness in your life, you must endure great pain and learn to forgive. You must do this so that you can fully understand the extent of Allah's mercy and love.

"But what about justice?" Al-Khalil pleaded.

"Allah will take care of that. Although Allah is the Most Forgiving, He said there are three sins that cannot be forgiven. One of those three sins is the killing of a believer—'Whoever slays a believer of set purpose, his reward is hell forever. Allah is wroth with him and hath cursed him and prepared for him an awful doom.'"

"So if Allah will not forgive the killing of a believer, why do I have to forgive those who killed my parents? Both my mother and father were believers. Hamas even called them martyrs."

Angie considered his question. She leaned back in thought and gazed skyward. Her eyes widened, and she leaned back toward Al-Khalil. "Let me tell you a story from the Hadith: A certain person had committed ninety-nine murders. He went to a scholar and asked, 'Is there any chance of my being forgiven?' The scholar said, 'No, you have committed too many crimes.' The man killed the scholar too, but his heart was restless, so he went to another scholar and asked the same question. He was told, 'Yes, but you must leave this town of badness and go live in the next town in the company of good people.'

"So the man set out to the town. On the way he died. A man passing by saw two angels arguing over his dead body. The angel from hell said, 'His body belongs to me as he had not done any good in his life.' The angel from heaven said, 'His body belongs to me as he had repented and was set out to be with good people.' A man who was a passerby said, 'Let us measure the distance of his body from the town he left and the town he was going to.' This was done. He was found to be nearer to the town he was coming from. Allah ordered the earth to shrink and make the distance smaller, so that he was admitted to heaven.

"If Allah could shrink the world in order to gain entry into heaven for a repentant murderer, why do you think Allah needs your help to avenge the death of your parents? Is it not better to leave to Allah the job of sending the killers to an eternal hell? Is it not better for you and Teeja to follow the path of forgiveness Allah has set out for you and enjoy the benefits and abundance Allah, the Most Generous, has provided for you?"

Al-Khalil felt that there was truth in Angie's words. The dam holding back his emotions developed a crack—the grief began to seep through. He got a smatter of the pain and a hint that grief also acts as a solvent on hatred, but he wasn't yet ready to let it show. He respected Angie's understanding of the Quran, and he knew that her only interest was his well-being. He was grateful to have such a wise guide to the mysteries of life.

"Thank you, teacher. I appreciate your words, and I will take them deep into my heart. I am still afraid of the pain, but perhaps this is my true jihad. Perhaps the signs that Allah has given us truly apply to us individually as well as to our tribes. I fear I have much to grieve, but I will have to leave that for another day. The Gordons truly have been kind to Teeja and me, and they have decided to have a party to celebrate peace. I will begin my repentance by being a good servant, in the name of Allah, the Most Merciful."

"You have learned the lesson well. So then, let us go inside and get to work."

The house was full of activity throughout the afternoon. Guests began to arrive at about 7:00 PM. There were Muslims, Jews, and Christians. There were members of the Knesset and the diplomatic corps. Guests were dressed in modern garb and traditional clothing. The party was a great success. All of the foods had been prepared with love, and so they were consumed with love.

People, who would never have talked to each other a year ago, were exchanging jokes as well as tragic or heroic stories. Finally, near midnight, the crowd began to thin out. The few guests that were left offered to help clean up, but the Gordons would have none of it. They showed their last few friends to the door; and Angie, Al-Khalil, and Teeja began to clear the plates and glasses.

"Angie, you sit down and relax. This has been a long day for you. It also has been a hard day for you, and you have packing in preparation for your flight tomorrow. I'll call you a taxi, and I want you to go home," Sarah Gordon said as she picked up the telephone to call for car service.

Max had a little too much to drink, and he was already asleep on the couch. Ben Gordon also felt the effects of a long day and wanted nothing more than to lay out, spread-eagled in his air-conditioned bedroom. Cleaning up could wait for tomorrow. He told Al-Khalil and Teeja to get some rest as well. He promised them the opportunity to get an early start on putting the house back together in the morning. They did not argue with him. Al-Khalil and Teeja walked down the hallway leading to their respective bedrooms.

The only thing worse than coming home from a vacation to a messy house is waking up in the morning after a party that has not been cleaned up. Sarah Gordon was the first one up the next morning. Max was still asleep on the couch. He had a smile on his lips, and Sarah could only wonder what he was dreaming. She shook him awake and suggested that he go to his bedroom to sleep for a few more hours. Then she looked around and took inventory of what needed to be done. As she was conducting her review, Al-Khalil and Teeja joined her in the living room.

"What a mess," said Teeja in her youthful innocence.

"Where would you like us to begin, Mrs. Gordon?" said Al-Khalil more respectfully.

"Teeja, why don't you start in the kitchen? We are going to have to bring all these glasses and plates in there, so we need counters cleared off before we can load up the dishwasher. Al-Khalil, you and I will start out here stacking things. Remember, we clean from the top down, so first things come off the shelves and tables; the floor comes last. Agreed?"

"Yes, ma'am," said Al-Khalil. "Would it be okay if I get a cup of coffee before we begin?"

"Of course, what am I thinking? Yes, let's throw together a quick breakfast. We've got enough work to do; it would be helpful to have something in our stomachs."

They worked together as a family would work together. Coffee was brewed, cereal was dispensed, the table was cleared and set, and they sat down to eat. Before the first bite, Sarah Gordon said, "Bismillahir rahmanir rahim. In the name of Allah, the Most Beneficent, the Most Merciful." Then she said in Hebrew, "Baruch atah Adonai Eloheinu Melech Haolam, borei minei m'zonot. Blessed are You, HaShem, our God, King of the Universe, who creates variety of sustenance."

As they were enjoying their breakfast, Ben and Max joined them. There was laughter and comfort except for one small fly in the ointment. Al-Khalil remembered the discomfort he once felt when Max had visited months before. Al-Khalil had been uncomfortable about the way Max spoke to Teeja, and he noticed something he did not like in the way that Max was looking at Teeja this very morning. Because they were dressed for working, Teeja was not wearing her traditional abaya. She was wearing one of Al-Khalil's t-shirts, a light headscarf, and loose linen work pants with an elasticized waistband. There was certainly nothing revealing about her dress, but Teeja was so curvaceous that her mature woman's body could not be hidden even under such loose clothing.

After breakfast, the entire group got to work, with the exception of Max, who was ordered to relax and enjoy the view from the deck. Eventually, the kitchen came back into shape; the dinnerware that was spread throughout the house was organized and washed. Once clean, Al-Khalil took the card tables and folding chairs to the outside storeroom while Teeja began returning items to the pantry. Al-Khalil returned and began vacuuming floors. After a few minutes, he looked around and wondered where Teeja was. He turned off the vacuum cleaner and called for her. She did not answer. He went to look in her bedroom, but she was not there either. He walked to the pantry door and opened it.

Teeja was in the back corner, facing outward with fear burning in her eyes. Standing in front of her, and blocking her escape, was the congressmen from New York City. He had his hand on her hip underneath the t-shirt.

Teeja was trying to push his hand down and kept repeating, "No—please—no. Please, don't do this."

"It's okay, don't worry about it. It's just a little game. No one will be hurt."

All thoughts of forgiveness were washed out of Al-Khalil's consciousness the way a flood washes away fields of grain. He reached into his pocket where he always carried a small .25-caliber automatic pistol. He ran to where Max was holding Teeja hostage. Al-Khalil grabbed Max's left shoulder and spun him around, pinning him to the wall. He pressed the small pistol up against Max's forehead. He pushed it with such force that Max knew there was no escape. Al-Khalil's finger tightened on the trigger.

"Brother! No!" Teeja exclaimed.

Hearing Teeja's voice distracted him for a moment. It allowed him to think about what he was doing—for a moment. It allowed him to remember the lessons of forgiveness—for a moment. And in that moment, the moment of indecision, Al-Khalil decided not to kill this lecher. Allah would take care of him—take care of the heathen monster. Allah would send him to eternal hell. Al-Khalil eased off the pressure, and then stepped back slightly and lowered the gun.

Max saw his opportunity to escape. He double chopped Al-Khalil in the chest with both hands. The moment he did that, Max knew he had made a grievous mistake. He knew that he had made a mistake because he heard the report of the gun, and he felt the searing pain in his groin. The bullet sliced through the corpora cavernosa of his penis, making any future erection highly improbable. The wound would prove to be life altering—but not fatal. All Max could do was slump to the floor and moan.

Al-Khalil went into a panic. He, a Palestinian, had just shot a politician from the United States of America in Tel Aviv. No one would believe that it was an accident. There was no way he could get a fair trial. Of this, he was certain.

He grabbed Teeja's hand and said, "Come, Teeja, we must go. There is no time to gather anything. We must flee; otherwise we will be put in prison—or killed."

Al-Khalil and Teeja ran out of the front door of the Gordons' house. As they ran down the pathway to the street, a taxicab pulled up. Angie was in the cab. She was on her way to the airport and had stopped to say good-bye. When she saw Teeja crying and Al-Khalil in such fear, she asked what was wrong.

"It was an accident! I didn't mean to do it! The gun—it just went off. That man from New York, he was trying to . . . he was trying to have sex with Teeja. I became enraged. I pulled my gun out. I was going to kill him, but I remembered what you said. I remembered how Allah would take care of him, and I stepped back. Then he struck me, and the gun went off. It hit him. I do not know where, but he fell to the floor, and he was moaning. I know the authorities will never believe me. Please, you must help us."

"Quick, quick, get in the car," Angie said.

They got into the cab, and Angie instructed the driver to take them to the public bus station, which was only a five-minute ride away.

As they approached the station, Angie said to them, "It is true. There is no way that you can get a fair trial under these circumstances. The only place that you can go is Gaza where you grew up. Perhaps there you will be able to find friends or some of your family to help you hide. When I get to the airport, I will call the Gordons' house. I will explain to them what happened. I know they love you, but I fear the police will not be sympathetic. When things calm down, maybe we will be able to work something out. After all, a congressman would not want you to testify about what he was doing in the pantry—to Teeja. For now, I will tell the Gordons that you decided to go to East Jerusalem in the West Bank. Perhaps that will throw the police off long enough for you to be able to get through a checkpoint and into the Gaza Strip."

The door opened. Angie reached into her pocketbook and gave them all the shekels she had and left them with these parting words, "Walk, do not run. Running will draw attention to you. May Allah be with you.

Al-Khalil turned and said, "And with you."

With that, they were off. Angie watched until they were out of sight. Then she told the cab driver to take her to the airport. She was so afraid for Al-Khalil and Teeja. She feared that what they had done would become an international incident, and they would be hunted. She could only call upon her faith. She clasped her hands tightly and looked up; she prayed for Allah to watch over them and to protect them.

A few hours later, the bus that was carrying Al-Khalil and Teeja approached the checkpoint leading into the Gaza Strip. The news of what had occurred in Tel Aviv and the identity of the possible suspects had not been broadcast yet. As their bus passed through the checkpoint into the Palestinian section, Al-Khalil and Teeja heard the haunting, yet beautiful, sound of the evening Call to Prayer.

CHAPTER 19

Universal love, empathy, and wisdom
are the keys to my Kingdom on Earth.

—*God*

The sound of the morning Call to Prayer forced its way through the window of Clay McRae's air-conditioned room. The Call to Prayer has exotic tones to westerners. At first, the strange sound startled him, but then he realized what it was and turned back into his luxurious bedding. It was his tenth day in Istanbul, Turkey, and he was still getting used to waking up without the sound of the rumbling clatter of Manhattan. He lay in bed quietly while thinking about the planned events for the day.

At 8:00 AM, he was to meet Mustafa for breakfast at an open-air café at the base of the Levitte Plaza on Caddesi Street. The five-star Swissotel Istanbul Bosporus in the Buyukdere section of Istanbul, where he was staying, was just a block and a half away. The café was across the street from the Türkiye Garanti Bankasi (Guarantee Bank of Turkey), the bank where he and Mustafa had deposited the hundreds of millions of dollars that would support him in his new life as an international man of means.

After a while, he slid out of bed and walked to the expansive windows of the hotel that overlooked sixty-five acres of parkland leading out to the Straits of Bosporus. He followed the sapphire blue waterway to its mouth at the Sea of Marmora. The Sea of Marmora ran into the Dardanelles, which joined the Aegean Sea, which eventually became the Mediterranean Sea. The dark blue water extended until it turned into the light blue sky at the horizon. He was looking westward, and so the rising sun behind him did not warm the cool blues in front of him, leaving Clay McRae feeling calm and tranquil. That was a good thing.

There were enough reasons for him to feel anxious. He was in a strange country with strange laws and strange customs. He had given all of his wealth, in trust, to a man he hardly knew. The only guarantee he had was a shared secret number that allowed access to the account. So many things could go wrong. On the other hand, perhaps it was arrogance, Clay just did not believe that anything would go wrong—for him.

Clay fixed a cup of American coffee using the small coffeemaker that was in the kitchenette. He sat in the comfortable armchair, looking out onto the city below and passed his time reading a *CultureGram* on Turkish customs and history.

When 7:30 AM arrived, he put his reading down and got dressed. The hotel was certainly first-class. He stepped into his walk-in closet, where the bellhop had arranged to have all of his hanging clothes pressed and hung according to type and color. He checked the digital display of the outside temperature and saw that it was to be a warm day. He selected a white cotton guayabera and a pair of cotton twill pants. He placed his passport, other identification, credit cards, and a little cash in a pouch that connected to a canvas waistband with a security clasp. He strapped the belt around his waist. The long tails of the Shirt-Jac kept the security device covered and hidden. He stopped by the full-length mirror to check his appearance, decided everything was in order, and turned to walk out the door.

When he reached Cadessi Street, he turned left. A few buildings down was the café Mustafa described. It was five minutes until 8:00 AM. The waiter came over, and Clay ordered a standard Turkish breakfast of white cheese, tomatoes, black olives, an egg, bread with honey and preserves, and, of course, Turkish coffee. The waiter brought the coffee out first along with a glass of ice water. He then brought a tray of olives, pita bread, and olive oil with various spices for dipping. Later, the plate came with the rest of the breakfast. Clay sat and ate slowly and pensively. Mustafa had not arrived.

Eight o'clock came and went. Then 8:30 AM passed. It was pushing 9:00 AM, and Clay was beginning to get nervous. He had never known Mustafa to be late; in fact, Mustafa honored punctuality. When finally 9:30 AM arrived, Clay paid for his breakfast and returned to the hotel. He went to his room and took out the list of contact numbers he had in case anything went wrong. First, he called Mustafa's numbers in Turkey and in the United States, and there was no answer. He then called Mustafa's son, Achmed's phone number in the United States, and there was no answer. Then he called the local Istanbul number, and a familiar voice answered.

"Achmed, is that you?" Clay asked with some urgency.

"Yes, it is. Is this Mr. McRae?" Achmed asked.

"Yes, it is. I've been downstairs waiting for your father at the café where we were supposed to meet. We were to meet at eight o'clock, and it is past nine thirty. I know that he's always punctual. Is something wrong?"

"Mr. McRae, thank Allah you have called. We were so worried about getting in contact with you. We did not have your phone numbers."

"Didn't have my phone numbers?" Clay repeated incredulously. "I gave them to your father on my way to the airport to catch my plane here."

"Then you are completely unaware of what has happened?"

The words Clay McRae focused in on were—"what has happened." What had happened? McRae began to feel the gnawing emotion of fear. He tried to get a hold on his feelings, but he felt his throat constrict, and his heartbeat began to increase.

"No, I am not aware of anything that has happened. Why don't you fill me in?" Clay demanded, barely able to keep the tremble out of his voice.

"I don't know how to say this other than to just tell you. My father was killed. He was shot and killed on the very day that you left New York."

"Shot and killed? What are you talking about? Why have I not been told about this? What's going on? Do you understand that he had the other half of the secret number to gain access to the account? Do you know how much money is in that account? This can't be happening. He must have told you what the numbers were. Why didn't you tell me all this happened?"

"We couldn't tell you because we didn't have your contact information. Remember, you gave that to him on the day that you left, and he was killed shortly after that. He never had a chance to pass it on to the rest of us. We were just waiting for you to call us. We knew that he had an appointment with you. We just did not know when. We figured that, sooner or later, you would go to meet him, and when you found him missing, you would call us. At least, that was what we were hoping, and thanks be to Allah, it has happened. Now we can try to figure out what to do."

Clay was beginning to wonder whether he should believe all of this. It seemed just too neat and clean a scam for it to be true. He wanted to see proof that Mustafa was dead. He didn't want to be taken over by a group of these Turks.

"You better come up to my hotel room and bring whatever proof you have of what you're saying. It's hard for me to believe that something like this could just happen by coincidence. I don't mean to be insensitive, but I'm sure that you can understand with so much money at stake, there has to be some verification."

"Oh please, Mr. McRae. Please do not be concerned with asking for some proof. I am sure that this must come as a great shock to you. It did to us as well. I will be at your hotel room in half an hour, and I will bring with me the newspapers from the day after his death. We could also go and visit his grave. I understand your concern, and it is my intention, as my father's son, to complete his obligations. That is our tradition, and that is our custom. I am the eldest son, and it falls upon me to make sure that any word or promise given by my father is completed and carried out. What you ask is not an offense. It is actually an honor to be able to complete the obligations of my father."

They hung up. Clay paced back and forth in his room. He no longer cared about the beautiful vista outside his window. He no longer cared about the service of the hotel or the plush surroundings of his room. All he cared about was gaining access to an account that had hundreds of millions of dollars in it.

Within twenty-five minutes, Achmed arrived. He had folded underneath his right arm several newspapers. Clay let him in and greeted him with the standard Turkish greeting he had learned from the *CultureGram*, "Nasilsiniz?"

Achmed was a little surprised at Clay's use of the Turkish word for "How are you?" Even though Clay's accent was a bit off, Achmed was impressed by Clay's courtesy in taking the time to learn about Turkish culture. He responded by saying, "Fine, thank you" in Turkish—"Lyiyim, tesekkur ederim."

Achmed then went over to the bed and opened up the papers he had folded under his arm. There was a copy of the *Daily News* and the *New York Times*. On the front of the *Daily News* was a black-and-white photograph that took up the middle half of the page. It showed chairs knocked over in a café. There were bloodstains on the floor. The headline read—"Cop and Owner of Greenwich Village Coffee Shop Shot." The date of the newspaper was the morning after Clay said good-bye to Mustafa. There was a smaller story on the front page of the *New York Times*. In the interior of the papers was more information.

Clay stopped reading halfway through the articles and just looked at Achmed. It wasn't enough proof. Oh, the photograph was taken inside Mustafa's Coffee House. Clay had been there himself. Maybe he just didn't want to believe it; maybe he just wasn't ready. Clay did recognize that Achmed may have actually lost his father. Considering that, Clay calculated that having an irate tone and being angry at this time would be counterproductive. Since he clearly wasn't going to be meeting Mustafa, he had to align himself with Achmed, and he adjusted his attitude to be more appropriate. It was a tactical decision—not a compassionate one.

"I'm sorry if I appeared insensitive when you first gave me this information. I guess I must have been in shock. I am truly sorry for the loss of your father. You say that his grave is here, I guess you had his body shipped back to Turkey?"

"Yes, we normally don't embalm bodies in Turkey. When people die, they are buried within fourteen hours. Of course, that was impossible in my father's case, and he had to be embalmed in New York City for the flight over. When he arrived here, we went through the traditional laying out of the body. The big toes were tied together, and he was wrapped in white cloths after being washed. He was placed in the coffin and carried to our family's graveyard. He's only been buried for a few days because of all the delay involved in the international transportation of bodies," Achmed said in a voice that broke slightly from time to time. His nose began to run. He took a tissue from Clay's night table and blew his nose.

"May I visit the grave to pay my respects," Clay said. Clay could not care less about paying respects. He wanted to go to the grave to make sure that Mustafa actually was in the ground.

Achmed said, "Of course, I'll take you there right now, and then on the way back, we can stop so that you can meet my family. I must apologize in advance for their appearance; they will all be wearing old clothing. That is our tradition for two weeks after the death."

"Yes, I would like that very much. I would like to meet your family, and also perhaps we can look around and see whether or not Mustafa left any information that would help us."

"You certainly are welcome to look through his personal papers, but we have spent a great deal of time looking for the information, looking for any indication that he might have hidden the numbers. It seems that he never, well, for that matter none of us, imagined that events such as these would take place. Who would have imagined that in a shootout a stray bullet would mortally wound my father?"

The two men left the room. When they walked out of the hotel, Achmed's car and driver were waiting at the entrance. Achmed gave instructions to the driver, in Turkish, to take them to the graveyard. When they reached the graveyard, the two men got out and walked along a gravel path until they came to a recently filled grave. There was a pot on the grave with fresh flowers. Mustafa's name was on the grave and the date of his birth and death, which were consistent with what Clay knew of his age. Achmed hung his head in sadness and let out a deep sigh or two. They stayed there until Clay felt the appropriate time to pay his respects passed, and they returned to the car.

They drove through different sections of Istanbul. Achmed pointed out to Clay items of historical interest. Clay pretended to give Achmed his attention, but his attention was really on how to get to his money. When they arrived at Achmed's house, there were many people in attendance. As Achmed indicated, all were wearing old clothes, most of them black. They were obviously still in mourning. One woman dressed completely in black and with a widow's shawl was in the back room. Suddenly, she let out a moan that was closer to a scream, and then she stood up, took a piece of her clothing, and ripped off a swatch. She ripped the material into smaller pieces then threw them down and cried out again. Achmed explained that the woman was his mother, and she still was trying to come to grips with the loss of her husband. They had been married for forty years, ever since she was fifteen years old. He had been the only man in her life.

A younger woman offered Clay a cup of tea and pastry dipped in syrup. He graciously accepted them, and then went with Achmed to Mustafa's study. The room had books open; papers spread about; and files laying on the desk, couch, and floor. Achmed explained that the disarray was simply how his father kept the workspace. Clay looked around and began to push some of the papers on the desk about. He could see instantly that looking for five numbers among all that was strewn about would be a difficult, if not impossible, task.

Clay turned to Achmed instead. "May we go to the bank now?"

"Of course. Let me just call ahead and tell them that were coming so that we can make sure the manager is there and not out taking a midmorning coffee break."

"Does the bank manager speak English?"

"He does. As a matter of fact, he was educated in England—at Oxford, I believe."

Achmed made a phone call. He talked in Turkish and then advised Clay that they were ready to go. The two men retraced their path back to Clay's hotel and then one hundred meters beyond. The car pulled over to the curb in front of the Guarantee Bank of Turkey, and the two men got out.

The bank was obviously prosperous. The floor was made of marble and was polished so brightly it reflected their images with the same clarity as still water. The interior lobby was spacious with large marble columns scattered throughout. Bank officials sat at desks far enough away from each other that there was no need for partitions or offices. The only negative of the construction was that there was a slight echo to every sound, but the ears quickly became accustomed to that and filtered it out.

Achmed led Clay over to one particular desk and introduced Clay to the bank manager whose name was Mehnteerah Soldanha. The manager motioned for them to sit at the seat in front of his desk. Clay spoke first.

"Mr. Soldanha, I have an account here with this young man's father. It is a joint account, and the problem is that both of us had part of the password, and his father had died. Can you look at our account and tell me what the status is?"

"Yes, Mr. McRae, I can do that, and please, call me Mehnteerah. I am well aware of your situation. Mustafa maintained an account at this bank for many years. We did not have a personal relationship, but we did have a long and trusting business relationship. I was saddened to find out about his death. Achmed has advised me of the predicament you find yourself in. I will try to work with you in solving it although there are difficulties involved. I can give you information about the status of the account by using your Social Security Number. The computer has all of the demographic information for both you and the other joint owner. It can therefore access information about the account; I just can't access the funds in the account."

The bank manager turned his attention to his computer terminal. He asked Clay for his passport, Social Security Number, and birth date. Once he pulled up the account information on the screen, he wrote the balance on a piece of paper, folded that piece of paper in half, and slid it across the desk to where Clay was sitting. Clay took the paper, opened it up, and saw that the correct amount was still in the account. That was at least some relief.

"Well, Mehnteerah, where do we go from here? As you have seen, this account is holding a substantial amount of money. I am most anxious to gain access to it. What can we do?"

"Mr. McRae, I am sure that you can understand that the entire reason we have created a system of password-controlled accounts is to provide the ultimate in privacy and secrecy—especially from prying government eyes of other sovereign nations. We make it clear to our clients that the password is vital to gaining access. Of course, we are not thieves, and it is not our intention to steal your money from you. On the other hand, we cannot release it for fear that the joint owner will make claim against it. The two of you have decided to split the information contained in the password. I understand that you did that to safeguard each other, but you also have set up a situation in which there is no immediate, instant, or current solution."

Mehnteerah's last few words felt like darts to McRae. He winced inside but maintained a poker face. "When you use the words—*immediate*, *instant*, and *current*—what are you speaking about?"

"Well, as I mentioned, we are not thieves. Situations like this have happened before, and we have a way of dealing with it. Access to the account is completely controlled by our computer system. I will open up a particular screen, and you will privately enter the information that you have concerning your password. The computer will check that information against your account and the other demographic information about you I have already entered. That will begin a clock ticking—"

Cutting Mehnteerah off, Clay said, "Then let's get to it."

"As you wish, Mr. McRae."

Mehnteerah called up the appropriate screen, and McRae entered the numbers.

Returning to his seat, McRae asked, "When can I return to set up a withdrawal and check writing privileges?"

"In three years, if no claim is made against the account, the computer will release all the funds in the account to you. I believe that it has something to do with what you refer to in the United States as—the statute of limitations."

"Three years? Are you kidding me? Are you telling me I have to wait three years before I can get to my money? It's my money.

You've got to be able to find some way to release some of it to me now. What do you expect me to live on?

Clay could not control the anger. He stood up from his chair, and his tone changed from talking to yelling. "I won't stand for it, I tell you—this is bullshit—there's no way . . ." Clay was spitting by now.

Achmed tried to tell Clay to calm down, but Clay ignored him. Mehnteerah signaled for the bank guard to come over. Clay became more agitated. Mehnteerah told Clay that if he did not calm down, he would be asked to leave the bank. Clay did not calm down. Another security guard stepped over to flank McRae. They each grabbed an arm, turned him around, and started walking him toward the door. Clay shook their hands off his arms and stormed out of the bank under his own power. When he got outside, Achmed joined him.

"Can you believe this? Can you believe what they're telling me? They're telling me that I can't have my own money."

Achmed replied in a very gentle tone, "Yes, Mr. McRae, I know what they're telling you. I understand what they are saying, and I understand what that means to you." Clay was pacing, only half listening as Achmed went on, "Mehnteerah had told this to me before, but I was certain you would have to hear it for yourself. At least, not all is lost. I know that three years is a long time, but you can spend that three years, knowing that the money waits for you. You know, the money that you can't touch, we can't touch either. I know that doesn't make you feel any better, but I hope it lets you know that I understand."

"Yeah, yeah, I understand. I'm going back to my hotel. I'll call you in a little while after I cool down. Maybe then we can figure out something else we can do."

McRae marched off down the street. Achmed watched until McRae was out of sight and then returned inside the bank. He walked directly through the lobby until he reached one of the private rooms set aside for people to go through their safety deposit boxes. He knocked on the door of the first of the rooms. The person inside opened the door.

"Father, he is gone. He has put the first numbers of the password into the computer."

"Good, good, I listened through the door . . . you did well. Now, let us finish the transaction," said Mustafa as he walked toward Mehnteerah's desk with a limp.

"Father, are you all right?"

"Yes, yes. I am still sore, but thanks be to Allah, the Most Merciful, for sending the ambulance so quickly. It is still a bit hard to breathe, but do not worry. I am okay."

"Father, are you sure that this is the right thing for us to do? You have always taught me to be honorable with my word and to follow up on all my promises."

Mustafa stopped and turned to his son with a smile on his face. "Did you not see all of the news reports of what that man did to the corporation he led? What happened to all of his employees and the loss of their pensions and retirements? He was a thief. Even in the day of the Prophet, may glory be upon Him, good men stole from thieves, especially if it was to benefit the poor. You know that as Muslim men, we are required to use the money we acquire only for the benefit of our family and to give alms to the poor. This American thief will help us do much good among the poor of our people. What can be bad with that?"

Mustafa wasn't sure his theology was right, or if the Prophet would approve his interpretation, but it sounded good for the moment. When they got to Mehnteerah's desk, the computer screen containing five asterisks where Clay typed in the first five digits of the password was still up. Mustafa typed in the second five digits, and Mehnteerah hit the enter button. The screen changed, and Mehnteerah put his hands back on the keyboard and asked where Mustafa wanted him to transfer the funds.

"Please transfer 80 percent of the account into my personal account. The remaining 20 percent may be transferred to any account you choose. I do consider myself to be a man of my word, and since my fee was 20 percent for helping the American thief transfer his money, it is only fit and proper that you take the 20 percent for assisting in the remainder of the transactions."

Mehnteerah began typing in the required information with the broadest of grins. When he was done, he printed out the requisite receipts, had Mustafa sign where necessary, and stood up to shake Mustafa's hand. Mehnteerah shook Mustafa's hand and shook it, and shook it until Mustafa had to stop him by using his left hand. Mustafa and Achmed said their good-byes and walked out of the bank. When they got outside, Mustafa stopped to soak in the midmorning sun.

"I suppose we ought to go home and tell your mother and sisters to get out of those old clothes. I would imagine we could take them on a shopping spree. What do you say to that?"

"Shouldn't we let them stay as they are for just a little while longer, Father? Perhaps Mr. McRae will revisit the house. If we are in celebration, he will suspect something."

"I think it will be all right. I don't believe that Mr. McRae will be visiting our house or, for that matter, any place in Turkey," said Mustafa with the air of knowing something that Achmed was not privy to.

*   *   *

When Clay McRae walked into his hotel, the concierge approached him. The concierge escorted him to the front desk and rang the bell. The attendant stepped out of the side office and walked directly up to where McRae was standing.

"I'm sorry to bother you, Mr. McRae, but it seems that the credit card that you provided us for payment has been terminated."

"That's impossible. That credit card has no limit. Run it through again."

"Mr. McRae, we ran it through and called for verification. We were told that the stop placed on the account was a private matter, and that you would need to call. We have the name, phone number, and extension of the gentleman with whom you need to speak. Would you be kind enough to make that call? The concierge will take you to a private phone."

McRae was speechless. He allowed the concierge to lead him through the lobby until they came to a small chair and table in a back corner. There was no one else around. Clay opened the paper given to him by the desk clerk and dialed the number written on it.

When he finally connected with the account executive handling his matters, he was informed that the IRS had frozen the account. McRae asked for emergency funds from his wife's account. He was informed that there was an annotation on those accounts specifically prohibiting Clay from access. The account representative was extremely apologetic but again told McRae that there was nothing to be done to lift an IRS freeze.

McRae got up and returned to the front desk. He noticed that a police car pulled up to the entrance of the hotel. The clerk asked McRae if he had any other credit card that he could use. He also informed McRae that, like in the United States, it was a crime to defraud an innkeeper by not paying a bill. Clay could see that two officers had gotten out of the police car and were beginning to walk into the lobby. McRae provided a different credit card. The desk clerk ran the new credit card through the slot of the reading machine. After a few seconds, one word was displayed—*Denied.*

The two Istanbul Police officers flanked McRae. As he reached for his wallet again, the officer on his right intercepted his arm with the open yaw of one side of handcuffs. When McRae heard the clicking sound of the cuff tightening around his wrist, he jerked back, "Wait, you can't . . ."

No other words were possible as the room spun for a fraction of a second until his right ear slammed down on the plush carpet and a hard boot pressed down on the left ear. He heard the sickening series of clicks come from the other half of the handcuffs. Hands under his armpits lifted him, dragged him out the door, and threw him in the back of the police car.

Clay wiggled his way to a seated position. The police officers got in the car and made a U-turn. Clay began to recover. "I am an American citizen. I demand to be taken to my embassy."

The officers laughed. The one in the passenger seat said, "I do not think that is where you wish to go, Mr. McRae. At least, if the Interpol flyer is at all correct." The other one added, "But you might—how you say—prefer, yes prefer that to a Turkish jail."

The officers went back to their laughs and remarks in Turkish. The police car drove past McRae's bank. McRae glared out the window. From the sidewalk, Achmed waived and Mustafa tipped his wide-brimmed white hat.

*   *   *

Jennifer McRae picked up the two-and-one-half-carat yellow diamond ring and tried it on. It was a perfect fit. She displayed it to the clerk and moved her finger around so that the diamond could catch the light from the spotlights above and sparkle, throwing dots of light all about.

"Will you need to have the ring sized, Mrs. McRae?" the clerk asked.

"No, I think it fits just fine. In fact, I think I'll wear it out. Would you put my old ring in one of those beautiful blue velvet Tiffany's boxes for me?"

Jennifer McRae thought to herself, *Does it get any better than this?* Clay was out of her hair. She had all the money she would ever want. The stock market was spiraling upward, and everybody just seemed to be so polite. Maybe, there really was a God although she wondered what she had done to receive such blessings. *Maybe,* she thought, *I was God's way of creating consequences for Clay McRae.*

She stepped out onto Fifth Avenue. There was a group of Hare Krishnas chanting and drumming on the street. There was a time, not too long ago, that they would have annoyed her. Today, however, she felt that it was a time to celebrate. She let her head bob to the beat of the finger cymbals and drum as she walked over and placed the blue velvet box containing her old diamond engagement ring in the open leather drum case.

"Hare Krishna" was the thank-you.

"Hare Krishna" was her reply.

EPILOGUE

It is a new day. Love each other.
Have fun and be happy.
—Mayor of New York City

They say that New York is the city that doesn't sleep. There is one moment, however, when it does take a nap. That moment is the subtle transition between night and day. That moment is the twilight minutes of dawn. In Times Square, there might be a few of the hardy-party people, or the most tenacious of the call girls, migrating to the entrances of the underground caverns leading to the subways. Most of the human movement is provided by homeless men and bag ladies picking through overflowing trash cans to find recyclables they can redeem for enough pennies to buy breakfast. It is far too early for the commuters to begin arriving. You might hear the swishing of circular, spinning brushes as mechanical sidewalk cleaners sweep the curbs. You might hear the hum of the neon lights that normally is drowned out by the honking and squealing of traffic. Unless the garbage is putting out its own odor, you can get a whiff of the steam that comes from sidewalk grates that vent the huge underground heating systems. It feels like a celestial referee somewhere had just called a time-out.

It was during one of those moments that preparations for the big "Celebrate God Party" on 112th Street began. Extra duty police officers from the 23rd Precinct set up barricades at the beginning and end of 112th Street to cordon off traffic. A large tractor-trailer turned off Lexington and pulled up in front of the First Baptist Church of Harlem. The moving crew got out and began to unload a huge soundstage that would mask the broad side of the church and extend halfway into the street. There would be five hundred folding chairs set out, courtesy of the local synagogue. Congregants of the church had already assembled to begin moving folding tables out to the street so that environmental groups and vendors would have a place to set up.

At Sandy's Deli, Habib Rashid had been directing his corps of volunteers, including Angie Gibran, since midnight. They had been slicing roast beef, bologna, turkey, and cheeses to provide food for the block party. No matter how many times they returned to the refrigerator, it remained full.

Heads of the street gangs, which now were called Community Clubs, were in a meeting at the 23rd Precinct with Captain Kaplan, getting instructions on how to be of assistance in providing information, crowd control, parking, and security. Artists and artisans began appearing in trucks and vans bringing their tables and tents to set up displays. Each church, mosque, and synagogue in the area had an assigned area to set up for the comfort of their faithful and to provide information and materials about their particular faith.

Two large portable billboards were set up for easy viewing. They listed the schedule of the day's events, which included concerts, appearances by local, national, and international celebrities, stand-up comics (PG rated, of course) and politicians. The First

Baptist Church of Harlem had formed a joint committee with a local mosque to decorate the street. Ladders were set up against streetlights, and people were stringing decorations across 112th from pole to pole.

The city of New York, which always touted its water as the best in the nation, brought in huge trailers to serve as watering stations for the expected crowd of over three hundred fifty thousand people. Less than six months ago, the city never would have joined an event that celebrated God for fear of crossing the line between church and state. Ever since President Edwards's speech and the decision from the Supreme Court (that it was a proper state function to develop ways of respecting the communications of God, in a nondenominational way), local governments all over the nation were declaring that God was a reality and, therefore, not a question of faith. The government still was careful to "make no law respecting an establishment of religion or prohibiting the free exercise thereof," as the Constitution required; but the government was free to celebrate God as a power for good.

At exactly 7:02 AM, it was time for the Muslim morning Call to Prayer. From the top of one of the ladders, a member of the mosque made the Call to Prayer in Arabic. All of the Muslims stopped what they were doing, kneeled wherever they were, and faced east toward Mecca. It was then that one of those little miracles happened—the kind people tell their children about. Every person on the street stopped, faced east, and in their own tradition—whether it was by kneeling, bowing their head in silent prayer, daviting, chanting, or saying the Rosary—prayed along with the Muslims. At the end of the prayers, the people turned to those closest to them and gave gentle hugs or shook hands in friendship. Many had tears in their eyes, and then they turned back to continue the work at hand.

The staging area for the parade, scheduled for eleven, was on 113th Street High schools and colleges, from as far away as Florida and Mexico, provided marching bands. Lavishly decorated floats lined up, ready to proudly awe the crowds. Interspersed among the flagships were simple floats, often nothing more than people in costumes riding in the back of a pickup truck. Anyone who wanted to participate could participate.

One of the most noteworthy groups was the Medina Marauders. When Claire Medina saw the difference that coaching could make in Joe Clidson's life, she and Tomás decided to make a very generous donation to the athletic program of the First Baptist Church of Harlem. The donation provided a handsome salary for a full-time coach. In gratitude, the church named its peewee football team after them. Joe was there, in his nifty new coach's uniform, trying to get the elementary school ball players into some semblance of order. Jimmy, his assistant coach, was laughing his head off.

"Just what is so funny?" asked Joe-24.

Hardly able to talk through his laughter, Jimmy said, "You sure are good on the field, but it's really funny to watch a bunch of little kids get it over on you. I'm beginning to think that you are really just a big old teddy bear. Here, let me show you how to do it."

Jimmy blew his whistle loudly and then circulated through the children whispering in each one's ear. The entire group of them calmed down and started to get into their parade positions. When he returned to where Joe was standing, Joe asked him what he said.

"I just told them that there were ice cream vendors out there, and if they didn't get themselves in order, they wouldn't get to see the inside of an ice cream cone."

"That's a bribe. You bribed them."

"Yeah, I guess I did," Jimmy said, chuckling.

At 10:00 AM, the celebration officially began. Father Abrahms stepped to the microphone of the soundstage with Lori at his side and gave a benediction. He was careful not to refer to any particular religion. He gave thanks to God—variously referring to God as Hashem, Allah, Yaweh, Krishna, Shangdi, Brahman, Great Spirit, and the Great Universal Intelligence. At the end of his prayer, the pastor proclaimed, "Let the party begin."

Lori stepped up to the microphone and sang an unaccompanied, hauntingly beautiful rendition of "Amazing Grace." She then said, "Tracy Chapman wrote a beautiful song that really asks the question of the day. It's called 'Change.' The song asks the question: 'If you knew that you could die today and saw the face of God and love, would you change?'" As the music started, Lori melted into the song.

As Ms. Chapman's prophetic words broadcast over the crowd, a member of the 112th Street Community Club was pushing Gee-spot of the 129th Street Club in his wheelchair to a booth. He was among members of both the 112th and 129th Street Community Clubs who were there to talk to youngsters about the dead-end life of gang members and the excitement of becoming the men God intended us to be.

The Manhattan district attorney joined Claire and Tomás in greeting the mayor when he arrived. They escorted him to the soundstage. The mayor had a speech prepared. He pulled his notes from his pocket and looked out at the crowd. There were peoples from all races, faiths, and nationalities. They all were celebrating their commonalities instead of their differences. The leader of the world's premier city could not have imagined the scene before him. Yet here it was, happening before him. There was nothing for him to do, and he had no words to add. He tore up his notes and threw them into the crowd. His entire speech came down to one line.

"It's a new day. Love each other. Have fun and be happy."

*   *   *

Half a world away, Al-Khalil and Teeja walked along a pockmarked road until they came to the narrow gravel path leading up to the hilltop cemetery where their parents were buried. Along the way, Teeja had collected a bouquet of wildflowers to honor the parents she barely knew. They picked their way up the road stepping around debris and over clumps of saw grass. Finally, they came to the top of the road. It had been so many years since Al-Khalil had visited the graves; he could not remember where his parents were buried. He held Teeja's hand tightly as they explored the graveyard.

Some of the graves were marked merely with a large stone. Some had rough slabs that only stated a name and date of death. Other markers included the signs of Hamas, other Palestinian militias, marks of faith, or martyrdom. Al-Khalil could not help but to think how many were there because of the conflict, because of the war, because of hate. Al-Khalil spotted his parents' graves, which, gratefully, were side by side. Because Israeli military action killed both of them, Hamas paid for the funeral and marked both as martyrs.

The two children of the man and woman buried before them stood silently. Al-Khalil began to cry. He remembered his father vaguely, but he remembered his mother with great clarity. He remembered her kindness and her bravery. He also remembered the moment that she was torn out of his hand by the Israeli missile.

Teeja was sad, but without having known either of them, it was hard for her to call up the same grief. She looked up and saw her brother crying. She squeezed his hand to comfort him. Al-Khalil could tell that the moment was much more emotional for him than for his sister. He wiped a few tears from his eyes and then leaned down to her.

"Teeja, I know that you don't remember mother and father, so you shouldn't feel bad if you don't feel as sad as I do. Would you do me a favor? Would you give me just a few minutes here alone with Mother and Father?"

Teeja nodded her agreement. She let go of Al-Khalil's hand and took her bouquet of flowers toward the graves. She laid the flowers down between the two strangers that had given her birth. It was then that she felt a stab of pain in her heart, but she wanted to give her brother the gift he requested. She let her curiosity guide her as she went off to look at some of the other grave markers.

Teeja came upon a grave that once had been marked with a Jewish star. The gravestone had been broken in half so only part of the star remained. On the broken marker, there were dried eggshells, bullet holes, and the sign of Hamas scratched into it. There were the dried bones of pig's feet pushed into the dirt of the grave and dried feces. Teeja remained there, examining the desecration of the grave, until Al-Khalil finally joined her.

"Look, brother," said Teeja, pointing, "They are hated even after they are dead."

Teeja then ran back to the graves of her parents. She picked two of the largest flowers out of the bouquet and ran back to the Israeli grave. She solemnly approached the grave and gently placed the two flowers upon it. The innocence and compassion of his younger sister moved Al-Khalil. He wished that he could take the final, the last step of forgiveness. He desperately wanted to fully divest himself of the last remnant of hatred.

They heard the sound of an aircraft overhead. Since no commercial airlines flew over Gaza, it could only be an Israeli jet. They looked up to the left; the sight of the F-16 confirmed Al-Khalil's fears. He began to look around for cover, but there was none, so they just stood and watched.

In the cockpit of the jet was Capt. David Nadav. He had followed his father, Capt. Moshe Nadav, into the Israeli Air Force. Since the closing of the settlements in Gaza and the shift in world consciousness, he no longer had to fly reprisal bombings as his father had. He only flew patrols. His father and he had often discussed the heartache that arose over having to bomb in the Palestinian sections. His father taught him from a young age that although killing might be necessary, it always carried great remorse. If one should ever take glee from destroying life, one would sever his connection with God. The Torah said that self-defense was allowed, but that did not give permission to kill in anger or hate. His father had always told him to respect those who died in the conflict regardless of the side they were on. He especially taught him to honor those they had killed themselves.

Capt. David Nadav had made it his habit to tilt his wings in salute every time he passed over a cemetery. He eased his flight stick to the right and touched his foot to the left rudder pedal. The right wing of his F-16 dipped in salute as the graveyard passed under him. He continued on his patrol with no further incident. He had no idea that, by a supreme irony, the two people watching him from the hilltop had been orphaned by his father. He also had no idea how important the gesture of his salute would be in closing the karmic circle.

Teeja may have been Al-Khalil's younger sister, but in some ways, she was more mature than he was. Because the same hatred did not infiltrate her emotions, she was more open to feel the touch and hand of Allah. When she saw the jet salute, she walked to her brother and stood before him face-to-face. She looked up at him, her dark almond eyes piercing his consciousness.

"It is a sign from Allah," she said solemnly and with certainty.

Al-Khalil had no choice but to agree with her. He put his arm around her shoulder, and they stood side by side looking out from the hilltop at the Mediterranean. The breeze began to kick up, causing their clothes to flap. It was a cleansing wind. In the overcast sky above, two clouds shifted slightly, allowing a shaft of light to shine down upon the water, which shimmered underneath it. Al-Khalil and Teeja looked at each other briefly, and then looked out again.

Finally, Al-Khalil was at peace.

A READER'S GUIDE

FOR

CHILDREN OF ABRAHAM

Questions for Discussion

A Conversation with the Author

QUESTIONS FOR DISCUSSION

1. Capt. Nadav is ordered to destroy an enemy headquarters, in spite of collateral damage. Is such a reprisal morally defensible? Spiritually defensible? What is the Jewish position on self-defense? Does it differ from Christian or Muslim philosophy?

2. Would God approve of warring between the children of Abraham? Between any groups? Where does the Biblical/religious/spiritual justification for war come from? Did Jesus change any philosophy derived from the Old Testament? Did Muhammad?

3. The word *Jihad* has different interpretations. Some Muslims believe it means taking up arms for a Holy cause. Others believe the word refers to the inner struggle between conscience and temptation—right and wrong. What does the Qur'an actually say about *Jihad* and how do people arrive at the different interpretations?

4. Contrast the life experiences of a Palestinian living in Gaza and an Israeli living in Tel Aviv. Is it possible for two peoples to believe the other is the aggressor?

5. Does Al-Khalil's decision to become a suicide bomber make sense, considering his experience? Was he crazy? Consider watching the Palestinian made movie *Paradise Now.*

6.   How would you react to a news report that God had left a message on the electronic news ticker on television? Why would such a message be inconsistent with Muslim belief?

7.   How does the Jewish history of slavery, oppression, and genocide affect their world view?

8.   Of hatred, greed, sloth, anger, pride, envy, and lust—which are the most susceptible to redemption? Which the least?

9.   What would be the legal implications if God's existence became a matter of fact rather than faith? How would it affect the separation between church and state? The first amendment rights of free speech and assembly?

10. When Tillie Clidson hears about the God messages she is not at all surprised. To her, God has always been known. Do you think her response is more typical or atypical of those who say they are people of faith? What does that say about faith?

11. Whether sex, drugs or gambling—what is the nature of addiction? How can it produce such self-destructive behavior? Does intelligence have any effect on addiction?

12. Do the issues that show up in the relationship between Tomás and Claire reflect issues within themselves and within their relationship with God? Can relationship be a path to self discovery? Does your relationship with a loved one teach you about your relationship with God?

13. Tomás seems to be most offended by those flaws of Claire that most closely mirror things he objects to within himself. Is this common for most human beings?

14. Tomás grew up in Chile during tumultuous years. The United States through the CIA contributed to the chaos that imprisoned his father and led, indirectly, to his mother's suicide. Is such involvement in other sovereign countries morally defensible? Spiritually defensible? Would God approve?

15. In Tomás's first fist conversation with Johnny there seems to be much innuendo and conversation about skirting the law. Did Tomás act properly and legally?

16. Claire has difficulty with confrontation. How powerful is the issue of confrontation to women's experience? Is it different for men?

17. Does chaos in early life, whether caused by circumstances or parents, affect men and women differently?

18. Clay McRae witnessed members of Congress making arguments that the God messages supported their particular political agendas. Do you think politicians would make such arguments? Do you think that once the proof became irrefutable they would become more solemn or respectful?

19. Are the actions of families, communities and nations governed by the same moral, ethical, and spiritual principles as individuals? Do nations reap what they sow?

20. Do you think that today God would choose one branch of the children of Abraham over another as his favorite? As his chosen?

21. Does redemption require that amends be made?

22. Claire seeks out the advice of a therapist. Is self-discovery circular—that is, can secular insight lead to a spiritual epiphany, and vice versa?

23. Joe and Lori both are beset by pride. Does pride present both a problem and a solution? Is there a difference between pride in yourself and pride in your relationship with God? How can pride sometimes keep you from healing and other times bring about healing?

24. Why was Pastor Abrahms the perfect person to help Joe reach his epiphany?

25. How does the advice given by Father Fitzgerald, Pastor Abrahms, Angie Gibran, and Mark Jacobs dovetail with the principles enumerated in Rick Warren's *The Purpose Driven Life.*

26. How do you discover your purpose in life?

27. Mark Jacobs described God as demonstrating the kind of parenting skills we should adopt in our own families. Considering the pain humans experience and the free choice we are allowed, was Mark correct?

28. Clair was highly impressed by Pastor Abrahms. Was he truly an extraordinary person? Why?

29. Angie counsels Al-Khalil from the Qur'an. Is her counsel different or similar to Christian or Jewish advice?

30. Did any, or all, of the characters get their just comeuppance?

31. Is it possible for the world's faiths to come into an accepting harmony?

32. Is *Children of Abraham*, ultimately, a novel of despair or hope?

A CONVERSATION WITH R.H. MARTIN

1.   When did you first decide to write Children of Abraham?

It was March of 2006. Although I can't say that I actually made a decision to write it. It was more just the way things happened. I had just finished working on a project in Costa Rica and I was back in the states without a job. The idea for this book had been bouncing around for a long time. My wife and I were visiting New York and I decided to look for some of the locales for the book. I found an area of Manhattan around 112th St in East Harlem that was perfect. It had the requisite combination of being multiethnic and home to both low-income housing projects and high-priced condominiums on the East River. It was a place where all my characters could come together as I had envisioned. When we came home I picked up a pad of paper and started writing. After that, it was off to the races. The fact that I started writing dictated that I take the time to write rather than having made a conscious decision to do so. Like many of the major decisions in my life, writing *Children of Abraham* seems to have been presented to me in a way that left me with little choice in the matter.

2.   Is there any other book on the market you could compare to your book?

Not really. There are other books that blend together the ideas of religion, mystery, and fiction such as *The Da Vinci Code* or the *Left Behind* series. There are other books that use the same technique of interweaving the lives of various characters as was done in the movie *Crash*. I don't believe there is anything out there that puts forward the premise of how the world would change if God were to make his presence undeniably known.

3.   How long did it take you to write the book?

It took 15 months to research and write, but that wasn't 15 contiguous months. I wrote for about 12 months and then experienced the famous writer's block. I had created the basic plot but came to a situation where there were a host of threads to weave and nothing seemed to come together. I had to walk away from the project for a few months and get a job. When I came back it fell into place. I finished the first draft of 118,000 words three months after that. The final draft runs a little over 100,000 words. Cutting out my own excesses was the most painful part.

4.   When you're writing, what does a typical day look like? (hours writing, early or late, etc.)

There's not a typical day. Some days I might write a paragraph or a page; other days I might write nothing at all. Some days I'll start out early in the morning and be amazed that it's become dark outside and it's way past bedtime. The days when I don't write actually tend to be the most productive because I'm in a freethinking mode when new connections and plot twists seem to bubble up from I don't know where. My wife, who is a very task-oriented and productive woman, would sometimes see me lying in bed, staring at the ceiling, and prompt me to get to work. I would reply, "I am working." She would shrug and walk off. I guess she just had to take it on faith. There were times, at night, after the lights were turned off that I would think about sending a character in a new direction. I'd turn over to her excitedly and tell her about my new insight, only to realize that she was already asleep. She was always kind under those circumstances and would tell me, "That's nice, Dear, that's nice."

5.   Do you work from an outline?

Yes. There are a couple pieces of software that I found very helpful. One is Storycraft and the other is Writer's Café. Storycraft is a program that guides you through the basic storylines of different genres and helps create the skeleton of your story. Writer's Café is an index card system that tracks storylines with electronic index cards that can be moved around and re-placed within the overall plot line. The outline was only a framework. I prefer to think that I work by inspiration.

6.   Where did you get the idea for your book?

I heard a song by Tracy Chapman called *Change*. It starts off, "If you knew that you would die tonight and stood in the face of God and Love—would you change?" I thought the question was fascinating. Living in the Bible Belt I came to know many sincere, devout people. However, I also often saw people who attended church and claimed to be people of faith, yet behaved in inconsistent ways. I thought it curious to hear preachers supporting divisive thinking and advocating war, while at the same time proclaiming the Prince of Peace to be their savior. I wondered why, if someone believed God was all seeing and all knowing, a person would sneak into a motel room to have an affair. Why sneak?

I didn't really think about it much more until 9/11 and the invasion of Iraq. At that point, conflicts between religions became a part of our everyday lives. In wondering what God would actually think of all the fighting that was being done in His name, I began to think of the question posed by Ms. Chapman. I began to wonder how things would play out in this day and age. That question gripped me and it was actually several years that thoughts were bouncing around in my brain. I would often ask people, "What do you think would happen if God were to make His presence known?" The question would often lead to interesting conversations and those conversations became the basis of the book.

7.   Did you have support from friends/family? Please share an experience.

Absolutely. My poor wife—every time I would write a few pages I would come running down the stairs pushing the papers in her face saying, "Here, read this. Read this." She would dutifully do so and encourage me. Finally she asked me to get the bulk of it written so that she could sit down and read it as a complete story. My daughter was very helpful in helping role-play parts and working out plot lines. She is an aspiring actor and enjoyed working on the creative aspects of the drama. My son enjoyed reading the book and giving me feedback. My sister-in-law, Ida, worked with me as my editor. We spent many, many days going over the manuscripts and correcting it. The acknowledgments at the beginning of the book cover four pages. That might give you an idea of how many of my friends contributed to the work.

8.   When you aren't writing, what do you like to do for enjoyment?

By profession I am a lawyer and therapist. The true blessing of my work is the opportunity to be with people at a time they are willing to share their lives and be receptive to guidance. That honor is a true enjoyment. Beyond that, when I'm not writing, I enjoy thinking about writing and going to movies. I believe that movies —at least well made movies—are underrated showcases of human dynamics. Through movies we can expand our repertoire of experiences and better understand human beings and the dynamics that drive them.

9.   What have you learned during the time you've been writing your book?

Two things. One, I learned how wonderfully complex human beings are. Second, I've learned how much fun it is to be an author and be in complete control of the world that you've created.

10. What suggestions would you have for someone who wants to write a book?

Be passionate. The first time you sit down to write a major work, be sure that it's about something that moves you emotionally, something about which you have a fire in your belly. You need to have the passion in order to carry you through the times where boredom and exhaustion set in and the remainder of the task seems to stretch out endlessly in front of you. It's passion that carries you through those times.

11. What are your future plans? Any more books, or perhaps a
     sequel?

Yes. I've got five other books I'm itching to get started on. One of
them is a fictional account of where Jesus may have been between the
last mention of him in the Bible at age 13 and his baptism at age 29.
Another is a work of creative non-fiction about a young lady who lived
in rural West Virginia up until the time she was recruited by Herbert
Hoover's FBI in the 1930s. I am also collecting lectures from a course I
teach at our community college called *The Art and Science of Happiness.*

12. Tell us a bit about your book.

The theme of *Children of Abraham* is driven by the question
of redemption, but the action is character driven. Most of the
characters are flawed, grappling with the seven deadly sins. Al Khalil
(hatred) carries around the wounds of having been orphaned by
Israeli military action. Louis the Cop (envy) is 20 years past burned
out and never got a break in life. Tomás (anger) vowed to never be
under anybody's thumb, yet finds himself losing control over his
life. Claire (sloth) can't stand confrontation, yet finds herself sucked
into enabling illegal behavior. Clay McRae (greed) a sociopath CEO
of an Enron-type corporation is trying to complete the rape of his
company before forces unleashed by the God messages catch up
with him. Max Silverman (lust), a Congressman who is also a sex
addict, tries to keep his addiction private in his very public life.
Joe 24 (pride), a Harlem football hero, who suffers a career ending
injury, can't seem to adapt to losing his celebrity status. Add to the
cast a mobster, gang-banger, Turkish money launderer, and others
wrapped up in a plot that takes unexpected twists and turns, thanks

to the messages from God and you have a fast-paced story that will surely entertain—and provoke thought.

13.   Who has been the greatest influence on your life?

I don't think there's any one person; certainly, my father. In a small, but significant way there was my third grade English teacher, Mr. Geezy, who gave me a pat on the back and an 'Atta boy!' when very few others had. He helped me to believe that I had some capacity for artistry—not in the visual sense, but with words.

14.   Tell us about the research you did, who you contacted, and why.

Research is vital in writing a book. First of all, the more research you do the more story you have. Every conversation leads to more information that can be wound into the plot of the book. The Internet is an invaluable source for information. If you need to know the map of a city, what a building looks like, or the name of a luxury hotel in Istanbul, Turkey, the information is at your fingertips. Beyond that, in this book I needed to know the nature and culture of different religions, beliefs, and faith systems. Not only between Christianity, Judaism and Islam but also the different sects within the branches. I interviewed pastors, imams, priests, and rabbis. I interviewed police officers for technical information, doctors for information about wounds, and judges for their opinions as to the legal ramifications of the God messages. I traveled to Washington, DC and watched sessions of Congress. I visited the offices of my Congressman to see how business goes on within the Rayburn office building. I walked the streets of Manhattan to find settings for the scenes. Not only was research involving technical questions important, but it was also important to get the input from women concerning my female characters (and I was often surprised to find out how much I didn't know).

15. What would you like to leave a reader with once he has read your book?

A commitment to understanding other faiths and finding ways of living harmoniously with people of different belief systems. What I discovered in writing this book is that there are differences between faiths in terms of history and culture, but there is a great deal of commonality between the faiths in terms of their values. We hear a lot about values these days, especially in the political races and campaigns. I think too often we overlook the sameness, that commonality between us because the differences are so much more obvious. Values like kindness, compassion, forgiveness, and empathy are fundamental to all belief systems. They are the signposts that lead us to find those golden seeds within us. I would like to leave readers with the hopeful feeling that by looking at what is alike among us, we will find it easier to overlook the superficial differences

16. Do you have a website?

Yes, please visit me at: *www.RHMartin.net*

17. Are you available for speaking engagements? If so, in what organizations do you envision yourself as a speaker?

Yes, I am available for speaking engagements. I would be more than happy to speak with civic groups, religious or church groups, book discussion or study groups. Any group that is interested in forwarding our progress towards a more peaceful loving world.

18. Is there any other information about yourself, your family, your faith that you'd like to share.

I'm not really sure about why I've come to write this book at this time. Although I thought about the story at great length, that's not unusual for me. I often think about projects and ideas without actually taking them on. Why I finally set my hand to paper and where I got the discipline to write a 350-plus page book is a question that I'm still not clear on. I'm not an overly religious person, although I do consider myself a spiritual person. Becoming a social worker gave me the skill of being able to sit with psychic pain, feel it, and understand it without wanting to run away from it. There seems to be so much pain in the world and so many of our systems seem to be breaking down. I guess I felt there was just something to say and what I wanted to say was, "It doesn't have to be this way—we can do better. There is something larger and greater than us in the universe." Where the rest of it came from, I don't know—but I don't want to start getting too 'new age' here.

19. Do you have hopes that this book will help people to .look at the religions of others in a different, more open way?

Yes.

20. You deal with religion delicately in this novel. Were you concerned about offending any reader's faith?

Absolutely, yes. I was concerned that it not be offensive. I intended it to be controversial, but not offensive. That's why I refrained from using any of the more serious curse words and from being negative about any religion or belief system. I did highlight some differences in belief but only because I was interested in how the message of hope, love, and redemption were expressed in the different faiths. I was not overly interested in highlighting the differences that might exist in culture or history. This is not a time for us to point fingers and say 'my way or the highway'. These times are times that call for us to understand each other on more deep and profound ways. Being offensive was not my intention. Being controversial, raising questions, and beginning a conversation was.

21. You've turned the concept of *Deus ex Machina* on its head by using God as the McGuffin. The idea of God communicating with us is fantastical—are the communications a metaphor for something more real?

In the ancient Greek plays, whether a comedy or tragedy, sometimes the playwright boxed himself into a corner. To get out of the dramatic corner and get on with the play he would have to do something fantastical to keep the plot going. They would take a crane and lower an actor dressed up like a god onto the stage and he would magically change things to get the plot back on track. That's where the expression of deus ex machina, God out of the machine, comes from. A McGuffin is a dramatic device that keeps the plot moving forward. In an Alfred Hitchcock movie perhaps the McGuffin might be a pearl necklace that is the object of everybody's attention. In the *Maltese Falcon* the McGuffin obviously was the falcon. By actually bringing God in as the underlying motivator in the plot does kind of stand deus ex machina on its head.

Is it a metaphor? Well, in terms of the plot it's not. In terms of the theme of the book, that we as human beings often have some hypocrisy in what we say we believe and how we actually act in response to the temptations we experience, there is metaphor. The messages, on some level, we intuitively know are the things that God would want us to live by. These are the messages that the quiet voice within us calls out to be listened to. So, whether these messages come from an outside intelligence, or whether they come from an intelligence that dwells within us is metaphor

22. Are any of your characters drawn from people you have personally known?

I am both a lawyer and a social worker, so the characters of the lawyer, Tomás and the therapist, Mark Jacobs, drew heavily on my own experiences. In the beginning of the book there is a disclaimer that says that the characters and places described are fictional and that any relationship between the characters in the book and real persons or places is strictly coincidental. I think I had best just leave it at that.

23. What does the R.H. in R.H. Martin stand for?

Robert Hall, but most folks call me Bob.